"Fortress of S IIIIIIII D1430161 "
and
"The Devil Genghis"

TWO CLASSIC ADVENTURES OF

DOC SAVAGE

REG. U.S PAT. OFF.

by Lester Dent
writing as Kenneth Robeson

with new historical essays
by Will Murray and Anthony Tollin

Published by Sanctum Productions for
NOSTALGIA VENTURES, INC.
P.O. Box 231183; Encinitas, CA 92023-1183

This Nostalgia Ventures edition is an unabridged republication of the text and
illustrations of two stories from *Doc Savage Magazine,* as originally published
by Street & Smith Publications, Inc., N.Y.: *Fortress of Solitude* from the
October 1938 issue, and *The Devil Genghis* from the December 1938 issue.
Typographical errors have been tacitly corrected in this edition.

International Standard Book Numbers:
Emery Clarke cover standard edition:
ISBN 1-932806-49-0   13 DIGIT 978-1-932806-49-6

James Bama cover variant edition:
ISBN 1-932806-24-5   13 digit 978-1932806-24-3

Series editor: Anthony Tollin
P.O. Box 761474
San Antonio, TX 78245-1474
sanctumotr@earthlink.net

Contributing editor: Will Murray

Copy editor: Joseph Wrzos

Cover reconstruction: Tom Roberts and Michael Piper
Cover lettering: John Workman

The editors gratefully acknowledge the contributions of James Bama, Brian
Kane, Ed Hulse and Rich Harvey in the preparation of this volume, Tom
Stephens for scans and OCR, and William T. Stolz of the Western Historical
Manuscript Collection of the University of Missouri at Columbia for research
assistance with the Lester Dent Collection.

Nostalgia Ventures, Inc.
P.O. Box 231183; Encinitas, CA 92023-1183

Visit Doc Savage at www.nostalgiatown.com

DOC SAVAGE VOLUME 1

TWO AMAZING ADVENTURES OF THE MAN OF BRONZE AND HIS IRON CREW!

Thrilling Tales and Features

Interior illustrations by Paul Orban

Introduction to FORTRESS OF SOLITUDE by Will Murray

It's almost impossible to overstate the impact of Doc Savage on the popular culture of the 20th Century.

From his first appearance in *Doc Savage Magazine,* March 1933, Doc was unlike any hero who had come before. Prior to the Man of Bronze, an adventure hero could be strong, smart, an expert in some line or profession. He might be uncommonly rich, or brave or a crack marksman.

When pulp writer Lester Dent accepted the assignment to flesh out Street & Smith's Doc Savage under the house name "Kenneth Robeson," he was handed a hero described as the "Supreme Adventurer." Dent made him much more. He transformed him into the bravest, richest, strongest, most brilliant man on Earth. The pulps trafficked in fictional supermen. Lester Dent took it one step further: he created the first superhero.

True, the Man of Bronze possessed no unearthly superpowers. The American public wasn't quite ready for that yet. Superman lay five years in the future. But the hyper-imaginative Dent pushed the heroic envelope as far as he dared. And he dared *far*.

Doc Savage was everything an aspiring hero could dream of becoming. Tall, physically powerful, emotionally reserved, yet a genius. He stood well over six feet, weighed 250 pounds, his physique so perfectly symmetrical that only by comparison to other objects did his sheer imposing size become apparent. They called Doc the Man of Bronze because his skin had been burnt a deep metallic bronze, the result of a lifetime spent under Equatorial suns and Polar climes. His hair was a dark metallic skullcap that was strangely waterproof. His eyes were like pools of flake-gold, always in motion, hypnotic and strangely intent.

Although the world's preeminent surgeon, scientist and adventurer, Doc was modest. He never lied, nor swore, avoided killing, spoke in quiet, cultured tones and seldom lost his temper. The quintessential strong, silent type, he expressed emotion only through his animated eyes and a peculiar trilling sound which he made unconsciously, and which was invariably described in terms suggesting his exotic upbringing.

Dent called Doc Savage the "Man of Tomorrow." He was constantly coining colorful new descriptives—mental wizard, physical marvel, metallic giant, scientific Aladdin, Muscular Midas, "a colossus of brawn and brain," and any number of other pulp superlatives. This was pure unadulterated hyperbole on Dent's part, but it was also an expression of the desperate Depression times that birthed him. It was an era which celebrated its heroes. Charles Lindbergh had just crossed the Atlantic. Byrd and Perry were braving the Poles. The late Thomas A. Edison had been all but deified after his death, his inspirational genius driving a new generation of scientists. Lincoln was still remembered as the "Great Emancipator." America dubbed Lindbergh the "Lone Eagle." Babe Ruth was the "Sultan of Swat." On the front page of no less than the *New York Times,* Albert Einstein was grandiloquently described as an "explorer of the cosmos and champion of humanity." Even the criminals of the 1930's were shrouded in legend—"Scarface" Al Capone, "Pretty Boy" Floyd, and others.

"Doc" Savage and his men were walking tall tales. And that, as much as anything, inspired Lester Dent, who early on described him this way: "This man of mystery has been trained from the cradle, until now he is almost a super being." Furthermore, Doc "seemed to possess abilities beyond those of ordinary mortals."

From his superhuman strength and superkeen senses to his superplanes and supermachine pistols, everything about Doc was "super."

Doc Savage took Depression-era America by storm. Within a year he was on radio and later had his own comic book. Numerous imitations sprang up in the pulps, but it was on the comic book superheroes that the Doc Savage influence had its most profound and lasting effect.

Perhaps nowhere is this more evident than in the novel we've chosen to reintroduce Doc Savage to 21st Century readers. Everyone knows that the Fortress of Solitude is the Arctic retreat of Clark Kent, better known as Superman, the Man of Steel.

But Superman did not debut until 1938. Clark Savage's Fortress—the original one—was first mentioned in the premier Doc novel in 1933 as Doc's "rendezvous built on a rocky island deep in the arctic regions."

It was Doc's most closely-guarded secret. In *The Man of Bronze,* Dent revealed only this much:

> It was to this spot that Doc retired periodically to brush up on the newest developments in science, psychology, medicine, engineering. This was the secret of his universal knowledge, for his periods of concentration there were long and intense.
>
> The Fortress of Solitude had been his

father's recommendation. And no one on earth knew the location of the retreat. Once there, nothing could interrupt Doc's studies and experiments.

That was all. No hint of size or shape or construction.

Periodically, Dent teased readers with clues as to the Fortress' true nature. It was said to house the largest scientific laboratory on Earth. It was so remote that no one but Doc Savage knew its exact location. Once or twice, he considered taking Doc fans there. But Dent kept its actual nature to himself for over five years. Only a private notebook containing the secrets of Doc Savage held the truth.

In 1938, Street & Smith editor John L. Nanovic decided that the time had finally come. No doubt he was influenced by the successful unmasking of The Shadow the previous year. Probably the discovery by criminals of The Shadow's secret sanctum in *Crime, Insured* was another trigger. It was time for such an "event" novel in the Doc Savage series.

For this, Lester Dent sat down to create a foe brilliant and resourceful enough to penetrate Doc's holy of holies. He called him John Sunlight. Don't let the innocuous name fool you. As you will soon discover, John Sunlight is evil personified.

And curiously, the Fortress that Lester Dent finally unveiled in 1938 was not the same place he had imagined five years before. In that time, the idea had incubated. When at last the place stood revealed as … but why spoil the surprise? Read *Fortress of Solitude* for yourself and see.

So how did the Man of Steel come to possess a Fortress of Solitude all but identical in concept and location as that of the Man of Bronze? It's easy to point the finger of suspicion at Jerry Siegel and Joe Shuster, who created Superman circa 1934 as young boys who avidly devoured pulp magazines.

"Of course I read *Doc Savage* in those days..."

1934 house ad for *Doc Savage*

Jerry Siegel once admitted. How could he plausibly deny it? Both heroes sported an identical spit curl.

The parallels were not merely conceptual, but spiritual. Siegel once described Superman as "… a character like Samson, Hercules and all the strong men I ever heard tell of rolled into one."

Consciously or not, he was echoing Lester Dent, who once explained Doc Savage's genesis this way: "I looked at what people had gone for already, so I took Sherlock Holmes with his deductive ability, Tarzan of the Apes with his towering physique, Craig Kennedy with his scientific knowledge, and Abraham Lincoln with his Christliness. Then I rolled 'em all into one to get—Doc Savage."

On another occasion, Siegel put it this way: "The idea came to me in bed one night. A champion for good with the strength of Atlas, as invulnerable as a perfect Achilles, plus the morals of Galahad."

While Dent often likened Doc Savage to a "muscular Hercules," he also described him as "a modern Galahad." Street & Smith house ads trumpeted Doc as a "superman" and a "super-hero."

Siegel was hardly the only aspiring creator to be fascinated by this new kind of hero. Bill Finger, who with artist Bob Kane, created Batman in 1939, said this: "My idea was to have Batman be a combination of Douglas Fairbanks, Sherlock Holmes, The Shadow and Doc Savage as well."

By 1940, American newsstands were awash in a new publishing phenomenon—superhero comics inspired by Superman. They would give Doc Savage and The Shadow stiff competition over the next decade.

Dent himself acknowledged that he had created a startling new direction in fictitious heroes. Asked in 1945 about Superman and the others, he grumbled: "After the flood of super-people, phantoms, bat-men and such people that Doc started coming out of the cartoonists' and writers' ink-wells, my stomach kind of turned. ... And remember, I didn't have Doc brought from another planet the way Superman was. I just had Doc reared and trained by scientists, that's all."

But the Man of Steel did not start out as much of a direct imitation of the Man of Bronze as he later become. The man who injected extra doses of Doc Savage into Superman was not Jerry Siegel, but *Superman* editor Mort Weisinger.

Weisinger was a young pulp writer whom Lester Dent met in 1934, probably through Weisinger's roommate, W. Ryerson Johnson. Better known as "Johnny," Johnson was one of the first writers a busy Dent turned to for help writing the monthly Doc novels. When Johnny plotted his first one, Weisinger was at his side pitching in ideas.

Weisinger and Dent became friends, sometimes going on day trips on Dent's schooner, *Albatross.*

"He was like a corsair come to life," Weisinger recalled. "He was tall and he was brawny. And he was industrious. He knew mining and navigation. Dent had a formula he used for every one of his novels. He claimed you should always have an exotic locale, and the mystery should be: who did it? And the motivation: why did he do it? And a unique murder method: how did he do it? And in every book a unique treasure."

In 1940, Weisinger helped plot one of Dent's own Docs, and came within a whisker of writing it too. But Mort Weisinger's true forte was editing. During his stint on *Thrilling Wonder Stories,* he helped create the pulp hero Captain Future, which he frankly described as "a science fiction parallel to Doc Savage."

Then he was invited to join DC comics by editor-in-chief Whit Ellsworth. As Weisinger later related, "I said, 'What was the job?' [Whit] said, 'Be editor of *Superman.'* I said, 'What's that?' And he told me. But he said, 'What I want you to do is shape up *Batman* and other magazines because *Superman* is in a groove with Jerry Siegel. By the way, he recommended you.' Siegel and I were old friends. We used to work on a fan magazine together."

At DC, Weisinger's editorial duties expanded all through the 1940s and into the '50s, until finally, he had sole responsibility for Superman.

It was under Mort Weisinger's editorial

Lester Dent and future *Superman* editor Mort Weisinger set sail for adventure aboard *Albatross.*

guidance that Superman was given his Fortress of Solitude. The year was 1949. The final issue of *Doc Savage Magazine* was about to be published. Weisinger must have reasoned that Doc was a fading legend, soon to be forgotten. He never dreamed that fifteen years in the future, Doc Savage reprints would sell millions of paperback editions, earning the Man of Bronze a vast new audience.

It was a possibility that seemed to elude the otherwise prescient Lester Dent, as well. Mere months before his death in 1959, he said of his old Doc novels, "They would be so outdated today that they would undoubtedly be funny. Hell, when I wrote them, an airplane that would fly 200 miles per hour was science fiction. They would be of no interest any more."

Yet during the 1960s, when Hollywood brought Ian Fleming's James Bond to the screen, to make him more exciting they gave him Doc Savage-style weapons and gadgets by the pound. And when James Bond led to the hit TV show *The Man from UNCLE,* creator Sam Rolfe ransacked the *Doc Savage* novels he read as a boy for the new series.

> I lived for the monthly issues of *Doc Savage.* I saved every penny I could lay my hands on to save up the dime--then haunted the magazine stand every day for the week it arrived...*UNCLE* depended upon a very delicate balance between the absurd and the real. I insisted upon sticking a 'Normal' character into every episode, up early, who kept looking around at the things happening to himself and remarking that he didn't believe any of it—a person who always returned to his normal life at the end, having had a great adventure (I guess I was putting into my plays my old 'Doc Savage' daydreams).

During that Depression decade the future architects of the Marvel Universe, Stan Lee and Jack Kirby, also read *Doc Savage Magazine.* It was nowhere more evident than in their top creation *The Fantastic Four,* which was built upon the master blueprint Lester Dent had laid down thirty years before. Stan Lee recalls:

> I remember reading *Doc Savage* when I was young and being intrigued by his abilities and his characteristics as well as those of his teammates. Even though they didn't have super powers as such, they were more colorful and better at what they did than the average Joe and that's what made them so fascinating to me and to a legion of readers—and what has kept them fresh in my mind after all these years.

And now the original Man of Tomorrow has returned to thrill 21st century readers.

A complete
Book-length Novel

Fortress Of Solitude

Doc Savage's secrets revealed at last! And by a villainous mind of insatiable greed!

By

KENNETH ROBESON

IT was unfortunate that Doc Savage had never heard of John Sunlight. Doc Savage's lifework was dedicated to attending to such men as John Sunlight, preferably before they managed to get too near their goal. But Doc Savage did not hear of John Sunlight in time.

It was also too bad that John Sunlight was destined to be the man who found the Strange Blue Dome.

JOHN SUNLIGHT

It seemed from the first that John Sunlight had been put on this earth so that men could be afraid of him.

Russia was the first government to become afraid of him. It just happened that Russia was the first—John Sunlight wasn't a Russian. No one knew what he was, exactly. They did know that he was something horrible with a human body.

Serge Mafnoff wanted to give John Sunlight to a firing squad. Serge Mafnoff was the Russian official who captured John Sunlight and prosecuted him before the Soviet equivalent of a court.

"This thing known as John Sunlight," Serge Mafnoff said earnestly, "is incredible and shocking. We owe it to humanity to see that he is shot."

Serge Mafnoff was an honest, earnest, idealistic man. About John Sunlight, he was right.

John Sunlight took a silent vow to someday take revenge on Serge Mafnoff.

But the jury was soft. John Sunlight was accused of using blackmail on his superior officers in the army to force them to advance him in rank, and that might be only misdirected ambition. Serge Mafnoff knew it was more grim than that.

Anyway, John Sunlight didn't look the part. Not when he didn't wish, at least. He resembled a

gentle poet, with his great shock of dark hair, his remarkably high forehead, his hollow burning eyes set in a starved face. His body was very long, very thin. His fingers, particularly, were so long and thin—the longest fingers being almost the length of an ordinary man's whole hand.

The jury didn't believe Serge Mafnoff when he told them that John Sunlight had the strength to seize any two of them and throttle them to death. And would, too, if he could thereby get the power to dominate a score of men's souls.

John Sunlight went to a Siberian prison camp.

He had never, as yet, heard of the Strange Blue Dome. But he was determined someday to pay off Serge Mafnoff.

The prison camp was located on the outer northern Siberian coast. Hundreds of miles of impassable ice and tundra lay south; to the north was the Arctic Ocean and the North Pole. Once each year, an icebreaker rammed through to the prison colony with food and more prisoners.

No one had ever escaped the camp.

The icebreaker took John Sunlight to the Siberian camp one August. It came back.

The next August, a year later, the icebreaker sailed for the camp again. This time, it did not come back.

It was two months before the Soviets became excited and sent planes to see what had happened. They might have saved the gasoline the plane engines burned. For they found some piles of ashes where the prison camp had been, and nothing else.

They didn't even find an ash pile to hint what had become of convicts, icebreaker, and icebreaker crew.

SEVEN months later, John Sunlight stepped out on the bridge of the icebreaker, and forty-six persons sank to their knees in craven terror. This pleased John Sunlight. He liked to break souls to do his bidding.

No one had been killed yet. The forty-six included the crew of the icebreaker, and the convicts. For one of the queerest quirks of John Sunlight's weird nature was that he preferred to control a mind, rather than detach it from the owner's body with a bullet or a knife.

The icebreaker had now been fast in the ice for four months.

It looked very much as if they were all going to die.

None of them yet knew that the Strange Blue Dome existed.

Civan was John Sunlight's chief aide. Civan had helped in the prison camp break. It was he who emptied the powder from the guards' cartridges, working secretly over a period of days. Civan had fired the camp. Civan had a streak of sadism in his nature—he liked to destroy things. He had wanted to destroy the Soviet government. But he hadn't been in the prison camp for that. He had been there for destroying a man whose wife and money he coveted.

Civan was a bestial black ox to look at, but he did have a certain amount of brains. He had, however, absolutely no conscience. And so that strange and terrible thing, John Sunlight, had picked Civan to be his lieutenant.

Queerly, too, Civan feared John Sunlight infinitely more than anyone else. John Sunlight saw to that. Terror was the rope that John Sunlight kept around men's necks.

The icebreaker drifted, trapped in the arctic ice. They shot a seal now and then. But they slowly starved, too.

Women are supposed to be more hardy than men.

So the two giantesses, Titania and Giantia— these were their vaudeville names—did not waste away. Their great muscles retained the strength to open horseshoes and bend silver rubles double. Giantia and Titania—their other name was Jeeves. They were Americans. They were great women, very blonde. They were amazing women. They were a little queer, maybe, because all their lives men had been scared of them. They were such amazons.

They had gone to Russia with a vaudeville act, and had been accused of dabbling in a bit of profitable spy work on the side. They were quite guilty, so the United States government looked the other way when they were sent to Siberia.

Titania and Giantia were afraid of John Sunlight. They had never been scared of any other man. But they did not worry about John Sunlight.

Fifi—they worried more about Fifi, Titania and Giantia did. Fifi was their little sister, their tiny, cute, exquisitely beautiful sister. Fifi had been left in New York. Fifi was such a nitwitted little sweetykins, and they were bothered all the time they were in Siberian exile about how she would get along in big wicked New York. And they were still worrying about it.

It did look, though, as if they had troubles enough of their own.

Two months more, and they had surrendered themselves to all being dead in another month. But they didn't die.

Because they saw the Strange Blue Dome.

THERE was a fog, a low fog no more than twenty feet deep, and they could stand on the icebreaker upper deck and look out over it. So they first saw only the top of the Strange Blue Dome.

"Blue whale off the bow!" the lookout squalled weakly.

Titania and Giantia galloped to the upper deck as if rushing on a vaudeville stage to bend iron bars and do handstands before an audience. Some of the others had to crawl—ten couldn't make it at all. John Sunlight came walking with slow, cold ominousness, like a devil in black, or a Frankenstein, or a Dracula. They shrank away from him, and did not forget to sink to their knees.

They looked at the Strange Blue Dome for a long time. And they became very puzzled. It was no whale, blue or otherwise.

It was no rock, either.

It was like nothing that should be. Its height must be all of a hundred feet, and there was a shimmering luminance to it that was eerie, even if they had not seen it standing, as if completely disembodied, above a gray carpet of fog. Generally, it resembled the perfectly spherical half of an opaque blue crystal ball—of incredible size, of course.

They stood and stared, breathing only when they had to.

The crushing of the icebreaker brought them out of their awed trance. The icebreaker hull caved in. Suddenly. There was no warning, just a great grinding and screaming of collapsing metal, a popping of pulled rivets, the feeble screams of the men who had been too weak to come on deck and were trapped.

"Get those men out!" John Sunlight ordered.

He did not want men to die. A man dead was a man he could not dominate.

Ten had been below decks. They got six out, but four had been crushed to death.

"Get the bodies out," John Sunlight directed, a spark of awful determination in the eyes that now burned like sparks in the hollows of his dark, poetic face.

They did it, shuddering all the while, for they knew what he meant. There had been no food for days and days, not even boiled shoes.

The ice was piling up against a stone island, and this had caused the icebreaker to be crushed. They found that out soon.

The rocky island was as smooth as a great boulder, with no speck of soil anywhere, no chance of anything green growing. They crawled upon it in the fog, and it was more bleak and cold and inhospitable than they had believed anything could ever be, even after what they had been through.

They wanted to die, except for John Sunlight.

"Rest," he ordered. "Wait and rest."

He walked toward the Strange Blue Dome. It was now lost in the fog. John Sunlight went slowly, seeming to select and plan each step with care, for he was weaker than the others. He had taken less food than any of them, from the first, and the reason was that he did not want them to die. They were his, his toys, his tools, and he prized them as a carpenter values his best planes and saws, only infinitely more.

So he had given them most of his share of the food, to keep them alive, that he might dominate them. He was sustained now only by the power of the awful thing that was his mind.

This John Sunlight was a weird, terrible being.

At the outer edge of the bleak stone island—it seemed to be one great mass of solid gray rock—the wind had swept all snow away. But farther in, there was snow that got deeper, and was almost impassable to a man without snowshoes.

It was doubtful if a strong man of courage, well-fed, could have struggled through the snow to the side of the Strange Blue Dome.

But John Sunlight did so, and stood beside the fantastic thing and made a low growling sound.

Chapter II
A MAN'S BLACK GHOST

IT was still not too late, had Doc Savage known of John Sunlight. Doc Savage had the finest planes, and knowledge and courage and scientific skill. And he could have reached this arctic rock in time.

Doc Savage, combination of mental wizard, scientific genius, muscular phenomenon, would not have been too late—yet.

For John Sunlight could find no way into the weird blue half ball. He looked first at the base of the thing, but the glasslike blue walls seemed to continue on down into the solid rock.

John Sunlight clawed at the glazed blue. It felt as hard and cold as steel. He put his face against it and tried to see through the blue substance, whatever it was. It seemed that he should be able to peer through it—the stuff had a certain transparent aspect. But he could see nothing.

Next, John Sunlight made a complete circle of the thing. He found no door, no window, no break of any kind.

The blue dome was not made of bricks, or even great blocks. It appeared to be one solid substance of a nature unknown. Not glass, and yet not metal either. Something mysterious.

It took a long time to satisfy John Sunlight that he could find no door.

He went back to the others.

"Get sledgehammers off the wrecked icebreaker," he said coldly.

The sledgehammers were brought him. Titania

FIFI

and Giantia alone had the strength to fetch them.

John Sunlight took the heaviest sledge.

"Stay here." His eyes smoldered in the almost-black cups which his eye sockets had become. "Stay here."

He stood and gave each of them hypnotic attention in turn.

"None of you must ever go near that blue dome," he said with stark intensity.

He did not say what would happen if they disobeyed; did not voice a single threat. It was not his way to give physical threats; no one had ever heard him do so. Because it is easy to threaten a man's body, but difficult to explain how a terrible thing can happen to a mind. That kind of a threat would not sound convincing, or even anything but silly.

But they knew when they heard him. And he knew, too, that not one of them would go near the Strange Blue Dome. He had not exerted his hideous sway over them for months for nothing.

It took a longer time for John Sunlight to make his way back to the vast blue thing. He planted his feet wide, and raised the sledgehammer, and gathered all his great strength—his strength was more incredible than anyone could have imagined, even starved as he was—and hit the blue dome.

There was a single clear ringing note, as if a great bell had been tapped once, and the sound doubtless carried for miles, although it did not seem loud.

John Sunlight lowered the sledgehammer, examined the place where he had struck. He made his growling. It was a low and beastly growl, almost the only emotional sound he ever made. Too, the bestial growl was almost the only meaty, physical thing he ever did. Otherwise he seemed to be composed entirely of a frightful mind.

His sledge blow had not even nicked the mysterious blue substance of which the dome was composed.

John Sunlight hit again, again, and again—

He was still hitting when the Eskimo said something guttural.

IT was a sinister indication of John Sunlight's mental control that he did not show surprise when the Eskimo grunted. He did not know what the Eskimo had said. He did not speak the Eskimo tongue. And an Eskimo was one of the last things he had expected to appear.

Particularly a well-fed, round butterball of an Eskimo with a happy smile, holding a large, frozen chunk of walrus meat.

John Sunlight smiled. He could smile when he wished.

"How, Eskimo," he said. "You fella savvy us fella plenty happy see you fella."

The Eskimo smiled from ear to ear.

Then he spoke in the best of English.

"How do you do," he said. "One of my brothers reported sighting you landing from a wrecked ship, and stated that he believed you were without food, so I brought you some walrus meat."

John Sunlight's bony, dark face did not change a particle. He was not a man who showed what he thought.

"You live close?" John Sunlight asked.

The Eskimo nodded and pointed.

"Over there, a few hundred yards," he said.

"How many Eskimos are in your camp?" inquired John Sunlight.

"An even dozen, including myself," replied the Eskimo.

John Sunlight leveled a rigid arm at the Strange Blue Dome.

"What is it?" he asked.

The Eskimo stared straight at the blue dome, and looked faintly puzzled.

"I do not see anything," he said.

John Sunlight gave a violent start—in spite of the fact that he rarely showed emotion. This was different. Insanity was the one thing he feared. Insanity—that would take away the incredible thing that was his mind.

He thought, for a horrible instant, that he was imagining all this; that no blue dome was there.

"You do not see a great blue dome?" John Sunlight asked tensely.

The Eskimo shook his head elaborately.

"I see nothing of the kind," he said.

John Sunlight took hold of his lip with teeth that were unnaturally huge and white, and gave him the aspect of a grinning skull when he showed them.

"What do you see?" he asked.

"Only snow," said the Eskimo calmly.

John Sunlight moved quickly then. He seized the Eskimo. The Eskimo was round and strong and well-fed, but he was no match for John Sunlight's mad strength. John Sunlight hurled the Eskimo against the side of the blue dome. The Eskimo moaned and fell back to the snow, unconscious.

"That must have *felt* pretty hard, for something you couldn't *see,*" John Sunlight snarled.

He then dragged the Eskimo back to the others, along with the large chunk of walrus meat. There was not enough walrus meat for everyone, so John Sunlight divided it among—not the weakest, this time—but the strongest. He wanted to make them stronger, so they could overcome the colony of Eskimos. They cooked up the walrus meat, and the weak sat back in shaking silence and watched the strong eat, although they were starving.

John Sunlight did not eat any himself. He was a strange man.

Meantime, the Eskimo regained consciousness. He rolled his little black grape eyes and said nothing.

He still had said nothing, even after John Sunlight had kicked in half of his ribs. He only lay silent, coughing a little scarlet when he could not help it.

The Eskimo had not even admitted that he could see the Strange Blue Dome.

They had saved rifles off the icebreaker. They took those and went to capture the rest of the Eskimos.

THE capture was easy enough. They merely

APUT

walked in and presented the rifle snouts for the Eskimos' inspection, and the Eskimos, after first laughing heartily as if they thought it was one huge joke, realized it wasn't, and became silent and beady-eyed with wonder.

There were four igloos, very large and fashioned with picture-book perfection from blocks of frozen snow. Each igloo had a long tunnel for an entrance, and along these tunnels were smaller igloos used to store food. There were also other very small igloos scattered around, in which the dogs slept. There were not many dogs.

"What is that blue dome?" John Sunlight asked.

They stared at him wonderingly. "What blue dome?"

"Don't you *see* it?"

The Eskimos all talked like that, and it made John Sunlight more gaunt and grim, until finally, to satisfy himself of his own rationality, he broke down his order that no white person but himself should go near the Strange Blue Dome. He took Civan and Giantia and Titania and some of the others to the dome and made them feel of it, made them kick the sledgehammer out of the snow, pick

**John Sunlight hit
again, again ...**

it up and each strike a great ringing blow on the mysterious sides of the dome.

"You *see* it?" John Sunlight asked. "You *feel* it?"

"Dah, soodar," Civan said.

"Yes, sir," said Titania and Giantia, which was the same thing, only in English, not Russian.

John Sunlight thereafter felt much better, although there was no visible change in him. He knew now that he wasn't demented, or seeing something that wasn't there.

Two things were now possible: One, the

Eskimos were lying for a reason; two, they were hypnotized. John Sunlight knew something of hypnotism, knew more than it was good for any man of his kind to know, and he soon satisfied himself the Eskimos were not hypnotized.

So the Eskimos were lying. Not lying—just not admitting anything. John Sunlight began breaking them, and he found that breaking an Eskimo was not as easy as doing the same thing to a white man or woman. The Eskimos had lived amid physical peril all their lives; their minds did not get afraid easily.

The Eskimos got no more food. Fuel for their blubber lamps was taken from them. So was their clothing, except for bearskin pants. Naturally, John Sunlight seized their weapons.

Six weeks passed. John Sunlight, all those off the icebreaker, fared well, grew fat.

The Eskimos kept fat, too.

That was mysterious. It worried John Sunlight. The Eskimos got nothing to eat and thrived on it.

It was a human impossibility, and John Sunlight did not believe in magic. He wondered about it, and watched the Eskimos secretly, watched them a lot more than anyone imagined.

His spare time John Sunlight spent trying to get into the Strange Blue Dome. He swung the sledgehammer against the blue stuff for hours, and bored away with steel drills off the icebreaker, and shot a lot of steel-jacketed, high-powered rifle bullets against the mysterious material. The results—well, he would have had better luck with a bank vault.

The Strange Blue Dome became a fabulously absorbing mystery to John Sunlight. He kept on, with almost demoniac persistence, trying to get into the thing.

If it had not been for the Eskimos staying so fat, he might never have succeeded.

ONE night an Eskimo crawled out of an igloo and faded away in the darkness. It was not really dark all the time, this being the six-month arctic night, but they called it night anyway, because it was the time when they slept.

The Eskimos had been making a fool of John Sunlight.

He had watched them days and days. They were eating; they must get food somewhere. He had not seen them get it, and the reason was simple—a long robe of white arctic rabbit. When an Eskimo crawled away, the white rabbit robe made him unnoticeable against the snow.

This time, the Eskimo accidentally got a brown hand out of the robe.

John Sunlight followed the Eskimo.

He watched the Eskimo go to the Strange Blue Dome, stand close beside it; saw a great portal swing open in the dome and watched the Eskimo step inside, to come out later with an armload of something. The blue portal closed behind the Eskimo.

John Sunlight caught the Eskimo, clubbed him senseless. The stuff the Eskimo was carrying looked like sassafras bark—food. Compressed, dehydrated food, no doubt of that. But strange food, such as John Sunlight had never heard of upon this earth.

John Sunlight stood thinking for a long time. He took the Eskimo's white rabbitskin robe. He put it on. He stood against the blue dome where the Eskimo had stood.

And the portal opened.

John Sunlight walked into the mysterious Blue Dome.

It was now almost too late for Doc Savage, even had he known of John Sunlight, to prevent what was written on the pages of the book of fate.

JOHN SUNLIGHT vanished.

For a day, two days, a week, he was not heard of. Not for two weeks.

On the second week, he was still not heard of; but something incredible happened. Titania, Giantia, Civan, and some of the others saw an Eskimo turn into a black ghost.

The Eskimo who became a black ghost was the one who had vanished when John Sunlight disappeared and had not been seen or heard from, either.

It was night. That is, it was darker night, because there were clouds. Titania, Giantia, Civan and the others were wondering what they would do for food now that the supply taken from the Eskimo was running low, and they were standing on a small drift and discussing it, when they saw the Eskimo running toward them.

Screaming made them notice the Eskimo. He was shrieking—screeching and running. He came toward them.

Suddenly, the Eskimo stopped. He stood facing them, his arms fixed rigidly in a reaching-out-toward-them gesture. His mouth gaped a hole. Incredibly still, he stood. He might have been an old copper statue which was greased.

The next instant, he might have been made of black soot. The change occurred instantaneously. One instant, a copper man; the next, a black one.

Then smoke. Black smoke. Flying. Coming apart, swirling away in cold arctic wind; spreading, fading, going mysteriously into nothingness.

There was no question about it. The Eskimo had turned into a black smoke ghost, and the smoke had blown away.

Now it was too late for Doc Savage. And John Sunlight had not forgotten the score he had to settle with Serge Mafnoff.

Chapter III
IS A DIPLOMAT DEAD?

SERGE MAFNOFF was an idealistic man, a fine citizen of the Soviet, and ambitious—all of these facts his superiors in the Russian government recognized. They kept a kindly eye on Serge Mafnoff, and shortly after he did his fine stroke of work by catching John Sunlight and sending him to Siberia, a reward was forthcoming.

Serge Mafnoff's reward was being appointed as an important diplomatic representative to the United States of America, with headquarters in New York City. It was a pleasant job, one an ambitious man would like; and Serge Mafnoff enjoyed it, and worked zealously, and his superiors smiled and nodded and remarked that here was a man who was worth promoting still again. Serge Mafnoff was very happy in New York City.

Then one evening he ran home in terror.

Actually ran. Dashed madly to the door of his uptown mansion, pitched inside, slammed the door. And stood with all his weight jammed against the door, as if holding it shut against something that pursued him.

His servants remarked on the way he panted while he was doing that. They told the police, later, how he had panted with a great sobbing fright.

It was interesting. And Serge Mafnoff had servants who liked to gossip. They gathered in the chauffeur's quarters over the garage, the most private place, and discussed it. They were concerned, too. They liked Serge Mafnoff.

Everyone liked Serge Mafnoff. He was quite a newspaper figure. A fine representative of the type and character of man the Soviet is trying to create, he was called.

Liking Serge Mafnoff made what happened that night infinitely more horrible to the servants.

The house of Serge Mafnoff in New York City was one long popular with residing diplomats, because it had an impressive dignity and a fashionable location and other things that were desirable for a diplomat.

It was made of gray stone and sat, unlike most New York houses, in quite a considerable yard of its own in which there was neatly tended shrubbery. There were two gates. From one gate a driveway led around to the rear, where there was plenty of lawn and landscaped shrubbery and the two-car garage with the chauffeur's quarters above.

The other gate admitted to a walk which led straight to the mansion door. The house itself was generally square; had two stories and an attic, part of which Serge Mafnoff had walled off and air-conditioned for his private study. Behind the house was a sloping park which slanted down, unbroken except for two boulevards, to the wide, teeming Hudson River and the inspiring Palisades beyond.

Serge Mafnoff screamed in his study.

Every servant in the great mansion heard the shriek, and each one of them jumped violently.

The cook cut the forefinger of her left hand to the bone with the butcher knife, so great was her start. The finger leaked a thread of crimson for some time thereafter—which turned out to be important.

The scream brought all the servants running upstairs. They piled into the study. They stopped. It was impossible to believe their eyes.

Impossible to comprehend that Serge Mafnoff could have become a black man.

SERGE MAFNOFF was all black. Not only his skin, his fingernails, his eyes, his teeth—his mouth was open in the most awful kind of a strangling grimace. All black. That evening he had put on pants and vest of a gray suit, and a robe the nationalistic red color of the Soviet; but these were now the hue of drawing ink.

A jet-black statue, standing.

The butler moaned. The chauffeur made a croaking noise. The cook's hand shook, and her cut finger showered red drops over the floor.

"Comrade Mafnoff!" shrieked the maid, who was a Communist.

The black statue turned to a writhing black ghost. Or so it seemed to the servants. The whole man—they knew it was Serge Mafnoff, because the features of the all-black statue had been recognizable as his—appeared to turn into a cloud of sepia vapor.

A black ghost, it was like. It swirled and changed shape a little, then came swaying toward them, a ghostly, disembodied, unreal monstrosity.

Straight toward them, it floated.

The cook screeched and threw more crimson over the walls and floor. But the chauffeur snatched a pair of heavy pliers out of his hip pocket and hurled them at the black horror.

The pliers went through the thing and dented the plaster of the opposite wall.

Then, suddenly, impossibly, and before their eyes, the black thing silently vanished. It did not spread; it seemed to fade, disintegrate, go into nothingness.

"I killed it!" the chauffeur screamed.

Then the only sound in the room, for long moments, was the frightened rattling of the breath in their throats. The cook's hand dripped.

They were looking for some trace of Serge Mafnoff. Hurting their eyes with looking. And seeing nothing.

"I—I couldn't—have killed him," the chauffeur croaked.

"Ugh!" the butler said.

They were all primed for the next shriek. It came from downstairs, a man's voice in a long peal of imperative supplication and terror.

The cook barked out something hoarse, and fainted. She fell directly in the center of the door, just inside the attic den which was Serge Mafnoff's study.

The other servants left her lying there and raced downstairs to find out who had given that last scream, and what about.

There was a second bellow, just about the time all the servants, excepting the unconscious cook, reached the ground floor. This whoop was out in the backyard, and the whole neighborhood heard it.

Out into the backyard dashed the servants to investigate. They didn't know what they expected to find. Certainly it wasn't what they did find. Which was nothing.

Nothing at all. Only dark, cold night, and the gloomy clumps of shrubbery, which was evergreen and hence unaffected by the fact that the time was winter. Crouching black wads of bushes, and the sounds of the city—honking of automobile horns, a distant elevated, and the bawling of a steamship down on the Hudson.

The black statue turned to a writing black ghost.

They searched and searched.

Then they told the police about it. The police told the newspapers, who printed a great deal about the affair.

Doc Savage read the newspapers regularly.

Chapter IV
BRONZE MAN ATTACKED

NOT everybody in the world had heard of Doc Savage.

But too many had. Doc Savage—Clark Savage, Jr.—had of late been trying to evade further publicity, and he had an understanding, finally, with the newspaper press associations, with some of the larger newspapers, and with most of the fact-story magazines extant. They weren't to print anything about him. They were to leave his name out of their headlines.

Now, if anyone heard of Doc Savage, it would be by word-of-mouth only. "Haven't you heard—Doc Savage has invented a cure for cancer, they say." The surgical and medical skill of Doc Savage was probably his greatest ability. "I hear that new wrestler from Czechoslovakia is a human Hercules, built something along the lines of Doc Savage."

The physical build of Doc Savage got attention wherever he appeared, for he was a giant, although so well proportioned that, seen from a distance, he resembled a man of ordinary proportions.

Talk, talk—there was always plenty of talk about Doc Savage.

"I hear the Man of Bronze has invented an atom motor that could drive the Queen Mary across the Atlantic with a spoonful of coal." They called him the "Man of Bronze" because of the unusually deep-tan hue which tropical suns had given his skin. They—their talk—attributed fantastic inventions to him. Conversation made him a superman, a mental colossus.

Really, Doc Savage was a normal fellow who had been taken over by scientists as a child and trained until early manhood, so that he was rather unusual but still human enough. He had missed the play-life of normal children, and so he was probably more subdued, conscious that he hadn't gotten everything out of life.

Talk, talk—it attributed all kinds of fantastic doings and powers to Doc Savage.

But it was only talk. Nobody, for instance, listening to it, could find out exactly where Doc Savage was at a given time. No enemy could listen to the gossip and get enough real information to lay a plan to kill the Man of Bronze.

His enemies were many. They had to be. Because his lifework was an unusual one. That was why he had been scientifically trained; he had been prepared from childhood, in every possible way, to follow a career of righting wrongs and punishing evildoers, even in the far corners of the earth.

A strange career—his father's idea. His father who was no longer living. His father had located a fabulous source of gold in the Central American mountains, realized such wealth should do good, and had trained his son, Clark Savage, Jr.—Doc Savage—to use the wealth to do good. Also to use it to right wrongs.

This was the real Doc Savage, who found it safer not to be too well-known.

Doc read the newspaper account of what had happened to Serge Mafnoff. The bronze man often spotted unusual wrongs that could stand righting, from reading the newspapers.

Doc Savage did not know, as yet, about the man waiting in the lobby downstairs, or the other men looking at books in a nearby bookstall.

DOC SAVAGE was impressed by the Mafnoff thing.

He was so impressed that he did something which he only did in moments of great mental or physical stress; he made a strange, exotic trilling sound, a note that was created somehow in the throat, and which had a low quality of ventriloquism that made its vibrations seem to suffuse the entire surrounding atmosphere. The sound was often described as being as eerie as the song of some rare bird in a tropical jungle, or like the noise of a wind through an arctic ice wilderness.

There was nothing spooky or supernatural about this sound. Doc had acquired it as a habit in the Orient, where the Oriental wise men sometimes make such a sound deep in the throat—for the same reason, approximately, that the rest of us say, "Oh-h-h, I see. I see, I see-e-e," when understanding dawns.

Doc Savage had been seated at a great inlaid table in his reception room. He stood up quickly. Through the windows—this was the eighty-sixth floor of one of the city's tallest buildings—an inspiring view of Manhattan was visible.

Doc passed through a huge library crammed with scientific tomes, and entered a laboratory so advanced that scientists frequently came from abroad to study it. The bronze man picked up a microphone.

"In case you wish to get in touch with me," he said into the mike, "it is my intention to investigate the Serge Mafnoff story which is on the front pages of the newspapers this morning."

What he said was automatically recorded, could be played back at will. It also went out on the shortwave radio transmitter.

Doc Savage had five assistants in his strange work. Each of the assistants kept a shortwave radio tuned in on Doc's transmitter wavelength as much as possible.

The bronze man then rode his private speed elevator to the lobby.

He was instantly noticeable when he stepped out in the lobby. Not only because of his size. There was something compelling about his carriage, and also about his unusual flake gold eyes—calm eyes, fascinating, like pools of flake gold being continuously stirred.

THE man waiting in the lobby noticed Doc instantly. The man had been loitering there for hours. He was a short man, blond, with a face that looked somehow starved. His story was that he was a process server lying in ambush for one of the skyscraper tenants. When he told that, he spoke with a pronounced Russian accent.

The instant he saw Doc Savage, this man stepped outside, hurried a dozen paces to the door of a small bookstore, entered—and walked right out again.

Several men who had been pretending to browse over books in the store, followed him. These men began getting into taxicabs.

Taxicabs always waited in a long string before the skyscraper, because it was a good stand. The bookstore loiterers took the first four cabs, and these pulled away from the curb. This left the fifth cab in the line as the next one up.

The fifth cab was the one they wanted Doc Savage to take. Driving this machine was a vicious-looking, black ox of a man.

Doc Savage had walked out of the building by now.

Having accomplished the job to which he had been assigned, the fellow who had claimed to be a process server strolled away.

Doc got in the planted cab.

"Drive to the Hudson River waterfront," the bronze man directed quietly.

He had a voice which gave the impression of being infinitely controlled, a voice that could do some remarkable things if necessary.

The cab rolled among the high buildings, passed through the less presentable West Side tenement section, and neared the rumblingly busy street which ran along the Hudson. Here, it stopped for a traffic light.

The window between driver and passenger was open.

Doc Savage reached through this. He took the black oxlike man by the neck.

"That was an ambitious trick you tried to pull," the bronze man said quietly.

He squeezed the neck, trained fingers finding the proper nerve centers. The black ox fellow kicked around violently just before he became senseless.

DOC SAVAGE got behind the wheel, shoving the unconscious passenger over to make room. He kept a sharp lookout around about while doing this, but saw no sign of more trouble. No cars following. As an afterthought, he got out and examined the taxicab.

The bronze man's powers of observation had been trained from childhood, and he still took almost two hours of complicated exercises each day, aimed at developing his faculties.

He had to notice little things—like a man wheeling suddenly and walking from a skyscraper lobby when the bronze man got out of an elevator—if he wanted to go on living.

He saw, under the cab floor, lashed to the chassis, a thick steel pipe which was closed at both ends.

Doc snatched the unconscious man out of the cab, carried him, and ran away from the machine. This was a one-way street. He kept in the middle, so as to stop any cars that might enter. But it was a little-used street, and no cars came.

He waited.

The explosion was terrific. Doc stood at a distance from the cab, but the blast jarred him off his feet anyway.

The cab came apart, flew up in the air, some of the parts going so high that they became small. A deep hole opened in the street itself. Fragments of pavement went bounding along the street. After the first slam of the concussion, there was a ringing of broken glass falling from windows all over the neighborhood.

Doc Savage went away from there in a hurry with his prisoner. He had a high honorary commission in the New York police force, but there was nothing in it that said he didn't have to answer questions.

It was obvious, of course, that the bomb under the cab was attached to a time-firing device which was probably switched on when the driver took his weight off the cushions.

No doubt the idea had been for the driver to stop somewhere and go into a store to get something, leaving Doc in the cab to be blown up.

Doc Savage carried the captive around the block, north two blocks along the Hudson waterfront, and reached a warehouse. The sign on this warehouse said:

HIDALGO TRADING COMPANY

It was an enormous brick building which

appeared not to have been used for years. It was Doc Savage's Hudson River hangar and boathouse.

Doc carried the captive into the warehouse, closed the doors, put the man down on the floor and did things with his metallic fingers to the man's spinal nerve centers. The pressure which was keeping the fellow helpless could be relieved by these chiropractic manipulations.

Doc went through the man's clothing while he was reviving, found nothing except a flat automatic pistol. The dark ox of a fellow sat up. He batted lids over eyes that resembled peeled, hard-boiled pigeon eggs.

"Didn't I come to the end of the chain with a bang?" he muttered.

THAT was the first warning. In the case of this man, it was either one of two things: He was too stupid to be scared; or he had a brain that could control his nerves and make him wisecrack under circumstances such as this.

"Who are you?" Doc Savage asked calmly.

The man did not answer at once. He stared at the bronze man steadily. When he did speak, it was not to answer the question.

"They say no one has ever fought you successfully," he said slowly. "I begin to believe that—looking at you now."

Doc noticed the man's rather strong Russian accent.

"Atkooda vy pree-shlee?" Doc asked.

"Yes. I don't doubt that you would like to know where I come from," the man said. "But let's speak English."

He frowned at the giant bronze man, and could not keep a flicker of terror from his eyes. "You spoke that Russian with no accent at all," he muttered. "They say you can talk any language in the world."

Doc said, "We are not discussing what you have heard. The subject is—why did you try to kill me?"

The man shook his dark oxlike head. "We're

CIVAN

discussing," he said, "whether I had better talk—or tough it out."

"Talk," Doc said.

"Threatening me?"

"No." Doc said quietly. "It is becoming apparent that you are not the type of man who can be frightened readily."

The remark—it was merely a statement of truth as far as Doc Savage was concerned—seemed to shock the prisoner. His big white teeth set in his lips, and unexpected horror jumped briefly into his eyes.

"You don't know John Sunlight," he croaked.

Doc watched him. "John Sunlight?"

The man swallowed several times and forced the terror out of his eyes.

"No, no—you misunderstood me," he said. "I said: 'You don't know, so you lie.' What I meant is that you are trying to kid me along, telling me I'm brave. It's a buildup."

Doc said, "Why did you—" and the man hit him. The fellow hit hard, and he was strong. But the bronze man got his shoulder up, and the fist hit that instead of his jaw. Then he fell on the man. They stormed around on the floor; the man began to scream in agony.

"Why did you try to kill me?" Doc repeated.

"My name is Civan," the man began.

CIVAN sat up on the floor, inched back a few feet from Doc Savage, and felt over his bruises, wincing as his fingers touched the places that hurt. Two or three times he peered at the bronze man, as though puzzled and trying to fathom where such incredible strength came from.

"I was the strongest man in my part of Russia," Civan said stupidly.

Doc said, "Why try to kill me?"

"The man with the long nose hired me to do it," Civan said.

"Who?"

"Eli Camel was the name he gave me," Civan said. "He was a tall man, bowlegged, as if he had ridden horses in his youth. He had a high forehead, a mouth with no lips. And there was his nose, of course. It was very long, and kind of loose on the end, like an anteater's nose."

Doc Savage had never heard of an Eli Camel who had a long nose. But then, he had never heard of many men who might want to kill him.

Voice unchanged, Doc said, "What did this Eli Camel want to kill me for?"

"He did not say," Civan said. "He just gave me twenty thousand dollars, and I agreed to get rid of you. Then he sailed for South America yesterday."

"What about those other men—the ones who saw to it that I took your taxicab?"

"I hired them."

"Who are they?"

Civan shook his head. "I won't tell you. They're not important. They're just men I hired to help me."

Doc Savage did not pursue that point.

"Eli Camel of the long nose, sailed for South America, you say?" Doc asked.

"Yesterday."

"What boat?"

"The *Amazon Maid.*"

"That is all you know?" Doc asked.

"That's all."

Doc Savage went to the telephone. He knew there was a steamer on the South American run named the *Amazon Maid;* he knew what line owned her. He called their offices. When he explained who he was, he got service without delay.

"Yes," the steamship line official told him. "A man named Eli Camel sailed yesterday on the steamer *Amazon Maid* for South America."

"Radio the captain of the *Amazon Maid,*" Doc Savage directed, "and learn if the sea is calm enough for me to land a seaplane alongside his vessel and be taken aboard."

"We'll do that."

"I'll call you for the information later," Doc said.

Civan stared at the bronze man. "You're going after Eli Camel?" Civan demanded.

"What does it sound like?" Doc asked quietly.

DOC SAVAGE went next to a shortwave radio transmitter-receiver outfit—he had them scattered around at almost every convenient point, for he and his associates used that means of communicating almost exclusively.

"Monk," Doc said into the microphone.

The answer came in a squeaky voice that might have belonged to a child or a midget.

"Yeah, Doc," it said.

Doc Savage spoke rapidly and in a calm voice, using remarkably few words to tell exactly what had happened, and to give Monk instructions.

"Hold on!" Monk squeaked. "Let me get this straight. You started out to investigate this Serge Mafnoff mystery?"

"Yes."

"And this guy Civan tried to kill you, and you've caught him, and he's in the warehouse hangar now, and you want me and Ham and Johnny to drop by and pick him up?"

"Exactly."

"Doc, do you think there's a connection between the Mafnoff thing and this attempt on your life?"

Doc Savage did not answer the question. That was one of the bronze man's peculiar habits—when he did not want to reply directly to a query, he simply acted as though no question had been asked.

"Pick up this Civan," Doc said, "then go on out and investigate the Mafnoff mystery."

"Um-m-m," Monk said. "Where'll you be, Doc?"

At that point, the other telephone—there were several lines into the place—rang, and Doc said, "A moment, Monk," and answered the other instrument, listened for a time, said an agreeable, "Thank you," and hung up.

"Monk," the bronze man said, "the line that owns the *Amazon Maid* just called and said the sea was calm enough for a plane to land alongside the steamer and be lifted aboard with a cargo boom."

"Oh!" Monk said. "So that's where you're going—to get that Eli Camel who hired this Civan."

Doc asked, "You will be here shortly, Monk?"

"Shorter than short," Monk said.

This terminated the radio conversation.

Doc Savage tied Civan securely with rope and left him lying in the middle of the hangar floor, lashed to a ring embedded in the concrete.

The bronze man walked to a seaplane. A number of aircraft stood in the hangar, including a small dirigible, but the ship he selected now was small, sturdy, and designed for landing on bad water, rather than for speed or maneuverability in the air.

He started the plane motor, taxied out on the river, fed the cylinders gas. The craft got up on the step, lifted into the air and went droning away and lost itself in the haze over the Atlantic Ocean.

Civan lay on the hangar floor and swore long strings of very bad Russian words.

Chapter V
THE UNWILLING IDOL

MEN do things because of love. Always. Without exception.

Some men love to work, so they work; others love the things money will buy, so they work to get the money. There are men who love to loaf, and loaf. Slaves did not love to be beaten, so they worked in order that they wouldn't get beatings.

Doc Savage's five assistants loved excitement and adventure, and that bound them to the bronze man.

"Monk" particularly. Monk's looks were deceptive. He was one of the world's greatest industrial chemists when he took time off from his adventuring to putter around with test tubes and retorts. He looked rather like something that had been dragged out of a jungle tree recently. Startling near as wide as he was tall, with arms longer than his legs, too much mouth, small eyes, a furry, coarse reddish hair, he looked like a large ape.

"You look," said Ham, "like something an expedition brought back."

"It don't worry me," Monk grinned.

"I'll bet it worried your mother," Ham grinned.

"Ham" was Brigadier General Theodore Marley Brooks, who practically supported the fanciest tailor in the city with his patronage, who carried an innocent-looking black cane which was really a swordcane, and who was also admittedly one of the cleverest lawyers to come from Harvard.

"Listen," Monk said, "you keep on ridin' me, and I'll take you by the neck and shake a writ, a petition and a couple of torts out of you."

"Anytime"—Ham glared—"you gossoon!"

If these two had ever spoken a civil word to each other, it was an accident.

They drove past Radio City, and picked up Major Thomas J. "Long Tom" Roberts, who had been hired as consultant on an intricate problem having to do with television. They found a group of eminent electrical engineers staring at Long Tom Roberts in amazement.

No one would stare at Long Tom because of his looks. He was a scrawny fellow with complexion ranging between that of a fish belly and an uncooked mushroom. So they must be admiring his brains. They were. Long Tom had just pulled an electrical rabbit out of a hat.

Monk, Ham and Long Tom arrived at the warehouse on the Hudson waterfront, drove their car inside, got out and listened in amazement to Civan's swearing. None of them understood Russian. But they could tell that Civan was doing some very good work with words that were unlikely to be in the Russian dictionaries.

When Civan ran dry, they read a newspaper account of how Serge Mafnoff, the diplomat, had apparently turned into a black ghost and vanished.

"Very mysterious," Long Tom commented.

"I believe I'm going to like looking into it," Ham remarked.

"Then I won't like it," Monk said contrarily.

FIRST, they settled the question of what to do with Civan.

"Drown him," Monk suggested. "Tie Ham to him for a weight. Throw 'im in the river."

"That's very funny," Ham sneered. "I'll bet I come nearer solving this mystery than you do."

"You see what I mean," Monk told Long Tom. "Ham's opinion of himself is heavy enough to hold them both underwater."

They compromised by taking a hypodermic needle from an equipment case in the warehouse hangar, and injecting a harmless chemical concoction in both of Civan's legs and both his arms. They waited several minutes until the chemical took effect.

Thereafter, Civan could not move his arms or legs. He could only talk, and he did so, giving detailed opinions of them. Monk picked Civan up and sat him in various places, and Civan remained there; he could not stir. He sat stiffly, resembling an ugly image made out of dark meat.

"Kind of like an unwilling idol," Monk commented. "Only a little noisy."

They loaded Civan in their car and drove uptown to the home of Serge Mafnoff, vanished diplomat. Their credentials got them through the ring of police guards around the place.

"How much have you learned?" they asked the police.

"Are you gonna start that, too?" the cop demanded sourly.

"Then we are to take it you're mystified?"

"Look around," the cop invited. "We're always willing to learn. We'll watch."

They questioned the servants. They got a bloodcurdling, hair-curling description of the black ghost which Serge Mafnoff had become. Nothing else.

They pulled on rubber shoes and entered the attic study where the mystery had happened. The room was about thirty feet long, a little over half as wide, with a large gable window at each end, and small doors on each side. These doors admitted to the unused part of the attic, windowless and dark.

"There's been rats and mice running around here." Monk poked a flashlight beam over the rafters and sills in the unused part of the attic. "You can see their tracks in the dust."

"Yes," the cop said. "We found mouse and rat tracks, too."

"Your tone," Monk said sourly, "insinuates that I'm not gonna find anything you haven't."

The cop grinned. "I've always heard Monk Mayfair was a whiz," he said. "I'm waiting around to see a whiz working."

Monk did nothing to justify the cop's expectations in the attic study. In fact, he succeeded in confusing the issue a trifle. This happened when Monk put the pliers—the same pliers the chauffeur had thrown through the black ghost of Serge Mafnoff—under a microscope.

"Huh!" Monk squinted at the pliers. "That's strange." He took a file and rasped a nick in the pliers, then looked through the microscope at them again. "Yep," he decided. "I was right."

"Right about what?" Long Tom asked.

"The metal of these pliers," Monk said, "is strangely crystallized."

The cop said, "What do you mean—crystallized?"

Monk addressed the chauffeur, asking, "Have you been in the habit of using these pliers regularly?"

"Sure," the chauffeur said. "They're my favorite pliers."

"Do any hammering with 'em?" Monk inquired.

"Of course."

"Look," Monk said.

He tapped the pliers with his file, and they broke into several pieces. It was as though they were as brittle as glass.

"Why, that's funny!" the chauffeur gulped.

THEY turned up nothing else in the attic study, so they shifted attention to the scream which had been heard behind the house. First, they gave the backyard and the alley a thorough search. But all they got out of this was a good deal of exercise at squatting and peering.

"Blast it!" Monk complained.

The cop said, "I'm still waitin' for you guys to do somethin' to live up to your reputations."

When they stood inside the house later, and the cop was not with them, Monk confided to Ham, "That cop is gettin' in my hair, goin' around makin' cracks. He's beginnin' to think I'm stupid."

"The cop probably can't help it," Ham said, "after looking at you."

"I'm gonna show 'im up!" Monk squeaked. "He can't make a monkey out of me!"

"If he'd put you in a tree," Ham said unkindly, "I'd hate to try to tell the difference."

Monk grumbled, and stalked around peering in unlikely places for clues. He was in the kitchen when the cop came up to him.

"Look," the cop said, "I'm gonna have to help you out a little, whiz."

"You don't need to bother—"

"We found this," the cop interrupted, "in the backyard."

The article the policeman presented was a novelty pencil, a combination of pencil and tiny flashlight, and the clip which was designed to hold it in the pocket had been broken off close to the barrel. The clip had not come unsoldered; it had broken off.

"None of Serge Mafnoff's servants admits to owning this," the cop explained. "And it didn't belong to Mafnoff."

Monk took the pencil with bad grace. "I'll examine it for fingerprints."

"We've already done that," the cop said, "and found none."

"I'll do it scientifically," Monk said.

Monk had little confidence in the pencil as a clue; he carried it carelessly as he went back and joined the others, and he was thoroughly astounded when Civan gave a violent croak, pointed his popping eyes at the pencil.

They had set Civan on the floor, where he'd remained helpless, but occasionally quite noisy.

"That pencil!" Civan ejaculated. "Where did you find it?"

"The cops found it in the backyard," Monk replied. "What about it?"

Civan said, "If I wasn't in this too deep to help myself, I wouldn't tell you. But I saw Eli Camel with a pencil something like that. Hold it closer."

"Eli Camel was the man who hired you to kill Doc, eh?" Monk asked, and held the pencil close to Civan's eyes.

"Yes," Civan said. "That's Eli Camel's pencil."

Monk exploded, "Then Eli Camel was probably the man who screamed in the backyard here."

"Right," Civan agreed. "And now he's on the steamer *Amazon Maid* bound for South America."

Monk squatted in front of Civan and asked the man quite a number of questions, but added nothing to the plain fact that Civan knew this pencil had belonged to Eli Camel, the mysterious man with the long nose.

Monk was much pleased; he permitted himself to gloat. "Now I'll show that cop I'm not as dumb as I look," he chortled. He went looking for the cop.

Monk found the cop gaping in admiration at him.

Ham was saying, "The man you want is named Eli Camel. He is tall, bowlegged, has a high forehead, a long nose. And he is on the steamer *Amazon Maid* headed for South America.

"*You* learned all that?" the cop gasped.

"You bet," Ham said.

"Amazing!" the cop exclaimed delightedly

The cop then looked at Monk and sniffed.

"If you had lived up to your reputation, short-and-hairy," he said, "you'd have dug up something important, like Mr. Ham Brooks, here."

Monk glared at Ham.

"Glory hog!" Monk howled. "You knew I was tryin' to impress this cop!"

This was the beginning of a wrangle of some duration between Monk and Ham.

SEVEN other policemen were guarding the Serge Mafnoff diplomatic residence, the guarding consisting of turning back curious people who had read the newspaper stories and wanted to have a look at the house, and possibly play amateur detective.

Two officers stood at one end of the street, two at the other end; one was stationed at the northern extremity of the alley, one at the southern extremity, and the seventh watchman roved over the grounds.

They were surprised when two large touring cars rolled up, stopped, and a group of men alighted. The newcomers wore plain blue suits, and had rather grim faces. Their spokesman confronted the cops.

"We're special plainclothes men from the district attorney's office," he growled. "We're to take over here."

"But—"

"The D. A. isn't satisfied with the progress you've been making on this," the newcomer snapped.

There was never a great deal of love lost between the regular police and special detective squads. In this case, the uniformed cops were secretly enthusiastic about the idea of turning the Serge Mafnoff case over to specials. They were glad to pass the buck. The case was a lemon, utterly baffling.

"Luck be with you," the uniformed cops said, and betook themselves away.

The leader of the "special plainclothes men from the district attorney's office" beckoned his men together. His whisper was a hasty hissing.

"Them cops will find out we lied to 'em," he said. "We've got to move fast."

"Can't move too fast to suit me," a man muttered.

"Get Civan," the leader snapped. "Rescue him. That's the most important. Then wipe out these three Doc Savage aides."

"Rescue Civan," a man repeated, "then croak the Savage helpers."

Now that they all understood, they separated, quickly taking up positions at various points around the grounds of the Serge Mafnoff residence.

Inside the house, Monk was still lambasting the dapper lawyer, Ham, but the homely chemist was beginning to run out of breath.

"You know what a lawyer is?" Monk yelled.

"I'm not interested," Ham said.

"A lawyer," Monk roared, "is a guy who persuades his client to strip for a fight, then runs off with the client's clothes!"

Monk always bellowed when he got excited. Normally, his voice was a mouse among voices, but when he became agitated, or got in a fight, his howling was something remarkable.

Monk stopped for breath.

And all light disappeared.

Chapter VI
THE GRIM BLACK WORLD

ALL light disappeared. Nothing else quite described it, although it might have been said that the Serge Mafnoff house and its immediate surroundings abruptly and inexplicably became trapped in intense blackness. One moment it was a sunlight day, moderately bright; the next instant everything was blacker than black.

Ham's first thought was that Monk had hauled off and knocked him cold, and that the blackness was unconsciousness.

"You hairy hooligan!" he yelled.

He heard his own voice, so he knew he wasn't senseless.

"Has something grabbed you?" Monk demanded.

"Shut up," Ham said, embarrassed. "Can you see anything?"

"No," Monk said. "That is, I can see black."

They could all see black, and nothing else. They lifted their hands before their eyes, and discerned not the slightest vestige of their presence. Their first involuntary impulse was to try to feel the blackness, for it was so intense that it seemed solid; but it wasn't, for their fingers touched nothing more tangible than air.

Then their eyes began stinging.

"It's some kind of black gas!" yelled Long Tom, the electrical wizard.

But that was wrong, because they smelled nothing and tasted nothing.

Monk let out a frightened howl. He had remembered something—remembered the way they had been told that Serge Mafnoff had turned into a black ghost of a figure.

"Maybe we've turned into them black ghosts!" Monk shouted.

The terror of that held them spellbound—until Civan laughed. It was an ugly, delighted, much-relieved laugh that tore across Civan's lips.

That laugh was the wrong thing for Civan to do. Probably he couldn't help it. But it shocked Monk, Ham and Long Tom back to a grip on common sense.

"Grab that guy!" Long Tom yelled.

Monk sprang upon Civan. "I got 'im!"

Ham said, "We better lock the door. I don't know what this is about, but I—"

Ham never would have spoken another word, then, except that he wore a bulletproof undergarment of alloy chain mesh. Doc Savage and all his men wore them habitually, for they were light enough not to be uncomfortable. They were also knifeproof.

A knife blade struck Ham's chest, skidded on

the chain mesh, ruining his expensive coat and vest. Ham grabbed the knife-wielder's wrist, held it tightly, twisted and turned. An arm broke. The attacker started screaming, and kept screaming almost continuously

Fighting was suddenly all through the room. Fist blows, the *gr-r-it!* of knife blades striking chain mail, and shots. The shots were deafening.

A voice crashed out in Mayan.

"Gas masks," it ordered. "Put them on!"

It was Doc Savage's voice. Mayan was the little-known language which Doc and his men spoke—almost no one in the civilized world spoke it besides themselves—when they wished to communicate without being understood.

There was no time to be astonished that Doc Savage had turned up in the middle of this weird, black mêlée. He had a habit of appearing unexpectedly, anyway.

THE gas masks they carried were simple: Gastight goggles, spring-wire nose clips, and breath filters something like overgrown police whistles, which they held in their mouths. They were effective enough, providing you didn't snort off a nose clip, or get a filter knocked out of your mouth or down your throat. The goggles were nonshatterable, however.

Doc Savage called, "Where is Civan?" in Mayan.

Monk took out his breath filter long enough to say, also in Mayan, "Here."

Doc went toward Monk's voice—and straight into violent turmoil.

The assailants, apparently every one of them in the room, had charged toward Monk's voice. Probably because it was so distinctive. When Monk said something in a fight, there was no doubt about who said it.

Monk barked painfully—hit or kicked. His breath filter clinked against a wall. Monk fell down. He felt a powerful wrench on Civan, so Monk let Civan go. He thought Doc had taken the man. Monk was plenty willing to turn him loose; he wanted to fight.

There was no more shooting. But there was everything else. Blows. Furniture breaking. Someone tore the rug up with a ripping sound and plunged with it, upsetting people.

Doc Savage broke anaesthetic gas grenades. The stuff was extremely potent and abrupt; it would make a man unconscious, almost invariably, in less than a minute. But it didn't this time. It had absolutely no effect, except that Monk stopped howling and hitting and went to sleep, falling heavily.

The assailants wore gas masks, evidently.

They wore more than that, Doc began to have an ugly suspicion. His fight efforts were too futile. His senses, his muscles, were trained. He should be able to fight in the dark as well as the next man.

The attackers apparently could see in the blackness! And Doc couldn't. Nor his men.

Doc Savage plucked the breath filter from his lips and ordered, "Get into the next room, quick!" without taking gas-charged air into his lungs. He put the filter back.

He got down, felt, and found Monk. He dragged Monk to the door of the next room.

Long Tom and Ham were already in the next room. Doc joined them. They banged the door, and Doc found a key and turned it.

"Upstairs," he said taking the filter out of his mouth briefly.

They rushed across the room, through a door, found the stairs. Up these, they went. Behind them, there was a crashing as the locked door was caved in.

At the top of the first flight of stairs, Doc said, "Go on."

His men went on. Doc flipped a small high-explosive grenade down the stairs. He wore a padded vest which was mostly pockets to contain the gadgets.

Came a crack of an explosion. Crashing and splintering were mixed in with the blast. And the lower half of the stairs came to pieces and fell down.

A considerable number of bullets came up the stairway during the next three or four minutes. Then the strange attackers went away.

After awhile, it was suddenly daylight again.

DAYLIGHT brought stillness. It just had to. What had happened was so eerie, so impossible, that it left an aftermath of shocked awe.

Sunshine slanted in through the windows. Somewhere out in the shrubbery, a bird emitted a frightened cry. In the distance, city traffic still rumbled, and farther away there was a ghostly, undulating whining noise. Police sirens.

The walls of the room in which Doc Savage stood were papered blue, the ceiling was cream, the carpet was very dark blue and the furniture upholstered in plush. Monk lay on the floor at Doc's feet and snored. Around about was some debris which had flown up from the blasted stairs.

Doc held a long, thin, telescoping periscope at the door, and saw no one was now at the foot of the stairs. The lower half of the stairway was a complete wreck, scalable only with a ladder.

Long Tom and Ham were peering cautiously around an upper landing, where they had taken shelter. They came down.

"I thought you had Civan!" Ham exclaimed.

Doc Savage shook his head slightly. "Our own lives were more important."

"But—"

"They could see in that blackness," the bronze man said. "They concentrated on rescuing Civan. Then they were going to turn their attention to getting rid of us. We got away just as they started the last."

The tension of shocked awe subsided. Ham and Long Tom began to think of rational questions.

Ham pointed at Monk. "Is he hurt?"

Considering how the two quarreled, Ham's anxiety over Monk was surprising.

"He got some of the anaesthetic gas," Doc explained.

"Oh!"

Ham felt of his own person for damage. He groaned at the rip in his expensive suit. "You haven't had time to go to the *Amazon Maid,* Doc."

The bronze man shook his head slightly. "The *Amazon Maid* story was a gag."

"Gag?"

"To send us off on the wrong trail."

Doc flipped a small high-explosive grenade down the stairs.

"How did you figure that?" Ham demanded.

"Civan," Doc said, "was too eager to explain about a long-nosed man named Eli Camel, and the *Amazon Maid.* Moreover, his tongue slipped once—he mentioned someone named John Sunlight."

"John Sunlight?"

"The unknown quantity, so far," Doc Savage started mounting the stairs toward the attic. He explained. "Instead of flying to the *Amazon Maid,* I watched this place from a house across the street, to see what would happen."

Doc Savage reached the attic, looked out of the windows. They gave the best available view of the neighborhood. There was no sign of their late assailants; they had fled successfully.

THEY brought Monk up to the attic, administered a stimulant, and when the fogging effects of the anaesthetic gas had been knocked out of the homely chemist's brain, he sat up and made noises, then asked a question—the question uppermost in the minds of Ham and Long Tom.

"What was the black?" Monk demanded.

They all looked at Doc Savage; if there was to be an explanation, it would have to come from the bronze man. Monk, Ham and Long Tom were utterly at a loss.

Then they stared in amazement at the bronze man. His face—they had never seen quite such an expression on his face before. It was something stark. Queer. They could not, at first, tell what it was; then they knew that the bronze man was feeling an utter horror.

"Doc!" Monk gasped. "What is it?"

Doc Savage seemed to get hold of himself with visible effort. Then he did a strange thing; he held both hands in front of him and made them into tense, metallic fists. He looked at the fists. They trembled a little from strain.

Finally he put the fists down against his sides and let out a long breath.

"It cannot be anything but what I think it is," he said.

His voice had a hollowness. Such a macabre quality that the others were too startled to put questions. They had never before seen the bronze man this disturbed.

They knew, now, that he would not answer questions.

They watched him pick up the fragments of the pliers which had broken in such a brittle way when Monk tapped them with the file.

"Microscope?" Doc asked.

Monk's pocket magnifier had remained miraculously unbroken. He handed it over, and Doc examined the bits of shattered steel.

"Crystallized," he said. Which also seemed to be what he had expected.

Next, he gave attention to the unused part of the attic, the portion that was dark and windowless.

"Just mouse and rat tracks in there," Monk volunteered.

The bronze man examined the "mouse" tracks closely, and gave the homely chemist a shock.

"Some of the rat tracks," Doc pointed out, "are impressed in the wood."

"Huh?"

"They were probably made by small pieces of metal driven into the underside of boards, the boards having been laid on the rafters. Probably the metal bits were to disguise the fact that boards had been laid on the rafters for someone to stand upon."

Monk swallowed as he digested this. "You mean—somebody hid in there?"

"Apparently."

Doc Savage went next to the entrance of the attic study, where his interest centered on the crimson stains, now dried, left by the Mafnoff cook, who had fainted, they understood, when the shriek was heard downstairs.

There were two sets of the dark stains.

"Two stains," Doc remarked, "indicate the cook might have been moved while unconscious."

Monk eyed the stains, one in front of the door, the other to one side, until Doc's meaning dawned on him.

"Hey!" Monk exploded. "Somebody was hiding in the attic. The scream downstairs drew the servants away. Whoever was in the attic fled, moving the unconscious cook out of the way."

Ham said, "But why go to all of the trouble of moving the cook?"

"Perhaps the one who fled was carrying a heavy burden," Doc said slowly.

They could not get him to elaborate on this remark.

Chapter VII
BIG WOMEN

THE police came; so there naturally had to be extensive explanations, with much of the explaining devoted to making the police comprehend that the whole chain of events had happened. If there had been a shooting or a stabbing, the police would have accepted the fact that a crime had been committed. But this case was unusual. It was incredible. A noted diplomat, Serge Mafnoff, had vanished under—since he had apparently turned into black smoke—impossible-to-believe circumstances. A stranger with a Russian accent— that was Civan—had come to Doc Savage and tried to kill him.

"Wait a minute," the police captain said. "Why'd they try to kill you?"

"That can be part of the mystery," Doc said.

The attack on the Serge Mafnoff home to rescue Civan—the police could grasp that. But they couldn't grasp the strange blackness that had clamped down on the neighborhood; it was as bad as Serge Mafnoff turning into black smoke. It was impossible, it couldn't have happened, and there must be a catch somewhere.

Doc Savage left the representatives of the law with their headache. The bronze man, Monk, Ham and Long Tom went to their cars. They had two machines—one that Doc had driven, and the automobile used by his three men.

All three associates, it developed, wanted to ride with Doc and discuss the mystery.

"But someone has to drive the other car," Doc reminded.

"Let the gossoon do it," Ham suggested, pointing at Monk.

"We'll draw lots," Monk said promptly, which was wasted effort, because when they drew, Monk lost anyway.

Monk seated himself grumblingly at the wheel of the second car, and drove all alone in the wake of Doc Savage's machine. Because the mystery they were embroiled in was so fantastic so far that it completely confused him, Monk decided to keep his mind off it by thinking about something else. He thought about Ham. He tried to dope out a new insult to throw at Ham.

Ham was proud of his Harvard background, his membership in certain exclusive clubs. He often boasted to Monk that he was one of the Four Hundred.

"Four hundred!" Monk snorted. "He comes nearer bein' one of the fifty-seven varieties."

Thinking up verbal spears to stick in Ham was always an absorbing pastime with Monk. He grew completely occupied with the avocation. He paid no great attention to following the others; they were all en route back to headquarters, anyway.

Monk fell behind and entirely lost sight of the other machine containing Doc, Long Tom and Ham.

On a very deserted street, a shabby old sedan suddenly cut in front of Monk's car, and the result was a resounding crash. Both machines came to a stop.

MONK craned his neck.

"Blast women drivers!" he grumbled. "Er— that is"—he took another look to see if the woman was pretty, and she wasn't—"yeah, blast 'em!"

Monk's car was one of Doc Savage's special machines, body of armor steel, wheels of puncture-proof sponge rubber, and it had not been damaged. The other car had not fared so well.

Not one woman, but two got out of the other car. They came striding toward Monk's machine, looking apologetic.

"Gosh!" Monk said.

He was seeing two of the biggest women he had ever glimpsed in his life. Not fat women— big! Two Herculean females, not badly proportioned, but built with at least a triple or quadruple measure of everything.

"Woe is me!" Monk gasped, and hurriedly rolled up the bulletproof glass car windows.

However, when he heard the two feminine titans saying how sorry they were, he rolled down one window.

"We're awfully sorry," one female tower said.

"You bet we are," the other added.

Their voices were distinctly feminine, but as might be expected, had tremendous volume.

"Well," Monk said, "of course your car suffered the most—"

One big woman reached suddenly and got Monk by the hair. She held him.

"Search 'im, Giantia," she said.

The other female tower went through Monk's pockets, slapped the places where men generally carry guns. Monk's squawking and writhing didn't seem to bother her.

"Nothin' on 'im, Titania," she said.

Giantia released Monk's hair, simultaneously giving him a shove in the face. This skidded Monk over to the middle of the seat. One giantess got in on Monk's left, the other on his right, and they closed the car doors.

Monk howled, "Now, look here—"

Both big women put their arms around Monk, but they weren't hugging, exactly. They were squeezing. Monk heard his joints cracking, felt his breath whistle between his teeth and thought his eyes were going to pop out. When they released him the argument was all squeezed out.

"We used to wrassle a bear in one of our acts," Giantia said. "So we know how to handle you."

Titania looked at Monk speculatively.

"Only you're more like a baboon," she decided.

Monk felt of his neck tenderly.

"I can see I'm gonna like you two," he muttered.

Giantia started the engine, backed up, turned and drove away. It was evident to Monk that the two remarkable big girls intended leaving their own wrecked machine and taking him somewhere.

"What's the idea?" he asked fearfully.

Giantia said, "We're gonna make you tell us where we can find John Sunlight."

"John Sunlight?" Monk questioned. "What's that? Some guy's name?"

"Don't kid us," Giantia thundered.

"No," Titania rumbled, "don't kid us. We saw you goin' around takin' care of Civan. We know you're one of his pals."

"But—"

"Shut up," Giantia roared. "We'll tell you when to talk. And you'll talk then, plenty."

"I bet," Titania boomed, "that he knows John Sunlight grabbed our little sister Fifi and is holdin' her to make us keep our mouths shut."

"Sure," exclaimed Giantia. "I bet he knows it all. I bet he knows about the Strange Blue Dome, an' everything. Betcha he knows we only promised to throw in with John Sunlight an' help him so we could get back to New York an' take care of little Fifi."

Monk started off to do some roaring of his own.

"Fifi be danged—"

He got a slap that made his ears sound as though they contained steamboat whistles.

"Don't you talk that way about Fifi!" Giantia thundered.

"Dad blast my kind of luck!" Monk grumbled.

AS a driver, Giantia belonged decidedly to the Barney Oldfield school. When the speedometer needle got below fifty, it seemed to bother her. Monk was confronted with amazement as he watched speed cop after speed cop let them go by, with never an attempt to halt them, or even to follow. Then he remembered that the car carried the special Doc Savage plates which entitled the machine to make its own speed laws.

The destination seemed to be no particular place—just any remote spot where there was a thick growth of concealing trees. Monk began to have a grim suspicion that they were seeking a locality where his screams of agony would not be heard.

"There has been a little mistake," he ventured uneasily.

"Your mistake," Titania said, "was in being born."

"Judgin' from his looks," Giantia added, "there was a mistake somewhere."

Monk squirmed and debated mentally over the things he could do. Jumping out of the car was certainly not one of them, since the machine was now doing seventy-five.

"I'm one of Doc Savage's crew," Monk explained earnestly.

The two giantesses were puzzled, but not impressed.

"Doc Savage—never heard of him," Titania said.

Monk swallowed this pill of surprise. Persons who had not heard of Doc Savage, at least through rumor, were becoming scarce.

"Who is he?" Giantia demanded.

There was a subject on which Monk could wax eloquent. He had a sincere admiration for the bronze man—which very fact probably saved him a great deal of grief on the present occasion. His sincerity was expressed in his voice so effectively that Giantia and Titania were impressed. They stopped the car.

"Now tell us that again," Giantia ordered.

"Doc Savage," Monk said, "is a man whose business is helping other people in trouble. He was trained from childhood for the job. I know it sounds queer. But it's a fact."

Monk waved eloquent. He had a bill of goods to sell, and he suspected it was rather imperative that he sell it. Ham, the silver-tongued lawyer-orator, could have taken lessons from Monk's speech to the two Herculean women. Monk left out very little. Doc's scientific training, physical ability, his five assistants—Monk touched on it all with an earnestness that was completely effective.

"Strong man, eh?" Titania muttered, with an unmistakable gleam of interest.

"Yep," Monk said.

"How big did you say?" Titania asked.

"Bigger than you are," Monk assured her.

Titania sighed. "You know," she remarked, "I've never met a man I could fall—er—that is, a fellow who is as big as I am."

Monk took a deep breath.

"Doc," he said, "has never been able to find a girl quite his own equal, either."

Doc would probably exile him for that remark, if the bronze man ever found out about it.

Titania and Giantia were obviously intrigued. They exchanged glances which Monk had no trouble reading correctly.

"Maybe," Titania said thoughtfully, "this Doc Savage is the man to rescue Fifi from John Sunlight."

"He sure is!" Monk exclaimed quickly.

"We know all about this John Sunlight and the Strange Blue Dome, and everything," Giantia said.

"Doc will sure be glad to get the information," Monk declared earnestly.

Giantia stopped the car, turned it around, and headed back toward New York City.

"You tell us where to go," she ordered Monk.

MONK was expecting a sensation when he ushered Giantia and Titania into the presence of Doc Savage, Ham and Long Tom. He was not disappointed. Ham sprang up and dropped the sword cane.

"What's this?" Ham gasped.

"Little present I brought you," Monk

explained. He felt of his neck, which still ached. Then an idea hit him. He nudged Giantia and Titania, called their attention to Ham.

"When we rescue Fifi," Monk said, "you want to watch this shyster, Ham. He's a lady-killer from way back."

Giantia strode to the astonished Ham, gave him a shove, and Ham sailed back and fell over a chair.

"That," Giantia said, "is just a sample of what you'll get if you make one single sheep eye at Fifi."

"Wuh—wuh—" was the best the astounded Ham could do.

Giantia and Titania suddenly lost interest in Ham. They were looking at the Man of Bronze. They stared, not exactly with their mouths open, but with almost its equivalent.

Doc Savage wore tan trousers and a matching tan shirt which was open at the neck, and the effect of his metallic figure seemed unusually striking. His vitality, strength, size, and the quality of unbounded power which was somehow a part of his personality, were impressive.

Giantia glanced at Monk.

"You ain't the liar I thought you was," she said.

Monk performed introductions—Ham retreated to the other side of the reception room and acknowledged the introduction from that safe distance—and Titania and Giantia were left with nothing to do but stare at Doc Savage, which they proceeded to do with enthusiasm.

"Your accent indicates you have been speaking Russian recently," Doc Savage said.

There were some slight indications that already Giantia and Titania were beginning to make him uncomfortable. Women made Doc uncomfortable rather easily.

Monk said, "Doc, these two young women know all about this infernal mystery. They know all about Civan, and some guy named John Moonbeam—"

"John Sunlight," Titania interrupted.

"Suppose they tell us about it," Doc suggested.

Titania nodded. "It's a long story. It began in Russia where—"

"—where we got mixed up in a spy racket, were caught, and sent to Siberia," interposed Giantia, who seemed anxious to do any talking that was to be done to Doc Savage. "We were sent to Siberian exile, where we—"

"—we met John Sunlight," put in Titania, who seemed to have the same idea about monopolizing any talk with the bronze man. "John Sunlight organized an escape from the Siberian prison camp aboard—"

"—aboard an icebreaker," interpolated Giantia. "And—"

"Shut up, Giantia!" said Titania. "I'm telling it."

"Shut up yourself," ordered Giantia. "I can tell it as well—"

Doc put in quietly, "Perhaps if we closed the windows, there would be less noise to interfere."

Since the headquarters was located on the eighty-sixth floor, there was ordinarily not enough noise to interfere in the least with a casual conversation, but just now there was an unusual amount of uproar. Doc Savage stood for a moment at the window listening. His interest was caught.

A plane was flying slowly over New York City at an altitude of at least two thousand feet. It was a ballyhoo plane—one of the type that had a great aerial loudspeaker, or probably a battery of them, mounted in the cabin, their openings downward. Such a plane could fly a mile in the air and someone speaking into a microphone aboard it could make words heard by an entire city.

A ballyhoo plane over New York City was an unusual sight. There was an antinoise ordinance against them.

This one was talking.

"This is Fifi," it kept saying over and over. *"Giantia and Titania, please do not tell Doc Savage anything."*

It was a woman's voice.

Chapter VIII
QUEST FOR FIFI

THE idea of a ballyhoo plane flying over the city, warning someone not to talk to Doc Savage, was preposterously fantastic. Yet effective, too. More effective than newspaper advertisements, or any other quick way of giving warning.

Doc whipped the double soundproof windows shut. But he was too late.

"What was that?" Titania shouted. She flung the windows open again.

Giantia jumped to the window, too. The two big women listened.

"This is Fifi," said the voice from the sky. *"Giantia and Titania, please do not tell Doc Savage anything."*

Giantia and Titania stared at the ballyhoo plane with stark intensity, and horror came over their faces.

"Fifi!" Titania gulped. "Fifi's voice!"

"John Sunlight has her in that plane!" moaned Giantia.

They stood there, listening as if hypnotized, until the plane reached the far side of the city and banked around and came back. The ballyhoo craft was sweeping back and forth, covering the entire metropolis.

DOC SAVAGE and His IRON CREW

Never before has there been such a group of altruistic adventurers as Doc Savage and his five companions. Raised from the cradle for his task in life, Clark Savage, Jr., goes from one end of the world to another, righting wrongs, helping the oppressed, liberating the innocent. With limitless wealth at his command if he needs it, Doc has the best of scientific equipment and supplies. He maintains his

Doc Savage and his five aides

New York headquarters as a central point, but in addition has his Fortress of Solitude at a place unknown to anyone, where he goes at periodic intervals to increase his knowledge and concentrate. His "college" in upper New York is a scientific institution to which he sends all captured crooks, for there, through expert treatment, they are made to forget all of their past and start life anew.

Fighting these battles with Doc Savage are his five companions. Ham is Brigadier General Theodore Marley Brooks, the most astute lawyer Harvard ever turned out; a faultless dresser, and as adept with his ever-present sword cane as he is with words. Monk, his "sparring" partner, though he looks like a gorilla, is actually a most learned chemist— Lieutenant Colonel Andrew Blodgett Mayfair, one of the foremost chemists in the world. Ham, during the War, taught Monk some French words to use in flattering a French officer. The words weren't flattering, it turned out, and Monk spent some time in the guardhouse. Soon after, a supply of hams was missed, and all the evidence led to Ham, who denied his guilt. It gave him the name, and the cause for the continual battle between the two. Yet, when it comes to a showdown, they would gladly give their lives for each other.

Renny, or Colonel John Renwick, is a leading engineer. And his huge fists enjoy knocking through wooden panels. He likes a fight better than a slide rule. Long Tom, the electrical wizard, and Johnny, the geologist and archaeologist, complete the group. Johnny is William Harper Littlejohn; Long Tom is Major Thomas J. Roberts.

All of this group are famous in their own name, yet they find more joy in helping others than in adding to their own wealth. Under the guidance of Doc Savage, they form a perfect band of adventurers whose lives are one thrill after another.

Doc said, "Go ahead with the story of John Sunlight."

Giantia and Titania looked at him with their lips tight.

"We can't tell you anything now," Giantia said hoarsely.

"John Sunlight would kill Fifi," Titania added.

It was plain they had no intention of continuing with any story. Fears for their little sister's safety had silenced them completely.

Doc turned to Monk. "How much did they tell you before you got here?"

Monk scratched his bullet of a head.

"Not much, Doc," the homely chemist admitted. "They did say somethin' about a thing they called the Strange Blue Dome."

"*The what?*" Doc's face became frozen metal.

"The Strange Blue Dome," Monk explained. "Or so they called—"

The homely chemist stopped speaking, swallowed. For Doc Savage had spun, and flung into the library.

The bronze man snapped the library door shut behind him, then did nothing more exciting than stride to one of the great windows and stand stiffly, staring into the hazy northern sky. Doc's sinew-cabled arms were down, as rigid as bars, at his sides, and his powerful hands worked slowly, clenching and unclenching.

He was doing something that none of his men had ever seen him do before. He was taking time out to get control of himself.

Had his men seen, they might have guessed the reason. They were clever men, each one a headliner in his chosen profession. Probably they would have realized that Doc Savage knew more about the Strange Blue Dome than any of them dreamed he knew.

Monk, Ham, Long Tom—none of Doc's men had ever heard of any such thing as the Strange Blue Dome.

But Doc knew of it, obviously. Knew so much about it that he was shocked more profoundly than his men had ever seen him shocked before, by the mere mention of the Strange Blue Dome in connection with this mystery.

Strangest of all, Doc Savage seemed to be blaming himself for what was happening.

DOC went back into the other room.

"Ham," he said, "you and Long Tom watch these two women, Giantia and Titania."

Ham had no liking for that task. He gulped a hasty, "But—"

"Monk and myself are going after that ballyhoo plane," Doc said.

"Aw, O. K.," Ham grumbled.

Monk grinned derisively at Ham, touched his hand to his forehead in a boy-am-I-laughing-at-you gesture. Then Monk followed Doc Savage into the big laboratory. They wended through long tables laden with intricate glass and metal devices. Many cabinets stood filled with chemicals.

Doc opened a wall panel, disclosing a steel barrel several feet in diameter. There was a door in this, which he opened. He stepped through into a bullet-shaped car which was well-padded, and traveled through the steel barrel, driven by compressed air. When Monk got in, there was little room to spare.

Closing hatches, Doc pulled levers which tripped the air pressure on. There was a shock, a whining noise, and the vibration of great speed. Then they were jammed against the lower end of the cartridge-like car as air cushioned it to a stop. Holding devices clicked and a red light came on.

Doc and Monk stepped out in the bronze man's Hudson River waterfront hangar boathouse.

Monk ran for the plane which stood nearest the water, sprang in, got the propeller turning over.

"Hey, Doc!" he yelled. "Ain't you comin'?"

Doc Savage said, "You go after the ballyhoo plane alone, Monk."

Monk didn't understand why Doc wanted to remain behind. But he was not displeased. The prospect of chasing the ballyhoo plane, maybe an aerial dogfight, intrigued Monk.

"Keep your radio cut in," Doc called.

Monk's arm shot up to acknowledge that. He gunned the plane down into the water. The craft was an amphibian. When it got close to the big doors, it cut a photoelectric-cell-and-beam device, which caused the doors to open.

Monk's plane scudded across the river, and was in the air about the time the hangar doors were closing.

Doc Savage was already in a car in the hangar. He kept a car in the hangar for emergency use, and it was one of his fully equipped machines.

The car had, among many other gadgets, a very good radio direction-finder. A finder that could cover the entire band of ether wavelengths. Doc turned the tuning dial slowly, changed wave coils, kept on tuning. Carrier wave after carrier wave was picked up as a violent hissing.

Finally Doc picked up a transmitter which seemed to be sending nothing but—at intervals of two or three minutes—an apparently meaningless combination of dots and dashes.

The bronze man took a careful bearing on that station.

He started the car, drove furiously, covered about half a mile, and took a second bearing on the transmitter which was sending dot-and-dash combinations.

Doc watched the ballyhoo plane as he took this second radio bearing. The plane was a distant bumblebee against the sky. Another bumblebee— Monk's ship—was wheeling around it.

The ballyhoo plane changed its course in obedience to the dot-and-dash signal on which Doc was taking bearings.

The bronze man made his small, characteristic trilling sound briefly. It had a satisfied quality. His surmise had been correct—his suspicion that grew out of the fact that Fifi's voice, from the ballyhoo plane, *was repeating the same words over and over.*

Doc drew bearing lines on a scale map of New York City. The lines crossed in the section immediately below Forty-second street. He drove for the spot.

ONLY at street intersections could Doc Savage see Monk's plane and the ballyhoo ship. At other times, high buildings hid both craft.

Time after time, Monk flew around the loudspeaker ship. Doc was anxious about that, at first. But Monk was cautious; he did not get too close to the strange craft. This jockeying went on for minutes. Then it appeared that Monk had surrendered caution, and was flying very near the other ship. Monk's plane was on the opposite side; it seemed to blend with the ballyhoo craft, and then—

A splattering volley of dots and dashes came from the radio transmitter which Doc was tracking down with the direction finder.

Instantly, the ballyhoo ship exploded. Doc saw the flash, a flash that jumped in all directions; it was like looking at a distant mirror which had unexpectedly reflected sunlight into his eyes. The flash faded; Doc watched the smoke. It might have been from an Archie shell. Then came the blast sound, a distinct concussion, despite the distance. And echoes followed, bouncing around among the skyscrapers like thunder.

Then Monk's plane appeared. It had been safely beyond the other ship; only the distance had made it seem close.

Doc tuned the radio to Monk's wavelength.

"Damaged any, Monk?" he asked of his own transmitter mike.

"Startled out of six years' growth," Monk's voice stated shakily. "You know what, Doc?"

"There was no one in the plane," Doc said. "It was being flown by a radio robot. The girl's voice was coming off a record that was being repeated. And they exploded a bomb in the plane with radio control."

"You must be a crystal gazer!" Monk said.

His distant plane spun down in the sky and swooped in toward the Hudson River.

Doc Savage reached the spot where, as closely as he could judge, the radio-control transmitter had operated. He tried to tune it in again. It had been shut off. That was not so good; the plane might have been controlled from any building within a block.

Doc Savage made a quick survey of surrounding buildings, their height, their position with reference to the spot where the plane had blown up in the sky—a smudge of dark smoke still marked that point.

One tall building—it had to be that one. It was the only roof that offered a view of the spot where the plane had exploded.

Doc Savage drove away two blocks, parked, and got his makeup case from under the rear seat.

THE bronze man, getting out of the car some minutes later, was a large dark-skinned man with artistically long black hair, nostrils with an almost negroid flare—the celluloid nostril inserts did not hamper breathing and added a remarkable touch—and a nervous habit of twitching his lips.

Doc carried a leather tool bag which was worn.

He walked into the lobby of the building he suspected, saw no one there, entered an elevator when it arrived, and said, "Top floor."

From the top-floor corridor, a door gave into a flight of stairs that led up to the roof. The door to the stairway was open, and a man lounged there, obviously a guard. He was a thin dark man.

The lookout stared at Doc narrowly.

The bronze man walked up to the fellow, dangling his worn tool bag prominently.

"Have you noticed any peculiar smells?" Doc asked.

The other scowled.

"You've got me there, buddy," he said. "Smells?"

Doc said, "I am making a building inspection."

"So what?"

"You don't understand," Doc explained patiently. "There is a chemical firm on a lower floor of this building, and it is possible that a leakage of chemicals occurred. The chemicals form a gas, and it might have risen to the upper floors, following the elevator shafts. In such a case, it would be noticed here, or on the roof. Have you noticed anything?"

"Not a thing," the man said sourly.

He spoke with a strong Russian accent.

"Very well," Doc said. "The gas may not have reached this high yet. Or there may not even be any gas at all as yet."

The bronze man then walked, swinging his tool bag and whistling, to the stairway, opened the door, stepped through and left the door ajar a crack. He made tramping sounds with his feet so that it would appear he had gone on down the stairs.

Out of the bag he took a gas mask, which he donned. Then he took a gallon jug of villainously colored liquid from the bag and poured it on the floor.

He waited fifteen minutes, approximately. There was a strong draft up the stairs and through the door, and through the stairs that led up to the roof. The liquid Doc had poured on the floor slowly turned into gas and was swept up to the roof.

After the fifteen minutes were up, he went investigating.

There was one man asleep in the top-floor hallway.

There were six men and a girl asleep on the roof.

The girl was very small, very pretty—if you liked the Kewpie doll type.

Chapter IX
LOST WOMEN

DOC SAVAGE had a way, as those who knew him put it, of walking up and taking death by the beard. And not only getting away with it, but in unexpected fashions all his own, of leaving the old man with the whiskers and scythe wondering just whether he had been treated with disrespect.

But Doc's working methods were not as reckless as they appeared. He knew this strange trade which he followed; he had received years of training for it, and he carried with himself always an astounding number of scientific gadgets calculated to cope with emergencies.

Whenever possible, he tried not to do what was expected of him.

There was a portable radio transmitter of some power standing on the roof. In a case beside it was the additional mechanism necessary to make an ordinary radio into a plane control.

Doc freed Fifi—she was bound and gagged—and left both rope and gag lying on the roof.

Doc carried the men from the roof to the top-floor hallway, and put all seven of them in the freight elevator, which operated automatically and thus did not have an operator.

Next, Doc carried Fifi down and put her with the others. He had no doubt that he was carrying Fifi.

He locked the door leading to the roof, then sealed it with a bit of chewing gum. Not ordinary gum, exactly. This would turn white when he touched it with a drop of chemical; and if it didn't turn white, he would know it was different gum.

Fifi had the cutest form of any small girl Doc had ever seen. Short girls are usually spread out a bit.

The bronze man got down to the alley, got his car around there, got his passengers loaded into it without attracting anyone's attention. He drove toward his headquarters.

Fifi slipped over and her head rested against his shoulder. She was the type of little thing that could look delicious when she was sleeping.

Doc's car traveled quietly, and did not take long to reach the high building which housed his headquarters. The machine rolled into the private basement garage.

He loaded the seven prisoners into the speed elevator. Then he put Fifi in.

Fifi seemed, if anything, smaller and more exquisitely pretty. She looked like trouble. She looked like nothing else but trouble.

Doc piloted the elevator and his load up to the eighty-sixth floor and got out. He began unloading.

Neither Ham nor Long Tom came out to help him.

Suddenly concerned, Doc Savage hurried to the door, opened it and went into the reception room. He stopped, stared about in astonishment.

Two thoroughly angry bulls might have put the place in the shambles he saw before him. Two bulls—it was hardly likely one could have done as thorough a job.

Ham and Long Tom were skinned, lacerated, contused. They had black eyes, were minus some hair, and their noses leaked crimson. Another expensive suit had been ruined for Ham.

The two were also bound and gagged.

DOC untied them.

"Titania!" Ham yelled.

"Giantia!" Long Tom shouted.

"They got away!" they groaned in chorus.

Doc Savage's metallic features did not change expression, which was a tribute to his self-control.

Titania and Giantia had been going to tell everything about John Sunlight, the instant they knew their sister Fifi was safe. Well, Fifi was safe; she would have no more than a slight headache when she recovered.

"How did it happen?" Doc asked quietly.

"They saw that plane explode—the plane Monk was after," Long Tom muttered.

"And they went wild," Ham added ruefully. "You never saw such a performance. They landed on us before we knew what'd happened. Insisted we had gotten Fifi killed. They thought she was in the plane, you know. Well—that is—anyhow, they got the best of us."

"They left," Long Tom explained, "swearing they were going to join John Sunlight and help him get you, to pay you back for causing Fifi's death in the plane."

Ham stood up, felt of himself, ran to a mirror and got a good look at the damage which had been done to his garments. He made a croaking noise. He loved his clothes as if they were his children.

Another hideous thought hit Ham. Monk—if Monk heard of this, the homely ape would have the time of his life kidding Ham. And he was certain to hear of it. Ham's groan was so loud it sounded like a honking.

Doc Savage said nothing more on the subject of the two giantesses escaping. He never criticized his crew for errors or shortcomings. The bronze man made mistakes himself.

Mistakes—his metallic face settled into the grimmest of lines. Mistake! This whole thing was the result of a mistake he had made. A horrible error. He had not told them that as yet, but the fact

After the fifteen minutes were up, Doc went investigating.

had taken shape in his own mind, and was there whenever his thoughts relaxed, to torment him like a spike-tailed devil.

In grave silence, the bronze man carried the captives into the laboratory. Ham and Long Tom helped him.

Before the job was done, Monk put in an appearance with an aviator's helmet and goggles perched on his bullet head. He listened as Long Tom told what had happened. Then Monk looked at Ham and roared with mirth.

"You look like an accident goin' someplace t' happen!" Monk howled.

"At least," Ham said unkindly, "I don't look

and act like something six months out of a jungle."

Monk scowled. "Listen, shyster, my ancestors came here on the *Mayflower*."

"It's a good thing," Ham sneered. "The country has immigration laws now."

They did not notice Doc Savage closing the laboratory door. And later, when they tried the door, it was locked, and although they called out, the bronze man returned no answer from within.

They sat down in the reception room to wait, puzzled.

DOC SAVAGE preferred to work alone

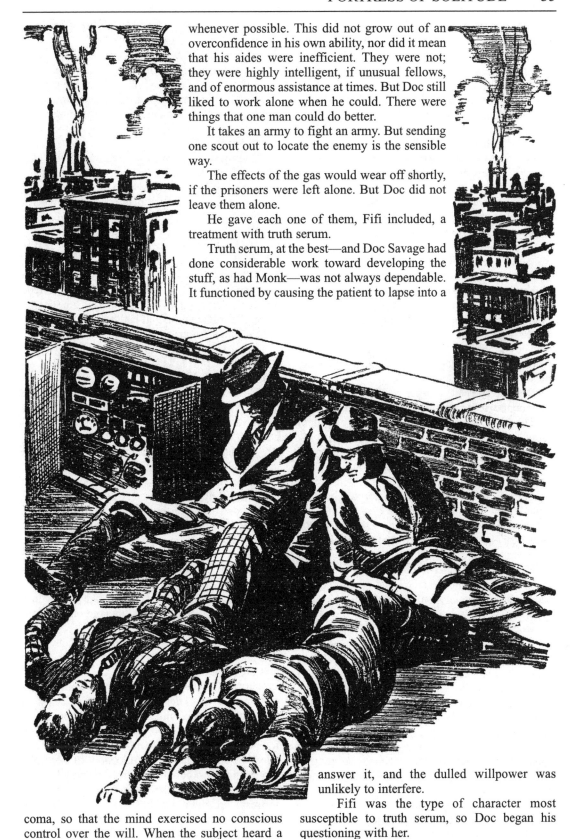

whenever possible. This did not grow out of an overconfidence in his own ability, nor did it mean that his aides were inefficient. They were not; they were highly intelligent, if unusual fellows, and of enormous assistance at times. But Doc still liked to work alone when he could. There were things that one man could do better.

It takes an army to fight an army. But sending one scout out to locate the enemy is the sensible way.

The effects of the gas would wear off shortly, if the prisoners were left alone. But Doc did not leave them alone.

He gave each one of them, Fifi included, a treatment with truth serum.

Truth serum, at the best—and Doc Savage had done considerable work toward developing the stuff, as had Monk—was not always dependable. It functioned by causing the patient to lapse into a

coma, so that the mind exercised no conscious control over the will. When the subject heard a question, put insistently, the impulse was to answer it, and the dulled willpower was unlikely to interfere.

Fifi was the type of character most susceptible to truth serum, so Doc began his questioning with her.

Fifi knew absolutely nothing of value.

Doc went to work on the others.

He kept questioning them for almost an hour—

And when the bronze man unlocked the laboratory door, there was an expression on his face which shocked his men. It was a stricken look— one of such intensity that it was startling, for Doc Savage so rarely showed his emotions.

"Doc!" Ham gasped. "What—"

The bronze man shook his head.

"We haven't much time," he said. "You might help me."

They carried the men prisoners out, one at a time, and put them in the speed elevator.

Monk maneuvered himself into carrying Fifi.

"Not a bad little number," he said admiringly.

"Keep her here," Doc said.

Monk burst out in a big wreath of grins.

Ham complained, "That ugly clunk is havin' all the luck—"

Doc said, "Ham, you and Long Tom stay here. Be ready for a call."

They nodded, puzzled. The strangely set expression on his face deterred them from asking questions.

Doc Savage got a larger makeup box out of the laboratory. He also took two equipment cases.

Then he lowered the prisoners to the basement garage, loaded them in the car, drove back to the building where he had captured them, and managed to return them to the roof, still without being noticed.

The prisoners lay limp and snored where he placed them. He put the thin dark one at the foot of the roof stairs. He scattered the others over the roof, near the radio plane control, where he had found them.

He emptied another bottle of chemical on the roof. At once, the air became filled with a reeking odor which certainly smelled like a chemical vapor potent enough to overcome men.

Doc Savage then left the roof.

Chapter X
WAR LORDS

THE first John Sunlight man to sit erect on the roof looked around himself in a dazed way. His next act was an impulsive glance at his wrists, as though he expected to find handcuffs there. He began shaking his head.

"Hey!" he yelled. He shook the limp form nearest to him.

The shaken man groaned.

Doc Savage's skill with drugs was highly developed; he had calculated the combined dosages, in proportion to the bodily resistance of the men, so closely that they were all reviving at approximately the same time.

Half an hour saw them all on their feet, stumbling around, asking each other foolish questions. Then the man came crawling up from the stairs.

"Gas!" this man gasped. "Gas that came from a chemical firm downstairs. The fumes musta got us!"

"How'd you know that?"

"There was an inspector come around just before I keeled over."

A man rubbed his forehead bewilderedly. "I kinda feel as if somethin' happened to me when I was unconscious," he mumbled.

"What?"

The man tried to think, gave it up finally. "Nothin', I guess," he said.

Which was as near as any of them came to imagining that they had been taken to Doc Savage's headquarters, had talked under the effects of truth serum, and had been returned.

"Where's the girl?" one yelled suddenly.

She wasn't there, obviously.

"She must 'a' failed to get as much gas as we did, and crawled off," one man decided.

They saw the ropes and gag lying where the girl had been. But no girl. There was a furious rush in search of the girl, and when it netted them nothing, they were uneasy.

"John Sunlight ain't gonna like this," seemed to be a general consensus.

They conferred, holding their heads, which ached splittingly, and decided there was nothing to do now but take their radio outfit and leave. They did this. Their cars were parked in a nearby side street.

They drove north for over an hour along the bank of the Hudson River, then parked their cars at a wharf near the water's edge.

There was a speedboat tied to the wharf. Into this, they climbed. It carried them out on the river, and toward an island.

The island was mostly stone, although there was enough soil to support a few trees. The island was crowned by a house.

Crowned—there was no other word for it. Nothing else quite described how the house sat on the peak of the island, or described the house itself. The structure was like a crown, round, with four ornamental spires, one at each corner, and windows which, due to the reflections of afternoon sun from their colored glass, resembled jewels.

Of course the house could have been called a fortress, too. But not at first glance. The machine guns mounted inside the windows were not visible at any first glance.

The house might have been termed a spot for

a quick getaway, as well. But to realize this, it was first necessary to know that the big boathouse on the south held a fast plane, as well as a hundred-mile-an-hour speedboat.

John Sunlight did not believe in taking chances.

JOHN SUNLIGHT sat on a deep chair which was covered with a rich purple velvet cloth. He wore a matching set of purple velvet pajamas and purple velvet robe, and on the forefinger of his right hand was a ring with a purple jewel.

John Sunlight had very few changeable habits, but one of them was his fondness for one color one time, and perhaps a different one later. Just now he was experiencing a yen for purple, particularly the regal shade of the color.

The man could go in for colors like a male movie star, and still be dangerous.

He did not look dangerous as he listened to his men tell him they had been gassed on the building roof, and had awakened to find the girl, Fifi, gone, and that nothing else had happened to them—except that they hadn't succeeded in blowing up anybody with the bomb plane.

John Sunlight never looked dangerous.

"That is too bad," he said.

He resembled, with his thin aesthetic face, a dreamer of a poet who had listened to an editor turn down one of his rhymes.

"Too bad," he said. "You will have to be punished."

The terrified uneasiness which jumped over the faces of the gas victims at this was a tribute to the grisly qualities of the innocent-looking, tall, thin man before them. There was something hypnotic about it. He had not touched them, had not ordered them shot or even beaten.

"Put them each in a separate dark room of the basement," John Sunlight said. "After they have been there forty-eight hours, I will talk to them."

One of the men made a croaking sound. John Sunlight had done that to him once before, put him in darkness for a long time, then came and talked to him. And the talk of John Sunlight, spoken quietly and steadily, had contained such a combination of horrors and obscenities, ghastly implications and frightful verbal statements, that the man remembered he had been a gibbering wreck of terror for many hours afterward.

An impartial observer would have called John Sunlight's method a form of hypnotism.

The horrified gas victims were led away.

JOHN Sunlight was thorough. Attention to details, he had long ago learned, is important. Overlook a seed, and it may grow into a great tree

of thorns.

He consulted a Manhattan directory.

"Why," he said mildly, "there is no chemical firm registered as being in that building!"

He got on the telephone. He could speak English with almost no accent at all, so he made out fairly well with a deception that he was a Federal agent.

"Yes, do," he said.

Soon a voice said, "This is the Eureka Products Chemical House."

"What address?" John Sunlight asked.

The address given was the proper one.

"Did you have an accident there today?" John Sunlight inquired.

"Why, yes," the other said. "Some gas got loose in the plant, but as far as we can tell, it did no damage. We were afraid that it would rise to the upper floors, and cause people to become unconscious. However, the gas is harmless, unless one has a very weak heart."

"Thank you," John Sunlight said.

"Thank *you*," said the voice.

The voice was Long Tom. His thanks *were* sincere. He was still a little breathless from rushing around, warning the telephone people that there was a chemical firm in the building, in case anyone asked, and using his electrical skill to get a telephone connection in the building in a hurry. He hoped he had fooled John Sunlight.

He had.

John Sunlight was deceived, but he did not put the telephone aside at once, because he had another call to make.

"Hello, Baron," he said pleasantly, "I wonder if you could arrange to hold an immediate consultation with me?"

The "Baron" was silent, cautiously considering.

"Is it dangerous?" he demanded.

"It is to avoid danger," said John Sunlight, "that I wish to see you. This is very important, Baron. One of my men will call for you immediately in a car."

Again, the Baron thought it over.

"All right," he said finally, in a tone that said he doubted very much if it would be all right.

THIS Baron was one of John Sunlight's "contacts." John Sunlight had many contacts, more than anyone would have believed. He was not a young man, and he had worked all his evil life toward one hideous goal; and he had made his arrangements as he went along, always with an eye to the future. John Sunlight's idea about his destiny on this unfortunate earth was far from being as changeable as his fancy for colors.

The Baron was a representative of a Balkan

country. The secret representative. His position at home was high, but the work he did was of the lowest kind. He was the head of his nation's spy system; he also personally handled the purchase of information, or anything that would be of value to his vicious little government.

This Baron Karl—he was known as Baron Karl for short—was bosom buddy to the prime minister of his government, and the prime minister was as bloodthirsty and intolerant a tyrant as ever seized life-and-death control over an unsuspecting population. The prime minister had his eyes on his neighboring Balkan country, and he would willingly give the lives of a few hundred thousand of his soldiers to grab the other country.

The only redeeming feature about the situation was that the other Balkan nation was ruled by as vicious a rascal as either the prime minister or Baron Karl, who dominated the neighboring "democracy." The ruler was known to the world as the "playboy prince" because of his hilarious career. But what the world didn't know was that he was a bloodthirsty, power-hungry kind of weasel, and the first throat he wanted to cut was the neighboring "democracy" of the prime minister and Baron Karl.

Fortunately, the two countries, armed to the teeth, had so far been too evenly matched for either to risk a war.

But if anything gave either a balance of power, there would be a war at the drop of a hat.

No one knew that the so-called "playboy prince" had landed in New York yesterday. He was traveling incognito. Very much incognito.

This "playboy prince" was the next man John Sunlight called.

"I'll have my car call for you in about an hour," John Sunlight said.

John Sunlight made several other telephone calls and appointments. Each of these was to a representative of a government which wanted above all things to have the power to whip somebody else in a war.

Baron Karl arrived at six o'clock. It was getting dark around the island.

Chapter XI
ARCTIC RENDEZVOUS

BARON KARL was a smooth customer. He even wore a monocle. And, of course, the best of clothes. He was quite a hand with the chorus girls.

In the "revolution" in his country, it was rumored he had personally shot to death some fifty or so political enemies, having them brought, one at a time, to a dark little room under the castle. When he wished, he could look and act like a candy salesman. But when he relaxed, and was his normal self, he was so much like something made out of snake flesh that even his boss, the prime minister, didn't like to be around him socially.

Baron Karl sat with military erectness in the stern of the motorboat which brought him out to the island, and made rather a distinguished figure. He gave the island and its castlelike house a glance of approval. It looked like a safe place. As a matter of fact, his own castle in his native land was along the same order.

"Sometimes I think," he remarked, "that this John Sunlight is destined to be history's greatest evil genius."

He thought along that line while he was being led up to the castle. Like all evil men, he liked to think that other persons were worse than himself—and in the case of John Sunlight, he was eminently correct. Baron Karl was only a menace to a pair of small Balkan nations, whereas John Sunlight was a menace to practically all humanity.

Baron Karl made a little speech when he met John Sunlight.

"I salute again," he said, "the man who has inherited the qualities of the Erinyes, the Eumenides, of Titan, and of Friar Rush, with a touch of Dracula and Frankenstein."

"Those were very bad people," John Sunlight said dryly.

Baron Karl peered sharply at the other, a little apprehensive lest he had angered John Sunlight. He was afraid of the man.

"Let us call you a genius," he said, "and I say that sincerely. Er—may I sit down?"

He sat in a comfortable chair, crossed his legs, and dropped his candy salesman manner. He was ready to get down to business.

"What do you want?" he asked.

John Sunlight was blunt. "I wish to make an appointment to meet you at a point north of Hudson Bay in exactly five days," he said.

The stooge for one of Europe's worse tyrants looked startled. "Hudson Bay—you don't mean the Hudson Bay in Canada?"

"Yes. Our meeting place is near the Arctic Circle."

"You're crazy!" Baron Karl exclaimed. "Why, it's still winter up there. It's cold."

"Only about fifty below zero," John Sunlight said.

The other shook his head. "Meet you in the Arctic? Not me! Particularly not unless you explain why."

John Sunlight did not lift his voice.

He said, "This is very, very important. On your meeting with me in the Arctic will depend the future of your country."

"That is big talk," the European agent said dryly.

"Fail to meet me, and your country"—John Sunlight held up five fingers of one hand—"won't last that many months."

Baron Karl sat quite still and thought of the things he knew about John Sunlight, and of the whispers he had heard about the strange, terrible man. Baron Karl was given to quick, impulsive decisions. He stood up.

"I'll meet you in the Arctic," he said. "Although I'm mystified."

ROYALTY visited John Sunlight's island in the Hudson at ten o'clock that night, which was two hours after Baron Karl had departed in an extremely puzzled state of mind.

Royalty was the "playboy prince" who had come dashing to America in secrecy and much haste.

The prince sat in the launch and pouted as the boat sped toward the island. He was a large young man, and his personal opinion was that he was handsome. The newspapers called him "dashing." What they meant was that the things he did were dashing. Or sappy. It depended on how you looked at such things as drunken chorus girls bathing in champagne tubs on the royal table.

He had a mouth made for pouting, large wet-calf eyes, and in a few years, if he kept putting on weight, he would look like a large brown worm.

"My cabinet," he told John Sunlight peevishly, "advised me to come, as your message requested."

He'd filled his cabinet with the coldest, cleverest rogues in his country, and he had gumption enough to take their advice.

"One week from today," John Sunlight said, "I want to meet you at a rendezvous near the Arctic Circle, north of Hudson Bay."

The prince didn't like cold weather. He refused.

Then he listened to John Sunlight assure him that if he didn't keep the appointment, his country wouldn't last—John Sunlight held up five fingers—that many months. The prince thought of what his cabinet advisers had told him about this weird man before him, and remembered that they had assured him that if John Sunlight said a thing was important, it was assuredly important.

"How do I get there?" he asked grumpily.

"By plane—secretly."

That was all, and the prince left. He was mad at himself, because he was royalty, and here he was taking orders from a man who had no royal blood whatever. He was taking the orders simply because he had heard enough about the man to make him afraid not to do as he was told.

He was puzzled. He had no idea why John Sunlight wanted him in the Arctic.

As a matter of fact, the prince was not the only one who was puzzled. Andrew Blodgett "Monk" Mayfair was also baffled. And so was Theodore Marley "Ham" Brooks.

The two remarkable friends were stationed behind a bush on a cliff which formed a bank of the Hudson River opposite John Sunlight's island. Monk and Ham were behind the bush because they had received a radioed request from Doc Savage to appear there. They knew nothing more than that.

Monk and Ham had not seen Doc Savage since he had left headquarters with seven unconscious members of John Sunlight's gang. They did not know that Doc had taken the seven sleepers back to the same rooftop off which he had collected them. All they did know was that Long Tom had been left back at headquarters to watch Fifi. They weren't too happy about that. Fifi was pretty.

MONK had been prowling around, taking a brief look at their surroundings. The brush was thick, the night fairly dark, and Monk's mind was on Fifi.

When Monk came back to Ham, he grumbled, "I almost lost my way."

"You never had a way," Ham said unkindly.

Monk continued to think of exquisite Fifi being guarded by Long Tom.

"Thank heavens, Long Tom ain't got a way with 'em, either," the homely chemist said heartily.

Starting to sit down in the darkness, without having his mind on it, Monk had a rock roll under his feet, and he fell heavily.

"Oo-o-o!" he croaked. "I hit on my crazy bone!"

"Oh, dear," Ham said solicitously. "Your whole skeleton must hurt."

Monk was feeling around for a stone, entering vague ideas of seeing whether it would bounce off Ham, when the shadow of a boulder beside them seemed to grow much larger. There was no perceptible sound; the boulder shadow just seemed to grow mysteriously.

"Doc!" Monk gasped.

Doc Savage's quiet, controlled voice came from the shadow which had grown.

"Did you bring the equipment cases?"

"I'm sitting on them," Ham said. "Doc—where have you been? What became of the seven unconscious men? What—"

Doc said, "The seven revived on the roof, under circumstances which made them think the whole thing was an accident. They are now on that island you can see yonder. Fortunately, they did not see me following them."

"Oh! Then—"

"John Sunlight is on the island," Doc Savage interposed gravely. "It is up to us to raid the place and seize him."

They picked up the equipment cases—these were of metal, waterproof, shockproof, with handles for convenient carrying—and crept down the face of the cliff to the edge of the Hudson River.

Doc Savage stopped and gave a solemn warning.

"John Sunlight," the bronze man said, "is probably as complete a fiend as we ever met. He is extremely clever."

Monk spoke for himself and Ham. "We don't scare easy," he said.

Doc knew that. But he wanted to impress on them the need for caution—and success.

"Baron Karl does not scare easily, either," Doc said. "Baron Karl is the representative of a small war-hungry European government. Neither does the "playboy prince" scare readily."

"I've heard of them two guys," Monk admitted.

"They were enough afraid of John Sunlight that they came from Europe to see him, the moment he demanded it," Doc Savage said.

Monk peered in astonishment at Doc Savage.

"How come you know so much about what's been happenin' on that island, Doc?" he muttered.

Chapter XII
ISLAND RAID

MONK'S problem was solved shortly. Doc Savage opened one of the equipment cases they had brought, extracted diving "lungs" and they donned these. The devices—nose clips, breathing tube that ran to a chemical purifier pack—would enable them to remain under water for hours, if necessary.

They weighted themselves by carrying a rock under one arm, an equipment case under the other, and waded into the river.

Doc wore a luminous wrist compass. He consulted this until they reached the island, then turned the luminous compass face against his wrist, so it would not betray his presence in the darkness.

They climbed silently from the water and crouched in a river-worn pocket in the stone. Above them was a low cliff, standing limned in the faintest of light only at intervals, when it was touched by the beam from a distant navigation blinker far up the river. The castlelike house must be beyond that.

There was a faint click as Doc opened an equipment case again, then other clicks, and Monk and Ham found telephone headsets thrust into their hands. They put on their headsets.

"Civan," they heard a voice saying, "you recall what Serge Mafnoff meant to me?"

There was something about that voice that caused Monk and Ham to shove out their jaws, although they had never heard it before.

"Serge Mafnoff was your greatest enemy," Civan's voice said.

"Exactly," said that other voice, the hideous one. "And now I have another greatest enemy."

"Who?" Civan asked.

"Doc Savage," the other growled. "Civan, there is nothing I would rather do than stay in the neighborhood of New York and fight this Doc Savage to the finish. But it is not wise. I have other plans, and I do not want them ruined. Doc Savage might ruin them. Therefore, we are fleeing to the Arctic."

"Yes, sir," Civan said.

"I have made appointments with the men I wish to do business with," the other explained. "They will appear in the Arctic, one by one."

"I see," Civan said dutifully.

Monk and Ham bent close to Doc Savage, and Monk said, "Doc, who is Civan talking to?"

"John Sunlight," Doc Savage said.

"How—"

Doc explained quietly. "I managed to creep close to the walls and fasten supersensitive contact microphones to several of the windows. I did that as soon as I had trailed the men who thought they were gassed on the roof. It was impossible to get inside the house. He has every inch of the place under guard. For that matter, he has the entire surrounding river guarded by photoelectric-eye arrangements mounted in buoys. It would be impossible to approach unobserved in a boat."

Monk growled, "Ain't we wastin' time here?"

He never liked to put off a fight.

THERE was a guard at the head of the stairway that led up the last sheer few yards of rock to the castle front door. He was a dark man. He leaned on a rifle, and he was preoccupied with thoughts of the months he had spent on the icebreaker in the Arctic. He was recollecting some of the things they had eaten, and it had made him a little sick in the stomach.

"Beregeetes!" a voice ripped from a window. "Take care, fool! Don't you see that fire!"

The guard came to life with a start, saw a lurid red glow of flames a few yards down the trail, and raced to the spot. The fire was not much. The guard pointed a flashlight beam, saw a smouldering cigarette stub at the base of the burned wedge. He fell to stamping out the flames.

"Somebody threw a cigarette into the brush!" he shouted reassuredly.

By that time, Doc Savage, Monk and Ham were inside the castlelike house. Doc had started the fire, but not with a cigarette. The cigarette was just trimming.

Doc went ahead. He whipped across a reception hall that was as large as some schoolrooms. Knocking open the door with quick silence, he went through.

John Sunlight was not inside.

Civan, however, was.

Civan ogled Doc Savage, let out a howl, and dived backward for a door. Probably Civan had never seen a figure quite like the one the bronze man presented. Doc Savage wore a bulletproof helmet gas-protector, a transparent globe of a thing made of tough glasslike composition, holding the bronze man's entire head. The rest of Doc's great form was enveloped in a coverall garment of bulletproof chain mesh, there even being mesh gauntlets.

Civan got through his door, got the door shut just as Doc hit it. The panel was dark, old oak, studded with iron, and it held.

Doc dropped a hand grenade against the door, got back. The grenade let loose. Rock and wood fragments hit his armor grittingly. He went through the smoke, found the door and part of the stone frame demolished.

The bronze man had a stout canvas sack slung from a shoulder by a strap. From it, he began taking gas bombs. He broke these on the floor.

The bombs contained a gas that would take effect through the skin pores. The only protection against it was an airtight suit—a garment such as the rubberized lining of Doc's alloy mesh armor.

Doc reached another door, this one also closed. He reached into the canvas sack and brought out an object resembling a small metal apple equipped with a vacuum suction cup. He stuck that against the door.

The device was one of the supersensitive contact microphones, and a wire ran from it to an amplifier in the canvas sack; and from the amplifier, wires ran to a headset which Doc wore inside the helmet.

The mike picked up voices beyond the door.

John Sunlight said, "Don't fight them, you fool! Get the men out."

"Yes, sir," Civan barked.

Doc Savage threw small switches quickly, disconnecting his headset from the sonic amplifier and connecting it to a tiny microwave radio "transceiver" that had half the bulk of an ordinary shoe box. He spoke into a tiny mike mounted inside the transparent helmet.

"Monk! Ham!"

The two acknowledged over their own transmitter almost instantly.

"Get out of the place!" Doc ordered.

Monk howled, "But Doc, we've just started—"

"Out!" the bronze man rapped.

He retreated himself, and overtook Monk and Ham at the outer door. They went—as fast as they could in the darkness—down the path.

Behind them, the castle jumped off the top of the island.

MORE properly, most of the island tip went up, and took the castle with it. The blast seemed to knock the rocky earth down a foot, shove it sidewise—or maybe it was the impact of air against them that made the earth seem to shift.

Amid the castle sections, sheet flame stood or lunged. The flame sheets seemed to shove the walls and rooms apart, push them outward. The debris came showering down the steep slope, making a shuddering rumble.

Doc seized Monk and Ham, yanked them down in the narrow trench that was the path. They lay flat. Boulders flooded over them like water, and bounced on to land with splashing violence in the river. Smaller stones and earth settled on them until they were almost covered.

Toward the end of the holocaust, Monk made a remark.

"That John Sunlight," Monk muttered, "must like to destroy things."

With that comment, and without having seen John Sunlight as yet, Monk drew as true a word picture of the man's character as probably could have been drawn.

Doc said, "Down to the boathouse!"

They started leaping and sliding for the boathouse at the water edge.

It was then that the night suddenly got darker. Everything went intensely black. It had been a dark night without stars, but there were lights from distant houses, and lights on the river. Now these vanished.

Monk got out a flashlight—he and Ham both carried the canvas knapsacks—and thumbed the light switch, but nothing happened.

"My flashlight's broke!" Monk barked. "Ham, use yours—"

Ham said, "I'm trying, but it won't light—"

"The lights will do no good," Doc Savage said quietly.

They knew then; they had half guessed it anyway. The *black!* The eerie, incredible, impossible darkness that had enveloped Serge Mafnoff's mansion. It was here now.

Renny

They stood silently, gripped by awe in spite of themselves. And in that quiet, they were aware of a faint hissing in their radio headsets, a low windy noise, something close to static, but still different.

Doc Savage removed his transparent helmet. The thing would keep out sound as well as bullets. He listened.

From the river came another noise. This one might have been steam rushing. But it was a silenced airplane motor.

Monk and Ham took off their helmets, listened also.

"Doc!" Monk exploded. "That motor—that silencer—"

The homely chemist fell silent.

"Go ahead and say it," Doc suggested.

"It sounds like the type of silencer you use on your planes!" Monk exploded.

Doc Savage, instead of answering, made for a brief interval the small, exotic trilling sound that was his peculiar habit when mentally disturbed. The trilling was low, indescribably vague.

After that, they went down to the boathouse, and they could tell that it had contained a plane— probably the plane they had heard take off from the river.

The lights of distant houses, the lights on the river, were suddenly visible. The *black* had gone away.

Chapter XIII
ADONIS AND BEAUTY

DOC SAVAGE'S trained eyes picked up the stabilizer light of a plane, faraway in the sky. It was soon lost.

And as thoroughly as that airplane light vanished, so did all trace of John Sunlight, Civan, Giantia, Titania and all the rest of the Siberian convicts.

The island was a wreck; at least, the top part of it was. People who had heard the explosion came from miles up and down the river, and some of them put out in boats to investigate, while the others maneuvered their automobile headlights around so that they pointed at the island.

Doc Savage and his two men put on their hoods, and waded down the bottom of the river half a mile, came out unobserved, and went on back to their skyscraper headquarters.

Long Tom had been doing some investigating in their absence. This was at Doc Savage's suggestion.

"I've been talking to Moscow on the telephone," Long Tom said, "and I have learned—"

"Moscow—Russia?" Monk demanded.

"Of course," Long Tom said. "The Soviet officials furnished me with descriptions of the convicts who disappeared from that Siberian camp. There is no doubt but that John Sunlight's men are the same crowd."

"Well," Monk said sadly, "they got away from us."

"Where did they go?"

Monk looked at Doc Savage. The homely chemist had been told by Doc that John Sunlight had made appointments in the Arctic with at least two men—Baron Karl and the young European ruler known as the "playboy prince."

"Where was that meeting to be, Doc?" Monk asked.

The bronze man shook his head.

"I never did hear the exact spot," Doc Savage said quietly.

The calmness of his tone belied the importance of his words.

"You mean," Monk exploded, "that we're completely at a loss as to where John Sunlight went?"

"Yes," Doc agreed.

Monk groaned. "Blast it! Then we're stymied! We're out of luck!"

At this juncture, there was a plaintive feminine appeal from the library.

"What about poor little me?" was this helpless inquiry.

Long Tom made a face. "Ugh!"

"Whatcha mean—ugh?" Monk demanded.

"That's little honey lambkins," Long Tom explained. He made another face. "Fifi."

"You don't like Fifi?" Monk asked incredulously.

"Listen," Long Tom said sourly, "all the time you guys were gone, I kept trying to add things up so this mess would make sense. Everytime I came to Fifi, I added a zero."

"No appreciation of feminine pulchritude," Monk declared, and started in to comfort Fifi.

Ham put his hands in his pockets.

"It seems strange," he said unkindly, "that our friend here, the homely gossoon, should drop everything and go comfort Fifi."

Monk stopped, scowled, and pointed at Ham's pocketed hands.

"It ain't any stranger," he sneered, "than the sight of a lawyer with his hands in his own pockets."

Monk then stalked on in to comfort Fifi.

Ham, glaring, hurried to help with the job.

DOC SAVAGE seated himself at the great inlaid table in the reception room, with three telephones close at hand. He called the central telephone office, and placed, in quick succession, a series of transatlantic telephone calls.

At far as the world knew, Doc Savage worked at his strange career of righting wrongs and punishing evildoers, aided only by his five associates, of which Monk, Ham and Long Tom were three.

The two remaining members of the group of five were Major John "Renny" Renwick, the engineer, and William Harper "Johnny" Littlejohn, the archaeologist and geologist. These two were at present not in America.

Renny was in France, serving as consultant in the construction of a number of new flying fields designed for high-speed modern transport planes. Johnny was in Egypt, opening up another Pharaoh's tomb which had just been discovered.

Doc Savage consulted Renny and Johnny by long-distance telephone, and requested they make inquiries about the past of a man known as John Sunlight.

Next, Doc contacted the foreign representatives of a famous worldwide private detective agency. Doc had organized this agency. Its real work was to gather information for the bronze man. When not doing that, the agency did a very profitable business along regular private detective lines.

Doc put the private detectives to learning what they could about John Sunlight.

"John Sunlight is working on some kind of a plan," Doc explained. "If I can learn enough about his character, I may be able to guess the nature of his plan."

There was a lapse of time while Renny, Johnny and the private detectives worked.

Doc trusted his private detectives implicitly. And for a strange reason. Doc trusted each private agent because each one had once been a vicious criminal.

Whenever Doc Savage captured a crook, he sent the fellow to a strange institution in upstate New York, a place Monk and the rest called the "college." At the college, the crook underwent a delicate brain operation which wiped out all memory of the past, after which the patient was trained, taught to hate crime and criminals. The private detectives were all graduates of the college.

Reports began coming in from Europe by transatlantic telephone.

John Sunlight, it seemed, was more rumor than man. An evil rumor, a name that was whispered from mouth to mouth in the circles of international intrigue. The agents had found men who feared him, and would not talk. Many of those. But here and there they had unearthed a scrap of real information.

"You say," Doc Savage said, "that John Sunlight has always been hungry for power?"

"And money," the European agents explained. "It seems that he always believed that if he had money, he could get the power."

All the reports seemed to agree on that angle.

Renny and Johnny, having made inquiries of their own—they both had high government contacts in the countries in which they were

Johnny

working—verified the point about John Sunlight being hungry for power over men.

"That," Doc Savage said, "helps a great deal."

Long Tom, frowning at Doc in the New York headquarters could not see where the bronze man had learned much of value. Monk and Ham were interested in Fifi, but they could not see where Doc had learned so much, either.

Doc, however, seemed satisfied.

"Now," he said, "we find a king."

"A king?" Long Tom exploded.

"A king incognito."

THE "playboy prince" of European royalty— the newspapers called him the "former 'playboy prince'" because he was now a king—would have greatly enjoyed his incognito visit in New York, except for one thing.

He did not relish having to fly into the Arctic to keep an appointment with John Sunlight.

Tomorrow he would have to take off by plane for the arctic, and in the meantime, he intended to enjoy himself. His idea of enjoyment was a series of nightclubs, where he spent money furiously and drank himself loop-legged. He made a thoroughly disgusting spectacle of himself, and managed to indulge in repeated fights. That is, he started repeated fights. It was up to his bodyguards to finish them.

He'd brought his bodyguards from home. Two of them. They were big men, one a little larger than the other. They were obviously tough. Their hides seemed to be made of the same stuff as well-worn riding boots. They had enormous, scarred fists, and their faces were somewhat like the wax casts in museums labeled, "Head of a Prehistoric Cro-Magnon Man."

The fight in the Wacky Club was about typical of several the roistering prince started. Except that one small thing happened which was different, and queer.

It began when the prince spanked a showgirl. He liked to spank them. He thought it great fun. But in this case, he got hold of some young fellow's girlfriend. The prince was too intoxicated to notice the difference, and wouldn't have cared, anyway.

The girl's boyfriend knocked the prince over a table. The two hideous bodyguards sprang onto the boyfriend, knocked him down, began kicking him horribly. Someone unshaped a chair over one bodyguard's head, but it didn't seem to bother the fellow.

There was quite a bit of hullabaloo, before the nightclub attendants dragged the boyfriend out and got things quieted down, taking pains that the police were not called.

When the prince revived, he at once demanded a drink.

He was handed a drink instantly. One of the waiters in the nightclub did the handing, and the prince gulped the drink down at one swallow. Then the prince got up and cursed his bodyguards and threw bottles at them, and they took the abuse with stupid patience, because this mouthing, drunken fool was their king.

So far there had been nothing particularly queer about the incident.

The queer thing happened when the waiter drifted over and tapped on a door which gave into a private dining room. The door opened a crack.

"I gave 'im the stuff in his drink," the waiter said.

A banknote promptly came through the door. It was a fifty-dollar bill. The waiter picked it up and went away, well satisfied.

The private room had a window that opened into an alleyway.

THE prince was staying, naturally, in the city's most flamboyant hotel. He had the finest suite, and he had ruined most of the furniture in his wild orgies, and the hotel management was going to be heartily glad when he was gone, even if he had promised to pay for the ruined furniture.

The following morning, the prince awakened feeling badly. His conscience wasn't bothering him. It was his body. It ached, and judging from the taste, a cat had slept in his mouth.

He snatched a water carafe and smashed it against the door.

"Adonis!" he snarled.

"Adonis" was one of the two evil-faced bodyguards.

The fellow appeared, shuffling and kowtowing at every other step.

"Shut the damn windows!" the prince screamed. "The room is full of fog!"

The bodyguard shut the window, then stood looking uneasy and changing feet.

"May this humble one speak, sire," he asked fearfully.

"Speak about what?"

"There is no fog in this room, sire," the body-guard got around to explaining.

The prince did some cursing, and threw a telephone at the bodyguard. Then he got a little frightened, for it became obvious that there was really no fog. He could hardly see; the objects before him were discernible only as hazy presences.

He called a doctor.

"You must have got hold of some bad liquor," the doctor said. "Your eyesight is temporarily impaired."

"You blasted fool," the prince said. "Do something!"

The doctor explained stiffly that he could do nothing; it would just have to wear off.

The prince broke up some furniture, smashed a few pictures, and became resigned, if not pleased.

"Beauty!" he howled.

"Beauty" was the other bodyguard.

The prince heard someone approach, and there was a rather unpleasant gurgling noise.

"Talk up, you fool!" the prince yelled.

The voice of Adonis said, "May this lowly one advise you of an unfortunate fact."

"Eh?"

"Beauty had his throat hurt last night," Adonis said fawningly, "and now it seems he cannot talk. But he is here and ready to serve you, sire."

The prince was delighted; he had that kind of a mind. He roared mirthfully, and forgot for a few seconds his own lack of eyesight.

Then he fell to whining and complaining and swearing.

"I've got to take off for the Arctic today," he grumbled. "And here I cannot see!"

"Sire, you cannot go," Adonis said.

The idea of a vassal bodyguard telling him what he could not do enraged the prince.

"Get my clothes on me!" he snarled.

They got his clothes on him. Then they led him down to a taxicab, and the prince told the driver where to go.

"Newark Airport!" the prince ordered.

The cab drove for a long time—but it did not go to Newark Airport. It went, instead, to a smaller field on Long Island.

The cab went to the other field principally because Beauty sat in the front seat—and Beauty was holding a large pistol against the ribs of the taxi driver.

THE prince got out of the cab cursing the fact that he could not see.

"Is the plane I ordered here?" he yelled peevishly.

"Yes, sir," said a crisp voice.

"Who're you?"

"I'm the pilot," the crisp voice said.

"You have plenty of fuel?"

"Yes, sir."

"Get me in the cabin, then. And take off."

"Where do you wish to fly to?" the crisp voice asked.

The prince said, "I'll tell you that, you fool. It's a latitude-and-longitude figure."

"Very well, sir," the voice said.

No doubt the peevish prince would have been rather astounded had he known that the crisp voice he was hearing came from the hideous lips of the fellow he had been calling Adonis.

They got in the plane, and it took off.

The prince was spared further surprise by not realizing the plane was being flown by the creature who had been making the croaking noises, the one he had called Beauty.

As a matter of fact, only the prince, Adonis and Beauty were in the plane as it flew northward.

The prince was a complaining, quarrelsome passenger, and when he was not abusing Adonis, he insisted on drinking, or howling obscene tunes at the top of his lungs.

Later, Adonis went forward to see how Beauty was making out with the flying.

"Doc," Monk, who was Beauty said, "I don't envy you the job of takin' care of that thing back there."

"He has given me the latitude and longitude of the place where we are to go," Doc, who was Adonis, said, and wrote the figures on the chart board. "Think you can find the spot, Monk?"

"Swell!" said Monk in a squeaky voice. "Now I'm in favor of dumpin' 'im overboard."

"No. We'll continue to be his bodyguards."

Mention of the word "bodyguards" seemed to arouse a bit of musing recollection in Monk's mind.

"Doc, I guess the two real bodyguards are arrivin' at our college about now," he said thoughtfully. Then he grinned. "I'll never forget what a job we had knockin' 'em senseless when we called 'em to the door of the prince's suite last night."

"The chemical we had the nightclub waiter put in the prince's drink had exactly the effect we hoped for," Doc said. "There is not much chance of his recognizing us."

"I don't think he'd recognize us anyway, considerin' how we're disguised to look exactly like Adonis and Beauty."

"Probably not."

Monk flew in silence for a while. Then he sighed.

"What burns me up," he complained, "is the idea of Long Tom and Ham followin' in another plane—with Fifi."

"Fifi will be left in some little town upstate," Doc assured Monk. "She will be safe there."

LATER, a plane piloted by Long Tom, with Ham and Fifi as passengers, was circling a tiny landing field near a small town in Vermont.

Ham had been making headway with Fifi.

"Landing!" Fifi exclaimed. She gave Ham's arm a squeeze. "You didn't tell me we were going to stop anywhere."

Ham took off and put on the natty aviator's helmet which he wore.

"Er—I—we—" he said. "Well—it's not my idea."

"Aw—tell her we're leavin' her at a little hotel here!" Long Tom snapped.

"Oh, but I don't want to be left!" Fifi gasped. She gave Ham her most toe-curling look. "You don't want to leave Fifi, do you?"

"Er—it may be too dangerous up north," Ham said weakly.

"But you're going!" Fifi pointed out.

"That's different," Ham said.

"Aw—throw her out!" Long Tom flung in disgust.

Ham patted Fifi's arm, scowled at Long Tom. Ham enjoyed having Kewpie doll girls hanging onto him.

The plane landed.

And Fifi changed her tactics. She showed an unexpected bullheaded streak.

Fifi screamed, "Listen, you two! I'm going along! I want to help my sisters! Now get this: You leave me behind and I'll tell John Sunlight what you're doing—"

Long Tom glared at her. "You want me to fan your skirts with a frying pan?"

Fifi glared right back at him.

"I'll trade John Sunlight information about you for the release of my two sisters!" she shouted.

"You don't know where John Sunlight is!" Long Tom yelled.

"I'll advertise in the newspapers!" Fifi screamed. "I'll broadcast on the radio!"

"Women and trouble!" Long Tom groaned.

He turned on the shortwave radio and contacted Doc Savage.

"Doc," he said, "Fifi has turned cocklebur."

"How is that?" Doc asked.

"The nitwit says if we don't take her along, she'll trade information about us to John Sunlight for her sisters' freedom."

"That is bad."

"It's terrific," Long Tom said sourly.

"Bring her with you," Doc said reluctantly.

As Doc Savage made the decision, Monk groaned.

"That burns me up!" Monk complained. "The idea of Ham followin' in that plane—with Fifi."

"If we understood women, we might have argued her out of it," Doc said.

"Huh!" Monk said disgustedly. "That Ham understands 'em too well."

Chapter XIV
SPOT IN THE ARCTIC

THERE is something completely monotonous about riding in an airplane. Certainly it is fully as uneventful as a train ride across a Nebraska prairie, despite even the mental pastime in which the most seasoned air traveler finds himself engaging—the pastime being to pick out possible landing fields on the earth below.

In the case of the prince's plane flown by Doc and Monk—they managed to go on playing the parts of Adonis and Beauty—air travel became doubly monotonous because, from the time they left New York City's cloud-tickling spires behind, there was a blanket of haze over the earth that, at the height they were flying, made the wooded hills and rivers an unending gray blur which might have been anything.

The prince was as peevish as an ugly baby, and seemed satisfied only when they gave him his bottle—not milk—for if not satisfied then, he at least occupied himself only with thinking up loud, profane opinions of the kind of scheme that would let him, a king, get in a shape where, when he put his hands before his eyes, all he saw was a dark blur that might have been his hand or, as he expressed it, a dirty buzzard. Just why he referred to a dirty buzzard in that connection was obscure, unless it was simply he subconsciously connected the hands with something they had done in the past.

The plane seemed slow. Doc Savage and Monk were accustomed to the specially designed speed ships which the bronze man used. This was an ordinary type of craft, and comparatively clumsy, and conceivably not nearly as safe; but they had not thought it wise to substitute one of their own, because such a ship would have been distinctive enough to attract suspicion.

It began to get colder.

They stopped twice and refueled, and it was very chilly, and there was snow on the ground at the last halt, where they took plane skis out of the cabin and fastened them to the landing gear. Hereafter, landings would have to be made on snow.

They flew on for hours, and Doc Savage knew they must be getting near the Arctic rendezvous with John Sunlight.

Doc contacted Long Tom and Ham by radio.

The prince sat back in the cabin, but could not hear because the plane was so noisy.

"Long Tom," Doc said, "what is your position now?"

THERE was a "scrambler" here in Doc's plane, and another one in Long Tom's ship; one scrambler mixed up the voice until it was an unintelligible gobble, and the other unmixed it and made it understandable. That was so John Sunlight could not comprehend, in case he did tune in on them.

Long Tom's position proved to be approximately one thousand miles southward.

"Stay back about a hundred miles," Doc directed, "once you draw near the rendezvous. Land and wait for some word from us."

"O. K.," Long Tom said. "Maybe once we get down on the snow, Fifi will cool off."

"Fifi? What is wrong with Fifi?"

"Listen, Doc, that Fifi is a pain," Long Tom complained. "All she does is cuddle up against Ham and wail, 'Poor little me'!"

Monk heard that, and he was so indignant he forgot himself and snatched the microphone out of Doc's hands.

"Did you say Fifi is cuddlin' up to Ham?" he howled.

"Yes. And—"

"You tell Ham to cut that out!" Monk squalled wrathfully.

Long Tom evidently conveyed the order to Ham, because he came back to the mike in a moment with an answer.

"Ham says," Long Tom explained, "for you to go jump in a snowbank."

Monk collapsed and made strangling noises, opening and closing his hands as though he had his fingers around the neck of his favorite enemy. His agitation must have been considerable, because he came to the point of criticizing a Doc Savage tactic, something he rarely did—not because Doc couldn't take it, but because the bronze man's judgment was usually first-rate.

"Doc," Monk said, "why the dickens didn't we leave Fifi in New York?"

The bronze man had explained that before, but he expounded it again for Monk's benefit.

"Fifi," he said, "is our hold over her two freak sisters, Giantia and Titania, who are probably with John Sunlight."

Monk subsided, since only the future would show whether Fifi would be of any value.

THE prince grew worse. They hadn't thought that possible, but the prince demonstrated that it was. He howled and roared.

Doc Savage was kept very busy. Doc had to be the pilot as well as Adonis, the bodyguard. Monk had to be only Beauty, the other bodyguard, but that grew complicated when the prince began to express an insane desire to choke Beauty and see if that would bring back his voice.

Monk could not afford to have Beauty's voice brought back, because he could not speak Beauty's language.

"Where's that Beauty!" the prince screamed. "I'll beat a voice back into him."

Doc Savage said, using the imaginary pilot's voice, "I think we are approaching the landing place."

The prince jammed his face against the cold plane windows and swore at his inability to see.

"What is it like?"

Doc Savage scrutinized the terrain through the plane window. He saw an expanse which appeared to be nothing but pack ice covered by snow. A cold, white waste across which swirling ghosts of snow were carried by the wind.

Doc described what he saw.

"You fool!" the prince screeched. "This can't be the place."

"We are within fifteen minutes flying of the spot to which you have directed us," the bronze man explained. "I have checked the latitude-and-longitude figures carefully."

"Call me," the prince snarled, "when you reach the spot. I want you to describe what you see!"

Doc went back to the cockpit. Monk flew on. Monk had drawn a black dot on the chart, to mark the latitude and longitude of their goal, and a red line to indicate their progress. The red line had about reached the black dot, and Monk was wondering.

"This territory is all unexplored," he remarked. "Has been, for the last thousand miles."

Doc did not comment on that.

Monk had evidently been thinking about their chance of getting back, in case they had engine trouble, for he continued.

"This is about the most remote corner of the earth," he grumbled. "They talk about the polar seas being explored, but believe you me, that's an exaggeration. Nobody is supposed to have ever been within a thousand miles of this point."

Doc Savage was silent. His strange flake gold eyes were focused ahead rather intently.

"There," he said, and pointed.

Monk grabbed a pair of binoculars, knowing very well that his own vision was not equal to the bronze man's trained eyes. Monk focused the glasses, peered into the misty grayness that was the perpetual Arctic daytime.

"Blazes!" he croaked.

He stood up and leaned forward in an effort to see more of the strange object he had sighted.

"What—what is that?" he gasped.

Doc said nothing. And in a moment, Monk emitted an astounded gasp, and sagged back on the cockpit seat.

The Strange Blue Dome!

FOR miles and miles in all directions the white waste looked absolutely barren—except directly ahead, where there was obviously an island.

The island seemed to be solid stone, with no

bit of soil and no vegetation. Just a high, bald knob of stone. A mass of rock rearing up from the floor of the Arctic Ocean. It must be as solid as Gibraltar, for it stood firm against the ice pack. The ice had piled up against the island, and for leagues it was broken in great bergs. The floes had squeezed and piled one on top of the other, and the ice had lumped up in masses that were sometimes as large as factory buildings.

The Strange Blue Dome stood, a weird-looking thing, on the rock island.

It was like half a blue agate marble.

Like a marble that some fabulous titan had lost here in this unknown part of the globe, to become buried in stone and surrounded by fantastic ice.

It was strange.

Lying where it did, it should logically have been about the most completely lost thing upon the earth.

"Uh—I—well," Monk said. "Uh—that is—hmmm!"

He fell silent.

Then he looked at Doc Savage—stared at the bronze man's face at close range. And suddenly, he knew! He was positive. Doc Savage, not even Doc, could maintain composure in the face of such an incredible discovery as that queer blue thing yonder—unless Doc had known it was there.

"Doc," Monk said.

The bronze man did not seem to hear.

"Doc!"

The bronze man's eyes left the blue mystery.

"Doc," Monk said, "what is that thing?"

The bronze man was silent and grim-faced.

Monk suddenly seized Doc Savage tightly with both hands, and all the puzzled amazement came out of him in a shouted demand.

"You know what the blue thing is!" Monk bellowed. "What is it, Doc?"

Doc never answered.

Because the prince shoved his head into the pilot's compartment.

"I heard you!" he said loudly.

Chapter XV
HALF A BLUE BALL

THERE was—Monk was a long time forgetting that moment—an interval when it seemed certain that their hoax was discovered, that all their careful planning had gone for nothing. Then:

"I sometimes talk to myself," Doc Savage said quietly in the pilot's voice.

Monk held his breath.

"Oh," the prince said. "I could only get a voice. The damned plane makes so much noise."

Monk began breathing again. It was all right.

The prince was too stupidly drunk to fool them.

"What do you see below?" the prince demanded.

"There is a rocky island," Doc said quietly enough. "And on the island is a strange-looking blue dome."

"A blue dome?"

"It seems a very queer thing to find in the Arctic," Doc said.

The prince announced in a profane, inebriated voice that he didn't like queer things, and the thing he liked least of all was the fact that he had come here without knowing why he was doing it.

"Land!" he ordered.

"Very well," Doc said.

Monk itched to ask a legion of questions, but the prince stood close, and he dared not speak.

Completely flabbergasted, Monk examined the blue half-sphere. The plane was dropping now. The ice waste, the solid rock island, the blue mystery, seemed to swell as they came upward. The berg pinnacles appeared to grow. It was startling. The pack ice was even more formidable than it had appeared from a great height.

It occurred to Monk again that this was as inaccessible a spot, probably, as existed on earth.

"You had better get back in the cabin," Doc told the prince, "and fasten your safety belt. Have your bodyguards help you."

Monk helped the prince back into the cabin, doing his best to seem like two men. Handling the prince was about like handling a warm worm, Monk thought.

Then Monk went back to the cockpit and stood by for the next move in their plan.

HE watched the island. Snow covered most of it, and in places there was ice; obviously it was no spot for a landing, except along the southern edge, where there was a level area where the snow looked deep and level—a smooth white stretch which terminated against a ridge of high, broken pack ice that had jammed up against the island.

The plane leveled, skimmed the gleaming ice fangs, swung past the blue dome—Monk was made breathless by the queer shimmering luster of the thing—then the craft dipped for the level area of snow.

There would be no room to spare. But the less room the better, for what they had in mind.

The plane skis touched. The craft landed fast: Too fast. Doc knew that; he deliberately had too much speed.

"Monk!" he rapped.

Monk knew what to do. He jerked his fascinated gaze off the blue dome, dashed back to the rear, then came rushing forward again, doubled low so he could not be seen from outside. He had a bundle—a strange man-shaped bundle.

Monk slapped the bundle in the spare pilot's cockpit seat.

The plane slid on across the clearing. It climbed up the side of an ice pinnacle, moving slowly now. It slid sidewise, turning. One ski runner snagged. The plane went over, a wing buckling.

The craft dropped down behind an ice ridge, somewhat of a wreck.

Monk snatched the prince, dragged him out of the door. He pulled behind him one of Doc's equipment cases of metal.

Doc wrenched at a tab overhead in the pilot's cockpit. He tore the tab off. Gasoline burst through from the tanks in a flood that soaked the cabin.

Standing in the plane door, Doc struck a match, tossed it. With a low *whoop,* flames enveloped the plane interior. Doc bounded backward, but not before he was singed enough to make it convincing—the fur burned off around his parka hood, his bearskin trousers scorched and smoking.

Doc gestured at the case.

Monk let the prince drop in the snow, carried the equipment case to a snowdrift near by, made a hole with great haste, and buried the box. Monk used his hands to scoop great banks of snow over the case, then went back to Doc.

"Our nest egg," Monk whispered, "is all planted."

Fire devoured the plane with roaring greed. In the cockpit particularly, it burned and blackened the long bundle which Doc had left there—a fake thing made of beefsteak, imitation bones of composition, enclosed in a pilot's flying suit.

They had to have some way to account for no pilot getting out of the plane.

THE prince showed further that he was a spineless, cruel fool. The roaring flames scared him, and he ran away, or tried to, clawing at an ice ridge and slipping back, screaming all the while.

"Adonis!" he screeched. "Beauty!" Then: "Where's the pilot?" he wanted to know.

"The pilot did not get out," Doc said, using the voice of the bestial Adonis.

"It serves the clumsy so-and-so right!" the prince gritted. "I hope he burns to death."

A moment later, Civan appeared.

Giantia and Titania were with Civan. So were some others. But no John Sunlight.

Their coming gave Monk a vast start; he had no idea from whence they came.

They came in haste, plowing in the snow, slipping on ice where it was bare. They had guns, big revolvers with mechanisms that would not freeze and become useless in this cold, as automatics sometimes did. The guns went back into clothing

when Civan recognized the prince, and gave the word.

They got the odor coming out of the burning plane. There were also faint cries for help coming from the plane now.

"The pilot's burning to death!" Civan bawled.

"Let him burn!" the prince snarled.

After a while, the low, awful cries that seemed to come from the plane were no longer audible.

Doc Savage was a skilled ventriloquist, and he had done a very good job putting the cries for help into the plane; but he did not believe in pushing his luck too far, and anyway, it was about time they thought the pilot had burned to death.

Civan looked over the damage.

"Kakoi srahm!" he said. "What a shame! It was a good plane."

He gave Adonis and Beauty a close inspection. They did not look at all like Doc Savage and Monk Mayfair to Civan. They looked like two tough lads with whom it might be a good idea not to be found alone.

"Who are these cookies?" asked Civan, who could speak American slang with a Russian accent.

Adonis and Beauty were not supposed to be able to speak any English, and they murdered their mother tongue when they spoke it. They merely glared at Civan and made ugly noises.

"They are my bodyguards," said the prince sharply. "Take me to John Sunlight!"

Civan turned and walked back the way he had come. The fact that he slipped almost at once and fell flat on his back did not improve his dignity, but seemed to do no harm to his disposition. It developed that progress on the ice was likely to be a succession of spills, none of them expected. The prince cursed everytime he fell down, and struck his bodyguards.

"Oh, boy!" Monk said. "What can that blue thing be, anyway?"

Monk did not say this out loud, but Doc Savage was lip reader enough to catch the words, even though Monk's lips looked stuffy and unnatural because of an injected chemical which produced a harmless form of swelling, and was infinitely better than internal padding of paraffin or some other substance which might be discovered.

The bronze man did not explain about the blue dome.

JOHN SUNLIGHT had covered his planes with white tents. That was why they had not been discernible from the air. There was a wind of some force blowing, and the air was full of driving snow, and that had helped make the tents invisible.

The men seemed to be camped in white tents, fully a quarter mile from the weird blue edifice.

Covered planes, white house-tents, and igloos were located on the south side of the level, natural landing field in the Arctic pack ice.

The prince was conducted into one of the tents. Civan made an effort to prevent the two hideous bodyguards from sticking with the prince, but he got a shove that sat him down in the snow for his pains.

"They cannot understand English!" the prince said indignantly.

John Sunlight sat in the largest of the white tents. He had caused a block of ice-hard snow to be cut and brought into the tent, and he had spread a polar bearskin over this to make a seat.

Doc and Monk stared at John Sunlight in astonishment. The prince would have stared, too, only he couldn't.

John Sunlight wore light duck trousers and a white silk shirt which was open at the neck. Tropical attire! And yet it must be thirty below zero outside. A warm day in the Arctic for this season. But still thirty below.

John Sunlight was not unaware of the effect. He liked effects. Probably his whole weird, macabre life was devoted to getting them.

"Sit down," he said politely. "And do only one thing—do not ask questions about the blue dome."

Then the placidity left his dark poetic face and burning eyes, for he could see that something was wrong with the prince's eyesight.

"Your eyes!" he rasped. "What is it?"

The prince said a great deal that was uncomplimentary about the brand of liquor served in New York.

"How long will you be blind?" John Sunlight demanded.

"About twenty-four hours more, the doctor thought," the prince explained.

John Sunlight was not pleased, but there was nothing he could do about that.

"You will have to wait," he said grimly, "until your vision has returned."

"Wait? Wait for what?"

"My demonstration."

The prince was befuddled. Why he had come to the Arctic was still a complete mystery to him, and he had come only because his ministers at home had told him anything in which John Sunlight was involved would be important.

"Demonstration?" the prince repeated. "What kind of a demonstration?"

"You must see it to appreciate its value," John Sunlight said.

"See what?"

"The thing," John Sunlight said, "for which you and your government are going to pay me ten million dollars."

Chapter XVI
SNOW TRICKS

THAT was all the satisfaction the prince got. He yelled and swore, and John Sunlight gave him liquor to quiet him. Usually John Sunlight could quiet men without using outside means, either liquor or a club, but in this case the prince couldn't see John Sunlight.

You had to see John Sunlight to appreciate him.

The prince was shoved into a tent, Doc and Monk were shoved in with him. This was not to their liking, and they started to come right out of the tent.

A guard put the muzzle of a rifle close to their noses and waggled it.

"In the tent you stay," he growled. "And if you go near the Strange Blue Dome, you'll get plenty dead. Savvy?"

Doc and Monk sat down on polar bearskins. There seemed to be nothing else to do for the time being, and it was bitterly cold.

The prince howled and sang, and swore for a while, then fell over in a stupor, and they rolled him up in more bearskins.

Doc and Monk began talking with their hands.

"This is insane business," Monk fingered.

"Not so crazy," Doc replied. "John Sunlight feels safe this far from New York City."

They were skilled in use of the finger alphabetic system used by deaf-and-dumb persons.

"But what's he doing here?" Monk demanded.

"Making arrangements to sell something to various European nations, it would appear," Doc responded.

"Doc, that blue dome—"

Monk did not go any further into this at the moment because there was an interruption. Giantia and Titania came into the tent. One carried a kettle of what seemed to be hot stew, and the other had cups and a pot of hot coffee. Steam from the warm food boiled around the two big women.

"Cooks!" Giantia grumbled.

"Here!" Titania snapped, and shoved the food at Doc and Monk.

Evidently the large ladies were not satisfied with their lot.

They looked Monk and Doc over with distaste, but no fear. The two big women seemed to have infinite confidence in their own ability to handle any situation. No normal women could have looked at Doc and Monk—in the kind of disguises they now wore—without feeling frightened.

Suddenly, Doc straightened, looked interested in something outside, and cupped hands to his ears. His pantomime was plain; he meant that he had heard something outside, very faint, and he was listening.

It was perfectly natural that Titania and Giantia should also listen.

There was, at the moment, a lull in the Arctic wind.

A voice drifted to them. It was a voice that could be unmistakably identified as belonging to John Sunlight.

"GIANTIA and Titania," this John Sunlight voice said, "are fools. They do not know their sister, Fifi, is safe and in the hands of Doc Savage's men."

There was a mumbling answer, no words distinguishable. Both voices seemed far away, reaching the tent only through some freak of the lulling wind.

But Giantia and Titania were staring at each other with the most stark shock that Monk had ever seen.

"Fifi—alive!" Giantia croaked. "But she was in that ballyhoo plane. Doc Savage blew her and the plane to bits."

Titania said, "I—" then went silent, for the John Sunlight voice was going on.

"As long as the two fool women think Doc Savage got their sister killed," the voice said, "they will work with me. They may be useful."

The voice cackled delightedly.

"I've even made them think," it ended, "that Doc Savage blew up that ballyhoo plane. They don't know there was a radio-controlled bomb in the plane, and that Fifi wasn't even in it—that her voice was coming off a phonograph record."

That was the end of the John Sunlight voice, for the Arctic wind had started to blow again with whining chill.

Giantia and Titania stood and stared at each other in incredulous amazement. Delight—it had soaked in that Fifi was alive—leaped over their faces, and Titania opened her mouth, doubtless to emit a yell of joy. But Giantia stopped her by clapping a hand over her mouth.

"Fool!" Giantia hissed. "Do you want him to know we've learned the truth?"

Titania subsided. She assumed an expression of grim purpose.

"I'm gonna break John Sunlight's back with my two hands!" she gritted.

Giantia shook her head warningly. "Sh-h-h. Too risky. I don't think we could get away with it."

"Then what'll we do?"

"I don't know," Giantia said. "We'll think it over. But one thing sure—we'll do something."

The two huge women stumbled out of the tent.

Monk waited until they must be well away. Then rolled over close to Doc Savage.

"Doc," Monk breathed, "that was as nice a job of voice imitation and ventriloquism as I ever saw."

"It should do no harm, at least," Doc admitted. Which was probably as close as he ever came to admitting that he considered he had done a difficult piece of work rather well.

Monk still had the Strange Blue Dome on his mind.

But again he was sidetracked off that subject. He listened. Then he threw a quick glance at Doc Savage, half suspecting the bronze man might be imitating this new sound. But obviously he wasn't.

"A plane!" Monk muttered.

Then abrupt anxiety seized him.

"Maybe it's Ham and Long Tom!" he croaked. "Maybe they misunderstood instructions and have come on here!"

THE arriving plane did not carry Ham, Long Tom and Fifi.

It carried Porto Novyi—that was the man's name, although his name wasn't important, since this was the only time he stood out particularly in the grim scheme of things. The rest of the time, he was just another harpy in the pack of soul snatchers. Porto Novyi was a squat, wide man who had not been a Siberian convict, and had not been on the icebreaker. He was a freelance pilot, a swashbuckling daredevil who fought in wars for hire, or did any other kind of flying that paid well.

Neither laws nor human rights meant much to Porto Novyi. He was scared of only one man in the world, and that was John Sunlight. There was probably not a living person he would not have double-crossed for money—except John Sunlight.

The plane swung down and landed. It was a slim ship of remarkably advanced streamlining. It was painted a color which camouflaged it against the sky; it could hardly be seen from the earth when it flew at any considerable height. Moreover, the two motors were scientifically silenced.

Flying two miles up in the sky, this plane could be a ghost.

Porto Novyi bounded out of the plane. He was excited. He ran, a roly-poly figure in flying furs, to the tent occupied by John Sunlight. He even neglected to give the blue dome thing his accustomed number of puzzled looks.

John Sunlight looked sharply at the pilot.

"Did something happen to Baron Karl?" John Sunlight demanded.

The aviator shook his head.

"I took Baron Karl to a Montreal airport," he said.

John Sunlight still looked concerned. Baron Karl had been here to the Arctic rendezvous, and John Sunlight had put on a demonstration of what he had to sell, and everything had gone off well.

Baron Karl had seemed satisfied. Enthusiastic, in fact. That was important. John Sunlight needed ten million dollars from Baron Karl's government. He needed, of course, infinitely more money than that—for what he had in mind. But ten million of it was to come from Baron Karl's government, and it was imperative that nothing should interfere with that.

Baron Karl had promised to buy what John Sunlight had to sell.

So it was very essential that Baron Karl remain satisfied.

"I landed Baron Karl at Montreal," the pilot repeated. "He was enthusiastic about your proposition."

John Sunlight frowned. "Then what," he demanded, "are you worried about?"

"A plane," the flier growled.

"Plane? What's wrong with that ship you're flying? It's the best—"

"I don't mean that one," he growled.

"You—"

"I refer to the plane," the flier said, "which is resting on the snow about a hundred miles south of here."

John Sunlight looked dumbfounded.

"But I know of no such plane!" he exclaimed.

"That's what I was afraid of," the pilot agreed.

John Sunlight got up and took a quick turn around the tent, his feet causing the frozen snow under the tent floor to make squeaking noises. It was bitterly cold, and he had been putting on a show, going around in light trousers and thin silk shirt, pretending not even to notice the chill.

But now he forgot himself and gave a violent shiver. He shook, in fact, until he all but fell down. Then he got control of himself and glowered. It always aggravated him to have his control of himself slip.

"It will be dark soon," he said. "Judging from the clouds it is going to be as dark as night before long."

Porto Novyi looked up through the misty grayness at the dark clouds gathering on the southern horizon and climbing up into the sky like stalking animals.

"As dark as night," the pilot agreed.

"We'll drop some men off by parachute," John Sunlight said, "and have a look at that mysterious plane. You marked the location exactly, did you?"

"I can take off blindfolded and find that plane," the flier said, "because it's standing beside an open lead in the ice, the only open water I saw for a thousand miles."

Chapter XVII
DELILAH

LONG TOM and Ham were finding it comfortable waiting beside the open lead in the ice.

The open "lead" meant open water—a crack where the ice pack had spread apart, leaving a narrow, salty lake which had not frozen. Long Tom and Ham had landed on this water, after first looking it over to make sure there were no floating ice blocks. It was the only suitable landing place they had been able to find. So they had come down, although the spot was too close to a direct line to the southward for their liking.

Their plane was a type that could land on water, snow or earth.

The cabin was snug, and readily kept warm. Moreover, they wore special arctic gear which Doc Savage had developed—garments that were chemically heated.

The plane stood on the ice. They had driven it up there with the motors, and it was poised for a quick takeoff, should the ice lead threaten to close, or should they get a call from Doc Savage.

Fifi was pouting. She had turned out to be consistent with her pouting, and it aggravated Long Tom, although Ham didn't seem to mind. Ham, indeed, seemed to enjoy listening to Fifi's complaining.

Just now, Long Tom was listening to Ham tell Fifi what a sweet, pretty, brave, patient little creature she was.

"Ahr-r-r!" Long Tom said disgustedly.

He got out of the plane. Wind caught his clothes and shook them, and the snow particles stung his face. He walked around the plane, to make sure that no light was showing from the shaded windows.

It was intensely dark; the clouds that had been hunched in the south, now turned the whole sky black. The small waves in the open lead made slapping noises. From time to time, there was a long rumbling grunt as the ice floes cracked; sometimes the ice made gunshot reports, a characteristic of freezing floes.

Long Tom felt along the side of the plane for a wire. He found it. But an instant before, just as he came near the wire, there was a whining sound inside the plane.

The wire was spread in a huge circle around the plane, in the same fashion that cowboys spread a rope around their bedrolls when they bed down on the range, thinking to keep away the snakes. But this wire was more efficient.

The wire was a capacity burglar alarm; if anyone came near it carrying a rifle or some piece of metal of like size, a delicately balanced electrical field around the wire was disturbed, and carefully adjusted apparatus in the plane would give an alarm.

Satisfied the alarm was operating—the machine pistol Long Tom carried in an armpit holster was metal enough to set it off—the feeble-looking electrical wizard climbed back into the plane. That capacity alarm was his pet; he had an infinite amount of confidence in the thing.

They were just deciding to go to sleep when the buzzer whined again.

HAM and Long Tom went into action as if a starting gun had fired. Ham sailed into the cockpit, grabbed switches. The big motors—chemical heaters had kept them warm—exploded into life.

Long Tom landed spread-legged in the center of the cabin, knocked another switch. This ignited flares. The flares had been planted in the ice near the plane; they were high on light, collapsible rods, and reflectors threw the light away from the plane, kept it from blinding those in the craft.

A glare as white as the sun spread hundreds of yards in all directions from the plane.

The white blaze disclosed three fur-clad figures. They were about seventy-five yards distant. Friends? No. That was soon settled. Down they went; their rifles came up. And jacketed bullets began hitting the plane.

The lead slugs made big drumstick noises, but did not come into the plane, because its cabin was alloy-armored.

"Take off!" Long Tom yelled.

Ham barked, "There's only three of—"

"Take off!" Long Tom roared. "I don't like this!"

Ham fed the engines gas.

Long Tom picked his machine pistol out of its holster, used the muzzle to prod open the lid of a firing port in the plane cabin. He latched the pistol in single-fire position. He shot. The gun noise was not big, but the sound its bullet made was astounding. The slug was high-explosive. A cloud of ice flew up in front of the three riflemen.

Long Tom shot again, this time at one of the men. This second bullet was a "mercy" slug; it would cause unconsciousness without doing much damage. But apparently he missed with that one.

The third shot, he put in front of the trio. This bullet hit and became a cloud of black smoke.

That was how the supermachine pistol charge alternated—one explosive, one mercy, one smoke barrage.

The plane tore its runners loose from the ice, wallowed forward like a duck, splashed into the water.

"We'll lay 'em out from the air!" Long Tom yelled. "But first, we gotta find out what this means!"

The plane scudded along the lead. The water was black, heaving, ominous in the light. But it was good enough for a takeoff.

Good enough water, but the plane never made it. The reason it didn't was a bomb. A bomb that fell from a plane which came down in a silent dive. The bomb was almost a direct hit.

A geyser of water climbed, the plane almost in the middle of it. The plane wings folded downward like a sick bird. Then the plane seemed to complete a convulsive jump, and fell over on its back.

Porto Novyi, war pilot for money, was good at his trade.

Water gushed into the plane cabin. The bomb had opened a rip in the side.

"Help!" Fifi screeched. "Help! Help!" And she went off into senseless, hysterical shrieking.

Ham and Long Tom fought to get the girl to the plane door, to get the door open. The door on that side had jammed. They tried the other. Water pressed against it; then they got it open and water jumped in with a great gurgling whoop, and mauled them around in the cabin.

They fought back to the door, hung to its edge, pulled themselves—and Fifi—outside. The plane was under, sinking. The water felt incredibly cold, for they had been warm and comfortable in the plane. It chopped at them like a million knives, that water.

It seemed frozen ages before they got to the surface.

THE three men with rifles were standing on the edge of the ice. One lifted a rifle, and the bullet, hitting the water beside Long Tom's head, sounded as though a firecracker had gone off.

"Hold it!" one of the riflemen shouted. "Savage isn't there!"

No more bullets hit. The men with the rifles gestured, shouted.

There was nothing to do but for Long Tom and Ham to swim to the men, hauling Fifi. She screamed and tried to climb on top of them. She fought them madly.

Overhead, the plane came diving back. Its superbly silenced motor made a noise only a little greater than the wind. Satisfied, the pilot made another circle, then came down in a landing glide toward the open lead of water. That plane, too, was equipped to land on ice, snow, water, or earth.

"Come out!"

The rifleman who gave that order was Civan.

Climbing out of water onto slick ice was hard work. Long Tom and Ham, knowing how it was done, threw their arms up on the ice, and waited for the quick cold to freeze the fur of their garments to the ice. Then they got themselves out and dragged Fifi onto the ice.

Fifi kicked and struck at them, cried at the top of her voice.

"Stop that!" Long Tom gritted.

She paid them no attention.

"You little idiot!" Long Tom hissed. "You made us bring you along!"

She kept on squealing.

Civan growled an order. One of the two riflemen went away and came back shortly dragging three parachutes—obviously 'chutes by which the men had descended quietly from the plane.

The plane taxied up. A man out on the nose kept it from bumping the ice too hard, using a boat hook.

Porto Novyi, the pilot, put his dark, unpleasant face out of the cockpit windows.

"Are those flares about burned out?" he demanded.

"Just about."

Porto Novyi turned on his plane landing lights, and thereafter these illuminated the scene.

"Question them," Porto Novyi ordered.

"I'm running this!" Civan said.

Civan jabbed his rifle at Ham and Long Tom.

"Strip to your underwear!" he gritted.

Ham was cold, but he suddenly got much colder.

"We'll freeze!" he gasped. "You can't—"

"I'd love to see you freeze!" Civan snarled. "We'd all love to see you freeze. Strip!"

Ham and Long Tom got their soaked fur garments off, after which they knew they would freeze to death in, at the most, half an hour.

"Where is Doc Savage?" Civan demanded.

THAT, obviously, was a question that Long Tom and Ham could not afford to answer. They were actors enough not to glance at each other, not to give any sign that they were making up a story.

Turning slowly, Ham stood shivering and looking at the dark, squirming water of the lead. He did nothing but that for a moment. Then, suddenly, he fell to his knees and broke into realistic sobs.

"Don't take it so hard," Long Tom said miserably.

"I kuk-can't huh-help it," Ham sobbed.

"What the hell is this?" Civan snarled.

"Doc Savage was in that plane," Long Tom gulped. "He was killed by the bomb."

This was an out and out untruth, but under the circumstances Long Tom did not feel like letting a lack of veracity trouble him.

"Doc Savage—dead?" Civan began to grin.

"Yuh—yes," Ham sobbed. Suddenly Ham sprang to his feet, and gave every indication of intending to spring upon Civan and the others in a grief-crazed rage. "You killed Doc!" he shrieked.

It was good acting, and Civan was convinced.

"All right," he said. "We might as well shoot them and finish off all the blasted trouble they've caused."

Long Tom, suddenly relieved, said, "Thanks."

"Thanks?" Civan was startled. "What for?"

"For shooting us," Long Tom said grimly. "I wouldn't care about being left to freeze to death. I figured that was about your caliber—so thanks for the shooting."

"Go ahead," Civan ordered. "Shoot them!"

Fifi screamed then. All her other screams were mere kitten mewings compared to this one. If there were polar bears within miles, they must have started running.

"No!" she screeched. "You—they lied to you! Doc Savage wasn't in the plane!"

Long Tom yelled, "Shut up—"

But Fifi was scared; she didn't see the slightest chance of going on living. She didn't know that Ham and Long Tom were gathered to leap backward into the water, and that they had other plans if that was successful.

"I can tell you where Doc Savage is!" Fifi screeched.

"Where?" Civan demanded.

Fifi was not too scared to bargain.

"You take me to John Sunlight," she gasped cunningly, "and I'll show him Doc Savage."

Civan said, "Take her in the plane!"

They boosted the cute little Delilah into the plane. Civan and the other two riflemen climbed into the craft.

"Hey!" Long Tom squalled. "You said you wouldn't leave us to freeze and—"

"I change my mind sometimes," Civan shouted at them.

LONG TOM and Ham stood, in thin cotton underwear and woolen socks, on the ice, and watched the plane scud down the lead and take the air. The craft, once it was off, cut its lights; so that there was only the hissing of engine exhaust to mark its presence. Then that sound left, and there remained nothing but darkness and intense cold, the noise of waves slopping the ice, and the chill whining of the Arctic wind that blew interminably, carrying a fine fog of snow particles that hit their naked skin and felt like needles.

In that chill darkness, in this lost waste, there was one thing that stood out with the staring certainty of death: The nearest civilization was thousands and thousands of miles to the south, and they were two practically naked men left alone.

"Swell!" Long Tom said.

"It could be worse," Ham admitted. "Say, if you hadn't given him that speech about not leaving us to freeze, I don't think he would have done this."

"Contrary, isn't he?" Long Tom remarked. He had a little difficulty with his speech, because his teeth insisted on hitting together.

"Let's get busy," Ham croaked, "before our teeth get knocked flat."

They walked, judging their directions carefully in the darkness, until they reached a drift of snow. They kicked into the drift, scooped with their hands, searched.

Hidden in the drift was the cache of equipment they had placed there against possible emergencies. Taking a leaf out of Doc Savage's book, they had overlooked no bets. They found the cache.

There was clothing, food, a tent, rifles, a sled. The sled could be covered with the tent, thus converting it into a boat with which they could cross open leads. There was a compass, sextant, for finding their way to a destination.

They dressed, then ran and jumped until their circulation was restored.

Best of all, there was a portable shortwave radio with which they could contact help.

The plane came back while they were setting up the radio. It dived, dropped a flare. The flare swung from a parachute, and stayed in the air a long time, and when it hit the ice, the plane dropped another one. The plane also dropped a few bombs, and sent down many bullets.

Long Tom and Ham eventually had to throw away their rifles and hold up their arms. Otherwise, they would have died.

The plane landed on the lead, and Civan came to confront them and cackle pleasantly.

"I got to thinking," Civan growled, "about the reputation this Doc Savage crowd has got. They didn't get that rep for nothing, I thinks. So we came back. Lucky for us, eh?"

Long Tom and Ham were loaded into the plane and tied hand and foot.

"You see," Civan explained, "we contacted John Sunlight by radio, and he says to keep you alive. We may be able to use you as hostages to keep this Doc Savage off our neck, if worse comes to worse."

Fifi whimpered in the cabin.

"I wonder if we shouldn't just shoot you and put you out of your misery?" Civan growled.

"But I'm going to show Doc Savage to you!" Fifi wailed.

One of the bullets Ham and Long Tom had fired up at the plane had damaged the wiring of one motor. It could be repaired, but it would take a little time.

Porto Novyi, the pilot, set about making the repairs.

Chapter XVIII
THE POISONED SEAL

JOHN SUNLIGHT, having contacted Civan and the plane by radio, knew about the delay caused by the necessary motor repairs. He said pleasantly enough that he didn't mind. But he did. He spoke pleasantly, because he considered that his expedition had done a very nice piece of work. Wasn't Fifi going to show them where Doc Savage could be found?

Of course, the silly little fool of a girl wouldn't tell anybody but John Sunlight. She probably thought she could save herself in that fashion.

Fifi did not know John Sunlight very well.

John Sunlight took a walk over to the tent wherein slept the prince. He kicked the prince in the ribs, got him awake.

"Can you use your eyes yet?" John Sunlight demanded.

The prince did not relish being kicked in the ribs.

"I can see much better!" he snarled.

John Sunlight was pleased.

"In half an hour," he said, "I shall make my demonstration for you."

"You mean," the prince gritted, "that you'll show me why I made this crazy trip up here?"

"Exactly."

John Sunlight then walked out of the tent.

The prince, still rankling over being kicked in the ribs, rushed over and kicked Monk—Beauty—several times to relieve his feelings.

"I'll kick your voice back into you!" he roared.

He had no success, but he felt better.

"Get out of here!" he screamed. "I hate the sight of your ugly faces!"

Doc and Monk did not like the sight of the prince's face any better by now, and they were very willing to get out of the tent—providing the guard outside would let them. They scrambled out through the tent door—and confronted John Sunlight.

John Sunlight stood, a tall dark tower of a figure; he had given up his show of not feeling the cold, and had donned dark clothing and a black cape and an aviator's black helmet. He presented a picture that was not in any sense pleasant. He showed his teeth.

"Your master treats you roughly," he said.

He spoke these words in the tongue which Adonis and Beauty were supposed to use.

Doc replied. He spoke the tongue fluently, as he spoke many others.

"Our lot is not a bad one," Doc replied in the language. He used the illiterate form of the tongue, as Adonis might be expected to do.

"You have been with his highness long?" John Sunlight asked.

"A long time," Doc replied promptly.

He didn't know whether that was the correct answer; there had been no time to check on all details of the prince's two bodyguards

"Where were you born?" John Sunlight asked.

Doc immediately named a small mountain town in the prince's native land.

"I have heard of the place," John Sunlight said. Then he added, "Well, you will be out of the cold weather before long. Your master will probably start back at dawn. I shall send you all in one of my planes."

He walked away.

Monk breathed, "Doc, we could grab him now—"

"No," the bronze man whispered. "We have to learn exactly what he is doing. We have to be sure. We suspect the truth, but we are not sure."

"O. K.," Monk said. "But this prince is gonna get strangled if I hafta bodyguard 'im much longer!"

Doc said, "We had better make a try for that equipment case."

"Want me to help—"

"You go get it," Doc said. "I will stay here and try to alibi your absence, in case you are missed."

DOC SAVAGE watched Monk move away. The homely chemist was lost in the blackness of the brooding dark clouds almost at once, and the drifting snow covered his footprints.

There was no sign of the guard who had been watching the tent, and Doc wondered about what had become of the fellow. That mystery was not long being clarified.

There was a sudden, frightened outcry from a nearby igloo. There was genuine horror in the voice. It was the guard.

The fellow had evidently gotten cold, crawled into an igloo to keep warm, and dozed off. John Sunlight had found him missing, and put men hunting for him.

Another guard appeared shortly. He had an electric lantern, and he was too concerned over the failure of the other guard not staying on the job to order Doc back in the tent.

"The poor fool," the new guard muttered. "He should have known better."

Evidently, he referred to the other guard.

Monk would be coming back soon. Something had to be done about that.

Doc began to sing. There was not much music in his singing, but there was volume—and sense, if one understood ancient Mayan, the language which he and his men used for private conversation. Over and over, he told Monk to be careful, to wait until a propitious moment to show himself.

Doc allowed plenty of time—time enough that he knew Monk was lying low, out in the darkness.

Then the bronze man took a coin out of his pocket and began to play with it. He tossed it high, and caught it, cackling like the half-witted oaf he resembled in his disguise.

Directly, what looked like the inevitable happened. The coin flew over, hit the side of the tent, and skidded down into the snow.

Doc gasped, ran to look for the coin. The guard watched idly. When Doc beckoned him to help, the man came over on that side of the tent and began kicking around in the snow.

"Monk—your chance!" Doc called in Mayan.

He made it sound as if he were saying something disgusted about losing the coin.

When Doc found the coin and entered the tent, Monk was inside, looking innocent. The guard, thanks to the diversion, had not seen him return.

THE prince apparently had rolled up in his blankets again and gone back to sleep. He must be a physical wreck. It was not hard to believe. Doc shook him gently, and the dissolute fellow snored. He was asleep.

"Where is the case, Monk?" Doc breathed.

"It's cached in a snowbank about forty feet from the tent," Monk whispered. "If you could follow my tracks, you can find—"

"All right," Doc said. "You hold the fort down for a while now."

"But how you gonna leave? That guard—"

Doc used a sharp knife—he and Monk had not been searched—and opened a slit in the rear of the tent. He opened it close to the floor, and after he crawled out, tied the canvas together again with a spare four inches of shoestring. Monk, inside, placed bearskin sleeping covers against the spot, and it was temporarily unnoticeable.

Doc faded away quickly in the darkness, keeping low. He circled, and found, not without some difficulty, Monk's tracks. The wind was filling them rapidly.

It was only by bending low and watching the reflection of the tent guard's electric lantern that Doc was able to locate Monk's footprints at all.

Once he had found them, he managed to help along the business of following the prints by utilizing the sense of touch.

Later, the bronze man located the equipment case which Monk had buried. Carrying it, Doc retreated a short distance, then opened the case.

Principal item in the equipment box was a portable shortwave radio outfit.

Doc spent ten minutes in a futile effort to contact Ham and Long Tom.

He was worried enough over that, after he had checked the radio and was sure it was putting out a signal, to make his strange, low trilling sound. He made it unconsciously, and the instant he realized what he was doing, he stopped. The exotic note had an unusual carrying power; he listened, but it was evident no one had heard.

Probably everyone but John Sunlight would have been astounded at what Doc Savage did next, and what happened as a result.

Doc concealed about his person such articles of equipment as he might need. There was nothing astounding about that, nor about the fact that he concealed the radio outfit in the snow again.

Next, the bronze man moved off in the darkness, crawling much of the time, and came to an igloo. It was an Eskimo *igloovegak*—an igloo. Doc found the long tunnel that was part of the igloo entrance, crept in, and moved past small food-storage igloos—called *suksos*—into the bigger room of iceblocks where the Eskimos lived.

There were animal skins on the floor, the walls and ceiling had been darkened by blubber lamp soot, and around the smoke vent in the ceiling a swelling of frost had gathered. Almost circling the interior of the igloo was the ice-block shelf which served the same purpose for the Eskimos as the studio couch serves New York apartment dwellers.

A blubber lamp burned in the center of the igloo, giving off a dark worm of smoke. There were sleeping forms around the shelf.

Doc went to one of the sleepers, touched him.

"Aput," the bronze man said. "Do not be alarmed—I am Doc Savage."

Aput opened his eyes. He was a sturdy man whose face was rutted by the years. He stared at Doc Savage unbelievingly.

"Doc Savage!" Aput muttered. "You do not look—but it is your voice."

APUT was one of the group of Eskimos whom John Sunlight had found living on the rocky island of the Strange Blue Dome. Aput was one of those who had first looked John Sunlight in the eye and insisted they could not see any weird blue

dome; that it didn't even exist. That had been, of course, a clever trick to further bewilder and confuse John Sunlight.

Aput was a venerable man, still a great hunter in spite of his years, and a man who was looked to for advice and leadership. He was not, correctly speaking, the chief, because this little group of Eskimos had no chief.

The Eskimo word *angakoeet* better described Aput's position among his people. *Angakoeet* was the vernacular for "medicine man," which meant that Aput was a combined oracle and father-confessor, the man who had the most influence.

Aput knew Doc Savage very well—obviously. It was several moments before Aput recovered from his astonishment at seeing the bronze man.

"*Chimo!*" Aput muttered fervently. "Welcome!"

"Thank you," Doc Savage said quietly in the Eskimo tongue. "It moves me deeply to hear you make me welcome when it is plain that I have caused you much sorrow and trouble."

Aput shrugged, and got out of his sleeping skins, took Doc Savage's hand and shook it.

"We have been hoping you would come," he said. "*Elarle!* Indeed, yes!"

Doc saw that Aput had nothing to wear but a sealskin singlet.

"Your clothing?" the bronze man asked.

"This John Sunlight," Aput said, "took away our clothing long ago. It is to prevent our escaping. They count each bearskin and sealskin daily, so that we will not be able to make any of them into garments. We are given clothing to go out to hunt, and armed men go along; and after the hunting, our clothing is taken away again."

Doc Savage was grimly silent.

"When did Sunlight come?"

"*Akkane,*" Aput replied.

The word akkane meant last year.

"THEY were on a great boat, a boat as big as a hundred *umiaks,*" Aput continued. "It was crushed in the ice. They come ashore. We take them food. But this strange dark one, called John Sunlight, got to want only to enter the Strange Blue Dome."

"That was bad," Doc said.

"Very bad," Aput agreed. "John Sunlight tried to starve us into telling him what the Strange Blue Dome was. We pretended to be very ignorant Eskimos."

"That was good," Doc said.

Aput smiled wryly. "We were doing as you told us. We were doing the thing for which you brought us here. We were following your orders not to allow anyone to enter the Strange Blue Dome."

"And to take care of what was inside the dome," Doc said.

Aput nodded. "Yes. But we failed. For John Sunlight watched one of us, and saw that the secret door opened when we came near it with the white rabbit cape. He seemed to guess how it operated—"

"John Sunlight," Doc said, "is clever enough to know all about magnetically operated relays and door-openers, particularly since he would have little difficulty finding the tiny, permanent magnets sewed in the lining of the white rabbit cape."

Aput was silent a moment. His face clouded with grim memory.

"This John Sunlight got into the Strange Blue Dome," he said, "and thereafter weird and horrible things began to happen." Aput closed his eyes and shuddered. "There was the time one of my people turned into a black ghost of smoke and blew away."

"That happened to an Eskimo here?" Doc asked.

"Yes," Aput said, and shuddered again.

Doc Savage's metallic features went grave.

"John Sunlight was making a test," he decided.

"Test?" Aput was puzzled.

"You do not understand, Aput," Doc said quietly. "There are many mysterious and terrible things in that Strange Blue Dome. You would not understand them." The bronze man shook his head slowly. "Few people in the world would understand many of them. So it is too bad that a man with John Sunlight's type of mind had to discover the dome."

Aput's curiosity was sharpened.

"What were those things in the dome that you told us never to touch?" he asked.

"Things that the world was better off without," Doc said.

"I do not understand," Aput said.

Doc Savage patted the old medicine man's shoulder.

"If you found a seal that was poison, Aput," Doc said, "what would you do with it?"

Aput answered promptly.

"I would bury the poisoned seal," he said, "where none would ever find it."

Doc made a short, grim sound.

"That was my idea, too," he said.

He went on—he spoke quickly, for time was getting short—and advised Aput how to help when the fight against John Sunlight started. Aput said he would spread the word among his people to be ready.

Chapter XIX
DEMONSTRATION

WHEN Doc Savage—his Adonis disguise was holding up very well in the cold—crawled back into the prince's tent, he had hardly replaced the slitted canvas when there was a commotion outside. It meant that John Sunlight's men had come for the prince.

"Monk!" Doc breathed. "Ham and Long Tom did not answer my radio call."

Monk's mouth fell open.

"But what on earth could 'a' happened to 'em?" he gulped.

There was no time to discuss that, because a swarthy head shoved into the tent and said, "John Sunlight wants the prince."

The prince was still in his drunken sleep.

Monk winked slightly at the others, then gave the prince a terrific kick on the part of the anatomy most generally kicked. Monk sprang back, looked quite innocent as the prince awoke and turned the adjacent Arctic air blue with profanity. Monk had been aching to kick the besotted prince.

They were not taken to a tent. Their escort led them to an igloo, a large one, made expertly of snow blocks well-frozen. Actually, there was one large igloo, and three more built against it, like a cluster of grapes with one big grape.

John Sunlight lost no time in getting down to business.

"I am going to tell you a story," he said.

The prince blinked stupidly. "Story?"

"It concerns an amazing man," John Sunlight said. "This man was—"

"Do I have to listen to your bragging?" the prince asked impolitely.

John Sunlight frowned, and looked as though he had made a mental note to raise his price to the prince an extra million dollars for that crack.

"This is not the story of myself," John Sunlight said coldly. "No one will ever know that story. This is another tale, a brief synopsis of the fantastic life of one human being. It is a story which illustrates to what extent a human mind can be developed."

"I'm not very interested," the prince said.

John Sunlight ignored the interruption.

"This man," he said, "was taken from the cradle, literally, and put into the hands of scientists, who were ordered to train the child. They did so. And the child grew into a young man who possessed a fantastic brain. People sometimes call him superhuman. But he is not that—he is only a scientific product."

"Humph!" the prince grunted. "About that demonstration—"

"This scientifically trained young man," John Sunlight continued, "dedicated himself to a strange career. A career of aiding mankind and of increasing his own knowledge that he might help the human race. In other words, this young man continued to study—study—study—"

The prince shook his flabby shoulders impatiently.

"It sounds damned dry and uninteresting to me," he said.

John Sunlight's dark, poetic face remained composed.

"Study," he said. "Study—study—that was the young man's occupation in every spare moment. The most intense kind of study. Study that demanded solitude, no interruptions."

The prince shrugged, lit a cigarette.

"Solitude," said John Sunlight, "was what this unusual young man had to have. So he came here into the Arctic, and found this island."

THE prince abruptly became interested. "Here?" he said.

"Yes."

"Say, who is this—this scientific marvel you're talking about?"

"Doc Savage," John Sunlight said.

The prince started violently. "Doc Savage!"

"You seem to have heard of him," John Sunlight said dryly.

As a matter of fact, the prince had heard of Doc Savage—and so had the rogues who composed his cabinet in his native land. A number of times they had discussed Doc Savage, and the possibility of the Man of Bronze appearing in their nation to attempt to remedy certain cruel malpractice on the part of the prince and his government.

Doc Savage had a habit of doing such things, they'd heard. And that was why a strict censorship had been clapped down on news that left the country. They didn't want the mysterious, almost legendary, Man of Bronze to learn too much about the succession of political assassinations in the land.

"I have heard of Doc Savage," the prince admitted. "Er—faintly."

John Sunlight smiled wolfishly. "I imagined you had."

The prince swallowed uneasily. "Doc Savage—you mean—" He scratched his head, worked his loose mouth around in several shapes, then got an inkling of the truth. "You mean that Doc Savage—he constructed that blue dome?"

"The blue dome," John Sunlight said, "is the Fortress of Solitude."

"Fortress of—huh?"

"The Fortress of Solitude," John Sunlight said, "is the place which Doc Savage created so that he would have a place to do his studying in solitude."

The prince gulped and muttered, "That—it all seems fantastic."

John Sunlight nodded. "You must understand that Doc Savage is something of a fantastic person, a man who is many generations ahead of the day in scientific knowledge. This place here— this Fortress of Solitude—was unknown to the world. It was built by Eskimos under Doc Savage's direction, with materials brought in by a huge transport plane. The construction took a long time."

At this point, Monk Mayfair realized his mouth was hanging open, and he closed it. This story that John Sunlight was telling might sound fantastic to the prince; Monk, however, knew it was true. He had known the Fortress of Solitude existed. He had not known where it lay, or exactly what it was.

Doc Savage had never told. The bronze man simply disappeared from his usual haunts, sometimes for months at a time, and during these absences, it was absolutely impossible to get in touch with him.

When Doc came back from these absences, he explained simply that he had been at his Fortress of Solitude—and usually, too, he brought back some new invention, or the solution of some complicated problem of science or surgery.

The Fortress of Solitude!

Monk knew it must be a marvelous place. A great laboratory, probably. Monk, who was something of a chemical wizard himself, had often wished he could see what kind of a chemical laboratory Doc kept in the Fortress. It must be amazingly complete, undoubtedly the finest in existence.

An interruption shocked Monk out of his reverie. A plane! There was a plane circling in the Arctic gloom overhead.

A man put his head into the big igloo.

"Civan and the others are arriving in the plane," he announced.

JOHN SUNLIGHT gathered his dark-red cape around him. He had worn black earlier in the evening, but now he had changed colors again, and wore an impressive, bloody-red ensemble. It gave him the aspect of a satanic alchemist. He was probably aware of that.

"Bring Civan and the others here," he ordered, "as soon as they land."

He laughed then. A laugh that was a quick, ugly report.

"I want everyone in the plane here for my demonstration," he added.

The messenger went away.

"Now," John Sunlight continued, "I shall finish my story of Doc Savage and the Fortress of Solitude—which the bronze man thought no one would ever discover."

The prince licked his lips uneasily. He was learning for the first time that he was involved in something that concerned Doc Savage, and the idea was giving him a worse case of the jitters than he had ever gotten out of a bottle.

"For some time now," John Sunlight said, "Doc Savage has been following his unusual career. And in the course of it, he has captured a number of amazing inventions."

The prince's mouth fell open.

"Inventions," said John Sunlight, "which Doc Savage considered a menace to the world. Among these is the machine which through creation of an unusual type of concentrated magnetic field, stops atomic motion entirely."

Monk took a deep breath. A great many things were coming clear to the homely chemist.

John Sunlight said, "I'll explain about atoms." He took a one-cent piece out of a pocket. "This coin, for instance, is made of copper. And copper is made up of molecules. The molecules are in turn composed of atoms. And each atom is a nucleus of electrons. Just what the electrons are composed of is a matter about which science is not certain, but it is believed they are electrical in nature. At any rate, the electrons travel in gravitational orbits, with a good deal of space between them, somewhat like our solar system—the earth, the moon, sun and planets.

"In case," John Sunlight went on, "the motion of the electrons is stopped, the result is to all practical effects and purposes a complete disintegration of matter."

Monk swallowed. That stuff about molecules, atoms and electrons was straight stuff—so was the surmise about what would happen if electronic movement could be stopped. But, as far as Monk knew, no one had ever stopped it. Still—

John Sunlight was continuing.

"Doc Savage perfected a device," he said, "which, by creating a magnetic field of superlative intensity, completely stops atomic motion, and results in the collapse of any matter in that field."

The prince wrinkled his bulbous forehead. "What is this leading up to?" he demanded.

"You read about Serge Mafnoff, the Russian diplomat?" John Sunlight demanded.

"I—" The prince looked stunned. "Look here, did—"

"He did. Serge Mafnoff was the victim of Doc Savage's death machine, as we will call it." John

Sunlight moved his red cloak a little. "You see, I had a score to settle with Serge Mafnoff, and I also wished to call the world's attention to my mur—ah—death device."

At this point, the plane, which had been circling repeatedly, landed. It taxied up outside, its motors died.

"Excuse me," John Sunlight said.

He went out. He was gone about five minutes. Then he came back in.

Several of his men trailed behind, all carrying rifles. Along with them, they brought the prisoners—Ham, Long Tom and Fifi.

NO one happened to be looking at homely Monk at that instant. That was fortunate. Because Monk's self-control slipped; he couldn't help showing his shock at seeing Ham and Long Tom prisoners.

Doc Savage's metallic features remained inscrutable. Having failed to contact Ham and Long Tom by radio, he had half feared something like this.

"Line them up!" John Sunlight growled.

The prince looked at the captives, and was puzzled. He had never seen them before.

John Sunlight asked, "Where are Giantia and Titania?"

"They're in their igloo," a man said. "I looked a minute ago."

"Go and make sure," John Sunlight ordered. "They must not know that this sister, Fifi, is alive. They would turn on me. Later, we will take care of them."

The man left to see about Giantia and Titania.

"Now," John Sunlight said, "we'll proceed."

The prince put in peevishly, "Why not get around to the demonstration, whatever it is? This is getting me confused."

"You realize," John Sunlight said sharply, "that I have just described a scientific death machine to you."

"So what? I don't see—"

"War."

"Eh?"

"War, you fool. War."

The prince yelled, "Who you calling a fool? I'm a king; don't forget that!"

John Sunlight's grip on his patience slipped a trifle, and the snapping evil of the man showed in his eyes. He calmed himself.

"With this electron-stopping war machine," he said, "you can conquer your neighboring nation ruled by the prime minister whose agent is the Baron Karl. I believe you would like to do that."

A flash of greed jumped over the prince's dissolute face. "That," he said, "is true."

"I'll sell you the war machine," John Sunlight said, "for eleven million dollars."

"Eleven!" the prince ejaculated. "You said ten, earlier."

"I hadn't been insulted then," John Sunlight told him calmly.

Whatever the prince was going to say—it was obviously to be explosive—remained unuttered, because a man dashed wildly into the igloo. He was the fellow who had been sent to see about Giantia and Titania.

"The big women are gone!" he squalled.

JOHN SUNLIGHT'S poetic face became ugly. "I thought you looked into the igloo a few minutes ago?"

"They had piled up snow under their sleeping robes," the man groaned. "Made it look like they were asleep!"

John Sunlight yelled orders.

"Civan!" he howled. "Take four men with guns and begin hunting those women!"

Civan shoved four men out of the big igloo, and followed himself.

John Sunlight had been trembling a little. He was a nervous man, and when excitement came, he sometimes lost some of his control. He forced himself to become calm.

"Now," he said, "I shall—"

"If you think I'll pay you eleven million for anything, you're crazy!" the prince yelled.

John Sunlight looked at the poor sample of royalty, and being short-tempered at the instant, he did not mince words.

"Remember the newspaper stories about the mysterious blackness that appeared around Serge Mafnoff's house in New York City?" he asked.

"Yes," the prince growled. "But that—"

"That was another war machine," John Sunlight snapped. "The blackness was caused by a combination of short electrical waves, and high-frequency sonic vibrations, which paralyze the functions of the rod-and-cone mechanism of the optic nerves in eyes. In other words—a blinding ray."

"I—"

"That, too, is a Doc Savage invention."

"But—"

"I sold it," John Sunlight said, "to Baron Karl and your enemy, the neighboring nation. They will use it against you."

The prince blanched. His mouth worked, could not make words.

"You will have to buy the electron machine," John Sunlight said coldly, "to defend your country."

The prince looked around for a seat, and sagged to it.

"Damn you!" he gritted.

John Sunlight was satisfied. He jerked his head slightly. "Now we show the prince what happens when the electrons are stopped in a human body," he said. "I suppose we had better tie the victim."

John Sunlight slanted an arm at the huge, grotesque creature whom the prince had accepted as his bodyguard, Adonis.

"We will use that man—Doc Savage," John Sunlight said. "Fifi, he is the one, isn't he?"

"Yes," Fifi said. "That is Doc Savage."

Chapter XX
MAD HOUR

THERE were a few occasions in his life when Doc Savage had been caught flat-footed. This was one of them.

He began doing things about it.

Rifles were coming up. Doc whipped forward. He made for John Sunlight.

But the strange poetic-faced man with the distorted mind was fast. He was faster than even Doc had dreamed. He pitched sidewise, got behind some of his men, went on—toward the snow hole that led into one of the smaller connecting igloos.

A rifle crashed. The bullet hit Doc's chest, and he would have died then, except for the bullet-proof vest from the equipment case which he had donned. As it was, the slug tilted him sideways.

Doc went on down, hit Ham and Long Tom's ankles. They toppled. Doc had a knife out of his clothing by then. His speed was blinding. He slashed, got Ham's wrists loose—Long Tom and Ham were bound with ropes.

Doc left the knife in Ham's hands, left Ham to finish freeing himself and Long Tom.

Monk had hold of a man now. The hairy chemist's great hands made the victim scream. Monk lifted the fellow, slammed him against others.

Two men fell on Doc. They tried short-range clubbing with rifles. Doc rolled with them, all in a tangle. The bronze man was trying to reach the hole into which John Sunlight had gone.

Unexpectedly, John Sunlight came back out of the hole. He came fast, and an instant after he was through it, a gun blasted in the smaller igloo which he had just left. The bullet missed John Sunlight, but a man in the larger igloo screeched and started a jig, trying to plug a leak in his chest with his hands.

Titania came out of the small igloo. She had a rifle. Her huge sister, Giantia, was close behind, also with a rifle. They both shot at John Sunlight again. But he got out of the big igloo into the Arctic night without being hit.

Giantia and Titania ran to their little sister, Fifi, and thereafter gave no thought to anything but protecting her.

Monk, Ham, Long Tom were all fighting now. Not a man was on his feet. They flailed around on the floor, and a gun banged now and then.

Doc got on his feet, turned around and around like a discus thrower, and slammed his two opponents against the ice walls of the igloo. They dropped back somewhat broken.

Then old Aput, the Eskimo, came through the igloo door like a greased brown bullet. He had few clothes, but he did have a short *oonapik,* the little hunting spear of his people.

Other Eskimos followed, some with *oonapiks,* others with only the small half-moon knives used in domestic work, called *ooloos.* They joined the igloo fray. There was no real need of Doc after that.

John Sunlight was outside. So was Civan, the pilot Porto Novyi, and—Doc did not know how many others. But a score, at least. The men who had been on the Soviet icebreaker on which the convicts had escaped from Siberia. How many of those would turn against John Sunlight now was a question. Some of them, surely. Then there were the rest of the Eskimos—friends, but unarmed.

The odds were still terrible.

DOC dived into the adjoining small igloo into which John Sunlight had tried to get. His guess was right. The apparatus for stopping electronic motion—the machine that had killed diplomat Serge Mafnoff—was there. The powerful coils and tubes were heating. That took a little time. John Sunlight had evidently switched on the device.

But Giantia and Titania had been hiding in there, and had driven out John Sunlight.

The device operated from heavy high-voltage storage batteries.

Doc picked up a battery, smashed it down on the contraption; picked up the battery, smashed again. Crushed, broken, destroyed. Until finally the death machine was a hopelessly ruined tangle that would never function again.

It was not as mad as it looked. The scientific device, as remarkable as it was, had no great value as a weapon.

John Sunlight had been perpetrating a species of hoax on the prince. For the electronic-stopping machine would not work at a distance of much more than twenty feet.

When it had killed Serge Mafnoff, it had been hidden in the unused part of the attic. The marks on the sills had been left by boards on which the device stood when it killed. It had killed through the attic wall, for it was only where the magnetic

and sonic beams met, their focal point, that the effect was obtained.

Having smashed the apparatus, Doc picked a single bar of steel—a permanent magnet—out of the mess.

Then he dived back into the larger igloo.

Fighting there was done. Victims were spread out on the floor, and Monk was dancing around, tying himself into knots in an effort to learn the depth of a cut he had received in the back.

"John Sunlight!" Doc rapped. "Get him!"

Old Aput, before Doc could stop him, shot for the igloo door, hit on his stomach, sledded. He must have gone out of many an igloo in a hurry in his time to become that skilled.

A rifle whacked.

Old Aput came sliding back in, just as fast, and when he stopped sledding, began trying to straighten out his right arm, which a bullet had broken.

"They wait with guns!" he yelled.

"Back wall!" Doc said.

They went to work on the rear wall. Ice blocks were thick. There was no time to chip. They hit the wall, Doc and Monk, who were strongest. They learned that ice could be like steel. Then the ice broke, a great mass of blocks toppling outward, and they landed in the snow and cold.

FOR forty yards or so, Doc and the others traveled with all their speed; and Doc covered the whole distance before some of the others made half of it. Then they were down behind an ice ridge.

Giantia and Titania had remained in the igloo with Fifi.

There was a crash. A grenade. The igloo jumped apart, blocks of ice flying.

Then Giantia and Titania came running and dragging Fifi. Guns snapped, but they made it, and got down behind the ice ridge with Doc and the others.

Doc lifted his voice.

"Turn against John Sunlight now," he called, "and you will be free of the fellow."

The bronze man's voice was enormous, a rumble that carried with the volume of a public address loudspeaker.

His words were for the benefit of those who had courage to turn on John Sunlight. And they had an effect. A rifle banged, and a man screamed.

A man—it was Porto Novyi, the pilot—set off a flare, hanging it by its parachute from one of the plane wings. The glow ignited the fighting. Half a dozen men, or more, had turned on John Sunlight's group. They were fighting a strange kind of civil war of their own in the icy wind and drifting, flour-fine snow. Eskimos came running to join the fray.

Monk reared up and roared, "Boy, I ain't gonna miss this!"

"Upwind!" Doc ordered. "We have some gas grenades."

But the gas grenades did them no good. John Sunlight saw them running, guessed their intent, and shouted orders.

John Sunlight and his faction broke away and fled in retreat toward the Strange Blue Dome that was Doc Savage's mysterious Fortress of Solitude.

IT was a chase, then. A wild, mad race, with death made of lead passing through the air, of hitting ice and glancing off with violinlike whining.

It was dark, the polar sky packed with clouds. That was why John Sunlight and his men managed to reach the Strange Blue Dome. Had there been light, they would have been picked off.

Doc, racing furiously, taking chances, saw the panel in the side of the Strange Blue Dome closing. It was shut when he hit it. He snatched the permanent magnet from a pocket. It was the magnet he had taken from the Death device. But it had no effect when he held it close to the door-opening mechanism.

Inside, they had jammed the door apparatus.

Doc whirled, met Monk and the others.

"Back!" he rapped. "Get way back!"

He was running with the words, going out across the stone island in what was apparently a senseless direction. Most of them stared at the bronze man in amazement. But Monk, making speed with his short legs, trailed Doc. He lost ground steadily, and began to think that Doc was going to continue out across the Arctic ice.

But Doc stopped, and when Monk reached him, the bronze man was on his knees at the edge of the rocky islet. Doc was knocking snow aside with his hands, maneuvering the naked stone, obviously searching.

Monk watched. There was silence, except for his breathing, and the breathing of the bronze man. The steaming plumes of their breath blew away from their lips. Once, far out in the ice fields, there was a cannon report as a floe cracked.

Then Doc found what he was seeking. A crack, apparently. He began to lay the permanent magnet on various parts of the stone, as if he were using its attraction to work a combination.

There was a crunching, and a section of the rock flew up, lid fashion. Doc dropped into the aperture.

It was only a box. In it were two switches. Doc threw one of them.

Monk, knowing something was going to happen, turned his eyes toward the great dome of glasslike blue. He waited, seemingly an age.

Finally, "Doc, nothing—nothing—" he breathed, and couldn't find the words to go on.

"Gas," the bronze man said in a low voice. "It may work; may not. When the place was built, the gas was installed against such an emergency as this."

The bronze man suddenly looked weary and battered.

"The trouble was," he added, "the place was so remote that I got to thinking no one would ever find it. So I stored those infernal machines here. I should have destroyed them."

Monk said, "We've captured some pretty devilish scientific devices in our time."

"Yes, Monk," Doc said queerly.

The strangeness of the bronze man's tone caused Monk to glance at him.

"Are all those contraptions in that blue dome, Doc?" Monk asked wryly.

"Every one of them," Doc said hollowly.

They waited. There was no sign of life from the arching blue half-sphere of the Fortress of Solitude.

Ham and Long Tom and the Eskimos, tired of waiting, moved back, some of them, and went to inspect the igloos and tents of John Sunlight's camp, searching for enemies, treating the wounded, and binding those who might offer resistance.

Later, Ham approached Doc Savage.

"The prince got his," Ham said grimly.

"Yes?"

"That grenade John Sunlight's men threw into the big igloo," Ham explained, "probably killed the prince instantly."

Chapter XXI
WILL TERROR COME?

THIRTY minutes later, Doc Savage opened the Fortress of Solitude.

They had to destroy a plane to do it. They sent the craft full speed against the side of the Strange Blue Dome—Doc Savage did this, selecting the spot, then leaping out of the racing craft—and the impact of the heavy motors smashed a hole large enough for them to crawl inside, one at a time.

Only Doc, Monk, Ham and Long Tom were allowed to enter. They wore gas masks. They had found the masks in John Sunlight's equipment.

Once inside, they saw senseless forms lying about, and knew the gas had been effective.

They had often wondered—Monk, Ham and Long Tom—what this Fortress of Solitude was like. They saw now, and it exceeded, if anything, what they had imagined.

Monk saw a chemical laboratory which, for completeness and advanced equipment, was far beyond anything he had ever seen, or expected to see. In America and abroad, Monk had a reputation as one of the greatest living chemists, particularly in advanced chemistry. But here, in this laboratory, he saw apparatus after apparatus so advanced that the nature of which he couldn't even grasp.

"Blazes!" Monk breathed in awe.

Long Tom, the electrical wizard, saw an electrical experimental setup which took his breath. It made his fingers itch, drew him like a magnet. His own laboratory in New York City, and the one Doc maintained in the New York skyscraper headquarters, was a child's experimenting set, compared to this.

Ham, the lawyer, did not see any law books. Ham was no great enthusiast as a scientist.

So it was Ham who wandered around gathering up the unconscious John Sunlight faithfuls, and passing them out through the hole in the side of the blue dome.

The construction of the dome, the strange, blue glasslike material of which it was made, did interest Ham. He asked Doc about that, and learned it was a form of glass composition which could be welded with heat, and which had strength far beyond that of true glass. The welding operation explained how the dome had been constructed without joints. The stuff had the advantage of being a nonconductor, which meant that it kept out the cold.

But construction details suddenly ceased to worry Ham. He ran to Doc Savage.

"Doc!" Ham exploded. "John Sunlight—he's not here!"

"John Sunlight—not here!" The bronze man sounded incredulous.

Then they searched. Searched furiously. Doc Savage, who knew every cranny of the Fortress of Solitude, went over everything repeatedly. He examined the prisoners, to make sure none of them was John Sunlight in disguise.

Then, with breathless intensity, they began a widespread search.

They did not find John Sunlight. They did not find his body.

IT was Doc Savage who located footprints that must have been John Sunlight's. And by the tracks, they knew that John Sunlight had not entered the Strange Blue Dome with his men. He had gone around the Dome, and hidden in the snow. Then, when he saw his men had been defeated, he had fled.

John Sunlight's tracks led out across the Arctic ice pack.

Doc Savage followed the footprints for two days, and came to a patch of frozen red gore on the edge of an open lead in the ice. There, beside the water, the traces showed that a monster polar bear had come out of the lead and attacked John Sunlight.

They found John Sunlight's rifle, a little of his clothing. That was all.

Standing there on the edge of the lead, wondering if they were faced with evidence that John Sunlight had finally died, Monk sighed deeply.

"I pity the bear that eats that guy," the homely chemist muttered.

Doc Savage spoke quietly.

"If John Sunlight is not dead," the bronze man said, "we may have something pretty terrible ahead of us."

They stared at him. "What do you mean, Doc?"

Then he told them something they had not known before.

"There were almost a score of deadly scientific devices stored in the Fortress of Solitude," he said. "They're gone."

That didn't quite soak in.

"You mean—"

"I mean," Doc said grimly, "that John Sunlight removed the death machines from the Fortress of Solitude and hid them somewhere. If he is alive, and recovers them—"

The bronze man turned away without finishing.

The pursuit party returned to the island with subdued spirits. They returned quickly—a plane came out for them. They could not help but wonder, and the wondering was not pleasant. Evidence that John Sunlight had been killed by a polar bear seemed conclusive, and yet—

They landed on the island and guided the plane into a great hangar-room in the side of the Fortress of Solitude. It was from here that John Sunlight had secured his first plane, the craft in which he and his party had flown to New York. Doc always kept two extra planes on hand at the fortress, one a spare craft, and the other an experimental machine on which he tried out new aeronautical developments.

For the next three weeks, Monk, Ham and Long Tom flew over the Arctic, searching vainly for some trace of a cache where John Sunlight might have hidden the death machines he had stolen from the Fortress of Solitude.

They never found a cache.

"What about the darkness-maker that John Sunlight sold to that Baron Karl?" Ham demanded one day.

"We will have to recover that," Doc said grimly, "as soon as we can."

THERE was one other problem they had to settle. Most of the value of the Fortress of Solitude lay in its existence remaining unknown to the world.

Many people now knew about it. The Eskimos did not count; they had always known, but they lived here and took care of the place. Doc had trained them for that, and they would continue, for they were well satisfied.

But the others—

"They won't keep their mouths shut," Monk muttered. "Not every one of 'em."

Doc Savage was thoughtful. When all gathered for the next meal, the bronze man made a talk. It was probably the most compelling speech Monk, Ham or Long Tom had ever heard the bronze man make.

Doc pointed out that the whole experience, from the time the convicts escaped the Siberian prison camp was so terrible that their minds would be better off if all memory of the past was wiped away. Then he explained about his brain operation, guaranteed no one would die, and promised that all memory of the past would be gone. Incidentally, no one would recall the Fortress of Solitude, either.

He sold the memory-wiping operations en masse. It was such a good talk that Monk and Ham and Long Tom were almost impelled to join in.

"It's a swell idea—for Monk!" Ham said enthusiastically.

"Why me?" Monk demanded.

"Rid your mind of the idea," Ham said, "that you're evolution's gift to the ladies."

Ham left Monk sputtering, and went away to make a little progress with Fifi. After all, Fifi had repented; and after all, Fifi was a very cute trick. Not to add that pretty soon she was going to be relieved of her memory. What more could a confirmed bachelor such as Ham look for?

The flies in the ointment—elephants in the ointment was more like it, Ham thought ruefully—were Giantia and Titania. Ham thought he'd better get on the good side of Giantia and Titania, before proceeding with Fifi.

Ham went looking for Giantia and Titania to discuss the matter.

Ham was minus a front tooth when Monk saw him next.

"What happened?" Monk asked.

"Giantia," Ham said ruefully, "cracked a smile."

"Huh?"

"My smile," Ham explained.

THE END

The almost impossible has happened! A man who battled Doc Savage not only lives, but lives to battle him once more! None other than John Sunlight, who broke into Doc Savage's secret Fortress of Solitude, faces him once more in an even more amazing battle. This complete novel,

The Devil Genghis

comes to you replete with thrills, mystery and action, and even more astounding surprises and disclosures than in *Fortress of Solitude*!

INTERLUDE

From the start, Lester Dent planned to bring John Sunlight back for another round with Doc Savage. At the end of his outline to *Fortress,* Dent left the fiend's final fate wide open, signaling his intentions to *Doc Savage* editor John L. Nanovic with the following note:

> John: This gag may help carry over readers, if you don't object to trying it. In the next story, I'll have John Sunlight trying to steal back all the inventions he sold, then organize a warlike Himalayan tribe into a world-conquering unit.

This was a Doc Savage first. No foe defeated by the formidable Man of Bronze had ever escaped to battle him again. But John Sunlight was no ordinary enemy.

Nanovic was cautious about running anything that smacked of a continued story. Serials were against Street & Smith policy. He gave Dent his blessing, but with reservations. John Sunlight could return, but not in the next issue. This would forestall any reader complaints over continued stories.

Here exact details are murky. Street & Smith records show that Dent was paid for *Fortress of Solitude* on March 25, 1938. He outlined a sequel, which he called *The Devil Genghis.* This manuscript was paid for on April 1st—only a week later.

While Lester Dent was capable of writing a Doc Savage novel in seven days flat, the payment may represent an advance paid against the outline.

For on April 6th, Dent, his wife Norma, and Dent's secretary, Evelyn Coulson, had set sail for Europe on the luxury liner *HMS Queen Mary.* The Dents were visiting the Continent for the first time. It was supposed to be an extended vacation, but Lester scrupulously produced five pages per day, without fail.

Early chapters of *The Devil Genghis* take place on a luxury liner crossing the Atlantic, then shift to London, Dent's first European stop. It seems odd that he would write about a locale when he was on the verge of seeing it firsthand. So it's reasonable to speculate that *The Devil Genghis* was actually written during the stormy (a ferocious 80-mile-an-hour gale blew for 24 hours straight) six-day Atlantic crossing, and air-mailed back to Manhattan upon Dent's arrival in Plymouth, England, on April 11.

But the version of *Devil Genghis* Dent ultimately produced was not quite the same story he had planned to write. Nanovic had scheduled a Doc Savage novel entitled *The Green Death* between *Fortress of Solitude* and *The Devil Genghis.* It had been ghosted for Dent by his friend, newspaperman Harold A. Davis, and turned in simultaneously with *The Devil Genghis.* No doubt it helped to finance Dent's trip, the true purpose of which, he prophetically told friends, was "to study the locale of the next war."

The slotting of this stand-alone story forced Dent to abandon most of the first half of the outlined plot, which left a few plot threads hanging. To reveal the details here would spoil the novel which follows. But we'll pick up that tale when we delve into the story behind John Sunlight immediately following *The Devil Genghis.*

As for the Dent party, they toured Europe for three months, taking in England, Paris, Austria, Holland, Switzerland and Germany firsthand. Of the Nazi capital, Dent wrote: "My impression of Berlin was—soldiers. Hard jaws and grim eyes under iron helmets. The kind of thing I can just remember seeing on the Liberty Loan posters during the World War."

Repulsed by the daily sight of German soldiers marching on parade with fixed bayonets, he concluded that another European war seemed likely, and confessed his opinion that Chancellor Hitler wasn't exactly rational. Germany had just "annexed" Austria. A real-life John Sunlight had begun his brutal march toward world conquest. The world was about to be forever changed.

The pulp world changed too. The Dents landed back in Manhattan on July 4th. During those three months, the earliest issues of *Action Comics,* starring Superman, had been released to an enthusiastic response. America had a new superhero. Synchronistically, the Man of Steel first rolled off the presses at the exact same time *Fortress of Solitude* was emerging from the Dent typewriter.

Before long, Lester Dent discovered Doc Savage faced a new rival. One neither creator or creation could beat.
—Will Murray

Norma and Lester Dent on the deck of *HMS Queen Mary*

THE DEVIL GENGHIS

John Sunlight crosses Doc's path again. Who will win this second encounter?

By KENNETH ROBESON

Chapter I
A MYSTERY MOVING SOUTH

IT was too bad the dog could not talk.

The dog came yelping and kiyoodling across the ice at a dead run. It was an Eskimo dog. The dog stopped in front of an igloo and had a fit.

The dog seemed to be trying to bite something in the air above it. It kept jumping up and snapping its teeth. For hours it just sprang high and snapped its jaws.

The Eskimos stood around and wondered what on earth.

Or maybe it would not have helped if the dog could talk.

The Eskimo could talk. It didn't help in his case.

The Eskimo was a hunter named Kummik. He could speak the Eskimo language, and he could also say, "Hello, baby, how about a nice juicy kiss?" just as plain as anything.

An explorer with a certain variety of humor had taught him that, and told him it was the proper way to greet a white man. Kummik

A complete Book-length novel

could also say, "By Jiminy, you're big and fat and as ugly as a mud fence!" The explorer had taught Kummik those words, also, and advised him they were the correct greeting for a white woman.

This Eskimo named Kummik went out hunting on the Arctic ice.

It was not particularly cold. A white man, an inhabitant of Missouri, for example, would have thought it was pretty chilly; but in the estimation of the Eskimos, it was just good hunting weather. Only about fifteen below zero. It was cloudy and rather dark, for the six-months-long winter had begun. The wind, which was getting a running start up around the North Pole somewhere, blew hard and scooped up much snow and drove it along in stinging, stifling clouds, so that the effect was something like a western Kansas dust storm. Except that this was snow.

The Eskimo came back as naked as the day he was born.

He still had his spear.

If he had just been naked, and carrying a spear, the other Eskimos would not have been particularly shocked, although they might have done some wondering. These Eskimos lived farther north than any others, so no one bothered them, except a genuine explorer now and then— but only genuine explorers.

The drawing-room explorers never got this far, not only because it was a long way north, but because this spot in the Arctic was surrounded by some very tough traveling. At any rate, the Eskimos had escaped the white man; so they had escaped modesty.

Hence the Eskimos did not have any modesty to be shocked when their fellow citizen named Kummik came galloping back to the igloo village without a stitch of clothes—rather, without a hair of clothes, since his garments had been made of furs.

There was plenty else to shock them.

THE spear Kummik carried was the short type of hunting spear called an *oonapik*. It was made up of a wood shaft—wood was very valuable here in the ice wastes—and a point of bone, which was not so valuable. The spear was used to harpoon *ogjuk*, the seal, was employed to stick *nanook*, the bear; and occasionally, it was used to give little *innuks*, the kids, a few chastising whacks.

Kummik was using his spear to jab, stab and belabor the air over his head.

Now Kummik had always been a *sennayo*. A sennayo is a good worker, a family man, an excellent provider. A *sennayo* is the equivalent of a good Missouri farmer who is on the school board. And Kummik was a *sennayo*.

It was unusual for a fellow like Kummik to be stabbing at the air over his head with a spear.

Moreover, there was nothing but air over his head.

It was so strange that a legend was at once made up about it, and will probably go down through time to puzzle and awe future generations of little *innuks*.

Kummik, the Eskimo, kept jumping around and wielding his spear. He fought a great battle right there among the igloos, surrounded by astounded Eskimos. He fought for hours. He seemed unaware of the other Eskimos, and he did not call on them for help. He went at it on his own. He would jab with his spear, leaping up. Then he would retreat, holding his spear ready, and suddenly stab again with all his might.

It was comical; but nobody laughed.

The expression on Kummik's face kept anyone from laughing. The expression was horrible. It consisted of rage, desperation and utter terror.

Kummik's fight was so real, but nothing was there for him to fight.

Kummik never uttered a word.

There probably is not a primitive people who do not believe an invisible devil drops around to haunt them occasionally. In the case of these Eskimos, this undesired fellow was an evil spirit called Tongak.

The existence of *Tongak* had been vaguely discussed at times by the Eskimos, and he'd been used as bogey man to frighten little *innuks* out of wandering off bear hunting with their toy spears.

But here was a grown man fighting *Tongak*, the evil spirit.

"What will we do about this?"

Decision was simple. Only Kummik saw *Tongak*, so the spirit devil must be after Kummik alone. Better let him have Kummik. Better stop Kummik from fighting the devil, before the devil got aggravated about it. Better cooperate with the devil, and please him, in hopes he would go away.

So the other Eskimos grabbed Kummik, tied him hand and foot, and left him.

Sure enough, very soon the *Tongak* got Kummik's spirit, and went away to Eskimoland again. At any rate, Kummik died.

An American doctor, skeptical about *Tongak*, would have said Kummik froze to death.

AN American doctor would have done something with Kummik that was probably more terrible than what his fellow Eskimos did to him.

An American doctor would have put Kummik in an insane asylum. Like the English doctors did to Fogarty-Smith, for example.

Fogarty-Smith was an aviator, and a capable

one, who had a reputation for brave flying, as well as being known as the man who at one time held the England-to-Australia speed flying record. He was a tall, quiet man, well-liked.

It was Fogarty-Smith's job to fly supplies to the English weather observing station on the Arctic ice pack in the far north. There was currently an international epidemic of Arctic weather observing, and the ice pack station was England's contribution. Fogarty-Smith flew food and fan mail up to the meteorologists.

One gloomy day, Fogarty-Smith took off from the ice pack weather station to fly back to England. He left in his plane. Fourteen hours later, Fogarty-Smith came back to the weather station—on foot.

He had his clothes. He didn't have his plane.

The behavior of Fogarty-Smith completely confounded and horrified the Arctic weather station personnel, from head meteorologist to newspaper correspondent.

But then, the same kind of behavior had confounded the Eskimos.

There seemed to be nothing in the air for Fogarty-Smith to be fighting, either.

He had saved some cartridges for his pistol. He shot those away at nothing overhead. He began hurling his empty gun at whatever it was. He would throw the gun as hard as he could, then run and get it and throw it again.

Fogarty-Smith never uttered a word.

They never found Fogarty-Smith's airplane.

The meteorologists turned seamsters and made a straitjacket in which Fogarty-Smith was taken to England, where he was confined to a padded cell while learned psychiatrists and doctors examined

TONI LASH

him, shook their heads, gave out statements full of technical multisyllabic onomatopoetic nomenclature which didn't mean a thing.

The English believed that a man could suffer such shock and exposure that he would go insane.

The Eskimos had thought an evil spirit called a *Tongak* could get after a man.

One was as screwy as the other, in this case.

The mystery was moving south.

IN the south of France there is a pleasant spot known as the Riviera, a delightful stretch of seashore widely renowned as a spa, a watering place, a playground for grown-ups, a lovely section which probably is to Europeans what Florida or southern California is to those who live in the United States. If the alluring printed descriptions of the Riviera are to be believed, this balmy Valhalla combines the good qualities of both Florida and California, with some added. Here Europe goes to bask in the sun, to make love.

Park Crater was there to make love.

The sun didn't intrigue Park particularly, and certainly he didn't need it, because he always seemed to look as though he had a strikingly healthy suntan. Park had a little Latin blood in him. The Latins are reported to be great lovers. In Park's case, there wasn't any doubt.

No other lad had ever made the grade with Toni Lash.

Park Crater's business was making love. He didn't need to have any other kinds of business. A young man who had a father who'd drilled two thousand oil wells and struck oil with one thousand of them did not need to have any other business. Park Crater's father had done that.

Park Crater was so handsome that the other boys all threw rocks at him at school. Park threw just as many rocks back at them, and later practiced up until he was intercollegiate boxing champ. He was no sissy.

Park was a nice guy. He was many a mother's idea of first-class son-in-law material.

Toni Lash liked Park Crater. Whether Toni Lash's feelings went any deeper, whether she loved Park, only she knew. It was certain that no one else knew, because Toni Lash was an unfathomable person.

Toni Lash was the current mystery woman of the Riviera. The reigning sensation. She was tall, dark-haired and—well, striking was the only word. She struck the men breathless. She made the other women, especially the married ones, feel as though they were being shot at.

"Great Jehoshaphat!" gasped Park Crater when he first saw her.

Cleopatra could take a back seat. So could all the current beauties of stage, screen and society, as far as Park was concerned. When Toni Lash smiled, every man in sight felt his toes curl; and Park discovered himself getting selfish and wishing that the toe curling could be confined exclusively to himself.

"Love!" exclaimed Park. "It must be love."

Park Crater and glorious Toni Lash had been seeing a great deal of each other for about six weeks.

One night Park arrived, carrying a club, unable to speak a word, and wearing an expression of indescribable terror.

Park was using the club to fight the empty air about his head. Toni Lash, with presence of mind, tried to quiet him, calling her servants to help, and later she summoned the best doctors. They tried holding Park Crater in a bathtub full of warm water for hours, a treatment which will usually calm the most violent cases of insanity.

But it was of no appreciable benefit in this instance. Park Crater went to the best Riviera hospital, with six strong men holding his arms and legs.

Toni Lash went into seclusion in her villa. After she had grieved two days, she had a visitor.

"Oh," she said. "I saw you last week. I thought you had gone away."

Park Crater was using the club to fight the empty air about his head.

AS the young woman looked at her visitor, there was awe and dislike on her grieved face, but fascination, too, almost as though the visitor were a serpent and she a weakened bird.

The visitor did not have a snaky look. There was something about him that was a great deal worse. But it was hard to define. At first glance, the man just seemed to be a long sack of bones with a thin, poetic face and a pair of smoldering, compelling eyes.

Toni Lash said, "I checked up on the newspaper stories after I saw you last week. You are supposed to be dead."

Something strange and hideous appeared, as a brief flicker of emotion, on the man's long poetic face. It was as though his face had turned fiercely animal for a moment.

"Perhaps I am dead, and come back to haunt people," he said. Then he laughed grimly.

He wore solid gray. Every article of clothing on him was gray—shoes, socks, suit, tie, shirt, hat—all exactly the same shade of gray.

"You were wearing all the same shade of blue the last time I saw you," Toni Lash said. "You seem to—"

"Let us not talk of small things," the long, sinister man said quietly. "I have heard of your grief."

Toni Lash bit her lips.

"You loved Park Crater, did you not?" the man asked.

Toni Lash nodded quickly, and tears came.

"You should forget," the man said. The awful expression flickered on his face again. "Will you do a job for me?"

"Is it dangerous?" the girl asked.

"Very," the man said frankly.

"I'll do it," Toni Lash said with a kind of desperation.

One day soon, the sun worshipers of the Riviera noticed that the windows of Toni Lash's villa were boarded up tight. Toni Lash had gone away.

The impression got around that Park Crater had gone mad—over beauteous Toni Lash.

The idea was as screwy as those about the dog, about Kummik the Eskimo, and about Fogarty-Smith the inventor.

The mystery had only moved southward.

Like something that had taken three great strides, the mystery had come south as far as the Riviera. Starting in the vicinity of the North Pole, it had left a grisly footprint at the Eskimo village, another footprint at the English weather station on the ice pack, and a third track on the Riviera.

It was gathering itself now, getting ready to spring all the way across the Atlantic and stamp with both feet on a man in New York City.

Chapter II
A MYSTERY IN GOTHAM

DARKNESS had fallen over New York City, the sky having turned into a murky mantle on which a myriad of pleasant stars were scattered, while the lights of the city, particularly those in the theatrical district along midtown Broadway, were so clustered and brilliant that they threw a soft glow high toward the night heavens. The streets were a happy rumble of traffic sounds, for this was the hour around eight o'clock in the evening when Gothamites went to the theater.

Clark Savage, Jr., rode through the city in a taxicab.

The giant man of bronze, who was better known as Doc Savage, was breaking a personal rule, doing something he almost never did. He was preparing to appear on a stage, before an audience, and exhibit one of his many abilities.

Now he rode in a taxicab, heading toward huge and famous Metropolitan Hall, where he was to stand on a stage and play a violin. Later in the program, he understood he was scheduled to "lick a licorice stick" and "send out with some hep cats," which was the current slang way of saying he was to play a clarinet with a good orchestra. He did not mind mixing classical music with popular "swing," because he had no false, highbrow ideas about what music should be.

Still, he would as soon not have done this.

There would be an audience—his appearance had been advertised in the newspapers—and among the audience might possibly be some enemies. A great many men would like to see an end to him, he knew. This was natural, because of his unusual career of righting wrongs which the law did not seem able to remedy.

He did not feel any special fear, for he had been in real danger too many times before. Also he had learned that fear was a bad thing to allow in the mind when one followed a career such as his. For the rest, he knew he would enjoy the program tonight, because he liked all types of music, although he rarely had a chance to enjoy it.

Doc Savage had not been able to enjoy many of the pleasant things in the life of a normal man. From infancy, he had been trained by elderly, learned scientists who had forgotten how to play; and sometimes he wondered if this unusual upbringing didn't cause him to unconsciously regard men and women with reference to the psychological classification of their minds and how many chemical elements their bodies contained.

Tonight, he would enjoy himself.

He was appearing in Metropolitan Hall because the proceeds were going to a really deserving charity.

His appearance was scheduled for late in the program, and he intended to find a quiet spot in the audience where he could sit unobserved and enjoy the early numbers.

He did not expect to be noticed. As a matter of fact, he had no public reputation at all as a musician, so he doubted very much that his name among the artists would bring anyone near Metropolitan Hall tonight.

As the taxicab drew nearer Metropolitan Hall, it began stopping with increased frequency. Traffic was becoming unaccountably thick. Finally, the cab became wedged in a traffic jam and could not move.

"Just what," Doc Savage asked, "seems to be wrong?"

His voice was deep and gave an impression of controlled power.

"There's umpteen thousand people," the taxi driver explained. "Lookit 'em! The whole block is packed."

This seemed to be a fact.

The taxi driver said, "Pay me, if you don't mind."

Doc paid him. The taxi driver then got out and slammed the door.

"I'm gonna go get a look at the guy, too," he said.

"A look at who?" Doc asked, surprised.

The driver snorted at such ignorance.

"Doc Savage is gonna be here tonight," he said. "Who else d'you think that mob is waitin' to see?"

The driver left, horning people aside with his elbows.

DOC SAVAGE sat in the cab a few moments. He made, unconsciously, a tiny trilling note which came from deep in his throat somewhere, a sound as weird and exotic as the call of a strange bird in a tropical jungle. This sound was an absentminded habit when he was mentally perturbed.

He began to feel an attack of stage fright. During the taxi ride, he had looked forward to enjoying some music quietly. He was in a mellow, human mood, and it was a shock to find a packed, shoving throng hoping to get a glimpse of him.

Maybe the taxi driver was wrong.

Doc turned up his dark coat collar, pulled his black hat down, tucked violin and clarinet under an arm, and got out of the cab.

He accosted a man with, "Just what is going on?"

"Doc Savage is to be here," the man said. "Damn the luck! I don't think I'm gonna be able to get within a block of the door."

That was that.

Realizing that his height put him head and shoulders above the crowd, Doc assumed a stoop.

The crowd milled and shoved. Policemen blew whistles and were helpless. At the entrance to Metropolitan Hall, a battery of powerful mercury-vapor floodlights blazed so that motion pictures could be taken, and a number of movie cameras were visible, mounted on top of cars.

Doc's stage fright got worse. He had always been embarrassed by public attention, and right now the last thing he felt like doing was to run a gauntlet as this one.

He discovered himself retreating, toying with the idea of telephoning that he was ill, a thought he put aside at once. He had promised to appear, and he always kept a promise.

He turned and walked, unnoticed, into the back street which ran along the rear of Metropolitan Hall. It was dark here, and there was no crowd, because there was no door into the Hall.

There were windows, however. But the lowest one was at a height about equal to a third story, and between it and the sidewalk was naked brick, evidently the back wall of the stage. Apparently ingress here was impossible.

Doc examined the wall, particularly a point where the bricks were outset a trifle in a kind of old-fashioned ornamental corner-piece. He was pleased. Removing his belt, he used it to sling violin and clarinet cases over his back.

Then he climbed. An observer would have said it was impossible—incredible. But the observer wouldn't have realized the kind of strength a lifetime of training had given the bronze man.

Having mounted carefully, Doc swung over to the window, found it unlocked, and entered. He stood now on a catwalk beside the huge scenery curtains. An iron stairway led downward, and he descended.

He was greeted profusely by the charity organization officials.

"So you came early and secluded yourself upstairs!" they exclaimed.

Doc let it go at that.

An usher was dispatched to the entrance to announce that Doc Savage had arrived, and that there was no more standing room, and that the doors would be closed.

The audience inside heard the announcement and broke out in applause.

One in the audience did not applaud. This person was a woman. She looked incredulous, then disappointed, and springing to her feet, hurried to the front of Metropolitan Hall and began trying the doors of offices used by the management.

Visitors on the French Riviera a few weeks

CAUTIOUS

ago would have recognized the young woman as Toni Lash.

THE young woman found an unlocked door, stepped through it into an empty office. Her first glance was to see if there was a window. There was.

A small flashlight came out of her bag. She went to the window, got her bearings and centered her attention on a second-story window in the building across the street.

She began blinking her flashlight, spelling out words in code.

"You fools," she flashed. "He is already inside."

The building across the street was of brick, many stories high, the first floor being occupied by a used car show window. Adjoining the showroom, and also a part of the used car establishment, was a doorway through which cars could be driven across the sidewalk into the building—or from the building to the street.

The girl stopped sending.

A light flashed from the window of the used car building which she was watching.

"He could not be," the light signaled. "We have watched the entrance."

The girl's light replied in a long string of flashes that meant nothing but rage.

"Keep watching," her light ordered. "We may be able to get him when he leaves."

"O.K.," the man signaled from the used car building window.

He shoved his flashlight in a coat pocket. He was a squat man with long arms, a reddish face and a tangle of blond hair. He was very well dressed. The tips of all ten of his fingers were masses of scar tissue—they had been burned with acid sometime in the past to destroy his fingerprint identity.

"Now what do you know about that?" he said disgustedly.

He had spoken to himself; there was no one else in the barroom with him. The one door stood open.

The man ran a hand absentmindedly over the military type of machine gun which stood, squat and blue and ugly on its spraddled tripod, on a low table in front of the window, the muzzle pointing down into the street. The ammunition belt of the gun was draped across the table like a snake of brown canvas with lead-and-brass striping.

The cartridges in the belt were "mercy" bullets, a type of slug consisting of a hollow shell which contained a powerful drug that would cause unconsciousness rather than death.

On the other end of the table lay a gas mask.

The blond man with the marred fingers picked up the gas mask and dangled it from one hand as he descended the stairs.

An armored truck stood inside the closed doors which led to the street. The truck was painted white. Lettered on each of its sides was:

AMBULANCE

The white paint and the name on the armored truck gave it enough resemblance to an ambulance to fool casual observers.

"What's the word, Cautious?" greeted one of the men in the ambulance-fortress.

Cautious scowled at the men. There were four of them, assorted sizes. They wore white coverall suits to disguise their clothing. Bulletproof vests made their bodies bulky. Gas masks hung ready from their necks.

"Savage got in the Hall, somehow," Cautious explained sourly.

Chapter III
BRONZE MAN TAKEN

THE four men in charge of the ambulance-fortress frowned at Cautious. They were nervous, on edge; they did not like the idea of things going wrong.

"Thought you knew this Doc Savage by sight?" one growled.

Cautious looked them over. Cautious had a mobile face and he could make his expression vicious.

"I've seen his pictures," he said. "He didn't go in the front door. And, buddy—just remember who's running this."

"We ain't in no army!" the other said sourly.

Cautious took a flat pistol out of a pocket.

"At a time like this, there's only one answer to argument," he said, hardly changing tone or expression.

The other man swallowed. It suddenly dawned on him that he should be frightened.

"I ain't arguin'!" he said hoarsely.

Previously, he had known Cautious only by reputation. Cautious was not a gangster; as to just what Cautious was there seemed to be some doubt. Cautious had the habit of disappearing from New York for long periods, and was reputed to be something of an international gadder.

The four ambulance-fortress attendants subsided. Cautious had hired them, but they knew he was working for the girl, Toni Lash. They were to seize Doc Savage—a job they did not like, since they had heard a great deal about Doc Savage. That they had been offered a startling sum of money to help was all they knew. Why Doc Savage was to be seized was a mystery.

"You took this job," Cautious told them grimly, "and don't think you won't go through with it!"

They looked at his gun, then assured him they would go through with it.

Cautious put the gun away and went back upstairs to the window. Standing beside the machine gun, he watched the entrance of Metropolitan Hall with fixed intensity.

He could hear a roar of applause coming from the Hall.

The applause was filling the interior of the great hall with deafening volume. There was hand clapping, whistling, stamping.

Doc Savage, on the stage, did not look nearly as ill at ease as he felt. He had been trained to conceal his emotions. And certainly the skill with which he had played his classical number on the violin left no suspicion that he was not perfectly at home. The quickest and loudest applause had come from the members of the audience who really knew music.

Now the bronze man played the clarinet number with the swing orchestra. The result was a joyful uproar. No one had to have an advanced education in classical music to know here was a number well done. In the vernacular of swing, the boys "sent gate," "slapped jibe on the dog house," "busted hide" and "gripped that git box." They went to town. The "jitterbugs" in the audience got

DOC

up and danced in the aisles. It was a tremendous success.

Doc Savage, putting his instruments in their cases, and walking along a passage to the front entrance, was in a thoughtful frame of mind. Suddenly, he was realizing just how far from normal was the life he had lived, and was living.

The gobble of the machine gun across the street was a complete surprise.

THE gun burst was short. Ten shots. Doc went down.

One moment, he stood at the top of the entrance steps. There was an open space around him—police were holding the crowd back. Then he was tumbling down the steps.

He landed loosely. His great bronzed hands gripped his legs. He'd been hit only in the legs. He started to get up. His knees buckled. He crouched, still gripping his legs.

Then he slumped, a giant limp form. Turmoil had the crowd now. Some surged forward. Others fled. The police were helpless. There was screaming, yelling, angry shoving and frightened scrambling. The surface of the throng became a storm-tossed human sea.

Into that bedlam came the armored truck that looked like an ambulance, moving slowly. It had been equipped with a regulation siren, and now this moaned steadily. The vehicle nosed the crowd aside, reached Doc Savage.

The attendants sprang out. Their white coveralls gave them somewhat the appearance of ambulance attendants. And they had left their gas masks inside. There had, as yet, been no need to use tear gas.

"Stand aside!" they yelled. "We've got to get him to a hospital!"

Doc Savage's limp form was rolled onto a stretcher, lifted into the fortress-ambulance. The attendants got in. So did two cops. That was not so good. But nothing was said.

The ambulance rolled. The siren frightened a path through the throng. Gathering speed, the disguised armored car rolled north.

"Hey!" exploded one of the two policemen riding inside. "You're not going toward the hos—"

A blackjack blow over the ear put him to sleep. Simultaneously, the other cop got the same kind of an anaesthetic.

Cautious peered back through the bars which separated the driver's seat from the rear of the armored truck. Cautious had managed to get aboard, and was riding with the driver.

"There's two squad cars of cops followin'," he said grimly. "Lay a few eggs."

The "eggs" were tear gas bombs. The men tossed out a few. One police car left the road and knocked over a telephone pole. The other one stopped, and a few bullets from police guns hit the armored steel sides of the truck harmlessly. Then pursuit was left behind.

"Slow up," Cautious ordered, "and dump the two cops out."

This was done.

The ambulance-fortress drove north at high speed, turned left, entered a dark patch of woods, and the men transferred Doc Savage to an innocent-looking sedan. The bronze man was still limp.

"Everybody been wearin' gloves?" Cautious demanded.

They had. White gloves. No fingerprints had been left.

"Make sure Savage ain't dead," Cautious ordered. "Sometimes the dope in them bullets is strong enough to kill a man."

"He's still alive," a man advised.

"Swell. Let's get going with him."

They went on in the sedan. Doc Savage made a considerable bulk on the rear floorboards, and they tossed a lap robe over him. The car traveled decorously enough so that no speed cops would be interested.

IT had been a roadhouse. It was off the busy roads and patronized during the summer months by a certain type of clientele who did not care to be seen in the more popular places, but in the off-season such as this there was not enough business to keep open. So the dive was closed.

It was a rambling, unlovely building which stuck on the side of a hill. There was a rain barrel under one eave's spout. There were scrubby, wooded hills all around.

Cautious knocked open the door, and they carried Doc Savage inside and lifted him onto the table.

One of the men drew back, looked at the bronze man, and rubbed his jaw uneasily.

"I've heard a lot about that guy," he muttered. "If I thought half of it was true, a team of mules couldn't have pulled me into this."

"He's helpless enough now, isn't he?" Cautious demanded.

The other shrugged. "Just the same, the sooner I'm through and get my dough, the better."

Cautious laughed.

The laugh seemed to irritate the four men who had been hired to handle the ambulance.

"Just why," one demanded, "did we grab Savage?"

"Because you're getting paid for it, I thought," Cautious said dryly.

"I don't like your sass!" the man snapped.

"Suit yourself," Cautious replied, shrugging his shoulders. "But why Savage was grabbed is something you'll have to take out in guessing. I'm not putting out."

There was some scowling, but Cautious had a reputation with a gun; furthermore, he was the man who was going to pay them, so the four hired men subsided.

"In the back room," Cautious said, "is a box. We'll bring that in."

"That box is damned heavy," one of the men complained.

"I'll help you," Cautious offered.

They all started for the door, then Cautious turned and came back to the table on which Doc Savage lay.

"I'll leave this stuff here," he said, "so it won't get broke."

From his pocket, he drew a package, paper-wrapped, which he placed on the table.

All the men disappeared into another part of the unused roadhouse.

Doc Savage rolled over on the table and sat up.

THE giant bronze man showed no indication of having been drugged, or of any other injury. Nor was he excited. His only emotion seemed to be an alert interest in what was going on. Listening, he could hear voices in a distant part of the roadhouse—Cautious was explaining how they would carry the box.

With movements that were astonishingly swift without appearing to be so, Doc Savage untied the cord around the package and removed the paper.

A mass of cotton was revealed, and inside this, a hypodermic needle and a glass bottle containing a colorless liquid.

Doc uncorked the bottle, tested the odor of the contents at a distance, then at close range.

Swinging off the table, Doc went to the front door, moving with the practiced silence of a jungle thing. He emptied the bottle, dipped water from the rain barrel, rinsed the bottle thoroughly, then filled it with water and corked it.

Back again in the roadhouse with ghostly silence and speed, he heard Cautious swearing at a man and accusing him of not lifting his share of the box. While that was going on, Doc whipped off the trousers of his dress suit.

The bronze man then removed a pair of under-trousers that somewhat

The gun burst was short . . . Doc went down.

resembled the lower portion of a suit of old-fashioned long underwear—except that this garment was made of a light, alloy chain mail that would stop a revolver bullet dead, and considerably discourage a rifle slug. It bore some smears where the mercy bullet had been stopped.

Doc dropped the mail garment in the rain barrel. With his fingers, he broke his leg skin slightly in three places, just enough to make it appear that the mercy bullets might have damaged him.

He was back on the table, looking as unconscious as ever, when Cautious and his men came in, panting and stumbling with the weight of the box.

They put the box down where Doc could see it through narrowed lids.

The box was slightly less than eight feet long, over three wide, not quite as high, and made of oak. It had brass handles.

Cautious wiped off perspiration, came over, examined Doc Savage. He tested the wrist pulse, then felt the hardness of the bronze man's muscles, astonished.

"I'd sure hate to be in the ring with this guy," he muttered.

He tugged up Doc's trouser legs and examined the broken places in the skin which were leaking a little crimson.

"Never seen them mercy bullets work better," he said. "I had a guy fix 'em up for me one time when I had a contract to get some live animals out of Africa for a zoo." He laughed grimly. "That was when I had an attack of conscience, and made an honest living for a while."

Cautious stopped reminiscing and turned to the package, which Doc had rewrapped. After shaking the bottle, Cautious filled the hypo.

He emptied about half the contents of the small bottle into Doc Savage's cabled forearm.

One of the others asked, "What is that?"

"It's a drug," Cautious explained, "that will knock him out for about a week."

Cautious opened the box. It was perforated with ventilating holes. Inside was an ordinary cheap coffin, also equipped with ventilating apertures.

"Gimme a hand," Cautious ordered.

They put Doc Savage in the coffin. Then they began nailing the lid.

"He'll keep swell in there," Cautious declared, "and I'll take a look now and then to be sure he's all right."

There is something about being nailed up in a coffin that plays hob with the strongest kind of an intention. Doc Savage had resolved to play along with these fellows in hopes of solving the complete mystery of what it was all about. But if Cautious had not spoken assurance that they intended to keep their "corpse" alive, Doc Savage would probably have made a break for freedom.

IT must have been six hours later when Doc Savage heard Cautious say, "O. K., boys. Here's where he stays parked for the next week. I'll pay you off now."

In the six hours, the rough box and the coffin had been lugged out of the roadhouse, hauled some distance in a truck, unloaded, rolled around on a hand truck, and finally deposited with a thump, no way of knowing where.

Doc lay still, giving Cautious time to depart. To his ears, very faintly, came a deep moan. This sound repeated after a moment.

The bronze man shifted around, set himself, and began trying to break out. Coffins, fortunately, do not have locks. But the nails in the rough box lid were a different proposition, particularly since it was a matter of forcing all of them at once.

He turned over, arched his back against the lid, and mighty muscles coiled in bunches. The lid nails pulled out, squealing.

Doc stepped out of the coffin.

Darkness surrounded him, and it was rather smelly. Conscientious exercise had given Doc's nostrils a sensitivity equal to that of many animals, and he identified the odor in the air as salt water, bilge, cargo and tarred rope.

He appeared to be in a steamship hold. The moaning sound came again, a steamer foghorn.

Moving around in the darkness, exploring, he learned that the coffin was part of a general steamer cargo. He climbed over boxes and bales toward the glint of stars, reached a hatch.

He climbed out on deck. It was a large ship, apparently a passenger liner which carried only a small amount of cargo. The bridge stood gaunt and white in the murk, and cargo booms stuck up like great stiff wooden fingers beside the hatch.

The eastward sky had a ruddy, blushing tint that indicated the hour was near dawn.

Doc Savage swung hand over hand down a mooring line to the covered dock, and became a silent, moving part of the darkness.

Chapter IV
ESCORT FOR A COFFIN

LIEUTENANT COL. ANDREW BLODGETT "MONK" MAYFAIR had once been approached by a motion picture producer who had assured Monk that he could make a fortune as a cinema actor. Monk, who had always had an eye for a pretty girl, thought of all the beauteous damsels in Hollywood, and grew rather enthusiastic about the idea. However—

"Why," the producer said, "you'd make Frankenstein and King Kong look like pets for babies."

So Monk grinned his homely biggest to cover his broken heart, and turned the film offer down, explaining that he already had made a fortune.

Monk was not really sensitive about his looks. In fact, his homeliness seemed to be an advantage with the fair sex. It hypnotized the girls, or something.

Monk already had the fortune, too, every nickel of which he'd made himself. He was one of the world's greatest industrial chemists, although he didn't look it, being almost as wide as he was tall, equipped with a bullet head, an oversized mouth, a coat of reddish hair, and other apish characteristics.

Monk also had a swell time out of life. He loved excitement.

He was an assistant to Doc Savage, so he got plenty of excitement.

Just now, Monk Mayfair was jumping up and down in Doc's headquarters, shaking both fists over his head, and roaring like a foghorn.

"You shyster!" he howled. "You've swindled so many clients you just can't get outta the habit!"

The man who confronted Monk was lean-waisted, rather handsome, with the large, mobile mouth of an orator. The striking thing about him, however, was his clothing. His garments were impeccable perfection. He carried a black cane.

This man was Brigadier General Theodore Marley Brooks, called Ham by people who thought they could outrun him, and by his very close friends. He was a noted lawyer, another Doc Savage aide, and did not like the nickname of Ham, which had arisen out of a distressing incident in his past that had to do with hogs.

Ham shook his cane at Monk.

"You gossoon!" he yelled. "I'm good at adding!"

"At adding insult to injury, maybe!" Monk roared. "I claim you gypped me!"

Monk normally had a small, childlike voice, but when he got excited, his listeners felt inclined to put their fingers in their ears.

"I paid close attention to the bill," Ham snapped.

Monk snorted his loudest. "There's only two ways of gettin' your attention," he barked.

"And what are they?" Ham demanded loftily.

"Flutter a skirt, or rattle money."

Ham flourished his cane.

"I am on the verge," he said grimly, "of whittling an arm off you!"

"Whittle away, ambulance-chaser!" Monk invited.

They had been threatening to slaughter each other ever since anyone could remember. Any small item in their lives was good for a rousing squabble. Just now, it was a matter of three cents sales tax out of which Monk claimed Ham had gypped him when they settled the restaurant check for their breakfast.

Since they were threatening to mangle each other over three cents, they were obviously the best of friends.

They suspended their quarrel to look at Doc Savage, who had just entered.

MONK pointed at Doc's legs.

"You fall down and tear your pants?" the homely chemist asked.

Except for being a little disheveled, Doc Savage was outwardly undisturbed. But there was a certain lively interest in his eyes. They were strange eyes, like pools of flake gold, and when the bronze giant was animated, the flake gold seemed to be disturbed by tiny winds.

"Evidently," Doc said, "you have not read the morning newspapers."

Monk shook his head. "We just got out of bed."

Doc Savage spread a morning newspaper on the inlaid table which, with the great safe, comprised the principal furniture in his headquarters reception room. Monk examined the newspaper. While he was reading, morning wind came in through the window and stirred the apish chemist's rusty-red hair.

Below the windows the city was spread, the tops of the skyscrapers blushing crimson in the morning sun. All the buildings seemed to lie below the window, for the Doc Savage headquarters occupied the top floor of one of the tallest buildings in the city. High up here, the wind was strong and pushed coolly against Monk's astonished face.

"Blazes!" Monk exploded, as he read:

DOC SAVAGE BELIEVED KILLED;
MACHINE GUNNED AND
BODY STOLEN

The headlines were all over the front page in black letters three inches high.

"Blazes!" Monk said again. He looked disappointed. "Daggone it! I've been missin' excitement!"

Rapidly and briefly, Doc Savage narrated the night's happenings, beginning with the machine gun blast when he walked out of Metropolitan Hall, and ending with his being deposited, encased in a coffin, in a liner's cargo hold.

Monk swallowed several times, got his astonishment down.

"Doc, that's some story!" he gulped. "But one thing is missin'."

"What?"

"Reasons—why'd it happen?"

Doc said, "I never heard of this fellow, Cautious, before."

"Then why should he try to grab you?"

Doc did not answer.

Monk continued, "Where in blazes were they gonna take you in that coffin?"

"The liner is scheduled to sail to Mediterranean ports," Doc said.

The bronze man went into the adjoining rooms, a vast library, then into an amazingly complete laboratory. He began assembling the assortment of metal equipment cases which they usually took with them on trips.

Monk grinned, shadowboxed around Ham.

"Gitcher extra shirt, shyster," he said. "The one you wear on a boat."

Ham had never gone anywhere equipped only with a mere shirt. A wardrobe trunk the size of a piano box was his idea of a minimum wardrobe for an ocean voyage.

HAM had fourteen suitcases and two trunks sent to the liner. Then he discovered that they were to keep undercover, and he would have no opportunity to flaunt his wardrobe.

"Haw, haw!" Monk said.

Doc Savage visited the hold and placed a piece of apparatus in the coffin. The mechanism consisted of a storage battery which ran a motor that slowly opened and closed a bellows of a type used to blow smoke into beehives.

When the coffin was nailed up again, the bellows made sounds very much resembling someone breathing inside the box.

"But this Cautious," Monk ventured, "is liable to open the thing up to feed you. He's gonna be right disappointed to find that gimcrack."

"Chances are Cautious will not try to feed me for a day or two," Doc explained. "We will watch him. When we see him get food, I will accommodate him by getting back in the coffin."

The liner sailed at noon.

Doc Savage and his two associates concentrated on learning what was behind Doc's being seized, drugged and taken abroad in a coffin.

As Monk remarked, "The reason is as hard to find as a lawyer's conscience."

The remark caused Ham to go around muttering to himself.

THE ship was the *Maritonia.* She was a new craft, built after the European nations had given up the race to see which could construct the biggest sea-going white elephant. The *Maritonia* was several hundred feet long, a well-made boat, and while she wasn't likely to gain the transatlantic speed record, neither did her aft sections shake like a carnival South Seas dancer while she was steaming.

Ham had favored the royal suite, but there was a little cluster of three cabins, set apart by themselves, and the bronze man had engaged those.

They kept under cover the entire first day at sea. The next afternoon, Ham killed time by taking his wardrobe out and arranging it. There was plenty of time.

Doc stated, "We do not want Cautious to get scared, and have a plane come out and take him off the liner."

"You think we'll learn something by watchin' him?" Monk asked.

"He thinks he is taking me to Europe," Doc explained. "If we play along with him, we should learn something."

Monk spent the afternoon teaching Habeas Corpus new tricks. Habeas Corpus was Monk's pet pig. Habeas was not exactly a pig in age, for Monk had picked him up years ago in Arabia. But the vicissitudes of Habeas's youth—Ham insisted it was the hog's natural cussedness—had stunted him, and Habeas was pig-sized, with long doglike legs, and ears which resembled misplaced wings.

Ham, the dapper lawyer, also had a pet—Chemistry. Chemistry was a chimpanzee. At least, Ham insisted Chemistry was a pedigreed chimpanzee, although Monk called Chemistry the "What is it?" and other things. Monk didn't care for Chemistry; nor did Chemistry care for Monk, or for Habeas Corpus, Monk's pet. The four of them, Monk, Ham and their pets, all squabbling at once, was a bedlam worth hearing.

It was an extremely calm afternoon, with the ship hardly rolling, so it was probable most of the passengers would turn up in the dining room for their dinners.

SHORTLY before dinner time, a steward delivered a wheelchair to Doc Savage's cabin.

"What the blazes!" Monk said.

The reason for the wheelchair became apparent when Doc put on a white wig, a pokey-looking old hat, and wrinkled his face by applying a coat of colloidal substance which, as it hardened, he molded into wrinkles; then he applied ordinary theatrical makeup to get a natural enough effect. Disguised as an old lady, Doc sat in the chair, tucked the steamer rug in around his legs.

Doc rolled, in his wheelchair, to the dining room, where he sighted the man who called himself Cautious.

That night, Cautious haunted the bar, drank sensibly, attended the ship's movie, strolled the deck in the chill moonlight—and paid a short visit to the box in the hold. Around midnight, he sat in the bar and toyed with a nightcap, apparently making innumerable wet rings on the table with the glass. Then he went to bed.

Doc rolled his wheelchair past the table where Cautious had sat, but his trained eye picked up no trace of any kind of message.

"That's too bad," Ham said when he learned results of the sleuthing. "I drew the same thing, sitting here looking at Monk."

"Drew what?" Monk demanded.

"A blank," Ham said unkindly.

The following day was an innocent one for Cautious. He did the ordinary things—except for another short visit to the hold. That night, he again sat in the bar with his nightcap and made circles with the bottom of his wet glass; then he went to bed.

This time, Doc rolled his wheelchair to the table that Cautious had vacated. The table stood in a secluded corner.

Doc drew a bottle out of a pocket, wet a napkin with the contents, and blotted the table top, dampening it. Then he sat watching.

The bottle contained one of the common chemicals used to bring out secret writing. The stuff was much used by spy operatives.

Faint marks appeared on the table.   Only

Ham

chicken tracks at first; then they filled out and became a message. Doc read:

> He's all right. Can hear him breathing in the box. Will meet you 2 a.m. in cabin D 27.

With the napkin, Doc wiped the message away. On the chance that Cautious had been using this method to leave a message for someone, Doc had provided himself with some of the chemical used to make the writing. With this, he replaced Cautious's message, imitating the handwriting.

He rolled his wheelchair across the room and waited.

WHEN he saw her, he felt the same thing that other men always felt. He was human, in spite of the training that had tried to make him a scientific product. And she was beautiful. She was probably, he thought, the most striking feminine creature he had ever seen.

She came into the bar quietly, and although she made no effort to be conspicuous, it was as though a magnet had come into the room. Every eye followed the girl—but only one drunk stared openly, because there was a regal air about her that said, "Kindly keep your distance."

"Who is she?" he asked a waiter.

The question was appropriate enough. Anyone would want to know the identity of such a girl.

"Her name," the waiter said, "is Toni Lash."

It was obvious that a number of others had asked the same question.

Toni Lash sat alone. Doc admired the way in which she brought out the message, and read it. Had he not known what she was doing, he would hardly have noticed.

"This woman," he said to himself, "has been an espionage agent. And she is very clever."

He watched, without appearing to do so, as she finished a glass of wine, paid her check and left. An unusual stillness had held the bar, but it was noticeable only by the sudden hum that was audible after she had gone. Low voices, murmuring in admiration about the beauty of that girl.

Doc Savage rolled his wheelchair to a dark corner of the deck, made sure no one was near, and shucked off his disguise. He left the parts of the disguise—the wig, loose frock, shawl, smoked spectacles, gloves for his hands—lying in the chair, so he could don them later.

He went below and found cabin D 27. It was a cabin in a corner, corridors on two sides. Adjoining it on a third side was one of the passenger bathrooms.

A stateroom on the fourth side seemed the logical place to eavesdrop, providing it was not occupied. He listened. People who slept usually breathed loudly, and he could hear no such sounds inside. He tried the knob.

The door was unlocked and he went in silently.

Flashlight glare blazed into his eyes, blinding.

"I have a cautious nature, don't you think?" a feminine voice asked.

Doc remembered the calmness of that voice for a long time. He had known the girl was dangerous.

Toni Lash held a strange-looking weapon—a thing that had two barrels, one above the other, the lower one like an ordinary air pistol, the upper barrel fatter, the end closed by what appeared to be a seal of soft wax.

She moved her queer weapon slightly.

"Maybe you never saw one of these before," she said. "The lower barrel discharges a dart that will break your skin, and at the same time the upper barrel shoots a stream of hydrocyanic. It's complicated, but it will kill you almost instantly."

Doc said nothing.

The girl tapped on the cabin wall.

Cautious came in, gasped and popped his eyes at Doc Savage.

"Turn around," the girl ordered.

Doc turned.

"Handcuff him, Cautious," she directed.

Cautious handcuffed Doc Savage, using bracelets which the girl gave him.

Toni Lash looked at the bronze man regretfully.

"I'm afraid," she said, "that the world has seen the last of a very clever man."

Chapter V
CLOWNS ON A SHIP

MONK and Ham were bound to Doc Savage, if one excluded their intense admiration for the bronze man, by a common love for action. Both liked excitement. That was a liking held by all the bronze man's aides, including the three who were absent—Long Tom Roberts, Renny Renwick, and Johnny Littlejohn.

There were only five men associated with Doc Savage, and each was a specialist in his profession.

Long Tom Roberts, electrical wizard, was at present in Alaska, laying out a hydroelectric project.

Renny Renwick, who was famous for his big fists and his engineering skill, was in France, serving as consultant in the establishing of a chain of ultramodern airports suitable for high-speed planes.

Johnny Littlejohn was in Egypt, indulging in his specialty, archaeology. Someone had found another ancient Pharaoh's tomb, and Johnny was showing them how to read the hieroglyphics therein.

Monk

That had left only two aides, Monk and Ham, available in New York for work on this present mystery.

And Monk and Ham were getting to the point where they didn't care for the whole business. Not enough action. No action at all, was more like it.

"Fooey!" Monk said, looking at Ham.

"My sentiments exactly," Ham agreed miserably. "If it wasn't for being cooped up with you, I could stand it."

"What's wrong with me?"

Ham surveyed his companion in misery at some length.

"I don't feel like writing a book," he said, "so I won't go into that now."

Monk was so disgusted by the lack of action that he refused to rise to the insult. He kept silent.

Ham asked, "How do you figure this mystery out?"

"I haven't figured it."

"Well, what do you think?"

"I ain't a lawyer," Monk said unkindly. "I can't even talk without thinkin'."

They eventually got a half-spirited quarrel going, and entertained themselves until three o'clock in the morning, when they gave it up as a bad job and crawled into bed.

The nonappearance of Doc Savage did not alarm them particularly. They took it for granted that the bronze man was merely keeping a vigil on Cautious.

Some of their unconcern departed when they awakened and found no Doc on hand.

By noon, they were frankly worried.

"This begins to get me," Monk muttered.

"I never expected anything but a zoo to get you," Ham said.

He did not manage to get much enthusiasm into the dig.

They sat there and worried. Doc Savage had advised them not to go about on the ship, because both of them were fellows who looked conspicuous enough to be readily recognized by anyone who had taken pains to learn the personal descriptions of the bronze man and his associates, and it had previously become evident that Cautious had done that.

They worried. And their worrying was probably mild to what it would have been had they known of the weirdly terrible thing that had happened to Kummik, the Eskimo hunter, or to Fogarty-Smith, the aviator who had been flying supplies to and from the weather station on the Arctic ice, or to Park Crater, the young American millionaire visiting the Riviera, who had made Toni Lash care more for him than she had ever cared for any other young man.

But Monk and Ham, as yet, knew nothing of the fantastic fate of those three men who had been victims, apparently, of a fantastic horror that came out of the polar regions in three long steps.

Still, by midafternoon, Monk and Ham knew they had better be doing something.

FIRST, they did the natural thing. They went to the hold, listened to the box. The breathing sounds were audible inside, so lifelike that they were not sure whether they were made by Doc or the "breathing" gadget they had rigged, until they opened the coffin.

Doc was not there.

A note was. It lay on the gadget, and read:

> You won't see me for a while, but I will be all right. Don't worry. Get out and enjoy yourselves. Doc.

"That's Doc's handwriting," Ham said.

"Yep," Monk agreed. "I'd know Doc's fist anywhere."

They did not know, then, that expert forgery was another accomplishment of the amazing girl, Toni Lash.

"Getting out and enjoying myself," Monk said gleefully, "is the thing I do best."

They returned to their cabin and Ham donned his most resplendent ship-going garments. Monk, just to be contrary, put on an old and extremely fuzzy tweed suit which, by no stretch of the imagination, fitted him.

"You look," said Ham disgustedly, "like you'd run through a flock of colored sheep, and some of their wool stuck to you."

Monk admired his woolly effect in the mirror.

"Betcha," he said.

"Betcha what?"

"I get a date with the prettiest girl on the ship," Monk offered recklessly, "before you do."

Ham dry washed his hands delightedly. "What do you want to bet?"

Monk gave the subject deep thought, and ended up by cocking an eye on Chemistry, the pet chimp belonging to Ham. Monk had never cared for Chemistry, because he knew very well that Ham had acquired the chimp because of the startling resemblance the thing bore to him—Monk.

"If I win," Monk said, "I get to drown the what-is-it?"

"Drown Chemistry?" Ham exploded.

"Sure. The thing I've been lookin' forward to doin' for some time."

Ham swallowed, and he fell to eyeing Monk's pet pig, Habeas Corpus.

"And if I get the first date with the prettiest girl," he said, "I get to have Habeas for breakfast bacon?"

Monk winced, then nodded.

"Bargain," he said.

"Bargain," Ham echoed.

He started for the door.

"Where you goin'?" demanded Monk.

"To find which cook can butcher a hog," Ham said enthusiastically.

They were quite elated over the bet. Whoever lost would naturally refuse to pay off, so they would be supplied with ammunition for weeks of argument.

TONI LASH was inevitable.

Monk and Ham merely asked a first officer, "Who's the prettiest girl aboard?"

"Toni Lash," the officer said.

And so they lost no time heading straight for trouble.

Their first sight of Toni Lash brought an argument about who was to approach the woman first. They were entranced by her beauty.

"Oh, boy!" Monk said. "Me first! It was my idea."

"You first—nothing!" Ham gritted. "Over my dead body, you'll be first, you missing link!"

"Afraid of my power over women, eh?" Monk asked loftily.

Ham managed a violent sneer.

"I don't want her scared into a nervous wreck by seein' you around," he said. "I want her healthy, so I can enjoy her company."

"Toss a coin for first?" Monk suggested.

"O. K."

Monk put one hand in his right pants pocket, the other hand in his left pocket, and felt for a coin.

"Heads or tails?" he asked.

"Heads," Ham said unwarily.

Monk took the coin out of his right pocket. That one had tails on both sides. The coin in his other pocket had heads on both sides.

"Ouch!" Ham groaned when tails came up. "Oh, well, I'll go tell the cook to have scalding water hot for that hog!"

Monk had learned very early in life that, being so astoundingly homely, he must use a technique on femininity that was different from the common approaches used by the good-looking fellows. Monk had worked out a system. Habeas Corpus, the pig, was part of the system.

Toni Lash was reclining in a deck chair, reading a book.

Monk walked past her, apparently unaware of her presence. At Monk's heels trailed Habeas Corpus, the pig.

In front of Toni Lash, Habeas stopped, sat down. The pig had done this often enough to learn his part of the act.

Habeas said, "Oh, gracious me!"

Or at least, it certainly sounded like Habeas spoke the words.

"Come on, Habeas," Monk said.

"I can't," Habeas said. "I'm hypnotized."

"You're what?" Monk demanded.

"I'm helpless," Habeas explained. "I never saw such a pretty girl in my life, and I'm helpless."

"You tramp," Monk said, "you've got no manners!"

"Scat. Go roll your hoop." Habeas looked at Toni Lash. "Say, baby, how about a little walk around the deck."

Toni Lash smiled slightly in spite of herself.

"Sir," she told Habeas, "I'll have you know I'm a lady."

"I know it," Habeas replied. "If I intended to walk with a man, I'd stay with this big hooligan I'm with."

Toni Lash broke out in laughter.

"Look, baby," Habeas said, "I'm afraid I'm gettin' stuck on you."

"So I suspected," Toni Lash smiled. "I noticed your eyes had been glued on me for some time."

Then the ravishing beauty looked at Monk, and burst forth in more laughter.

"You're quite a ventriloquist, aren't you?" she asked delightedly.

MONK looked around and was very pleased to note that Ham was exhibiting traces of an impulse to tear his own hair out by the roots.

Monk was more tickled than he would have been in a barrel of feathers. The old system had worked. It never failed.

Monk sank into a deck chair at Toni Lash's elbow.

"Hey, you homely gassoon!" Habeas said. "I saw her first!"

Monk indicated Habeas and remarked to Toni Lash, "Don't you pity me, having to put up with a heckler like that?"

"I certainly do," the young woman laughed.

"Pity me enough to give me a date for the dance tonight?" Monk asked.

Monk was nothing if not a quick worker.

"I guess so," Toni Lash said, still laughing.

Habeas eyed Monk.

"You viper," the pig said.

Fifteen minutes later, Monk escorted the exquisite Toni Lash up to Ham.

"Mr. Brooks," Monk said cheerfully, "this is Miss Toni Lash, with whom I have a date for the dance tonight. Miss Lash, this is Ham Brooks, a lawyer"—Monk almost forgot to add the false-hood he always told pretty girls about Ham—"who has a wife and fifteen children at home."

"Good afternoon, Mr. Brooks," Toni Lash said.

"The wife and fifteen brats," Monk added maliciously, "probably explains that vinegary expression on his face."

"Don't you think," pretty Toni Lash asked, "that Monk here is the most delightful ventriloquist?"

Ham made a series of strangling sounds, and ended up by whirling and rushing off down the deck.

"Why, where can he be going?" Toni Lash asked wonderingly.

"Probably to find a fire hose," Monk explained, "and turn it on himself to get cooled off."

THE entire afternoon passed before Monk managed to wrench himself away from the hypnotic company of Toni Lash. He found Ham in their cabin. Ham gave him a glassy-eyed glare.

"I trust," Monk said cheerfully, "that you had a pleasant afternoon."

Ham said, "I looked for some trace of Doc Savage."

Monk's homely face sobered. "Find anything?"

Ham frowned uneasily. "I found the wheelchair Doc was using; also the white wig, shawl, the rest of his disguise—but no Doc."

Monk sank down on the bunk and pounded one knee anxiously with a large, furry fist.

"I'm worried about Doc! Still, that note did say he would be all right."

"I guess," Ham said, "there's nothing we can do."

Monk sighed, got to his feet and assumed a cheerful look.

"There's somethin' I'm gonna do," he said.

He took a lead sounding weight out of a coat pocket, along with a length of cord. He hefted the lead, testing its weight.

"You think this will sink the what-is-it?" he asked.

"You're not gonna drown Chemistry!" Ham yelled.

"I won the bet, didn't I?"

They discussed that warmly through dinner, and desisted only when Monk took time out to dance with Toni Lash. The young lady danced exquisitely, and there was no question about it— she was the most consummate bit of femininity aboard.

Monk was spending one of the most glorious days in his life. He had thwarted and confounded Ham at every turn, and had met the most sublime girl of his career.

However, about eleven o'clock that night, a fly came buzzing around the candy bowl.

"I think your friend Ham should join us," Toni Lash said.

"Aw!" Monk groaned.

Thirty minutes later, Ham had joined the party, and he and Monk and Toni Lash were headed, chatting and laughing, for the young woman's cabin. She was going to show them a frock she had designed.

Toni Lash had explained that she was a fashion designer employed by an exclusive Park Avenue shop. Monk was disgusted. Ham's interest in clothes was giving him something in common with the young woman.

They entered the young woman's cabin.

"The model is in this cabin, here," she said.

She went over, opened the closet door, stepped back.

Cautious came out of the closet. In each hand, Cautious held a single-shot pistol of large caliber, equipped with silencers.

"We're playing for keeps, boys," Cautious said, ugly-voiced.

Toni Lash went to a drawer, got out her hydrocyanic gun, and explained to Monk and Ham what it was.

"Luckily," she said, "I took the trouble to learn descriptions of all Doc Savage's men."

Chapter VI
THE FIRE ALARM

TONI LASH saw Monk and Ham handcuffed, wrist and ankle. To discourage picking handcuff locks, she taped their fingers together with adhesive tape, made wads of tape around the locks. She also plastered tape over their mouths.

"Cautious," she said, "you can get their pets."

Cautious showed no elation. "Aw—you mean the runt ape and that pig?"

"I think I would rather like to have them," Toni Lash said. She added sharply, "Go get them!"

Cautious, with no love for the assignment, disappeared from the cabin. He was gone fully a quarter of an hour, and came back looking as though he'd had a disagreement with several tomcats. He carried two suitcases from which came, respectively, pig grunting and chimp chattering.

"Dang it!" he complained. "I hope somebody else has to catch 'em next time."

The girl ignored his remarks. "You hold down the situation," she directed.

She left Cautious in that cabin to watch Monk, Ham and the pets, and walked down the corridor to another cabin, which she entered, closing the door behind her and switching on the lights.

Doc Savage lay on a berth in the cabin. Handcuffs secured his wrists and ankles, as well as great masses of adhesive tape. The mattress had been removed from the bunk, and he was lashed to the bunk stringers by many turns of rope.

He could roll his eyes, but that was about all the motion he could manage.

Toni Lash went over, tested the bronze man's bonds, satisfied herself as to their tightness.

"Hooray for our side!" she said dryly.

Doc Savage's flake gold eyes appraised her with intense interest. The more he saw of this unusual girl, the more amazed he became.

Toni Lash drew a chair near, seated herself, lighted a cigarette.

"I had a suspicion," she said, "that you weren't alone."

She took the cigarette from her lips, looked at the glow, and blew ashes off it.

"Monk and Ham," she said, "are rather entertaining fellows."

The smoke crawled up and made tiny, wriggling gray ghosts above her cigarette.

"Unfortunately," she said, "we don't need them."

Doc Savage's flake gold eyes fixed. They asked a question which, being gagged, he could not ask any other way—Did she mean that Monk and Ham were to be—

She understood.

"I don't know," she said. "Whether or not they die, will depend on the word from the higher up."

TONI LASH had told the truth. This was evident when she went to the radio room and dispatched a message in code.

Three hours later, an answer came. The girl, reading it, bit her lips. Tears came into her eyes. With a pencil, she wrote a translation of the code message on the lower part of the blank. She carried this to Doc Savage, held it before his eyes.

Doc read:

Want only Doc Savage. Drown the other two, but be careful.

"I'm sorry," Toni Lash said.

She was crying.

After she had left the cabin, Doc Savage lay in grim immobility. He would have to change his plan—and he had been following a plan, even lying here bound and gagged to log helplessness.

Doc was still adhering to his first purpose. That was to find out what this was all about by letting himself be taken, as a prisoner, to wherever he was to be taken.

The bronze man made a mental inventory of possible methods by which he might escape. The list was not encouraging. If he had been wearing his own clothing, it would have been easy, for he always carried gadgets. But Cautious had taken his garments, giving him in return a pair of grimy, blue denim overalls and a jumper.

Doc had been working his fingers. Now, twisting and wrenching, he got the fingers of his right hand free of the tape. He was still manacled, lashed with ropes, could not move the right hand except below the wrist.

The lashed hand was close to his side, near the side buttons of the overalls. He got hold of a button, tore it off. It was a large metal button, as heavy as a marble.

Doc got the button between thumb and crooked forefinger, marble-shooter fashion, turned, took careful aim.

His target was in the center of the ceiling. Not the light—it was the little ceiling doodad of the liner's automatic fire alarm system. The device consisted of two spring electrical contacts held apart by a transparent marble-shaped thing, which would burst when the temperature reached a certain height.

Doc shot the button at the marble. He missed.

He tried again. Another miss. There were three buttons on that side of the overalls. He couldn't reach the other side. This time, he had better hit. He did.

There was a hissing sound. Water showered into the room from the automatic pipes. Somewhere an alarm bell rang. There were calm orders. Men running. The door burst open.

"I'll be darned!" somebody said.

THEN Doc Savage was cut loose. Trying to stand up, he fell, arms and legs stick-stiff. Even his trained muscles had become stiff. He kneaded himself, eventually managed to get on his feet.

"The captain wants to question you," he was told.

Doc Savage made known his identity. The officer was not impressed. He seemed to consider Doc some kind of crook. So they went to the bridge and saw the captain.

"You're being very silly, mister!" the captain told the officer. "This man is Doc Savage, and he probably has more real influence than any one man in the world."

The bronze man glanced around. There was warm air whipping across the bridge, and the night was very dark. The heavens were full of stars that were like sparks, and out behind the ship the wake stretched, a widening swirl touched with phosphorescence.

"Where are we?" Doc asked.

"We've just entered the Mediterranean," the captain explained.

Doc Savage nodded grimly.

"A girl named Toni Lash," he said, "is holding two of my friends, Monk and Ham, and is planning to kill them. We have got to find them."

The captain swallowed. "I'll assign you a searching party."

Doc Savage left the bridge.

The captain bit his lips, got out his pipe, stuffed it and lighted it. His hands shook. He seemed to be having a violent inner debate with himself.

"She's too lovely a girl," he muttered. "He can't be right!"

The captain went to a telephone—the boat was equipped with a telephone system to all cabins—and called Toni Lash.

"A man named Doc Savage is hunting you," the captain said. "He's accusing you of a terrible thing."

Toni Lash's voice was apologetic, concerned.

"I'll come and see about it at once, captain," she said.

The young woman hung up. But she made no move toward going to the bridge to see the captain.

"Doc Savage is loose," she said.

Cautious jumped up, looked as though someone had shot at him.

"Huh?" he croaked.

"He's started to search the ship," Toni Lash explained.

"But—how—uh—ugh—" Cautious, trying to speak, ended up with a string of noises.

The girl wore a faraway look. She contemplated her fingernails, polished one of them thoughtfully on a sleeve, and seemed wrapped in abstract thoughtfulness.

Cautious recovered, barked, "We're trapped!"

The girl, looking at him, shook her head. "No," she said.

"You're crazy!" Cautious gritted. "They will find us! They will find Monk and Ham! I tell you, we're sunk!"

The girl shook her head again.

"No," she said. "I have an idea."

She went to the two prisoners, Monk and Ham, and bent over them.

"We'll have to work fast," she said.

Chapter VII
AT MONTE CARLO

DOC SAVAGE was also saying, "We had better move fast on this."

They went first to the cabin which showed in the records as the one Toni Lash had engaged. It was empty. They tried other cabins—they went over the ship, the first time rapidly, covering the whole vessel.

They found nothing.

The second search of the ship was more systematic.

The third search missed nothing whatever.

Not a cabin, not a closet, not a single ventilator interior escaped their scrutiny. They took the dogs out of the kennels in the baggage hold and searched there. They opened flour sacks, probed into innumerable pieces of baggage and freight in the holds, and scrutinized every passenger closely.

Of Toni Lash, Cautious, Monk and Ham there was no trace whatever.

"Why, that's incredible!" the captain said. He meant it. He leaned on the bridge rail for a long time and contemplated the sea. His eyes were sad and his heart heavy. He was convinced that Toni Lash had gone overboard, had committed suicide to avoid capture. There seemed to be no other explanation.

Doc Savage, certain finally that his men and his quarry both escaped the ship, went to Toni Lash's room—the cabin she had engaged for herself. A guard had been left over this. The bronze man began searching the young woman's luggage in quest of a clue—any kind of a clue.

The frocks in Toni Lash's wardrobe were expensive. Doc probably knew less about such items than he knew about any other subject, but he was sure the stuff was exclusive.

For a long time, the search brought forth nothing that was of value. Then he found the envelope.

The contents of the envelope were puzzling at first. Why, for instance, should a girl like Toni Lash keep several stubs of theater tickets, a few menus printed in French, some pressed flowers of different kinds, and one note? The note was addressed to Toni Lash, at a hotel on the Riviera in France. It said:

> Tonight at seven. Love you a lot.
> Park Crater

Doc Savage realized suddenly that the articles in the envelope were souvenirs of some love affair. Some of the items, the note in particular, bore stains; and after he applied a chemical test that showed a saline content in the marks, he knew they were tear stains.

Toni Lash had shed tears over these pitiful souvenirs.

Doc Savage went to the *Maritonia* radio room, got a radio-land-line telephone hook-up to France, and began making calls.

It took him an hour to learn what he wanted to know.

"Can you put me off near Monte Carlo?" Doc asked.

"Yes, indeed," the captain said.

The captain of the *Maritonia* was in a state of mind where he wanted very much to get rid of this whole thing.

Doc Savage sent two radiograms. They were addressed to his two aides, Renny who was in France, and Johnny, who was in Egypt.

MONTE CARLO is a standing example of the axiom that a thing does not have to be large to be famous. The commonwealth of Monaco, containing Monte Carlo, is one of the smallest principalities in the world, yet few people have not heard of it.

The *Asile Blanc* is located on one of the steeper mountains. It is of stone. Once it was a castle; so it is high and grim. Steel bars have been placed over the windows, and the verandas and the edge of the roof are surrounded by high fences of steel bars, so that patients cannot leap to their deaths.

A low-slung, fast car went moaning up the winding cliff road and stopped in the afternoon sunlight that touched the barred gate of *Asile Blanc*.

Doc Savage swung out of the car.

A man jumped toward the machine. He was a big man, almost as large as Doc Savage; and he had a long, sad face and two fists which could hardly be inserted in quart buckets.

"Holy cow!" he ejaculated.

"Renny!" the bronze man echoed.

"I got your message to show up here," Renny said, "and here I am."

Renny was Colonel John Renny Renwick, famous as an engineer, also noted for his love of demonstrating how he could knock panels out of wooden doors with his fists. He was a Doc Savage aide.

Doc asked, "Any sign of Johnny Littlejohn? At the same time I radioed you, I also asked Johnny to come over from Egypt, where he's poking into a tomb."

"He's hardly had time to get here," Renny said.

He had a great rumbling voice that was something like the noises that might have been made by an angry lion that had fallen to the bottom of a deep well.

Renny boomed, "What's up, Doc?"

"Some unknown person hired a girl named Toni Lash to come to New York, seize me, and bring me to Europe," Doc explained. "We were playing along with her, but she outslicked us. She had a man named Cautious helping her. They seized Monk and Ham on the ship. Then all of them disappeared. Monk, Ham, the girl and Cautious—everyone vanished."

"Disappeared—how?"

Doc Savage's metallic features turned grim.

"That," he said, "hasn't become quite clear."

"You're sure," Renny said, "that they didn't just hide on the liner?"

"Positive."

Renny knew enough about Doc Savage's methods to be sure that, if the bronze man said the missing persons were not on the liner, they weren't on it.

"Holy cow!" Renny rumbled.

That was his favorite ejaculation.

Doc continued, "A search of the girl's cabin turned up some stuff indicating she'd had an admirer named Park Crater. And by radio-telephoning to the Riviera, it became evident that Park Crater is an American millionaire's son who recently went insane, and is confined here."

Renny looked up at the grim stone walls of *Asile Blanc.*

"I wouldn't want to be confined here," he rumbled.

PARK CRATER distended his mouth until all his teeth showed like fangs. He made his mouth a hole. In that hole, his tongue darted around like the head of an animal.

"Holy cow!" Renny croaked, and backed away. He didn't care about being around insane people.

Doc Savage said, "Will you remove Park Crater's straitjacket?"

The French specialist hesitated. The specialist knew Doc Savage by reputation, but this was the first time he had met this giant bronze man who was believed to be the greatest surgeon of them all; and he was awed.

"He is very violent," the specialist warned.

"So it would appear," Doc Savage said quietly.

The specialist gestured to two attendants, and they began removing the straitjacket from poor Park Crater. Toward the last, they had to struggle mightily to hold the patient.

Park Crater sprang onto the floor. He seized a chair. Those in the room retreated hastily. But it was not to attack them that Park Crater wanted the chair. He wanted it to fight the air over his head.

He fought the empty air with wild ferocity.

Park Crater had not been incarcerated here in the insane asylum many weeks, but already he had changed from the handsome, dashing young man who played so furiously and made love so irresistibly. His healthy, tanned color was fading, his cheeks were sinking, and his eyes were like white glass marbles in black teacups.

"Does he fight something over his head all the time?" Doc asked.

The French specialist nodded.

"A weird case, *M'sieu'* Savage," he said slowly. "It puzzles me. I never saw anything like it. I even took a trip to England to examine the similar case of Fogarty-Smith, but it puzzled me just as much."

"Similar case?" Doc Savage said.

"In London," explained the specialist, "at Admiralty Cross hospital."

Doc Savage turned abruptly to Renny.

"Renny," the bronze man said, "charter a fast plane and get to London as quickly as you can."

"London!" Renny boomed. "What can I do in—"

"Start guarding Fogarty-Smith twenty-four hours a day," Doc explained.

Renny rubbed his solemn jaw with one of his enormous hands.

"Holy cow!" he said. "Well—um—I'm London bound, I guess."

Chapter VIII
MADMAN VANISHING

AFTER Renny had lumbered out of the room, the French specialist studied Doc Savage in bewilderment.

"I do not understand, *M'sieu',*" he said thoughtfully.

Unfortunate Park Crater continued to strike madly at something imaginary over his head. Blow after blow he swung with the chair, striving to make each one harder than the first. When the chair happened to hit the wall, it broke, and he stood there hitting the wall with what was left of the chair, knocking plaster loose.

"We had better put the straitjacket back on him," Doc said.

They had some difficulty doing that, the two attendants attempting it first, but finding themselves unable to hold the madman; so that Doc Savage took over that part of the task, leaving the pair to apply the straitjacket.

"Can you arrange a diagnosis room for me?" Doc asked.

The specialist nodded. *"Très bien."*

Doc explained, "My bags containing the equipment necessary for a diagnosis of this young man's case are at an inn. I am going for them."

He was seating himself in his car—it was a machine he had rented—when a rattling taxicab arrived.

Out of the cab came a long head, a long neck, and a body that seemed to be of unlimited length. Probably the effect of extreme length was accentuated by the fact that the man was thinner than it seemed anyone could possibly be. Not only was he just a string of bones, but even the bones were thin.

This was Johnny—William Harper Littlejohn, who could look at a twelfth dynasty Egyptian hieroglyphic and tell how many years the man who wrote it had gone to school. His suit did not fit him. No suit would ever fit him.

Johnny was the other Doc Savage aide who had been abroad. Regarding Johnny's clothes, Monk often said that Johnny should try to wear a sheath, not a suit.

"An unprognosticatable eventuation," he announced.

That was his other failing: big words. He never used a little word if he could think of a jawbreaker.

Into the room came a young woman.

He could just as well have said that he hadn't expected what had happened.

Doc gave an outline of the mystery so far.

Johnny listened to the story in widemouthed silence.

"I'll be superamalgamated!" he said.

He fiddled thoughtfully with a monocle which dangled by a black cord from his lapel. Once he'd had defective sight in one eye, and had needed a monocle. But Doc had remedied the eye trouble, and Johnny still carried the monocle, although now it was really a pocket magnifier.

He was so confounded by the whole thing that he used little words.

"Does it make sense to you, Doc?" he asked.

"Not yet," the bronze man said grimly. "But a suspicion is beginning to form."

JOHNNY looked at Doc Savage sharply and demanded, "What kind of suspicion, Doc?"

The bronze man did not seem to hear.

"I asked you," Johnny said more loudly, "what kind of suspicion—"

He remembered, and did not finish the question. Doc had heard him the first time. This was the bronze man's habit, one of the few aggravating ones he had.

Doc Savage habitually did not voice his suspicions when they were only suspicions. Not until a theory had become a proven fact in his mind would he go into explanations. Until he wanted to talk, Doc would seem not to hear any questions on the subject.

"I'll be superamalgamated!" Johnny said.

"You go upstairs," Doc suggested, "and keep an eye on poor Park Crater while I go for my instrument case."

Johnny nodded, watched Doc Savage send his car down the steep cliff road with a speed that sometimes gave Johnny's stomach a suspended feeling. Then Johnny went into the *Asile Blanc* and mounted to Park Crater's room.

In two or three minutes, Johnny got enough of watching Park Crater. The young man's condition was so terrible that it gave Johnny creepy sensations.

Johnny backed into the other room, looked at an *Asile Blanc* attendant standing there.

"It's ultrainvidiousively harassing," Johnny remarked.

"Eh?" said the attendant.

"I said," explained Johnny, "that the young man's condition distresses me."

The attendant was a tall, thick-bodied man with more than a slight cast of the Eurasian to his features. He did not, Johnny reflected, look like the kind of fellow one would expect in the part of a male nurse. Riding a shaggy pony at wild speed over some Asiatic steppe appeared to be more his style.

The attendant took a black gun from inside his white hospital coat.

"This had better distress you, too," he said, moving the gun menacingly.

He spoke with a distinct Asiatic accent.

"Wuh—wuh—" Johnny swallowed. "What on earth?"

"Turn around," the attendant ordered.

Johnny barked, "What does this mean?"

The large words had been startled out of him.

"Turn around!" snarled the attendant.

Johnny didn't turn. He pitched for the man. It wasn't as foolish a move as it seemed. The gun pointed at Johnny's chest, and he wore a bullet-proof vest.

The gun banged. Johnny was twisting. The bullet missed him entirely, dug plaster out of the wall. Johnny got the gun arm, and went to work.

Johnny at work in a fight was something unique. He had the physical build of the type of spider called a granddaddy longlegs, and he was all bone and whipcord sinew. When he tied himself around an opponent, the foe immediately felt as if he had fallen into a tight-fitting cage of iron bars.

They hit the floor. The attendant lost his gun. He howled in an Asiatic tongue. It was very pained howling. Johnny rolled to the wall with him, began bumping the fellow's head against the baseboard. The man bleated.

Into the room came a young woman.

Johnny gaped at her. She was unquestionably the most exquisitely tall and slender young woman he had ever seen.

"Watch out!" Johnny shouted. "You'll get hurt."

He didn't want her to get hurt.

But then, men always felt the protective instinct when they first saw Toni Lash.

Toni Lash wound up like a softball pitcher and hit Johnny over the right ear with a blackjack.

By some freak of the instant, Johnny happened to be looking at a clock on the wall just before his consciousness was knocked into a black pit of silence.

The clock said 3:00—

JOHNNY, awakening, felt rather detached from reality, as well as confused, to say nothing of an unearthly aching inside his skull; and he looked around for something tangible upon which to fasten his attention—a kind of raft on the tossing sea of mental uncertainty to which he could cling until the storm blew over. He saw the clock.

The clock now said 3:30.

"I'll be superamalgamated!" Johnny mumbled.

Then he realized Doc Savage was crouching beside him.

"Johnny," Doc said, "can you understand me?"

"I understand your words," Johnny muttered. "But darned if I savvy what happened."

"They got Park Crater," Doc said.

"Crater—"

"They took him," Doc repeated. "Carried him away."

"Huh!"

"Describe that girl," Doc requested.

Johnny gave, considering the circumstances, an excellent idea of the young woman's appearance.

"Toni Lash!" Doc exploded.

"But she was on the liner—and—" Johnny held his head. "How'd she get here? And what became of Monk and Ham?"

Doc shook his head grimly, then wheeled, ran out of the room, went down stone steps with long leaps and flung into his car. Down the cliff road, he drove. Such natives as he passed turned pale, stared after him, holding their breaths and waiting for the crash. But he astonished them and reached the bottom.

Park Crater, Toni Lash and her helpers had been gone when Doc returned to *Asile Blanc* with his instrument case. They had left, according to the asylum officials, in a fast car, after menacing everyone with guns.

Doc stopped at a police station, and made telephone calls. He spoke French fluently, and he soon had *gendarmes* watching roads, as well as circulating in cars, looking for the machine in which Toni Lash had carried off Park Crater.

The *gendarmes* were efficient. They found the girl's car. It stood on a quay, and offshore from the spot a fast seaplane was scudding along, in the act of leaving the water.

Bystanders explained that a girl and a big Eurasian in hospital garb had transferred a man in a straitjacket from the car to the seaplane.

The plane was lost in the cloud ceiling over the Mediterranean when Doc Savage reached the spot.

The bronze man drove back to *Asile Blanc*.

"Oo-o-o, my head!" Johnny complained.

"Feel better?" Doc asked.

"I don't believe the X-rays!" Johnny groaned. "They say my skull is not fractured."

Doc talked to the *Asile Blanc* officials for a while.

"That Eurasian," Doc told Johnny, "was obviously posted here to watch Park Crater soon after the young man was confined."

Johnny felt of his blackjack souvenir. "It don't make sense to me."

"It makes this much sense," Doc Savage said gravely. "Park Crater was taken away so we could not have a chance to treat him."

"Which means—"

"It means," Doc said, "that he might have been able to tell us something if we had been able to bring him back to his normal mind."

Johnny pondered that.

"They've been telling me," he said, "about a man named Fogarty-Smith in London who had this same kind of insanity."

"Did you come from Egypt in your plane, Johnny?"

"Yes."

"Then we can use it to go to London."

"But what about Monk and Ham?"

"All we can do," Doc Savage said quietly, "is keep going on this madman mystery—and hope it leads us to Monk and Ham!"

JOHNNY'S private plane had been constructed after a design worked out by Doc Savage for his private use, being a low-wing, twin-engine job with retractable wheels and a body that was both a streamlined cabin and a pontoon for water landings.

It amused Johnny from time to time to notice the variety of furtive individuals who went to great pains to photograph his plane and take its measurements. His "spy magnet," he called the plane.

Over London there was a fog, for which the metropolis was noted.

To save time, they did not fly on out to Croydon Field, but dropped down and skimmed over the Thames River, high enough to clear the tower bridges.

"Use the black-light scanner," Doc directed.

Johnny did so.

The scanner was a contrivance, devised by Doc Savage, which utilized wavelengths of light outside the visible spectrum, light wavelengths which penetrated fog and smoke much better than ordinary light. To enable a man to see by this "invisible" light, Doc Savage had developed a type of scanning binocular, utilizing the principle of photofluorescent images mechanically displacing each other before the eye.

With the contraption, Doc Savage and Johnny studied the river. The plane volleyed along, buffeted a little by air currents out of the city streets.

"Johnny!" Doc Savage said suddenly. "That plane—see it!"

Johnny swung his scanner to the left. He saw a plane, not a large ship, but one that looked fast. It was a seaplane, and tied alongside a dock.

Johnny said, "I see it, but—"

"It is Toni Lash's plane," Doc said.

The next instant the bronze man yanked the controls, and the ship skidded around in the air, nosed for the water. He set the big wing flaps, so they could land at low speed. The ship knifed through a choking cloud of smoke from a tugboat funnel, hit the water.

Doc and Johnny threw aside the infra-light-scanning devices.

"Handle the controls," Doc directed. "Bring her in close to that ship."

Doc Savage gave the controls to Johnny, swung out of the cabin, ran along the wing, waited near the tip. Now that they were out of the air,

the fog seemed less thick. The riverbank loomed, and the dock, the other plane.

A man was standing half out of the other plane cabin, straining his eyes at the river, and listening. He had heard Doc's ship, obviously.

"You see that man?" Doc asked Johnny, low-voiced.

"Yes."

"That," Doc said, "is the man known as Cautious."

Chapter IX
LONDON GRIM

JOHNNY made an explosive, grim sound, and reached for a machine pistol. The weapon, resembling an oversized automatic, was capable of firing an astounding number of bullets in the course of a minute. It handled mercy bullets, explosives, gas shells and "smokers."

At that instant, Cautious recognized them. He hurled himself headlong into his plane cabin, came out with a rifle, lifted the gun, fired.

But Doc Savage was back along the wing—and down behind the motor of Johnny's ship. The big radial motor was the most effective kind of a bullet shield.

His plane moved steadily toward the one on which Cautious stood.

The bullets ate holes in the brick wall.

Johnny had pitched back, lay in the shelter of the other motor. This plane was not armor-plated, as were many of Doc's ships.

"What kind of a drum in your machine pistol?" Doc called.

"Explosives," Johnny said. "I was shooting at sharks for practice crossing the Mediterranean, and never changed drums."

"Shake him up a little," Doc suggested.

Johnny aimed carefully; his machine pistol made a bull fiddle moan—and that part of London was treated to a deafening uproar that must have reminded the inhabitants of World War bombing days. All bullets hit the water. A progressive geyser ran up to Cautious's plane, like a threatening monster. The plane pitched.

Cautious stumbled, went down, lost his rifle, but remained on the wing. He began bawling.

"Don't blast the plane!" he squalled. "Monk 'n' Ham are aboard!"

"I'll be superamalgamated!" Johnny howled delightedly. "Where's Park Crater?"

"He's on here, too!" Cautious shouted.

"Yeo-o-w!" Johnny yelled. "That's the plane they used to flee Monte Carlo! We got 'em cornered! Boy, what a break!"

Their plane droned toward the other craft.

Cautious, they suddenly perceived, was taking flight. He had kept down behind the cabin, crept out to the tip of a wing while thus sheltered, and with an agile leap, landed on shore. He ran.

Doc leaped to the controls of their own plane, changed its course, aimed it for the end of the dock. But it was slow. Moments passed. Then the bronze man leaped, got onto the dock.

Cautious had become a distant, speeding wraith in the fog. Doc flashed after him. He gained. Cautious turned right, around a corner.

A car engine snorted, began roaring. Gears rasped as they meshed, and tires whistled trying to get traction.

Doc reached the corner. It was fortunate he put his head around first, had the muscular agility to yank back quickly. Because an automatic rifle coughed out a clip of cartridges in one spasm. The bullets ate holes in the brick wall.

Cautious was riding in the backseat of the car. The man driving was bulky and appeared—it was hard to tell from that distance—to be some breed of Asiatic.

They got away. There was no other car in view, nothing in which to follow the pair.

Doc went back to the dock.

Long, bony Johnny was getting out of Cautious' plane.

"The liar!" Johnny grumbled. "The daggone prevaricator!"

Doc said, "Monk and Ham—"

"Not here," Johnny said. "Cautious just yelled that to keep us from shootin' at him!"

TWO London policemen in a patrol car arrived for the purpose of learning what had happened. Gun war on London streets was almost unheard of. Doc made explanations, identified himself, and borrowed the patrol car in which the two policemen had arrived.

The bronze man could borrow the police car, because he held an appointment to Scotland Yard, result of a service rendered in the past.

Gaunt Johnny sat back, watched Doc drive. Johnny happened to know the bronze man had not been in London for some time, but such was the trained retentiveness of Doc's memory that he took almost a direct line through what, to Johnny, was a confusion of streets. The fact that traffic took the left side of the street, instead of the right, as in America, led Johnny to repeatedly grab his hat in expectation of a collision.

"It looks," said Johnny, "as if this girl has the same idea we've got—get Fogarty-Smith."

Doc Savage nodded. "They flew straight here from the Riviera."

Johnny watched ancient, curious old buildings flash by. Antiques always intrigued him.

"I wonder," he muttered, "who that girl is working for."

Doc Savage, not answering, swung the car to the curb before a long, red brick building which had pleasing green boxes at the windows, and a general air of quiet comfort. A sign on the structure said:

ADMIRALTY CROSS HOSPITAL

"This is the place," Johnny said grimly, "where the French specialist said Fogarty-Smith was confined."

They entered, and in a moment the surgeon in charge was shaking his head slowly at them.

"Fogarty-Smith," he said, "is not here."

Doc Savage showed no visible surprise. His self-control was excellent. However, he did make, for the briefest of instants, the tiny, exotic, trilling sound which was his unconscious characteristic in moments of mental shock.

Johnny had no such iron grip on his emotions. In the space of hours, he had been blackjacked, thought he had found Monk and Ham, been disappointed, and now Fogarty-Smith wasn't here.

Johnny wrenched off his hat, slammed it on the floor, kicked it. His teeth made sounds like two rocks being rubbed together.

"That girl," he groaned, "is getting my goat!"

The surgeon wrinkled his brow in perplexity.

"There must be a misunderstanding," he said. "Over a week ago Fogarty-Smith was taken to Modernage Hospital. They have more advanced methods of treating at Modernage."

Johnny looked embarrassed. "Then nobody snatched Fogarty-Smith?"

"Snatched?" The surgeon frowned. "I—uh—snatched?" The piece of American slang puzzled him.

"Did Colonel Renny Renwick come here inquiring for Fogarty-Smith?" Doc demanded.

The surgeon said, "Renwick—you mean the man who had such large fists?"

"That was Renny," Doc said.

"He was here. I told him where Fogarty-Smith had been taken," the surgeon advised. "He left for Modernage."

Doc Savage was already leaving the room. Johnny whirled, legged after the bronze man. They landed in the car they had borrowed from the police.

"You know where Modernage is?"

Doc Savage nodded. "Not far."

At the end of the trip, Johnny was doubled over to keep from seeing things flashing by. He had perfect confidence in Doc Savage's driving ability, but still—a man sitting in a motion picture theater, when he sees a comic cannonball come toward him on the screen, knows very well he won't get hit, but he dodges anyway.

The Modernage Hospital was of white stone, as neat as a dice cube. The windows were round, like the pips on dice.

They walked through a door which had a modernistic chromium border.

Inside the door, a man lay on his back. His legs were rigid, and he was holding his head up and staring fixedly at a knife handle sticking out of his chest. The man wore a surgeon's garb, and apparently he was trying to figure just how much chance there was of the knife killing him.

"Don't try to pull it out!" Doc said sharply.

"I've got better sense than that," the man said, and bubbled a little crimson at his lips.

"What happened?"

"Upstairs!" said the surgeon with the knife in his chest.

DOC SAVAGE directed Johnny. "Wait down here. You may have to cover the rear door."

The bronze man went up dark-blue steps covered with a dark-crimson carpet. At the top he landed on a noiseless cork floor. There was one door. He hit it. Metal—and locked.

Doc began struggling with the door.

Down at the foot of the stairs, Johnny sank beside the knifed surgeon. "How did it happen?"

"Heard a noise upstairs." The surgeon spoke slowly through his red bubbling. "A man threw a knife."

"A girl threw it, you mean?" Johnny asked.

"No. A man. Eurasian."

At the top of the stairs, Doc hit the door. It held. He drew back, was pitching a shoulder at the door when it opened. He plunged into a room, twisting down and to one side. But that precaution was unnecessary.

The occupants of the room were obviously hospital people; about a dozen of them—doctors, nurses, interns and attendants.

They stood in a circle. A strange, silent kind of circle, around a chair. It was a shiny, chromium, modern chair, and on it sat a man.

The man on the chair was Renny. He sat very still, in an awkward position. His big hands were held, palms upward, fingers splayed, at about the level of his shoulders. His arms trembled a little with strain. It was as if his hands were supporting some tremendous, invisible, horrible weight. Renny gazed fixedly at the air over his head.

"Renny!" Doc Savage said.

Renny's lips parted, came off his teeth; he seemed to try to scream, but could not. Then suddenly he twisted off the chair.

He seized the chair with both hands, sprang up, began striking terrific blows at the empty air. Blow after blow he launched in a mad frenzy.

The hospital people scattered, getting away from him.

"That's the way we found him," someone told Doc Savage.

"Where is Fogarty-Smith?" Doc asked hoarsely.

"Carried off. We don't know by whom."

"When?"

"Not more than ten minutes ago."

Chapter X
THREE STEPS FROM THE ARCTIC

THE windows were open, and a cool gentle wind blew in and rustled the skirts of the nurses. Beyond the window was a park, with green grass and trees having leaves which had already turned the bright colors of fall.

The fog lay over the park, and the evening slanted down through the fog and gave it a sheen of bright silver. The city beyond was quiet with the stillness of approaching evening. Then there came from out in the city somewhere the slow striking of a clock which was not London's famous Big Ben, but a clock which struck slow, deep-throated notes that sounded very much like Big Ben.

When the clock ceased striking, there was

silence in the room where Renny stood. Renny had stopped smashing at the air with the chair. He stood on stiffly widespread legs, watching cunningly. He was waiting for the thing to get close enough for him to hit it again.

There was nothing in the air. But Renny's watching, his sly waiting, his conviction that something was there, was all so very real that those in the room could almost see the thing.

One of the nurses was brave. She took a paper booklet from the pocket of her uniform, tore out four sheets of paper and made four little sail darts such as students make in classrooms. She sailed the darts, one at a time, through the air over Renny's head, sailing each dart through a different spot. Renny did not stir nor show by any sign that he was aware of the darts, and none of the sailing papers were interrupted in anyway in their graceful arching flight.

"There's nothing—nothing—in the air," the nurse said.

Doc Savage spoke in a low voice to an attendant, and the man nodded and went out, returning in a few moments with a straitjacket of canvas and leather. Doc spoke again. The nurses got out of the room. All the male attendants surrounded Renny. The men took off their glasses and placed them where they would not get broken, and also removed their coats.

"Do not hurt him," Doc Savage said.

Doc's face looked, at this moment, as though it actually were made out of bronze. Each muscle seemed solidified by mental control so that it would not show emotion, lest horror, if it managed to set a single muscle quivering, might use that foothold to spring through the whole of the bronze man's great body, and his mind.

They closed in on Renny, seized him, and began the stupendous task of putting him in the straitjacket. Renny was a mighty man. The sheer brute force in his great sinews was enormous. And now, when his mind did not exert any mollifying control, each muscle put forth its fullest strength in each move. His strength now was the strength of an insane man. In his sane life, Renny had never been as strong as he was now.

They got down on the floor, a great mass of men who labored and groaned with their own terrific efforts. And finally they got Renny in the straitjacket.

"CAN'T you do something to help him, Doc?" Johnny asked hollowly.

Doc Savage, in a grim silence, carried Renny down to the car, placed him in the machine. Johnny also got in.

Johnny watched Doc's driving again, noted how frequently the bronze man took seemingly aimless turns. He realized Doc was throwing off possible pursuit.

They drew up, finally, before a little inn in a quiet section of the city, an inn which had a courtyard at the rear, accessible by car, so that their arrival attracted no attention.

Doc Savage was known at the inn. Apparently he had stayed there before. The proprietor was a large man, white-haired, pleasant of face, and sparing with his questions.

They carried Renny to a room. Renny had not spoken. But he heaved and strained against the straitjacket almost continuously.

"Watch him," Doc said grimly.

The bronze man drove, in the police car, back to the Modernage Hospital. The institution had quieted. The surgeon who had been stabbed was in the operating room, and the man nodded eagerly when he heard Doc Savage ask to handle the treating of the wound. The young man had read Doc Savage's surgical treatises—he knew that this giant bronze man with the strange, flake-gold eyes and the long-fingered, sinew-wrapped hands was probably one of the greatest living surgeons.

It was an hour before the bronze man said, "You will be as good as new in a few weeks."

"That's a bit of bally good news," the surgeon said. He was pale.

"Can you tell me anything more about what happened?"

"Only that the man who threw the knife was some kind of Asiatic. Mixed blood, I think. Eurasian."

Doc examined the knife. It was unusual. The blade was long, curved like a thin half-moon. The handle was of dark wood which had a knotty grain and was almost as hard as metal.

Doc took the knife.

Apparently the raiders who had carried off Fogarty-Smith had gained access to the hospital by climbing a stairway that led up to a rear balcony, from which a window opened into the room where Fogarty-Smith had been confined in a straitjacket.

That room was the same one in which Renny had been found.

There was no other clue of value. Doc did follow a vague trail across a part of the park to a driveway, where he found a few drops of oil leakage, indicating a car had waited there.

The police had learned nothing. Doc returned the police patrol car which he had borrowed.

The bronze man returned to Johnny, who was watching Renny at the inn.

"Renny," Johnny reported grimly, "is not a bit better."

There was a haunted look on the long, big-worded archaeologist's face. During part of the flight from southern France, he had kept his head shoved out of the plane in an effort to see what was below, and as a result, his face had been reddened by the wind, except for the small saucer-shaped areas around his eyes where goggles had protected his skin. The effect this gave his face was ghostly, and the stark aspect was increased by the strain on Johnny's face.

"Doc," Johnny continued, "did you get any trace of whoever took Fogarty-Smith?"

"No."

"THEN we're sunk," Johnny groaned. "I'll be superamalgamated! We're left without a single clue to the whole mad business. And it is mad."

Johnny spread his long, bony arms desperately.

"Mad, I tell you!" he continued. "A girl is hired to come to New York, grab you and bring you to Europe. Who hired her is a complete mystery. And why is also a complete mystery. Then you fight back, and the girl and her helper and Monk and Ham vanish off a liner at sea. How, we don't know. Then the girl turns up and seizes an insane man in France, then races us to England and seizes another insane man—and Renny—poor Renny—if that all isn't mad, I'd like to know what is."

The confusion of Johnny's words reflected the turmoil in his mind.

Doc Savage went down to the little bookcase in the comfortable inn parlor and ran a finger over the books. He was looking for a book that is a part of every Empire-conscious Englishman's library—an atlas of the world.

Opening the atlas to a map of the Arctic regions, Doc drew Johnny's attention to a spot well north of the Arctic Circle.

"That is the place," Doc explained, "where the English weather station is located. Fogarty-Smith left that spot in his plane. A few hours later, he returned on foot—and he was insane in exactly the same way that Park Crater later became insane, and in the same way that Renny is now demented."

"It don't make sense," Johnny groaned.

"Fogarty-Smith's plane was never found," Doc said.

Johnny looked thoughtful. "I—but what—"

Doc Savage again indicated the spot on the Arctic regions of the map.

"Johnny," he said, "it might be worth while if one of us went up there and looked around. It's dangerous country to fly over, so—"

"I'll go," Johnny said promptly. "You've got to stay here and doctor Renny."

Doc Savage nodded slowly. "All right. But—well, it will be dangerous flying." The bronze man took a pencil and drew a suggested route on the map. "You can arrange to get gasoline at the British weather observation station on the pack ice. My suggestion is that you use the weather station as a base for exploration flights."

"What do I look for?"

"Eskimos."

"Eh?"

"Question them."

"I'll be superamalgamated!" Johnny said.

He was about as completely puzzled as he could ever recall having been.

THIS was how a plane came to drop like an aluminum bullet out of the gray Arctic sky, circle the English weather station, and land on the ice. Johnny got out of the plane. He was expected. He had radioed in advance, and he was to use fuel stored here at the station.

"But just what kind of exploration are you conducting?" the meteorologists wanted to know.

"My lucubration thereon approximates pulverulence," said Johnny.

The long flight had calmed Johnny's mind enough that he had gotten back to using his big words.

There was a dictionary at the weather station, and consulting it, the meteorologists learned that Johnny had assured them he hardly had a particle of an idea himself why he was up here.

Johnny blocked off territory on his chart, calculated visibility, and began a survey. Just to make sure he was not missing anything, he took aerial photographs and examined them later with a magnifying glass.

He did not need an aerial photograph to find the Eskimo village. To land there, however, he needed the skill of a magician, and the luck of an Irishman. He had both, and the Eskimos dashed into their igloos, under the impression a winged *Tongak* was arriving.

"Kileritse!" Johnny shouted in the Eskimo dialect.

The word meant food, but it also meant, "Come here"—the Eskimos having combined the two meanings under one heading for some reason or other.

"Chimo!" Johnny also yelled. That was the word for welcome.

He had a little trouble. Not violence, but reluctance on the part of the Eskimos to credit the fact that this long, skinny *kabloonatyet,* or stranger, who came from the air was a fellow with whom it was safe to associate.

Johnny spoke their language, for the branch of

his archaeological work which had to do with the sources of the different races of the world, had made him proficient in the derivative tongues of the major languages. While he could not speak Eskimo well enough to fool an Eskimo into believing he had lived in a *tupik* and had grown up on seal meat, he could make himself understood. He produced a pail of hard candy and made it known that he wanted his friends, the Eskimos, to share it with him.

"Elarle! Elarle!" they shouted, which translated into something like, "Indeed, yes!"

On the good will built by that pail of candy, and another, Johnny Littlejohn got the story of the *Kingmuk,* the dog that had come back to the village and jumped and snapped at something in the air until the dog finally died.

And the story of Kummik, the Eskimo. That tale came out, too. Of how Kummik came back to camp as naked as the day of his birth, armed only with his *oonapik,* or short hunting spear, and kept stabbing and jabbing at something over his head, was the story that was told Johnny. The telling was done around a blubber lamp in an igloo, amid shadows thrown by the blubber lamp—so that the surroundings were spooky. Johnny got a case of the creeps out of the recital.

The body of Kummik, the Eskimo, had been sealed in an igloo of ice blocks, and when Johnny went there to have a look—not an Eskimo would venture within a mile of the place—he found Kummik as well preserved as the hour when he had frozen.

Johnny made sure that months and months had passed since Kummik's demise. The Eskimos said it had happened *akkane,* which meant last year in a general way, but whether one month ago or twenty-five was impossible to determine. Close questioning convinced Johnny that Kummik had been smitten more than six months ago, however.

Johnny borrowed Kummik's body and flew back to London with it. He did not relish any minute of the time he had to sit in the plane with a frozen Eskimo. He was convinced his short neck hairs stood on end the entire trip.

DOC SAVAGE said, "What you have accomplished, Johnny, is more valuable than anything that we have done so far." And it was obvious that he meant it. He never made statements for the mere purpose of praise. But this time he sounded especially sincere.

"I thought," Johnny explained, "that an examination of the Eskimo's body might show what is wrong with Renny, Park Crater and Fogarty-Smith."

"It will," Doc said, "if anything will."

Johnny sat down and polished his monocle-magnifier while he thought.

"Doc," he said, "it begins to look as if this might make sense."

"The mystery came out of the Arctic in three steps," Doc said.

"That's what I mean," Johnny agreed.

"A dog was the first thing stricken," Doc said.

"The dog was food, but it got away. Perhaps the mystery needed food."

Johnny tucked his monocle in the vest pocket of his coat, then took it out again.

"I'll be superamalgamated!" he said.

Doc said, "And the Eskimo's clothes were taken, Let us say the mystery needed clothes."

Johnny pulled his necktie. "Uh—"

"And the mystery moved south a hundred miles, where it got Fogarty-Smith's plane. Let us say the mystery needed an airplane."

Johnny made a platter of his left hand, a fist of his right hand, and smacked the fist into the platter.

"Yes," he said, "but what did Park Crater have? What did the mystery take from Park Crater?"

"Park Crater had Toni Lash."

"The girl?"

"Toni Lash had become convinced she was in love with Park Crater. The mystery wanted to hire her to come to New York, seize me and bring me to Europe. Intending to marry Park Crater, Toni Lash would have refused. The mystery could see that. So the mystery made Park Crater insane."

Johnny ran fingers through his hair. He insisted on wearing his hair at scholastic length.

"Now the mystery," he said. "What is it?"

"I'm afraid," Doc Savage said, "that the answer is becoming obvious."

Johnny started.

"I'll be superamalgamated!" he exploded. "What's obvious? Name me one obvious thing about it!"

"John Sunlight," Doc Savage said.

Johnny's mouth worked without making words.

"John Sunlight!" he managed at last, incredulously.

Moving as stiffly as a medical skeleton with wired joints, he backed to a chair, folded down into it. His face was stark.

"But John Sunlight is dead!" he said hollowly.

Chapter XI
JOHN SUNLIGHT'S GHOST?

THE devil had walked into that room. The door had remained locked, the window screen was fastened, and outside the window a bird went on singing merrily, unfrightened by anything. But inside the room, a Satan stood; and he was as vivid to Johnny Littlejohn as if he stood there in reality, surrounded by the odor of brimstone, and leaning on his thin, three-tined pitchfork, his long tail with the spike on the end looped over his arm.

Two words had conjured the devil: John Sunlight.

Johnny Littlejohn had never seen John Sunlight. He had missed the grisly adventure of Doc Savage's fight with John Sunlight. That had been months ago. That was when Johnny had first gone to Egypt, and he had been there doing archaeological work throughout the frightful days when John Sunlight had descended on New York.

Johnny had missed the incredible incident of the Fortress of Solitude.

But John Sunlight was supposed to have died in the Arctic those many months ago—

There was sound of an automobile horn out in the street. Doc Savage went to the window and moved the curtain back.

"There is an ambulance down there in the street," the bronze man said.

"What—oh!" Johnny yanked himself together. "Oh—that—that must be Kummik!"

"Kummik?"

"Kummik, the Eskimo. His body, I mean. I asked the airport officials to engage an ambulance and send the body here."

"You gave out word of where I am staying?"

Johnny shook his head quickly. "No. I said I had not seen you in some time. I said the Eskimo was a mummy, an archaeological specimen I was bringing in from Africa. I didn't even mention the Arctic."

Johnny went downstairs, and shortly returned, followed by four strong men carrying an Eskimo *kayak,* or small skin boat, around which canvas had been wrapped.

The four men deposited the *kayak* on the floor and left.

"I put the body in a kayak," Johnny explained, "because it was the next thing to a coffin."

He began untying the walrus-hide thongs and lengths of airplane piano wire which held the canvas wrapping around the midships area of the *kayak.*

"Wait," Doc said.

"Eh?" Johnny stopped untying knots.

"You tied those thongs yourself?" Doc asked.

"Why—yes."

"You tie a regulation sailor's square knot, do you not?"

Johnny examined the knots. He looked a little queer.

"These aren't square knots," he said. "They're grannies. They've been changed."

IT was evening, and although they had not realized it, the sun had gone down and twilight had fallen. And now, suddenly, twilight became darkness, for a bank of clouds must have moved up in the west to cut off the remaining illumination from the sun.

London, a vast city around them, was making the low, contented traffic sounds of a metropolis. The bird had continued to sing merrily outside the window, but now it suddenly stopped. And the blackening night was very still for a few seconds. Then the bird flew away, flew with a wild hastening flutter of wings. After that, there was stillness again. It seemed tense.

"Doc!" Johnny blurted. "I feel—I feel—"

Inside the *kayak,* a whistle blew. It was a police whistle, piercingly loud even through the skin hull of the *kayak.*

Johnny jumped a generous yard. If an Eighteenth Dynasty mummy had sat up and thumbed its nose at him, he would not have been more astounded than he was to hear the police whistle blow inside the *kayak,* where the body of Kummik, the Eskimo, was supposed to be.

"Doc!" he exploded.

A door caved in crashingly, downstairs.

A rounded metal object hit the window, broke out enough glass to come inside, hit the floor, made a popping noise and began to smoke. A tear-gas bomb.

Someone inside the *kayak* began trying to get out.

Johnny said, "It looks like Fourth of July is coming."

He took a machine pistol out of an underarm holster.

"They got a line on us from the airport," he added. "And that was my fault."

He caught a tiny, compact gas mask as Doc tossed it to him. The bronze man was already at an equipment case.

Doc Savage then caught Johnny's arm, yanked him back into the second room of the little suite they had engaged.

"Any smokers in that machine pistol?" Doc asked.

Johnny nodded. "Half a drum."

"Shoot them out the window!" Doc ordered. "Make as much smoke around the house as possible."

Johnny nodded.

He exploded his first smoke pellet against the window sill. Instantly, a black wad of smoke appeared around the window. That concealed Johnny from view as he knocked out a glass windowpane, shoved his machine pistol through the window, held the trigger back, and switched the gun briefly. The gun made a deep, bull fiddle moan, sprayed bullets as a hose throws water.

That side of the inn became enveloped in smoke.

WHIRLING, Johnny saw that Doc Savage was back in the other room. He leaped to help with whatever the bronze man was doing. He could hear the raiders coming up the stairs.

Doc Savage had put on his gas mask—nose clip, breath purifier and goggles.

The bronze man stooped, picked up the *kayak* and whoever was kicking and pounding inside, trying to get out. He carried the *kayak* to the hall door, knocked the door open, shoved the *kayak* through.

Bullets arrived, three or four. One slug spanked through the *kayak*. And inside the *kayak,* a bull-voiced Asiatic began squalling.

"Don't shoot me, you fools!" howled the man in the *kayak*. He said it in his native tongue first, then in English.

No more shots came.

But charging men reached the stairs. They were big, ugly fellows, thick through the cheeks, with slanting eyes.

Johnny—he had donned his gas mask—smashed a dozen smoke slugs in their midst. They turned, dived back down the stairs. They must have thought the smoke contained poison gas.

Doc gestured at the hall windows. Johnny could reach them now with safety. He ran to them, and a moment later, that side of the inn, and the ground for fifty yards away, was under a rolling, tumbling, growing blanket of black smoke.

Doc carried the *kayak* and the man inside back into their rooms—into the innermost room where the tear gas was not so bad.

Having dropped the *kayak* on the floor, the bronze man jumped around, shouted, knocked over furniture—fight noises. Then he ran to the window, and came back on his tiptoes, silently.

He barked harsh words in the Asiatic tongue which the man in the *kayak* had spoken.

"They got out the window!" he rapped. "After them!"

He had faked a capture of the room by the raiders for the benefit of the man in the *kayak.*

Doc removed the remaining walrus-hide thongs, untwisted the piano wire and removed the canvas covering from the *kayak.* It was wise that he had deceived the man inside into thinking he was in the hands of his friends. The fellow had a gun.

Doc's fist made a metal-on-flesh sound, and the big Eurasian lay back senseless in the *kayak.*

JOHNNY sent another dozen smoke pellets out the window. He ran into the other room, closing the door to keep out the tear gas, and sprayed the hall and more windows.

Downstairs, a voice was saying many profane things in the Asiatic tongues. Johnny didn't need to understand the tongue to know the voice was urging a charge.

It was a safe guess that this raid had been staged on the assumption that the Eurasian substituted for the Eskimo's body in the *kayak* would get Doc and Johnny covered with a gun. Failure of that scheme had thrown the raid out of kilter.

Johnny leaped back into the room where he had left Doc.

The bronze man was heaving the senseless Eurasian up through a small attic trapdoor in the ceiling. Doc got the fellow out of sight, set the trapdoor back in place, dropped to the floor.

"Get Renny," Doc rapped. "Put him by the window."

Johnny lunged to the bed which stood in the room. Renny lay on the bed, incased in a strait-jacket, his huge fists jerking inside the stout canvas as his disarranged mind still sought to fight something in the air over his head.

Doc was in the *kayak*. The *kayak* was not a dozen feet long, very narrow, and there was little room. Doc lay flat in the thing, squirming.

"Replace the canvas and tie it," he directed. "Then take Renny and do your best to escape with him."

"Leave you here in the *kayak?* " Johnny exploded.

"Make it fast!"

"But—"

"Quick! Tie the piano wires so they can't be untied. They won't have pliers. They'll have to leave in a hurry because of the police, and they'll take me, *kayak* and all!"

Johnny grew pale.

"That's a frightful risk!" he croaked.

"We've got to find their hideout someway," Doc said.

Johnny rolled the canvas around the *kayak,* tied the walrus-hide thongs, knotted the piano wires so tightly they could never be untied without pliers. Knives would not cut that wire.

"Luck!" he said grimly. "You'll need it!"

"You will need some yourself," Doc said from inside the *kayak.*

Johnny gathered up Renny. The big-fisted engineer was a burden. Johnny had been flying many hours, and had not rested; so he was tired. He gasped a little, swung a leg over the window-sill, balanced himself and the straitjacketed Renny.

This was a second-floor window.

The whole world seemed black. The smoke from the little bullets had risen, spread. The attackers would never see him, if that would help. He hoped it would.

Thinking of something, Johnny changed drums on his machine pistol. He put in a drum of mercy bullets.

He hung by one hand, held Renny with the other hand. He was convinced the weight stretched his bony arm a foot. He dropped—and landed on a man.

IT was a very hard-bodied man. The fellow was waiting there for someone to try to escape by the window. He had a gun. It banged. Johnny clubbed with one fist, knocked the man away. There were shouts. Other men were near.

Johnny crouched, clamped down on the firing lever of his machine pistol, and swung a complete circle as quickly as he could, while the gun hooted. The weapon could spew slugs faster than a military machine gun, some of which fired as many as six hundred bullets a minute. He had to turn quickly, before the ammo drum ran empty.

His burst of mercy bullets got a satisfactory chorus of howls.

Gathering up Renny, Johnny ran. His direction sense was confused. He banged into the house wall. Straightening himself out, he headed away from the inn. If he could just find the alley—

He found the alley, turned down it, put on speed. He was out of the smoke now, and he snatched off the gas mask. He needed all the air he could get. He made a grim resolution, if they ever got out of this mess, to suggest strongly that Renny go in for reducing. The big-fisted engineer seemed to weigh tons, and was getting heavier.

Staggering a little, Johnny came out of the alley. The side street looked clear. He turned right, because the nearest corner was in that direction, and ran.

He rounded the corner.

A car was standing there. A man got out of the car quickly and pointed a pistol at Johnny. The man was squat, had long arms, a reddish face, tangled blond hair. His fingertips were masses of scar tissue where acid had removed his fingerprint identification Johnny stopped.

The man said, "I'm the one they call Cautious."

Johnny looked at the gun.

"Put the guy with the fists in the backseat," Cautious ordered. "Then I'll let you ride with me."

Johnny obeyed. He was glad to do so, in a way. He had been sure he would be shot.

Chapter XII
SKY PASSAGE

"I'LL be superamalgamated," Johnny said.

Cautious grinned over his gun, and slid behind the car wheel. The machine was a sedan.

"Yeah," Cautious said, "I figured you for that one."

The starter growled like a disturbed bulldog, then the motor began purring. Johnny sat over as far as he could on the same seat with Cautious and watched the latter's gun.

"What one?" Johnny asked.

"The one with the words," Cautious said.

"Oh."

The car began moving. Johnny kept his eyes on the other's weapon.

"You're fixin' to get a job digestin' lead," Cautious said, "the way you're watchin' this gun."

Johnny said nothing.

"You roll down that window and hang your head and shoulders outside," Cautious ordered. "It'll be better for your health."

Johnny complied with the request. The man was right. He was in a state of mind where he would consider doing anything.

The night had not yet arrived with enough darkness to make automobile headlights necessary, nor was it light enough to do without them; but rather the twilight was at about that stage which leads motorists to switch on their lights, then because of the apparent inadequateness of the beams, wonder if they do not need new bulbs.

The car traveled slowly around the block and stopped before the inn. None of the inn was visible, being hidden in the black smoke screen.

Four automobiles stood in the street. Big men with high cheekbones and slant eyes were getting in the cars. Johnny saw them load the body of Kummik, the Eskimo, into one machine.

More men ran in and out of the smoke. They shouted, swore. There was some kind of dilemma inside the inn.

Cautious poked Johnny in the ribs with the gun. "Just keep your head out of the manger!" he said.

Cautious drove up before the inn and stopped. Two big Eurasians dashed up to the machine.

"Hoon mooshkeleeman choon!" one of the Eurasians gobbled.

"Aw, now," Cautious said, "you know I don't sabe that lingo."

"I am in fix," the man translated.

"What kind of a fix?"

"Our man in skin boat—we no get him out chop-chop," the other explained.

"Bring boat and all," Cautious ordered.

The Eurasian tore back into the house. A

moment later they came out with the *kayak,* placed it lengthwise on a touring car which had the top down. The cars all moved. Men held the *kayak* in place.

Johnny watched the inn drop behind. He could hear police sirens yammering in the distance, their sounds making him think of the coyotes that he had heard on the Wyoming range. The night was no darker, which did not seem reasonable, for Johnny had the feeling that hours had passed since the attack began. Actually it had only been minutes, because everything had happened with blinding speed.

Cautious had been listening to the police sirens. He shook his head, clucked uneasily.

The cars, the entire procession of them, had a definite destination. They lost no time in making for it.

The machines all stopped in a bit of grassy woodland which seemed to be a park. It was too dark to tell the exact nature of the place, and there were no lights of houses visible.

A FLASHLIGHT blazed against Johnny's face.

"That's one of them," Toni Lash's voice said. "But where are the others?"

Cautious made a sour noise.

"Doc Savage got away," he advised.

"How?"

"They made so much smoke around the place that the whole Chinese army could've escaped!" Cautious explained. "But we got this Johnny, and the big-fisted engineer called Renny." He was silent a moment, listening to the caterwaul of police sirens. "And we got trouble, it looks like. Hear it?"

Someone came up and issued orders. The speaker was a Eurasian, wider and taller than any of the others. He seemed to be in charge.

"The planes," he said in English. "We get in planes."

The girl was obviously surprised. "But I thought—"

"We leave England now," the Eurasian said.

The girl stamped her foot.

"I thought we were to stay until we got Doc Savage," she said.

The big Eurasian shook his head and scowled.

"I get order by radio from Genghis," he growled. "Order say leave."

"So you're going to give up trying to get Doc Savage!"

The Eurasian shrugged.

"Chalo!" he said. "Let us go."

The girl was startled. A visible tightness came over her. "I'm not going!" she said.

The Eurasian looked at her with slant-eyed inscrutability.

"The Genghis," he said, "orders you brought along."

The Eurasian was either a man of few words, or the increasing nearness of the police sirens chased away his patience. He barked orders, and more of his men appeared and also produced guns.

Toni Lash and Cautious walked away from the car. The Eurasians herded Johnny along, and more of them carried Renny's big form. The route led down a gently sloping bank to water, evidently a lake.

Little waves sloshed in the reeds that lined the bank, and a few yards offshore, the waves slapped against the thin metal skins of big amphibian planes. There were three of the planes, all large, modern, fast.

There was a great deal of splashing as everybody waded into the lake up to their waists and climbed into the aircraft.

Cautious got a chance to whisper to Toni Lash.

"What the blazes has this turned into?" Cautious demanded

The girl shook her head. She seemed frightened. "It don't look so good," she admitted.

"It looks like you have been demoted."

"The Genghis," she said grimly, "must be peeved about our repeated failures to get Doc Savage."

"In that case," Cautious said, "woe is us!"

The mixed crew of Asiatics and Eurasians were having trouble with the *kayak* containing, as they thought, their comrade. Inside the *kayak,* the "comrade" was abusing them in their native language.

"Toonkaman putavo!" he howled. "Hurry up! Get me out of here!"

Johnny decided Doc Savage was doing a very good job of acting inside the *kayak.*

By kinking the *kayak* in the middle with main strength—Doc Savage did a lot of roaring at that—they got the Eskimo's skin boat into a plane cabin. The planes took off.

JOHNNY, to his profound disgust, was confined in a different plane from the one which took off with the *kayak.* Renny was with Johnny.

Cautious was in the second plane.

Toni Lash rode in the ship which contained the *kayak.* Also in the craft which the young woman rode was the body of Kummik, the Eskimo.

The young woman saw this as she looked around. One of the Eurasians had propped Kummik up in the seat. Kummik had thawed out, but he looked like a very recent fatality, thanks to the preserving qualities of the Arctic cold.

The girl shuddered, and dropped into a seat. She fell to watching the *kayak.*

She saw a man kick the *kayak,* make the tight skin covering of the thing thump like a drum.

The voice inside the *kayak* bellowed a protest.

"Let me out of here!" the voice snarled.

The man kicked the *kayak* again.

"You fool!" he said. "You failed to hold Doc Savage at the point of a gun. It was because of you that he escaped."

The voice inside the *kayak* promised to take the other man's ears and tie them together under his chin—once he got out of the *kayak.*

The other laughed and flung himself in a seat. They had decided to let their associate stay in the *kayak* as a measure of punishment for his part in the fiasco at the inn.

Toni Lash fell to staring out the window. The plane had been climbing through the fog, and now it came out above the fog, into a brilliant silver moonlight which made the surface of the fog appear as an expanse of snow that spread for countless miles.

The plane climbed, and the motors moaned steadily. The ship gave a sharp little dip to the left as a down current caught that wing. The pilot leveled off again. Later, and at intervals for hours thereafter, the plane kept hitting air bumps, and the sensation was something like being in a car which was running into low ridges of soft sand that had drifted across a smooth highway.

The other two planes climbed up and flew abreast of this ship, and the three craft went roaring

Doc Savage got clear of the canvas.

across the English Channel and across Europe like big metal geese.

The voice inside the *kayak* had fallen silent.

Some hours later, another plane came up and buzzed around them. It was a small, fast, military pursuit ship which carried on its wings and fuselage the insignia of the Soviet army. The pilot made signals for them to descend, and fired a warning burst of tracer bullets.

Toni Lash knew they were flying over Soviet territory forbidden to planes, and she held her lower lip tightly with her teeth, wondering what the warplane would do.

The little fighter gave up the chase, dropped away, and was lost in the night.

After that, Toni Lash sat with her shapely chin cupped in a palm. She was thinking. It struck her that this was the first time recently that she had really been able to think. All the rest of the time, she had been hypnotized, in a sense, by the excitement of doing things. She liked excitement, or had always liked it in the past. But now she was beginning to wonder. She thought of Park Crater, of how pleasant he had been during those days on the Riviera.

Park Crater, she knew, was in one of those three planes. Which one, she did not know. It might even be this one. There was a compartment in the rear.

She was very still, thinking of Park Crater— she slowly grew tense, and her fingers bit fiercely at her cheeks; then realizing what she was doing, she took her fingers away and rubbed the small aching pits which her fingertips had pressed into her cheeks.

Suddenly she stood up, intending to go back and see if Park Crater were aboard this plane.

But a big Asiatic heaved up and scowled. The fellow's head was like an ivory cannonball. He had a beard, but it did not appear to consist of more than twenty hairs, and each was about two inches long.

"Uhin ruho!" the Asiatic said. "Stay here."

TONI LASH had a magnetic power, an ability to dominate. It was, she had always hoped, something in addition to her amazing beauty. There had been few times in her rather remarkable career when it had failed her.

"Bus!" she said sharply. "That will do!"

The man scowled.

"The Genghis," he growled, "said you were to be brought to him."

The girl showed scorn with her chin.

"Somewhere there is a donkey who has no brains," she snapped, "because he gave them to you."

The man shrugged. "A donkey that is hitched to a cart knows what will happen if he stops pulling."

"I also work for the Genghis," Toni Lash pointed out angrily. "He gave me a great mission. All he will ever hand you is a sword. Who are you to give me orders?"

The Asiatic was not as impressed as he should have been.

"With the sword handed me, I am a success," he growled.

Toni Lash stamped a foot.

"You let Doc Savage escape!" she retorted. "You and the others at the inn. The bronze man got away from you. When that is known, do you think the Genghis will stroke your long ears and turn you out to graze in donkey heaven?"

That gave the sparse-bearded Asiatic something to think about. He hitched at his belt uneasily.

"Muhesh!" he exploded. "It was a wise man who said that thornbushes and women grew from the same seed."

He made some faces, and came out loser in a staring match with Toni Lash, after which he felt a need of something to divert the young woman's anger from himself.

He decided to open the *kayak* and release the comrade he supposed was inside.

He went forward to the pilot's compartment, got a pair of pliers from the tool kit, and came back to cut the airplane piano wire which Johnny had tied so tightly around the canvas and the *kayak*.

Inside the *kayak*, Doc Savage made a snarling noise. He was still imitating, as exactly as he could, the voice of the man who had originally occupied the *kayak*.

"You will behave yourself when I release you," warned the voice of the man who was freeing him.

"Na!" Doc said explosively. "For keeping me in here, you shall have the pleasure of eating your own ears."

Doc was in a very tight spot. He knew that. He had no desire to be released just yet. So he made the threat sound as real as he could.

But the man outside either wasn't scared, or felt he had to show Toni Lash he was not afraid.

There was a metallic click.

"I have in my hand a gun," the Asiatic's voice said. "It is a wise rabbit which can recognize a wolf."

The canvas moved as the Asiatic started to whip it off.

Doc Savage came up with the canvas, trying to keep behind it, taking the long chance that he might fall upon the other man and the fellow would not shoot one he thought a comrade, before Doc got his gun.

Whether the man would have shot or not remained forever a mystery.

There was a gasp. A jar as the Asiatic fell. A shot.

Doc Savage got clear of the canvas and saw that Toni Lash had shoved the Asiatic, had pounced upon him, and had snatched his gun.

The girl leaped to her feet with the man's pistol. "I thought it was your voice!" she gasped.

She offered the gun to Doc Savage.

Chapter XIII
THE STOP-OFF

THERE was one thing that Doc Savage had always known he could not do, and he had never tried to do it, and right now he was glad he had never tried. He couldn't figure how a woman would act next.

He said, "Keep the gun."

Then he went forward, his destination the pilot's cockpit—the heart and brains of the plane.

There were six more men in the cabin seats, all of them Asiatics. He went plunging past them—they began leaping up and clawing for weapons—and hit the cockpit door. The pilot's compartment was closed off from the cabin, after the fashion of an airliner. He got the door open, dived inside.

The pilot was a beefy white man. When he turned his head, his teeth were showing. They were big, white false teeth. In each of the pilot's cheeks was a bullet scar which explained why he had to wear false teeth—his original teeth had been shot out of his mouth at some time in the past.

Doc clamped hands on the man, yanked him out of the seat. The fellow was strong. They fought, got down among the controls, broke some glass dials out of the instrument panel. Doc was stiff from being in the *kayak* so long.

Then Doc got the pilot's gun out of a belt holster and hurled the flier back into the cabin. The man went staggering, fell flat on his back.

The plane nosed down and went bawling for the earth.

Doc yanked at the control wheel. The plane's nose came up. Centrifugal force jammed the bronze man down in the pilot's seat. Strain made the plane wings bend. Then earth and sky had changed places, and the plane lay on its back, almost motionless.

Back in the cabin, there were howls and thumps—and the human cargo landed on their heads on what had been the ceiling.

Doc looked back. The cabin lights were on. He saw a hand sticking up, holding a gun. He fired once, hardly seeming to aim. The gun flew out of the hand, and the hand looked different.

The plane fell off, began a tailspin. Doc helped the spin along with the controls, the motors. Over and over, around and around, the ship gyrated. In the cabin, the Asiatics rattled around like whatever it is that makes the noise in a Spanish dancer's castanets.

Then he pulled out of the spin, put the nose of the plane straight down. Men came tumbling forward in the cabin, and three parachute packs and a man landed in the cockpit.

Doc clubbed the man with a fist. He came back on the wheel, and the big plane stood on its nose; men went piling toward the cabin rear, parachute packs hopping after them like playful pups.

A few shots had sounded, but had done nothing but make holes in the cabin.

The 'chutes gave Doc an idea. He could not go on with this forever.

He leveled the plane suddenly, and turning with the pilot's pistol, broke two arms deliberately.

"Put on the parachutes!" he shouted. "Jump!"

PROBABLY a combination of things made them take the order. These Asiatics were fierce hill fighters, at home on the back of a war pony, and the air was not their element. They had been treated to enough gymnastics from the plane to scare them badly.

Toni Lash stood erect in the rear of the cabin. She was disheveled, but she still had her gun. She pointed the weapon at the cabin occupants.

"Get the 'chutes on!" she ordered.

Her voice carried to the bronze man. The cabin of this plane, like the modern ships, was soundproofed.

A menace at either end of the cabin, and one of the menaces in control of the plane, decided the Asiatics and the beefy white pilot.

They put on the parachutes. There seemed to be enough 'chutes to go around.

At that point, Doc Savage made mental note of a rather surprising fact. The Asiatics all knew how to don the 'chutes. Not only that—it was evident they'd had training in parachute jumping.

That seemed a little unusual.

Out of the plane door they went, one after another. Doc watched them; realized that every man counted the exact regulation ten before he yanked the ripcord. Yes, they'd had 'chute training.

Eight white mushrooms floated below in the moonlight. That accounted for all the men, including the pilot. Toni Lash came forward and fell into the co-pilot's seat. She pointed. "It isn't over yet!" she gasped.

It wasn't. The other two planes—they had been circling, puzzled. But now their pilots guessed the truth, and they arched around, came diving.

Red whiskers of tracer bullets stuck out from machine guns in the ships. Six red whiskers from each ship. They were heavily armed.

Doc rolled his ship. Huge as it was, it handled easily. This was a warplane.

Phosphorus-laden tracers rattled on the right wing, mixed with yammering lead. Probably every fifth bullet was a tracer; the others plain, jacketed lead killers.

The yammering stopped. They were clear. Up and over went the big ship in an Immelmann turn—and the other two planes banked wildly to get Doc's ship back in their crossed sight wires.

Toni Lash sat tight in the other seat.

Doc felt for the Bowden trigger controls of his own guns, squeezed them briefly. The guns gobbled loudly. He fired only a short burst, to warm the weapons, soften the oil in their actions.

"You'd better be good," Toni Lash said grimly. "The Genghis has hired the best fighting pilots in the world. He pays them a thousand dollars a week, cash."

Doc had already realized he'd better be good.

RED yarns of tracer bullets stretched for them again. After the tracers passed, and went on ahead, they looked like fleeing red stars. Doc watched them.

He whipstalled. Brought the plane up, hung it by its baying nose, until the stars stood still in front of their eyes. Just before the big ship stalled, he let it reel off on one wing in a steep bank.

Now the other two ships were almost upon them. Doc took his time, got his ship turning slowly, aiming—then he came down on the firing levers. His guns clamored. He corrected a little by the tracers. His lead began eating holes in the right wing of one of the other crates.

The pilot rolled, got clear—then the ships were past. This fighting was done at well over two hundred miles an hour. It was lightning-fast business. Stab and go.

Doc wrenched the wheel, stamped the rudder, knocked the throttles wide. He got the tail of the plane to the left. Tracers raced at him. The other thing was a flying fortress.

There is a saying among combat pilots that the plane has never been built which does not have a blind spot, and Doc knew the design of these ships. He found it, hung on, kept batting the throttles with a palm to get them open their widest. He gained.

He drove a stream of lead into the streamlined cowling on one of the other ship's motors. Only a momentary burst. Then the other plane jumped up in a tight loop. But it scared the pilot.

In his present position, the bronze man could hang onto the tail of the other ship until gas gave out. But there was another enemy plane—and its lead began hammering at the cabin.

Doc banked away, as if seeking safety, then executed half an Immelmann and a wingover, and was, instantaneously, it seemed, nose to nose with the attacking ship.

Like fighting eagles, the planes charged head-on.

Toni Lash suddenly covered her eyes.

There was a jar. A report, really. Objects striking at four hundred miles an hour hit fast. And the combined speed of both planes was near that.

Doc looked back, wrenching open the cockpit window to do so, and examined his tailskid wheel. It was gone. Then he glanced at the other plane. There was a great rent in one of its wings where the tailskid had struck.

The three planes arched far apart in the sky.

Suddenly, a Very pistol ball climbed from one of the planes, burned red. The two pilots evidently had their code of signals, for both gave up the fight.

The two planes turned, pointed noses downward, and dived for safety.

Clouds were spread over the earth, a solid expanse, and these vapor masses swallowed the two planes.

Doc knew enough about flying to realize the uselessness of trying to follow them.

THE bronze man flew back, scanning the nodulose masses of cloud. He was seeking the spot—he had marked it by an upflung formation on the cloud surface, where the men in the parachutes had gone overboard.

Locating the spot, he went down. The clouds took him in, and it was very dark. He watched the altimeter.

"Know where we are?" he asked.

"Somewhere near Afghanistan, I should judge," Toni Lash said.

That did not help. There might be mountains below. The altimeter read sixteen thousand, but there were mountains in Asia higher than that.

Doc searched in the cockpit compartments, and found a parachute flare. He put that over the side, and followed it, spiraling slowly. The flare made a gray blur, and he kept above it.

Abruptly the light of the flare spread over a great area. It had dropped below the clouds.

There were mountains down there. Mountains that looked like the magnified tracks in the dried mud that animals make around a jungle water hole. No place down there for a landing.

"We'll have to let the fellows who used the parachutes take their chances with the natives," Doc decided.

He climbed the plane back through the strata of clouds. The moonlight hit the plane with rich silver when they came above the clouds, and the bronze man leveled. The compass dial had been broken during the fight. He consulted the heavens, spotted the Dipper, then Polaris, the North Star.

"What direction?" he asked the girl.

"East," she said.

The plane engines seemed to make a little more noise, but that was probably due to the bullet holes in the cabin. Also, out on one wing, a strip of metal skin fabric, bullet loosened, whipped in the wind and vibrated until it tore loose. The roaring rush of air got under edges of the rent, and there was violin-like humming. Suddenly, with a ripping report, another section of skin fabric came off.

"That is the trouble with metal covering on modern planes," Doc Savage said.

He decreased their pace to bare flying speed, kept an eye on the clouds below, watching for a gap in the floor. Sensible thing to do was to land, check over the plane.

Off to the west, he discovered the cloud field ended. He sent the plane in that direction, slid over the edge of the clouds and spiraled down.

There was desert, floor-smooth. He flew close to it, dropped a flare, and cranked down the retractable landing gear. His landing was good, for the sand was amply hard and the missing tail-skid wheel did not bother.

Doc began looking over the plane.

Monk and Ham, gagged, lay in the rear compartment. They were incased in straitjackets.

Chapter XIV
THE GENGHIS

MONK and Ham, in the straitjackets, looked like two stuffed canvas sacks—Monk a wide sack, and Ham a slightly longer and much thinner sack. Their gags were the most effective type, a dozen or more strips of adhesive tape which held wads of cloth in their mouths.

Doc Savage, looking at them, was suddenly tense with worry.

Monk and Ham were heaving with their arms, and it was very much as if they were striving to strike out at something unseen in the air above them.

The desert sand around the plane was almost as white as chalk dust, and the brilliant moonlight enhanced this whiteness. There was a wind, and it blew the fine sand along in little whirls that sometimes looked like white animals scurrying. The sand brushed against the metal of the plane with a ghostly whispering, and slowly filled the long,

strange-looking marks made by the plane's two fat tires, and the dragging, wheelless tail. In the east, a mile or two away, the clouds, over which they had been flying, lay like a herd of black sheep in the sky.

Except for the night wind and the whispering sand, there was everywhere the strange, breathless silence of deserts. A lifeless, abysmal quiet, depressing and unnerving.

When Doc Savage banged a plane door open to lift Monk and Ham out on the sand, still in their straitjackets, the noise the plane door made seemed to go a long distance and come back, in echoes, as of several plane doors banging open.

The bronze man somehow seemed larger than usual, an effect that came probably from the fact that he was in shirtsleeves. He wore dark trousers, a black shirt and black house slippers—the garb he had been wearing when surprised in the London inn.

Monk and Ham, when they were lowered on the sand, flounced about in the straitjackets.

Toni Lash got out of the plane. She watched Monk and Ham steadily, and there was horror on her face. She stood with her back against the side of the plane, her arms down rigid at her side, her lips parted slightly, and continued to watch Monk and Ham.

Doc Savage plucked off the gags.

"You mighta let us loose," Monk said indignantly, "so we coulda got in that fight!"

"Oh!" Toni Lash said.

She folded down on the sand in a faint.

DOC SAVAGE released the two men; they got up, but sat down again quickly, finding that confinement in the straitjackets had more or less ossified their muscles.

"Blazes!" Monk squeaked. "My legs have been asleep for a week."

Ham pointed at the girl. "What keeled her over?" he demanded.

"She was afraid you were insane," Doc explained.

Ham thought back over the incidents leading up to their downfall on board the liner *Maritonia*.

"I'm not surprised she should think Monk was nuts," the dapper lawyer said.

"How long have you been in the straitjackets, and gagged?" Doc asked.

"Ever since we clowned ourselves into being captured on the liner," Monk explained. The homely chemist eyed Doc Savage. "What did you mean—she thought we were insane?"

Doc Savage gave a clipped but complete description of what had happened. He told them how the trail had led to Park Crater who was mad, and who had been seized; of how the next clue was Fogarty-Smith, who had also been whisked away.

"That's all news to us," Ham said grimly. "They kept us tied up. In dark rooms most of the time."

"Did you overhear anything of value?" Doc asked.

Ham shook his head. "Nothing."

Doc Savage's metallic features were thoughtful in the moonlight.

"How did the girl manage to get you off the *Maritonia?*"

Ham grimaced, shook his head again.

"We don't know," he said. "She made us drink something that put us to sleep. When we woke up, we were in a dark room on dry land."

"That part sure puzzles me," Monk complained.

Doc Savage went to the girl, who was stirring a little. He rubbed her wrists to help the reviving along. She sat up finally, coughed a few times weakly, then buried her face in her hands and remained in that position for a time.

"I believe," she said quietly, "that is the first time I ever fainted."

Doc Savage had been thinking, and he had evolved a theory which might explain the way the girl had turned to his side.

"It was just beginning to dawn on you," he said, "that the Genghis made Park Crater insane."

The girl looked at him strangely, then nodded.

"Yes," she said. "Sitting there in the plane tonight, that came to me."

"Give us your story," Doc directed.

The girl nodded. "There's not much to it," she said in a low voice. "I was on the Riviera. I guess I was in love with Park Crater. I met the Genghis, but that first time we met, he didn't suggest that I work for him."

"The Genghis," Doc said, "is clever."

"Very clever," the girl agreed grimly. "He must have seen that I liked Park Crater, and intended to marry him—Anyway, Park Crater went—well, insane. I was grief-stricken. And when the Genghis offered to hire me, I took the job."

"And the job?"

"Was to come to New York, seize you, bring you to a Mediterranean port and turn you over to the Genghis' men. I hired Cautious to help me, and he engaged those other men in New York."

"What gets me," Monk put in, "is how you got us off that liner."

"I'll get to that." The girl looked at them, then dropped her eyes to the sand, and picked up white sand with both hands and let it sift through her fingers. "I've been an international spy for years. I have"—she grimaced a little—"rather a reputation as an espionage agent. Cautious had worked for me in the past. That was why I hired him." She looked up grimly.

"It was while doing espionage that I first met the Genghis," she said.

Doc Savage spoke quietly. "John Sunlight, you mean?" he said.

"Yes—John Sunlight is the Genghis."

HOMELY Monk came up off the sand as if dynamite had exploded in his hip pockets.

"John Sunlight!" he yelled. *"But he is dead!"*

Doc Savage shook his head.

"John Sunlight did not die on the Arctic ice that time."

They were all very still. The desert wind swept the white sand against them with gentle whisperings. The moonlight suddenly faded, for the cloud bank had crept closer and edged between the moon and themselves, and the clouds were not like dark sheep now, but seemed to have become huge, skulking monsters.

They were thinking, Doc Savage and his two men, of John Sunlight.

John Sunlight was one of the strangest, most sinister men they had ever encountered. Whether his real name was John Sunlight, no one knew, just as his past had always been more or less a mystery. He was a schemer, a plotter, a creature with a diabolically inhuman mind. The world knew that. A fantastic man, gaunt and bony, with the face and eyes of a poet, the ambitions of a Napoleon, the principles of a fiend. A man who liked to wear fantastic costumes of solid colors, changing them several times daily. A man who looked weak, but who had the strength of a Sandow in his hands. A man who liked to destroy souls, but who never destroyed a body—John Sunlight never killed a man if he could help it.

John Sunlight did not kill—he did the kind of things to his victims that he had done to Renny, Park Crater, Fogarty-Smith and Kummik, the Eskimo.

The world had first heard of John Sunlight when Soviet Russia sent him to a Siberian prison, from which he escaped with others in an ice-breaker which drifted across the polar regions with the Arctic ice—and was wrecked on the island where Doc Savage had his Fortress of Solitude.

It was unfortunate that John Sunlight was the man who found Doc Savage's Fortress of Solitude. The Fortress of Solitude was unusual. It was a sanctuary which Doc Savage had constructed for himself in the Arctic. It was where the bronze man went to study, to work out scientific experiments.

But most unfortunate of all, it was in the Fortress of Solitude that Doc Savage had stored inventions which were too grim to be in the hands of men.

War machines—death rays, hideous gases, fantastic weapons against which there was no defense—these were the kinds of things he had stored in the Fortress of Solitude. For the place was remote, and no one had known of its existence except the bronze man himself, and a few Eskimos who served as attendants.

Armed with the fantastic weapons he had found in the Fortress of Solitude, John Sunlight had descended upon New York. The fight that had followed was one Doc Savage and his men would never forget, and it ended—they had thought—when John Sunlight had been driven back to the Arctic and his followers overpowered, and the master fiend himself had fled into the polar ice wastes.

There had been almost undisputable evidence that John Sunlight had died. They had trailed him, and on the ice beside an open lead of water, they had found where a polar bear had set upon John Sunlight. There had been gore, scattered fragments of John Sunlight's clothing. They had thought John Sunlight had died there.

Monk broke the long, unpleasantly thoughtful silence.

"What gets me," he told Toni Lash, "is how you got us off that liner?"

"I radioed the Genghis' planes where to pick us up," the girl explained. "Then we went overboard with life preservers and a Very flare pistol with which to signal the planes. They picked us up."

MONK sat down on the sand again and treated himself to a belated shiver, thinking how large the Mediterranean was, and what would have happened if the plane which the girl summoned had not found them.

Doc Savage's flake gold eyes were steady on Toni Lash.

"What is John Sunlight—or the Genghis—trying to do?" he asked.

The girl shook her head miserably. "I do not know."

"He has those Asiatics helping him," Doc reminded.

She nodded. "He has established headquarters in the mountains beyond Afghanistan. That much I know. And those Asiatics—they are fierce, cruel warriors—obey his orders implicitly."

"The planes?"

"He has bought at least fifty of those big warplanes, and hired skilled war pilots to fly them. I told you that."

Ham had been listening with the attentive interest of a lawyer hearing the opposition outline an important case, at times giving his disheveled clothing a regretful examination. Rarely did a predicament become serious enough to make him forget his clothes-consciousness.

"As I see it," Ham said, "there are three things to be cleared up."

Monk eyed him. "What three, shyster?"

Ham held up one finger. "First, what is John Sunlight up to?"

He held up a second finger. "Second, what did John Sunlight do to Renny, Park Crater, Fogarty-Smith and Kummik, the Eskimo?"

Up went a third finger. "And why did John Sunlight want to get hold of Doc?"

Monk snorted.

"As far as I am concerned, there's not enough fingers in the crowd to illustrate the things I don't understand."

Doc Savage walked slowly around the plane, as though he wanted to think, to assemble the situation in his mind and analyze it. His metallic features were grave, and he made his tiny, exotic, trilling sound that indicated mental stress. The note had a tense quality.

The bronze man came back to the others. His flake-gold eyes went to Monk and Ham.

"You remember," he said, "the other trouble we had with John Sunlight?"

Monk pulled his homely face into a wry shape.

"I'll never forget!" he grunted.

"After it was all over, and we thought John Sunlight was dead, and when we searched the Fortress of Solitude"—the bronze man spread both hands palm upward—"we discovered that John Sunlight had removed many of the deadly inventions stored there."

"Sure," Monk agreed. "He'd been sellin' 'em to Balkan nations to raise money. But we put a stop to that."

"But we never did find many of the missing inventions," Doc repeated.

Ham had been rubbing his jaw; now he looked startled and took a step forward.

"Doc!" he yelled. "You mean that John Sunlight escaped from the Arctic, went back and got the inventions from someplace where he'd hidden them?"

"It begins to look that way," Doc admitted.

"In that case," Ham said grimly, "I can see where we're in for plenty of trouble."

Monk muttered, "We gotta get Johnny an' Renny away from that Devil Genghis, or whatever John Sunlight calls himself."

Toni Lash went to Doc Savage. She put both hands on the bronze man's arm.

"May I ask something?" she said in a low voice. Doc nodded.

"Let me help with this," the girl requested in a tight voice. "It was because of me that Park Crater is—well, I owe it to him to help all I can."

"We are going to need plenty of help," Doc Savage said quietly.

"Have you any kind of plan?" the girl asked.

"It might not be feasible to fly directly to John Sunlight's headquarters."

She shook her head sharply. "Suicide! He has thousands of Asiatic hill warriors as followers."

"Then there is another scheme we might try," the bronze man said.

Chapter XV
THE RIVAL GENGHIS

IT is said that the first principle of civilization is to live in peace with your neighbor—that every great war sets civilization back fifty years.

If this be, then there exists a region in Asia where civilization has a hopeless handicap. This spot is located in a mountainous section not far from Afghanistan—which is not exactly a land of peace itself—and also not distant from Tibet, where every man carries a rifle and, if he be true Tibetan gentleman, shoots at every stranger on sight.

In this section, civilization probably gets its fifty-year setback on a fortnightly average.

It is a mountainous district. A sheer five-thousand-foot cliff calls for no more comment than a cut bank beside a creek in Missouri. These mountains are bare, the principal vegetation being a scrubby sage called *tushkin,* and much of the year there is snow. They are great brown-and-red mountains, resembling Arizona's, except for the almost perpetual snow. There is little game, except for *ram chikor,* the snow partridge which clucks and whistles high on the stony steppes.

There are no roads, hence no automobiles, and one rarely encounters an *arabas,* or the lighter type of two-wheeled cart called *mapas.* Almost all traveling is done on the backs of wiry little Himalayan ponies called *tats,* or astride sure-footed yaks.

Two yaks and a pony were wallowing through the snow which choked a high mountain pass. The three animals crossed the pass and labored down into a deep *jilga,* a narrow and rocky valley.

The two yaks were ridden by men. A woman rode the pony. The men wore *pushtins,* the voluminous fleece-lined leather coats of Russian style, as well as felt boots, and they were wrapped in the yak felt coverings of *yurts,* for it was very cold. The woman wore a *burkha,* the long garment

favored by the women of India—styles had a way of traveling here, too—under heavy, fur outer garments. Her face was veiled.

As a protection against sun reflection from the blinding snow, the two men had tied strands of horsehair over their eyes, to shut out the glare. Snow blindness was a terrible thing here in this fierce land, where a man might need his eyes at any instant to look over his gun sights at an enemy.

The man riding the yak had been having his difficulties. He did not like yaks, and apparently the yak returned the sentiment.

The man resented the yak's natural gait, which seemed to consist of a trot with the front legs and a walk with the back legs.

"I been on these things before!" the man complained in a squeaky voice. "And I don't like 'em no better'n the first time!"

At this, the yak stopped. The rider drummed the creature's ribs vainly with his heels, then tugged on the rope attached to a ring in the yak's nose, but the yak's nose only stretched like rubber.

The rider rested both feet on the yak's horns, which stuck out like handle bars.

"By rights," he said, "Ham oughta be ridin' this mountain-climbin' buffalo."

"Monk, you matched him to see who would get the other pony," remarked the man riding the other yak, "and you lost."

"I know, Doc," Monk grumbled. "But I'm still tryin' to figure out that gleam Ham had in his eye when we was matchin'. I think he flimflammed me. I wonder if he used a trick coin?"

The woman spoke. "I don't believe he did."

"What d'you mean, Miss Lash?" Monk asked.

"Well, I saw Ham slip two coins out of your pockets, and I think he used one of them when you matched to see who would ride the yak."

Monk groaned.

"Them coins was my phonies!" he yelled. "I been rookin' Ham for months with 'em! Wait'll I get my hands on that shyster! Robbin' me like that!"

DOC SAVAGE, Monk and Toni Lash camped that evening in a *nullah,* a point where two canyons intersected. Monk unlashed a bundle of sticks—wood was almost as scarce here as it was in the Arctic—and tied the sticks together to make a framework over which they stretched felt coverings to form a *yurt.*

All three of them were disguised as Kalpaks, the fierce warriors of the north who were of Mongol descent. They hoped the disguises would suffice, and had reason to believe they would, judging from their success with such natives as they had encountered.

Monk drew a short sword, began to cut *tushkin* to make a fire. All of them carried so many weapons that they resembled armament salesmen traveling with samples.

"This scheme we're tryin'," Monk grumbled, "seems kinda slow to me."

Doc Savage nodded. "True. But we're four people against John Sunlight and thousands of men who have made a life business of fighting."

"As I said," Toni Lash put in, "it would have been suicide to fly in and try out-and-out fighting."

Monk jerked at a stem of tough sage.

"This Genghis, as John Sunlight calls himself, is hirin' combat fliers," he pointed out. "We coulda qualified, an' maybe got jobs with him."

Doc said, "He is clever enough to suspect that is exactly what we would do."

"You don't think he'll suspect this scheme?"

"Let us hope not." Doc Savage fell to studying the yaks thoughtfully, then changed the subject by reminding, "We get part of our supper by milking these yaks."

Monk grinned. "Well, Doc, since you're an old yak milker, it's up—"

"On the contrary," the bronze man said, "I never milked a yak in my life."

"Match you."

"Right."

They matched, and Monk lost. The homely chemist set about his yak milking. In a chemical laboratory, Monk could extract a very creditable imitation diamond from a lump of coal, but at the end of half an hour he had more yak milk on the ground and on himself than he had in his bucket.

"Fooey on this goin' native business!" he said disgustedly.

They ate raisins, dried apricots and the kernels of apricot stones which tasted like almonds, and brewed the buttered tea which was a staple of this section and of Tibet.

A small bevy of rifle bullets arrived during the last course.

MONK spilled hot buttered tea down the front of his *pushtin,* went over backward, hit the ground and came up with his rifle. Monk's rifle had been acquired for purposes of reality, and it was a huge thing, a muzzle loader with an octagon barrel that had a slight twist instead of rifling, and was so heavy that a pitchfork-shaped rest for the barrel was accessory equipment. Monk had not yet fired the blunderbuss, but he had been looking forward to it, he'd explained.

He raked a smoldering stick out of the fire. You had to have one of these, or a cigarette, to fire Monk's gun.

More bullets hit. The slugs glanced off stones with violinlike noises.

"In them rocks yonder!" Monk grunted.

In the dusk, they could see the rifle flashes. The scarlet tongues were jumping from a clump of boulders about two hundred yards distant, higher up on the slope.

A volley of fierce yelling sounded from the men who were doing the shooting.

"Do we shoot back?" Monk demanded.

"That seems to be the custom here," Doc advised.

Monk wriggled around with his gun, placed the forked rest for the barrel, aimed the piece, and fanned his smoldering stick to get the end glowing red.

"This is the way our ancestors fought the Indians," he explained.

He jammed the hot end of the stick in the match hole of his blunderbuss. Promptly, there was an earsplitting roar, and a cloud of powder smoke which enveloped the camp. The wind blew the smoke away. Monk and his gun were lying some distance apart.

"Who done that?" Monk asked feebly.

Either Monk's blunderbuss, or the slugs which Doc Savage and Toni Lash were driving from ancient Chinese military rifles, had an effect. The firing from the boulders stopped.

There was a piercing yell. To Monk, who did not understand the language, it sounded as though a wolf were howling.

"They want to come down and have dinner with us," Doc explained.

"They picked a fine way of openin' negotiations for dinner," Monk grunted.

"Oh, that is the custom of the country! They were just shooting in hopes of making us run off and leave our belongings. Now that they see we did not run, they consider us brave enough to be worth visiting."

Monk said something under his breath.

"I see I'm gonna like this country," he said skeptically.

Then he thought of something else, and turned suddenly anxious.

"I hope Ham makes it all right with his part of this job!" the homely chemist muttered.

THE hill fighters now arrived. They had mounted their ponies and rode up at a dead run, screeching at full lung capacity, so that the effect was about the same as that of the Indians coming into the big top in a Wild West show. Except that these fellows looked rather deadly.

Around and around the camp, the hillmen galloped, still screeching. They stood erect on their

Fierce yelling sounded from the men who were doing the shooting.

racing horses, did headstands on the animals, crawled under them, swung off and hit the ground with their feet, and bounced over the beasts and hit the ground on the other side. It was spectacular horsemanship.

"I hope," Toni Lash said nervously, "that this circus is not for my benefit."

She was obviously uneasy about attracting the amorous attentions of any of these gentlemen.

"I understand," Monk said dryly, "that it's O. K. here for a woman to have six or eight husbands."

"Oi-oi-oi!" the riders squalled.

Suddenly, they all reined to a dead stop. One man alighted and gave the accepted greeting—a deep bow with both arms folded across his stomach.

Next, the man stuck out his tongue. Doc stuck out his own tongue in return. All the riders stuck out their tongues.

"Out with your tongue, Monk," Doc directed.

"Huh?"

"The local equivalent of a handshake."

"Oh." Monk began putting out his tongue at the visitors whose looks he didn't like, which included practically all of them.

The guests gathered about and explained that they were a hunting party, then asked what Doc and the other two were doing and who they were.

"We are on a mission," Doc explained.

They were obviously curious to know what the mission might be, but when Doc Savage did not explain, they postponed further questioning about that.

The hillmen were eager for news from the outlying regions. Doc Savage, knowing that these people were inveterate gossips, had supplied himself with all the latest, which he related.

Monk, who could not understand a word that was being said, squatted beside the fire and fell to preparing buttered tea for the guests. When spoken to, he replied with surly grunts.

"My companion," Doc Savage explained, "is a fellow with an evil temper."

The bronze man then inquired for his share of the gossip. As he had suspected, these men were followers of the new Genghis. It had developed that they had never seen the new Genghis, however.

"Why do you follow the new Genghis?" Doc demanded.

"He is to rule," the hillmen replied. "The Powerful Ones have given signs."

The "Powerful Ones" would include, Doc Savage knew, whatever assortment of fakirs and medicine men who happened to be most influential at the moment.

"What kind of signs?" Doc inquired.

The hillmen looked at him in astonishment.

"Why," the spokesman said, "there were many signs. The Powerful Ones said so."

"Did you see any of the signs?" Doc persisted.

They shrugged. Of course, they hadn't seen any signs. This business of seeing signs was an activity confined exclusively to the Powerful Ones.

And anyway, they continued, what did it matter whether anybody saw any signs or not, in view of the fact that this new Genghis was going to lead them to victory in such a vast war that every man in the land would wind up as a prince at the least.

"War?" Doc Savage said. "The Genghis plans a war?"

"Aye," they explained. "A war in which he will use his magic. He is a man of great magic, this Genghis. His magic will overcome that of any man. The Powerful Ones have said so."

That made the immediate plan of John Sunlight clear. He had always been power-hungry, this John Sunlight, and his whole life had been one vast scheme to start out in a small way and become a conqueror.

Once John Sunlight had longed to emulate Napoleon. Now it appeared he had lifted his sights a little, and was hoping to follow the tracks made by the war boots of the Genghis Khan, that greatest conqueror of them all.

"Speaking of signs," Doc Savage said, "I have seen a sign."

NOW there were liars in this land, just as there are liars in every country, and Doc's remark first got a silence, then was the cause of a burst of skeptical laughter.

Doc Savage had a good idea of the psychology of these bushwhackers of the steppes; so he sprang to his feet, seized the hillman who laughed loudest, and hurled him at the others, knocking altogether half a dozen men sprawling head over heels.

They stopped laughing.

Playing the part of an offended hill fighter, the bronze man glared at them, fists jammed on his hips.

"I have seen a thing in my mind," Doc Savage said. "It is a strange thing I saw, that if I went to a certain spot, and found a rock that was as fire in the night, and smote this rock with a sword, I would release an All Powerful One who will be a savior of my people."

The listeners thought this over. Their general expression was something like that of a crowd on a Kansas City street corner listening to someone trying to say the earth was flat.

But nobody laughed.

"A rock that glows as fire in the night," one man said cunningly. "And you smite it, and an All Powerful One comes forth?"

"Ha," Doc Savage said. "Yes."

The men looked at each other slyly.

"We should like to see that," one of them said.

Doc Savage shrugged. "I have no objections. You go with me, and tomorrow night we find the rock."

The idea intrigued the hillmen.

Chapter XVI
GENGHIS MEETS GENGHIS

BY the following afternoon, Doc Savage's party had increased to more than fifty. It seemed that the word had gone around. The abrupt growth of the group, as curious hillmen flocked in, was somewhat surprising, because the country normally appeared to be almost uninhabited.

The affair had turned into a holiday. Around the evening campfire were pitched a number of felt *yurts.* Hillmen showed off their horsemanship, or wrestled with each other, or held footraces.

Monk, who could not speak the language, and Toni Lash, who could speak only a little of it, feigned bad tempers and managed to keep from talking.

Night came. It was cold.

The hillmen gathered around and suggested that Doc had better produce on what he had "seen in his mind." They had a strong suspicion that the whole thing would turn out to be imagination. Still, they were not too sure about that. They were superstitious, like all primitive people.

Without a word, Doc set out. He had his fingers crossed. He had better produce. Everything depended upon it.

In a long column, the party climbed a steep *tekree,* and high on the rocky slope, Doc Savage quickened his pace. He ran. The others tried to keep up, but in a short time they were outdistanced.

They yelled derisively, thinking Doc was trying to run away from his own lying.

Actually, the bronze man wanted to be sure that everything was set.

Unexpectedly, the hillmen caught up with Doc. They stopped. Mouths fell open.

"A *shoon che!"* a man croaked. "What is this?"

It was a rock that glowed like fire. No question about that.

What the hillmen didn't know was that it was a rock coated with a phosphorescent chemical.

"You see," Doc Savage said impressively. "It is as I saw in my mind."

If any hillman was breathing, the sound was not audible. Here was the totally unexpected. A miracle actually before their eyes. A miracle such as only the Powerful Ones were in the habit of seeing.

"In the future, I live a better life," a man muttered.

Doc Savage drew his sword.

Breaths were exhaled, they held again. Doc was to smite the flaming rock, and the new "All Powerful One" would materialize.

Doc lifted the sword, struck the rock. Following events were up to everyone's expectations, including Doc's.

First was the flash. It was an incredibly brilliant flash, all the world seeming to turn into utter flame. Every hillman was completely blinded.

What the hillmen did not know about the flash was that it had been produced by nearly twenty pounds of super-flashlight powder of photographic type.

As their eyes were able to see again, they perceived that the new All Powerful One had indeed appeared.

The All Powerful One had a gold body, but no face.

THE All Powerful One was a man, not a particularly large man, and one who had a thin waist. Most striking, however, was the lack of a face. Where the face should have been, there was only smooth golden flesh.

"I am the All Powerful One," this apparition said.

The voice, amazingly, seemed not to come from the figure, but to emanate from the air above its head. It was an eerie voice.

Doc spoke.

"The All Powerful One has no face with which to speak, so he has the winds speak for him," the bronze man explained, adding, "I see this in my mind."

The All Powerful One nodded with dignity.

"I shall show the power of my magic," the voice overhead said.

The All Powerful One then leaned over and touched the stone which glowed, and there was a sudden hissing and an intense bluish flame, and the rock slowly melted before their eyes.

Doc Savage, glancing around while the rock was melting, decided that none of these hillmen had ever heard of Thermit, the mixture of powdered aluminum and metallic oxides which burned with terrific heat.

Doc spoke again.

"The All Powerful One has no face," he explained. "He has lost his face because an impostor has come among you, his people. The impostor is the one you call the Genghis. Because you have accepted the Genghis as your ruler, you have helped the All Powerful One lose face. All this I see in my mind."

Again the All Powerful One nodded with slow dignity.

"It is as said," stated the voice from the air.

Doc Savage suddenly prostrated himself.

"I see in my mind that the All Powerful One is angry with us all!" he shouted.

The All Powerful One's nod was slow and wrathful this time.

"I shall shake the world a little to show my rage," the ethereal voice said.

Slowly the All Powerful One's arms lifted, and remained on high. Moments passed. The teeth of a few hillmen could be heard clicking in fright.

Then the earth shook. In fact, it gave a perceptible jump. And there was a great roaring, and a landslide down the steep slope.

A large dynamite charge, carefully time-fused, took care of that part of the demonstration.

That was enough. The hillmen were not only impressed; they were scared witless. This was a land where spooky stories were told around campfires, but here was the real thing, only worse than any current ghost yarns.

"I shall rest," said the All Powerful One's wind-voice. "Later, I shall see what can be done about regaining my face by ridding the earth of this Genghis fakir."

The upshot of this was that Doc Savage, Monk and Toni Lash were shortly resting inside their *yurt* with the All Powerful One.

"Doc, this gold-colored varnish, or whatever it is that you had me smear on myself, is making me itch!" complained the All Powerful One in a Harvard brand of English.

"It's probably your conscience makin' you itch, you shyster," Monk suggested.

The All Powerful One glared at Monk.

"The first thing I do when I start running this country is start a campaign to eliminate chemists," he declared.

"You hornswoggled me into ridin' that yak!" Monk gritted. "I'll never be the same after that yak ride."

"Then you'll be improved," snapped the All Powerful One. "Any kind of change would improve you."

"Listen, you ambulance chaser!" Monk squeaked. "Don't get to thinkin' you're such an All Powerful One. To me, you're just Ham Brooks, the pride of Harvard Law School."

And so on into the night.

DAWN. They put their heads out of the *yurt*.

"Blazes!" Monk gasped.

There was not a hillman in sight. Every man, pony and rifle had vanished, and the cold, reddish-brown mountains were naked of life.

"Doc, maybe we put on too good a show," suggested the All Powerful One uneasily.

"It is hardly likely, Ham," the bronze man replied quietly. "They have scattered to spread the news. They will return, bringing their friends."

Ham rubbed his featureless, golden face uneasily.

"You stick close to me when they come back," he requested. "Without that ventriloquial voice of yours I'm sunk. I can't speak their language."

Ham then retired into the *yurt* to adjust his faceless makeup, which consisted of a substance developed in Hollywood, a material that was applied as a semiliquid and molded as it hardened. Ham's breathing was done through a tube, and he wore goggles behind the makeup, which was applied thinly over the lenses, and being transparent, enabled him to see about as well as he could have with very dark-colored glasses. There was always brilliant sunlight in the daytime here, so the matter of vision would not bother him. It was the voice business that worried him—he had to have Doc Savage around, or he couldn't speak.

Doc's guess was correct.

Hillmen began swarming around the place all that day.

That night, the All Powerful One melted another rock, and also made some stars burn up in the heavens—the latter feat being accomplished with the aid of Monk, who fired a Very pistol star-shell from a distance.

The next day they moved toward the Genghis' headquarters. And by that night, there were at least five hundred hillmen following and staring at the All Powerful One in awe, frequently muttering, *"O mani padme hum!"* which was the local equivalent of "Forgive me my sins!"

The All Powerful One spent three more days impressing the countryside. By that time, Doc Savage judged that word of the All Powerful One's presence had penetrated to every region.

But Ham was impatient.

"This Genghis has Renny, Johnny and Park Crater, if he hasn't killed them!" Ham groaned.

"He hasn't killed 'em," Monk growled. "Not if I know my John Sunlight. He's crazy, but he don't kill people."

"But what he does to them is worse!" Ham reminded miserably.

"And what about our pets, Habeas Corpus and Chemistry?" Monk contributed.

The matter of the two pets had been frequently discussed. Toni Lash had explained that she had taken them along when they dropped overboard from the liner, and she was sure that the two animals had been in one of the three planes which

had taken off from London. But further than that, she did not know. It was recalled, however, that John Sunlight had been fascinated by the two unusual pets during their previous encounter with him in the matter of the Fortress Of Solitude, so it was possible that the animals were still alive.

"We will wait," Doc Savage said. "As soon as John Sunlight hears of the All Powerful One, he will send men to see him."

"Not to kill Ham!" Monk exploded.

Considering that he had spent most of the previous night explaining in detail how he was going to yank Ham's arms off, once they were clear of this mess, Monk's anxiety seemed inconsistent.

Doc said, "John Sunlight is clever enough to see that his best plan is to proposition the All Powerful One to throw in with him."

Monk blocked out his furry fists.

"Boy!" he muttered. "Just wait'll I get close enough to put my hands on this John Sunlight. He'll wish that polar bear had got 'im in the Arctic!"

THE messengers from John Sunlight arrived the next day. Ten of them. They were dressed in brilliant yellow—yellow boots, skintight trousers, neat jackets and skull caps. They rode horses equipped with yellow saddles and bridles.

The color scheme was effective.

They did their best not to seem impressed by the strange, golden, faceless All Powerful One. They did not quite succeed.

The Genghis would like to interview the All Powerful One. That was the gist of what they had to say.

The eerie voice came from the air around the All Powerful One.

"It is said that a worm remains a worm because he has no voice with which to ask forgiveness," it stated malevolently.

The men in yellow looked puzzled.

One of them said uneasily, "We understand you not."

"You follow the Genghis!" accused the voice from the air. "You are as the white sheep that follow a black one. It is not your fault, because your minds are as weak as buttered tea without butter."

Doc Savage, standing nearby and creating the All Powerful One's voice with ventriloquism, studied the yellow-clad men. They were uneasy. Obviously, they had heard enough about the magic of this All Powerful One to be impressed. That was excellent.

The fact that the Genghis' personal soldiers were impressed was an indication that the All Powerful One was having an influence over the hillmen—was making them wonder if they weren't walking the local equivalent of the road to hell, when they followed the Genghis.

"Even the lowly worm," said the ethereal All Powerful One's voice, "knows enough to crawl away from the sunlight before it is withered. O fools! Kneel for forgiveness!"

The men in yellow hastily got down on their knees.

In the background, Monk whispered to Toni Lash, "It looks like we're really underminin' John Sunlight's influence."

The march for John Sunlight's headquarters started. The horsemen in yellow rode in advance, forming a guard for the All Powerful One, and hillmen brought up the rear.

The cavalcade grew in size as it progressed. The way led upward through steep mountain passes, and each foot of altitude seemed to bring a dozen or so additional horsemen. It developed that the hillmen were concerned.

Finally, a fierce mountain fighter approached the All Powerful One. His attitude was awed, but also anxious.

"Teno mijaj thekane nuthee!" the man said uneasily.

Ham had no idea what the words meant, but Doc was fortunately close enough to overhear. The hillmen was explaining that the Genghis was in a very bad humor.

Doc replied with the ventriloquial voice.

"The fire that can burn stones does not fear the fire that can burn only a stem of dry grass," he said.

The hillman swallowed nervously.

"There have been mere men who desired to fight the Genghis," he muttered. "And the Genghis dispatched one of his own many spirits as a warrior to linger forever in the air above the victim, so that the poor man must fight always for his life."

"Make thyself clear, O man who surrounds his meaning with mud," the wind-voice requested.

The hillman then gave a graphic demonstration. There was no mistaking what he meant. The Genghis—John Sunlight—had been driving his enemies crazy, setting them to fighting something invisible in the air over their heads. The same fate that had befallen Renny, Park Crater, Fogarty-Smith and Kummik, the Eskimo.

"The Genghis," reminded the wind-voice, "is only a flame that can burn dry grass."

Chapter XVII
SINISTER MOUNTAIN

THE mountain looked, from a distance, like a steep volcanic cone that had a great white cork driven into its crater.

The cork apparently stuck up above the crater, in places as high as a hundred feet. However, when approached to within a mile or so, it became obvious that what seemed to be a white cork was actually a great castlelike building on top of the conical mountain. Or perhaps the building was not as much like a castle as it was like the lamaseries which stood atop many a mountain in this land and in neighboring Tibet.

Doc put a low-voiced question.

"Aye," he was told. "It was a lamasery before the coming of the Genghis."

"And that is headquarters of the Genghis?"

"Aye."

They sat their horses and their yaks a few hundred yards up the winding, steep trail that ran, like a coil bedspring, up the side of the cone. Doc studied the place thoughtfully. It was obvious that this trail could be covered, every foot of its length, by machine guns from the top.

There was a great deal of activity. Horses and yaks, burdened with great loads of merchandise brought in from the outside world through Turkestan, Afghanistan and Mongolia, were thick on the trail.

On the top of the cone, there was a sudden roaring, and plane after plane appeared, taking the air from what must be a landing field on top of the cone. The planes arched up in the rarefied, chilly air, and began to do practice formation flying.

John Sunlight had hired the best war pilots, and it was evident that he was making them practice regularly.

Doc Savage turned in the saddle to look backward.

Their retinue of hillmen had stopped at the foot of the cone. Seen from this vantage point, the actual number of the followers became apparent. There must be a thousand, at least.

Monk muttered, "Doc, you reckon they'll fight on our side if it comes to that?"

The bronze man was thoughtful.

"At least," he said finally, "we have started them doubting that the Genghis is any kind of a supernatural leader. How far they will carry that, we cannot tell, as yet."

They rode on, reached the top of the cone, and passed through an arched stone gate.

They found themselves between two long columns of uniformed men who were well-trained, and stood at attention.

"Tryin' to impress us!" Monk grunted. Then the homely chemist thought of something else. "Doc, all this costs money. Where in blazes did John Sunlight get the money?"

"You remember that he stole war inventions from the Fortress of Solitude and sold them to Balkan countries?" Doc reminded.

"Yeah."

"Well, he got many millions for them. Doubtless that is where the money for this came from."

Monk sighed. "It's lucky that John Sunlight sold those war devices in a way that kinda balanced. He'd sell one country something, then turn around and sell its neighbor something else, so that each was afraid to start fightin' the other." The homely chemist grimaced. "It was kinda like givin' both me an' Ham a gun. Neither of us would care to start shootin' because he knew the other had a gun."

Toni Lash said, "I'm afraid we're going to wish we had something stronger than guns before we get out of this."

THE buildings, contrary to the impression that distance gave, had been constructed around the edge of the flat cone top, low enough that their roofs were about level with the plateau. On this level area a landing field had been cleared, one that was large enough for the modern high-speed planes. There were many hangars.

The All Powerful One, accompanied by Doc Savage, Monk and Toni Lash, was led past the hangars and into the most impressive building on the cone top. Around them were walls intricately carved and gaudily painted. And abruptly they found themselves walking on thick velvet, passing through another door.

"These are your quarters, as guests of the Genghis," their escort advised them with dignity.

To their astonishment, they were left alone.

"I don't get this," Monk breathed.

"Sh-h-h," Doc warned.

They now stood in what proved to be a suite of great rooms with vaulted ceilings. The carving was artistic according to the local standards, and there were inlays of colored woods, mother of peal, and semiprecious stones. Deep rugs from Turkestan lay everywhere, and subtle perfumes were in the air.

"Lovely," Toni Lash admitted.

"I ain't in no state of mind to appreciate it," homely Monk muttered.

Ham contributed his bit, grumbling, "Brothers, what I think of this All Powerful One disguise by now would melt these rock walls if I repeated it."

It appeared that they were to wait for some time. Hours dragged past. An attendant brought food, and they eyed it longingly, because it was much better provender than the native diet on which they had been subsisting. But they passed it up.

"Drugged, possibly," Doc pointed out.

The bronze man went to a narrow slit of a window. The steep slope of the mountain stretched below, and on the trail pack animals still moved. The sun was dropping behind the snowcapped mountains.

Monk came and stood looking over the bronze man's shoulder.

"The more I see of this country," the homely chemist muttered, "the less I care for it."

"Is there a guard at the door?" Doc asked.

"Yep. Two of 'em."

"Big?"

"I'll say."

Doc Savage said, "We could do some exploring if we had a pair of those yellow uniforms."

"Now," Monk said, "you're talking."

THE guards were big, as Monk had said. Their yellow uniforms were neat and new, but they had detracted from the effect by shoving their belts full of pistols and knives, after the local style.

Doc Savage carried a tray of food to the door.

"We think this may be poisoned," he said grimly in the native tongue.

The guards looked at him and laughed. They proceeded to help themselves to the dishes. It was good food, and Doc had to retreat with the tray to prevent them from consuming everything.

The bronze man put the tray on a table.

"The food does not seem to be poisoned," he said. "We might as well eat."

Ham reached for the tray which the guards had sampled.

"Not that one," Doc said. "But the rest of the food is probably good."

"Aw, what'd you tell 'im for?" Monk exclaimed.

Ham scowled, puzzled.

"We put sleeping powders in everything on that tray," Doc explained.

They busied themselves eating—and shortly heard the two guards begin snoring. Hurrying to the door, they dragged the two watchers inside.

They began stripping off the yellow uniforms.

"We better take 'em in the back room, I guess," Monk said, glancing at Toni Lash. "They don't seem to be wearing any underwear."

Doc and Monk dressed in the gaudy yellow raiment. Doc's outfit fitted him much too tightly, and Monk had at least a foot too much length in his equipage.

Doc handed Monk one of the guard's rifles.

"You stay at the door," he directed.

"Huh?"

"Guard. Look better if there was a guard."

"Aw, blazes!" Monk was disappointed.

Doc Savage sauntered down the stone corridor. He moved quietly, but without appearing furtive. He turned corners, glancing into rooms, seeing native soldiers and a few white men—probably the latter were the hired pilots—but no trace of the Genghis, John Sunlight.

Unexpectedly, a man came up behind Doc.

"One side, you!" a voice growled. "Make way for the Genghis' supper."

Doc stepped against the wall, watched a fat native pass, followed by a file of men carrying trays.

The bronze man fell in behind the cavalcade. They tramped down passages, around corners, and walked through a door. Doc went on past the door, gave a quick glance inside.

John Sunlight—he sat at the head of a table at which were at least a score of others. John Sunlight! Doc knew that face. That gaunt and bony frame, the face that was the countenance of a poet, the hands that were so long and slender— Doc knew them all. They had not changed.

Only John Sunlight's hair had altered. It was white now, every hair of it. It must have turned in the Arctic, when he had undoubtedly undergone incredible sufferings on the Arctic pack ice.

John Sunlight still had his liking for strange costumes of solid colors. He wore white now, a bizarre outfit of white sandals with turned-up toes, white tights such as acrobats wear, and a loose blouse of white silk with voluminous, flowing sleeves. The white costume, with his white hair, made him striking.

Doc wondered, walking on, if John Sunlight's hair actually turned white; or had he dyed it white to match his fondness for one solid color in his dress?

THERE was another door. Doc doubled into it quickly, after noting no one was in sight.

He knew that he stood in John Sunlight's bedroom. Everything in it was white. Walls, floor, ceiling, furniture, rugs, coverings on the bed—everything was the hue of snow.

There were other doors. One of them was a closet. Doc examined it, saw that it contained dozens of riding suits, each a different color. The bronze man entered the closet. John Sunlight was not likely to examine his riding suits before he went to bed.

The bronze man sat there in the darkness. After about an hour, he heard a man stirring in the bedroom. The noises stopped.

Doc let another two hours pass. The building was quiet by now. He eased the closet door open.

The room was gloomy, a single candle in a far corner shedding light. Long, vague ghostly shadows climbed up and down the white walls, or darted from side to side as the candle flame guttered.

The white bed with its white covering was like a block of white marble, with a long ridge lying in the center. At the head of that ridge was a face, long, poetic, giving little hint from its shape of the sinister brain that lay behind it.

Doc Savage went forward swiftly and silently, and when he was over the bed, he leaned down and took hold of the neck below the poetic face with both sinew-cabled bronze hands.

Then he could tell—the knowledge was like lightning striking—that the head and neck were made of wax.

After that, the lights came on.

John Sunlight said, "The moment you let go of that thing you are holding, you will die."

Doc Savage looked at the wax likeness which he was gripping, holding a few inches off the white bed.

"It is wired to a device," John Sunlight's voice said. "Drop it and the device will kill you."

Chapter XVIII
A ROOM FULL OF DREAM

DOC SAVAGE turned his head slowly toward the voice, but he was careful, also, not to let go of the wax dummy which he held, because among all of John Sunlight's erratic, mad traits, there was one that could be depended upon—and that one was the fact that the fellow did not bluff.

John Sunlight did not have a gun. He stood, a lean tower, with arms folded. His garb was blue now, blue after the fashion of a sheik, with voluminous trousers, a loosely gathered robe, and a blue turban almost as large as a bushel basket, on the front of which scintillated a single blue jewel.

He was on the far side of the room, and there was no door near him.

He spoke again.

"One who lives by the sword comes to respect swords," he said.

His voice was deep, resonant and macabre. He was being calm and triumphant now; and the evil spell of him was going out into the room. Doc Savage, watching him, knew that the man was a student of hypnotism.

"In other words," John Sunlight continued, "he who uses his wits comes to be careful of the wits of others. Hence the trap, the trigger of which you are now holding."

Doc Savage said nothing. He was eyeing the wax figure which he held. Bending over, but still holding it up off the bed, he glanced under it, and the pale candlelight was sufficient to show him the thin, stiff steel rods that must run down to some kind of a firing mechanism contained in the mattress. He held the wax thing up with one hand, pressed the mattress with his other hand. It was hard.

"The mattress is one great shrapnel shell," John Sunlight advised grimly. "I dislike taking a life. But when an enemy tries to kill, one kills in return. That is the first law of nature."

The man had been speaking the hill dialect.

Doc answered in English, using his natural tones. His words were a criticism of his own impulsiveness that had gotten him into this predicament.

"Dogs who try to gulp bones," he said quietly, "are the dogs who become choked."

John Sunlight recognized Doc's voice instantly. This man whom Monk had called the Devil Genghis must have been haunted by that voice through many a nightmare, to know it so swiftly. John Sunlight fell back a pace, and his hands—he wore blue gloves—jerked up as though to fend off a blow. He fell to trembling and biting his lips, then pulled a great sob of air into his lungs and got control of himself.

The shaking of John Sunlight's arms and legs continued, but it was joy now. Utter, unrestrainable delight. So pleased he was that he tried several times to speak before he got out anything more than an incoherent gobble.

"Doc Savage!" he chortled finally.

Doc nodded.

John Sunlight looked at his shaking hands, then folded them.

"I am as a tree that shakes with joy in a balmy breeze of spring," he said.

Doc remained silent.

"While you stand there with death in your hands," John Sunlight continued, "I am going to show you how to keep life about you."

THE strange white room was as silent as frozen eternity, and the candlelight shadows cavorted on the walls like the shades of a past that might have come from John Sunlight's dark mind, come forth to dance in joy at another triumph in the twisted passages of the brain wherein they dwelt.

"You know, by now," John Sunlight said hollowly, "that I escaped from the Arctic. You probably thought a polar bear killed me on the pack ice." He glanced down at his long-fingered, strangler's hands. "Believe me or not, but I tell you that it was I who killed the bear, with my bare hands and a knife."

He pulled air into his lungs and let it out. "You will never know my suffering on the ice. No man will ever know that, nor could any ordinary mortal understand the full frightfulness of it."

Doc Savage said, "We have found out all that. We know how you took the clothes of Kummik, the Eskimo; took the plane of Fogarty-Smith; and took Park Crater away from Toni Lash so that she would be willing to work for you—to come to New York and seize me. We know what you did to all those men."

"You know *what I did?*" John Sunlight barked.

"It was hypnotism, aided by a drug," Doc Savage said. "You seized each of those men and treated them with a drug that paralyzed their minds. A drug that stopped their minds on one thing, as it were. And while the drug was taking effect, you used hypnosis as well, fixing in their mind the hallucination that they had to go on fighting silently against you as you stood over them."

John Sunlight shook his head in a slow, puzzled way. "You knew that—how?"

"Simple diagnosis," Doc said.

"But you had possession of your aide, Renny, who was afflicted, and you could not cure him!"

The bronze man admitted that. "There was no time," he explained, "to find the nature of the drug you used, or to perfect a treatment for it."

John Sunlight laughed fiercely, triumphantly.

"You are right, if it pleases you to know," he said. "There in the Arctic that time, I intended to use the combination of drugs and hypnosis upon your men—and I had the drug in my pockets when I escaped from you and your Fortress of Solitude."

Doc Savage nodded carelessly.

"Now that we have it cleared up," he said, "when do you try to kill me?"

John Sunlight shook his head quickly.

"Do you know why I had you brought from America?" he asked.

THE candle flame squirmed like a little scarlet goblin doing a jig on the tip of the long white candlestick, and all the evil elfin shadows around the white room sprang up and down and shuttled from side to side with unholy vigor.

"You have inventions stolen from my Fortress of Solitude," Doc Savage said.

"True," John Sunlight admitted.

"Some of the inventions," Doc continued, "are too complicated for the understanding of any scientist who could be hired by a man as vicious as yourself. You needed someone to make the death machines work. You plan a war upon mankind, and you need those infernal machines; so you hit on the idea of seizing me, bringing me here and forcing me to work for you."

"Not forcing you," John Sunlight said.

The wax form was a thing as still as stone in the bronze man's hands. It hardly moved, for Doc was holding it tightly, convinced that any major downward movement of the thing would shove down the thin rods and probably close an electrical contact which would detonate the shrapnel trap in the mattress.

"Not forcing you," John Sunlight repeated.

Doc remained silent.

"Because we have the same aims in life, you and I," John Sunlight said.

Doc Savage looked incredulous.

"The same aims, you and I!" John Sunlight repeated. "You strive to right wrongs. And I—I am trying to right the greatest wrong of all."

John Sunlight paused for emphasis.

"The wrong I am going to right," he said impressively, "is the fact that mankind lives under different flags and speaks different languages."

His voice became louder, acquired a kind of burning fervor. There was fanaticism in the voice.

"I am going to conquer the world," John Sunlight said.

He threw up his jaw.

"Then I shall disarm all of mankind," he announced. "I shall take every rifle, revolver, cannon and machine gun, and I shall make it a death penalty to own a firearm. Mankind has advanced far enough that it does not need firearms."

John Sunlight lifted both arms dramatically.

"Next, I shall make every person in the world learn to speak English," he shouted. "English shall become the common language of all mankind."

He shook his fists.

"I shall wipe out every state and national boundary. I will make all mankind of one nation, one language, and without arms."

He paused, lowered his arms and smiled.

"There will be no more wars," he said, "because there will be nothing left to cause wars."

There was a still moment in the strange, vaulted white room, and all the candle shadows seemed to stand motionless in awe on the walls. Outside, somewhere, there was a rattle of a sword on a stone wall, and the sound was a grisly intrusion into that moment of stillness in the white room, where Doc Savage and this fantastic being called John Sunlight stood alone with the echoes of the most Utopian of dreams that ever occurs to conquerors.

"A dream," Doc Savage said suddenly, "that many men have had."

"Eh?" John Sunlight scowled.

"It will not work."

John Sunlight drew himself erect. "You are mistaken. With these weapons which I took from your Fortress of Solitude, I can conquer, beyond a doubt. With your help, I cannot fail. You will help me. In return, I will bring your man Renny, as well as Fogarty-Smith and Park Crater, out of the drug-hypnotic spell. It is not difficult to revive them, when you know what antidotes to use."

Doc Savage shook his head slowly.

"Your plan," he said, "is unworkable. Millions would die, and violence is not the way to accomplish anything lasting. Look, for example, at the World War. Did it settle anything? No. The nations fought until they were exhausted, then were quiet only while they rested. Now they are getting their strength back—and the same hatreds."

"You won't help the world?"

"Only as much as it can be aided by eliminating John Sunlight," Doc Savage said grimly.

He grabbed a pillow off the bed and jammed it under the wax figure, to prevent the thing dropping back to the bed and firing the shrapnel trap.

Chapter XIX
DEATH IN BLACK

WHEN Doc Savage went away from the white bed—he did it in a long leap in case the pillow didn't work—there was no explosion.

He made for John Sunlight. He had both arms out ahead, and when he hit an upright partition of plate glass, he was not surprised. John Sunlight, for a man of cautious nature who never took chances, had been standing there too boldly.

Doc hit the glass wall hard enough to know that the stuff was bulletproof, in spite of its unusual transparency which had made its presence practically undetectable.

John Sunlight moved. He took off like a blue heron that had been hit with buckshot. He made a bleating noise of astonished terror. Rugs skidded under his churning feet, but he gained a door, sloped through.

Doc ran along the glass partition, jumping, exploring with his hand. No opening. No way over the top. He raced toward the door, scooping up a chair en route.

At the door, he turned, flung the chair at the pillow under the wax dummy on the bed. He got through the door before he saw whether the chair would hit the pillow and dummy or not—

But it hit. And there had been a shrapnel charge in the mattress. It exploded. The roar was earsplitting, and a small shower full of shrapnel stormed out of the open door.

Doc went back into the room. It was gorged with smoke, reeked fumes. The bronze man felt along the bulletproof glass again. The panel was easy to see now, because it was festooned with the small spiderweb cracks that come into a nonshatter windshield when it is hit by a rock. But the glass partition still held, and it was too strong for the bronze man's strength to smash.

Back out of the room, Doc flung. He tried doors; they were all locked. Big, strong, unbreakable doors. He raced down passages.

Men had appeared. They ran, shouted, did not suspect Doc's identity because he wore the yellow uniform and the disguise which made him seem a hillman.

"What—what—"

They meant the explosion.

"The Genghis," Doc shouted, "is trying to kill the All Powerful One."

That was true. And it would give them something to think about. The word spread.

"Genghis killing All Powerful One!" they relayed. From mouth to mouth, it went.

There was angry growling.

"I want no more of this Genghis!" a man shouted. "He is not of our people!"

Another man struck that one, knocked him down. The striker was floored by a third man, and a fourth took up the cudgels; and there was a free-for-all in that part of the Genghis castle.

Doc Savage reached the rooms where Monk, Toni Lash and Ham—the All Powerful One— were waiting.

"Fireworks have started," Doc said.

They raced out into the corridor. There was shouting and cursing and fight noises, and men running all through the great building. Bedlam. Revolution.

"Boy!" Monk said. "At last, I get a fight!"

A man ran up yelling, brandishing a short sword, and Monk jumped in, ducked, swung a big fist, and dropped the fellow.

"Wait!" Doc said.

The man Monk had hit lay on the floor. Doc seized the sword the fellow had dropped, stood over the man and held the point at the victim's throat.

"Words will keep steel out of your throat!" the bronze man rapped.

"Na!" the man screamed.

"Where is the prisoner with the big fists—the one who fights things in the air above?" Doc demanded.

He said the words in an ugly voice, with as frightful a facial expression as he could manage. The man on the floor was frightened into thinking he'd better talk to save his life.

The man spouted directions in the local dialect.

"Come on," Doc said.

IT took them about four minutes to reach Johnny, Renny, Park Crater and Fogarty-Smith. Three of those minutes they spent fighting, the other minute in running.

The door was big and iron-studded, also partially ajar. Knocking it open, they went in and joined another fight.

Men must have been sent by the Genghis to knife Johnny and Renny to death, and they had received a surprise—for Renny had suddenly stopped acting insane and had flung himself upon them.

There had been six in the execution party, and two of them were down, the lower part of one's face changed by contact with Renny's great fists. The other four were tangled with Renny on the floor, and Johnny was yelling big words and little ones and trying to get out of a set of rope bonds.

Doc leaped, got a knife wrist with both hands. The wrist broke almost as soon as he took hold of it. Monk came in and hit one man and kicked another—seeming to do both things at the same instant. There were not many rules in Monk's fights.

Renny took care of a third man.

Doc gathered up the survivor and held the fellow with one arm around his chest, and grasped the back of the man's neck firmly with the other hand. The bronze fingers worked, as though feeling for something, on the victim's neck. The man went senseless. Doc dropped him.

Renny got up.

"Holy cow!" he rumbled. "I began to think you fellows were never gonna show up!"

Monk said, "But I thought you were supposed to be crazy?"

Doc explained, "I was treating him in London. I had given him chemical antidotes for John Sunlight's drug, but it had not had time to work when he was seized at the inn."

"It worked," big-fisted Renny said. "I didn't see any need of lettin' John Sunlight know it had, however."

"I'll be superamalgamated!" Johnny yelled. "Somebody turn me loose!"

Monk began cutting Johnny free of the ropes which festooned him somewhat as though a granddaddy longlegs had gotten tangled in a spiderweb.

Doc drove a question at Renny.

"The inventions John Sunlight stole from the Fortress of Solitude—do you know where they are?"

"Holy cow!" Renny rumbled. "Come on an' I'll show you. But if you're figurin' on usin' any of 'em to help us outa this fight, it ain't no use."

"No use?"

"John Sunlight kept me locked in the room with them inventions," Renny said. "I was chained, and he thought I was crazy. But I picked the locks, and put every darn one of those inventions out of order."

"Ruined the death machines John Sunlight stole from the Fortress of Solitude?" Doc demanded.

"I sure did," Renny said.

Johnny got loose of the ropes, sprang to his feet, took a number of stiff jumps to get limbered up, then pointed both long bony arms at Ham, who was still faceless and in gold paint.

"Who the—the—superamalgamated—is that?" Johnny demanded.

"That," Monk explained, "is the All Powerful One."

"He looks like a guh-gilt-edged guh-goblin to me!" Johnny said.

THEY ran out and joined the fighting. Doc Savage, crowding close behind Renny, got in another question.

"Park Crater and Fogarty-Smith?" he asked.

Renny thundered. "They can be cured the same way I was."

Doc glanced at Toni Lash to see if she had heard. She had. She nodded gratefully.

A man came in, whirling a sword, and Doc went down and forward, feetfirst. His feet hit the swordsman's ankles. The man, upset, slammed his sword down on the stone floor so hard the blade broke.

"Wedge!" Doc said.

They formed a wedge, fought on. Men swarmed about them—and helped them fight. They packed closely, these men who helped, around the All Powerful One.

Doc gave a little moral assistance with the All Powerful One's wind-voice.

"The Genghis must be captured!" said the voice. "And those who follow him must be defeated!"

They got through to the doors of John Sunlight's chambers. Monk had acquired a submachine gun somewhere, a weapon of Chinese manufacture, but efficient. He turned the gun on the door, cut the lock away. The door caved open.

John Sunlight was in the room. The man called Cautious, too. And some white pilots. They opened up with guns. Doc threw the sword he was carrying, hit the cluster of candles which gave the only light. The candles scattered, went out, and there was intense darkness—and less danger from the guns of Cautious, the white fliers and John Sunlight.

Monk claimed later that the fight that followed in that room was the all-time high in fights. There just couldn't be another like it. Then there was no action, only groans and labored panting, and someone struck a match to see who had won.

Doc Savage's strange trilling sound came into being, a brief, startled note.

For John Sunlight was not in the room.

Leaping, Doc reached a door that stood open. It led into the white bedroom, into the part of it that was behind the bulletproof glass partition.

There was a window. The white draperies which had covered it earlier, shutting out every vestige of light, had been yanked back, uncovering a narrow slit of window.

John Sunlight's legs were just slipping out through the window.

Doc flung himself to the window, clutched, got an ankle. He set himself to yank. Outside, John Sunlight twisted up and saw who it was. He made a snarling sound, and fought.

They had always known that John Sunlight had a physical strength as unbelievable as his mind. But Doc had, even then, underestimated. For John Sunlight, wrenching and twisting, got free of the bronze man's hands.

John Sunlight had only a few feet to fall, and landed on the rocky earth at the edge of the great landing field which he had made for his airplanes.

He got up and ran toward a plane.

OTHER men were trying to reach the planes. The white fliers hired as war pilots. Some already had secured planes, were in the air. Roaring

motors made a bedlam. Planes with exhaust stacks moaning and slobbering flame dipped, diving and machine-gunning the crowd on the field. But it was too dark to do much good.

The mob boiled onto the flying field. Hundreds of them. Some flung themselves onto plane wings and broke the craft down by sheer weight. There were scores of private fights between followers of the Genghis and those who believed in the All Powerful One.

John Sunlight doubled low, tried to get through the mob. A man saw him.

The man stuck at least a yard of sword through John Sunlight's midsection.

"Jovoon!" the man screamed. "Look! He dies! Like an ordinary mortal, he dies!"

There was a roaring, a surging about the fallen Genghis. Men rushing in, waving swords, fighting with each other to be one of those who put sword to the Genghis.

"Forgiven are those whose blades enter his body!"

That cry got started somehow, and spread, and there was not enough of John Sunlight's body in that one place for all the swords to find it; so that suddenly it was in a dozen sections all over the flying field, where it was available to more swords.

Doc Savage, at the window, turned quickly and got the others back, particularly the girl, Toni Lash.

Monk rubbed the side of his homely face with a hand.

"The polar bear," he said, "would have done a kinder job on John Sunlight."

Chapter XX
BACK TO FIRE

IT was two days later. There were four thousand hillmen crowded on the flying field. They stood, for the most part, in awed silence. A few had climbed onto the metal skeletons of burned planes, the better to see.

On a small veranda, high enough that all in the crowd could see him, stood the All Powerful One.

The All Powerful One stared with his featureless face, and lifted both arms slowly to command silence. The stillness could not have been greater.

In a moment, the strange voice of the All Powerful One drifted over the throng.

"You are my children," the voice said impressively, "and I am proud of you."

There were a good many sighs of relief at that. So many of them that a low whispering swept across the throng.

The All Powerful One's voice spoke again.

"The Genghis is dead," it said, "and so I have

regained my face. I shall turn again into a rock, and when I have become a stone, I will put my face on again and sleep in peace, feeling confident that you can now carry on very well without me."

The crowd could not see into the shadowy doorway behind the balcony, where Doc Savage was speaking, perspiring a little with the effort of making the ventriloquial voice loud enough to reach the entire crowd.

Monk stood beside the bronze man, listening and hanging onto the pets, Habeas Corpus and Chemistry, which had been found safe.

"Doc," Monk breathed, "you'd better fix it up so we can get outa this place with Park Crater and Fogarty-Smith."

"Coming up," Doc explained.

The stillness of the crowd was broken again by the voice of the All Powerful One.

"I am going to show you my magic again," it said. "Bring to me the two who are insane."

This was the cue for Monk to drag Park Crater and Fogarty-Smith out on the balcony.

The pair had been treated by Doc Savage, and now were perfectly sane; but they went through all the motions of their previous condition, fighting the empty air furiously.

The All Powerful One leveled an arm at Park Crater and Fogarty-Smith.

"You are well," he said.

So they became well, and bowed, and backed off the balcony, still bowing.

"Later," announced the All Powerful One's voice, "all the others who have been made mad by the Genghis will recover."

They were fairly sure to do so, because Doc had treated them also. The crowd did not know that.

"Now," rumbled the voice of the All Powerful One, "I am going to leave you. I have sent the two men and the girl who were with me when I came here, and all of the white men, away on a mission from which they shall never return. It is my command that you let them go in peace.

"It is also my command that you do no more fighting with each other, except with your bare fists."

THERE followed a series of commandments which Doc Savage had improvised, in hopes of making the region a little more civilized in the future. They were workable commandments—the fighting with the fists instead of guns, for example. These people were exuberant souls who just

had to have a fight, and fist-fighting was probably the least disastrous form of scrapping in which they could indulge.

Explorers penetrating the area in later years, often remarked on what an amazingly workable set of commandments had been given these people by a vanished personage they referred to in an awed way as the All Powerful One.

"Now," ended the voice of the All Powerful One, "I come to my parting. But first, you will find a man in a dungeon under this building. Release him. He is a white man, a lawyer named Ham Brooks, and he will go on the mission with the other men and never return."

The All Powerful One lifted his arms.

There was a blinding flash, and an enormous mass of white smoke that puffed up around him and hid his figure and the entire balcony.

Under cover of the smoke from the flashlight powder, Ham ducked off the balcony, hurried down to remove his disguise and place himself where he could be found in the dungeon.

They had thought this the best means to account for an addition to Doc's party.

The smoke blew away.

Where the All Powerful One had stood lay a stone, a large stone, black and hard.

Johnny, the big-worded archaeologist and geologist, had done much nocturnal prowling the two previous nights, in search of a stone sufficiently impressive to become the All Powerful One.

AND so thereafter was in existence another sacred stone in another lamasery high in the hills of a land bordering Tibet, a black and hard stone which was kept resting on a dais of solid gold, and before which men came on festival and sacred occasions to salaam and ask in muted voices for favors in love and success in business. A stone that served, in its dark, inanimate way, as a warning to evildoers and an encouragement to those who lived righteously.

ALTOGETHER, everyone seemed satisfied, except Monk.

"It's too bad," Monk complained, "that Ham didn't really turn into a rock."

He advanced this opinion shortly after Toni Lash married Park Crater in New York City.

THE END

Postscript: JOHN SUNLIGHT'S SECRET by Will Murray

John Sunlight.

No adversary of Doc Savage, the legendary Man of Bronze, ever left such an indelible imprint on readers of the famous Street & Smith pulp series. Even if Sunlight had been bested after only one encounter, never achieving the distinction of having been the only villain Lester Dent saw fit to bring back for a second go-round with the bronze man, he would have gone down in pulp-fiction annals as Doc's greatest foe. For it was John Sunlight who was the catalyst for the most eagerly-awaited Doc Savage novel ever written—*Fortress of Solitude.*

It was a novel that, had Dent had his way, would never have been written. Initially, "Kenneth Robeson" had planned to take readers to the Fortress in *The Polar Treasure,* the fourth Doc novel. A planned chapter where Doc went to his North Pole retreat for resupply during the events of that bloody adventure never made it into the finished novel. Had it been otherwise, 1933 readers would have beheld an entirely different Fortress of Solitude, and there would have been no need, five years later, for a John Sunlight to discover the Strange Blue Dome in such a way as to make the readers' blood run cold.

For Lester Dent originally conceived Doc's Fortress of Solitude as hidden in an extinct volcanic cone on an Arctic isle protected from intruders by poisonous gases seeping from its base. Whenever Doc journeyed there, he was forced to land his autogyro on an ice lake in the dormant crater in order to avoid the toxic vapors seeping up from underground.* Dent described it in some detail in his personal files on Doc, but at some unspecified point rethought the design, coming up with the mysterious dome of welded glass that John Sunlight stumbled across in the polar waste. It's essentially an Eskimo igloo writ gigantic.

Editorial policy probably accounted for Dent's keeping the Fortress of Solitude an ongoing mystery for so long. Over in Doc's companion pulp, *The Shadow,* the true identity of the Master of Darkness kept readers reading long after the initial mystique of The Shadow had begun to wear thin. Doc Savage was sometimes called the Man of Mystery, but he really wasn't an enigma like the Master of Darkness. The fabled Fortress gave loyal readers something to look forward to.

*Readers caught a glimpse of the first Fortress in the prologue to my 1991 Doc Savage novel *Python Isle,* which was based on a Lester Dent outline from 1934.

Street & Smith certainly beat the drums in advance of the final revelation. For months leading up to the October 1938 issue of *Doc Savage Magazine, Fortress of Solitude* was trumpeted as forthcoming.

Obviously, no ordinary villain could be involved with so breathtaking an unveiling. When we first meet the curiously-named John Sunlight, he's a fugitive from Soviet justice, captaining a stolen icebreaker crammed with other Siberian exiles. We are told that Sunlight was convicted of blackmailing his superiors in the Red Army, but that he wasn't himself Russian. "No one knew what he was exactly," Dent hinted darkly. "They did know that he was something horrible with a human body." Dent went on to describe a weird being who took evil delight in dominating men, bending them to his implacable will, and breaking their very souls when it suited him. He possessed inhuman physical strength, but no other discernable ability beyond the irresistible hypnotic influence of his mind.

Dent seems to be describing a figure of malevolence somewhat like a cross between Rasputin and The Shadow. But nowhere in either *Fortress of Solitude* or its sequel *The Devil Genghis* is there an obvious clue as to his origin, his rather peculiar name or any clear source-figure for such a unique creation. Dent seemed to have plucked him from the one of the darker recesses of his fertile imagination.

Doc readers have long wondered what process led him to create so unique a foe, and concluded Dent simply needed a larger-than-life super-villain to penetrate Doc's greatest secrets.

But in Dent's outlines, there are significant clues. The outline to *Fortress of Solitude* begins:

> The story opens with a band of convicts who are making an escape from exile on the Siberian coast. They captured a small government ship which had put into the Arctic Sea with food.
>
> Leader of the escape was a strange, dark, moody, vile genius called, because of his black, brooding moods, John Sunlight.

In this simple assertion, Dent provided a major revelation that explains John Sunlight's name. It's a *nom de guerre!*

Unfortunately, Dent never revealed Sunlight's birth name. Perhaps that's just as well. It's much better left a mystery. Further along in the outline, Dent expanded on Sunlight's background:

John Sunlight was a man with an incredibly brilliant mind, an almost insane determination to do two things: First, he wanted the death of a man who had sent him to Siberian prison, a man named Serge Mafnoffsky, a high government official. Second, John Sunlight was mad for power; he was a small man, like Napoleon, and he wanted to follow in Napoleon's footsteps.

And there it was. The historical figure that inspired John Sunlight. Napoleon Bonaparte, the Little Corporal. Bear in mind that when Lester Dent first wrote *Fortress,* Adolf Hitler hadn't yet become the emblem of terror that he is now. On the European stage at that time, Napoleon's legacy of conquest still held that dubious distinction.

Obviously, Dent modified his vision of John Sunlight as he went from outline to the actual writing, making him tall and gaunt, after the fashion of Rasputin. But Dent's facial description of Sunlight—his high forehead and burning deep-socketed eyes—certainly mirrors the haunting visage of Napoleon Bonaparte.

The *Fortress of Solitude* outline ends very differently from the story itself. Here is what Dent planned for the last chapter:

> They corner John Sunlight, and he is apparently killed in an explosion.
> Doc Savage examines the vault where the death-dealing inventions were stored—and finds most of them gone, much to his horror. There are records, however, showing to whom the inventions had been sold.
> Doc says grimly, "Our next job, fellows, is to recover those infernal machines, and this time, we will *destroy* them."

Dent concluded: "But most grim promise of all, it is found that John Sunlight is not dead. He escaped, fled into the Arctic wastes, and they cannot trace him."

The outline to *The Devil Genghis* is actually quite a bit different from the novel Dent turned in. It begins with a mysterious raving man stumbling out of the Arctic wastes, who is captured and then temporarily confined to an asylum.

"He is John Sunlight," Dent wrote, "who has survived the trek across the Arctic wastes, and is now bent on stealing back the inventions he sold to warlike nations and warlords—in the last Doc yarn—and starting a campaign to follow in Napoleon's footsteps."

According to his plot, Dent intended to pick up the sequel exactly where he left off. Doc Savage is busy repairing his Fortress. His men scatter throughout the world, searching for Sunlight. Doc goes alone into the Balkans, attempting to recover the stolen war devices before a devastating ground war can break out among fractious nations, killing thousands. But Sunlight has beaten him to the punch, and successfully steals them back.

For reasons already explained, Dent ignored most of the first half of his prepared outline, picking up the action months after the events of *Fortress of Solitude* instead. In doing so, he let dangle the fate of these death machines, specifically the darkness-maker sold to the Balkan war minister Baron Karl, which Doc vowed to reclaim at the end of *Fortress*—an unrecorded Doc Savage adventure I may one day myself pen under the title, *The War Makers*.

Why was this European sequence abandoned? Besides the continuity issue, perhaps *Doc Savage* editor John L Nanovic reasoned that with Europe growing restless, a real war might flare up in the nine months it would take to get *The Devil Genghis* into print. He wasn't far off the mark. Having annexed Austria in March, Adolf Hitler seized a portion of Czechoslovakia in October. Poland would follow a year later. World War was coming.

As intended, the action shifts to Asia for the ultimate showdown. Dent had foreshadowed this denouement in his *Fortress* outline when he planned for Doc Savage to appear in the guise of Sat Sung, an Asiatic warlord. This imposture was dropped from the story, however.

The John Sunlight who returns in *The Devil Genghis* is markedly different from the being of evil who so dominated *Fortress of Solitude*. With a nod to Sunlight's Napoleonic origin, Dent wrote, "Once John Sunlight had longed to emulate Napoleon. Now it appeared he had lifted his sights a little, and was hoping to follow the tracks made by the war boots of the Genghis Khan, that greatest conqueror of them all." (Dent seemed unaware that "Genghis" was the Khan's given name, not his title. The novel actually *should* have been titled *The Devil Khan*.)

John Sunlight's ultimate goal is the same: to enlist Doc Savage in a fascistic-pacifistic scheme to remake the world. As he expressed it in Dent's outline:

> I am going to be the world's greatest benefactor. I am going to conquer one country after another with these inventions. I am going to take every gun, every war instrument, out of all those nations. I am going to make it a death offense to possess a gun. The world does not need guns. Without them, there will be no wars. Then I am going to make every nation, every person in every nation, learn to speak English. In five years, no one will be allowed to speak anything but English. Thus, the world will lose its national hatreds. The world will be one big, peaceful nation.

Not made clear in *The Devil Genghis* was Doc's view of John Sunlight's inner motives. In the outline, after Sunlight says, "Nothing is going to stand in my way of wiping out war by force," Dent added: "Doc seems to be the only one who does not believe the man is earnest; Doc knows that the man thirsts only for power."

John Sunlight was conceived as a modern Napoleon, a malevolent monster who desired nothing less than to bend humankind to his wicked will. He died attempting to become the next Genghis Khan. But to truly understand this creature whom one character in *Fortress of Solitude* described as "The man who has inherited the qualities of the Erinyes, the Eumenides, of Titan, and of Friar Rush, with a touch of Dracula and Frankenstein," his Napoleonic inspiration and his ultimate power-mad goals must be set aside.

Salted throughout both John Sunlight novels are certain traits that mark this evil genius as apart from other men. There is his penchant for wearing clothing of a single solid color at any one time—on some days purple, on others, white or scarlet. He is almost completely emotionless, expressing his feelings only by a low, bestial growl. He dislikes killing, preferring to dominate his victims.

Do you see a pattern forming?

John Sunlight said it during his last encounter with his polar opposite: "We have the same aim in life, you and I," he told Doc Savage. "You strive to right wrongs. And I—I am trying to right the greatest wrong of all...."

John Sunlight is Doc Savage's evil mirror image!

Consider: Where Doc is bronzed, Sunlight is spectrally pale. Sunlight growls rather than trills, affects exotic costumes of varying single colors in contrast to Doc's preference for conservative suits of solid brown, is a physical superman, and is in many other ways the negative image of the Man of Bronze. Doc's prodigious strength comes from a well-developed physique; Sunlight's might is entirely a function of his evil mind. Musculature alone cannot explain it.

It's tempting to imagine John *Sunlight* as an evil version of The *Shadow* as well. Likewise wiry and long-fingered, the Master of Darkness was also amazingly strong. His powers of mind and mental-control also smack of John Sunlight. Dent was of course very familiar with The Shadow, having written *The Golden Vulture*,* an early Shadow novel given him as a test before Street & Smith offered him Doc Savage. Weeks before Dent wrote *Fortress of Solitude,* his

Lester Dent circa 1938

Golden Vulture manuscript was rescued from oblivion by Walter Gibson, who rewrote it. Coincidence?

The Shadow and Doc Savage were polar opposites in their approach to the art of crime-fighting, much the way Batman and Superman later became. Exactly how The Shadow entered into Dent's calculations is impossible to say. And how much of this stark contrast between Doc Savage and John Sunlight was conscious only Lester Dent could answer. But keep in mind that Doc Savage—as his name implies—is an example of the perfect balance of mental and physical prowess a disciplined human being can achieve.

John Sunlight was all mind. His mind was unbelievably disciplined, and as Lester Dent makes clear time and again, the only thing John Sunlight feared was losing that brilliant mind of his. Perhaps Dent is saying that without the proper balance between mind and body, a superman is doomed to madness and delusions of grandeur. But for the spark of good that resided in the bronze man's soul, the training that transformed Clark Savage, Jr., into Doc Savage might just as easily have created another John Sunlight.

Will Murray is the literary agent for the Estate of Lester Dent, and collaborated posthumously with the Man of Bronze's principal author on eight Doc Savage novels, the latest of which is "The Desert Demons," forthcoming.

---

*Lester Dent's only Shadow novel *The Golden Vulture* was reprinted with Walter Gibson's *Crime, Insured* in Volume One of Nostalgia Ventures' Shadow reprints.

DOC SAVAGE RETURNS by Anthony Tollin

Doc Savage was one of the greatest publishing success stories of the 1930s. Launched in response to the runaway success of *The Shadow* and Street & Smith's revival of the single character magazine, *Doc Savage* was one of the top-selling hero pulps of the 1930s and 1940s, regularly selling nearly 300,000 copies each month. "Doc was a vivid splash of color in the emptiness of the Great Depression," Don Hutchison observed in *The Great Pulp Heroes.* "During the 1930s and 1940s generations of youth grew up under the spell of his far-ranging exploits."

Lightning struck twice when the Man of Bronze returned in 1964. The paperback revival of Doc Savage resulted in a publishing phenomenon that garnered major news stories in *Newsweek, Time* and *Publishers Weekly.* In 1971, *Time* reported that Doc's "10.5 million copies now in print have realized about $4.5 million in sales," and observed: "As stories, most of them are bloody good. He is a funhouse mirror of the America that loved him and apparently still does—a big square joe with the body of Charles Atlas, the brain of Thomas Edison, and the implacable innocence of Mickey Mouse."

Bantam's Doc Savage reprints launched the numbered series paperback adventure format that was later imitated by *The Executioner, The Destroyer* and *The Shadow.* The publisher eventually reprinted all 181 *Doc Savage* pulps (plus a "lost" novel) before commissioning new stories by Philip José Farmer and Will Murray.

Our inaugural Nostalgia Ventures Doc Savage volume is being released in two editions: the standard version reproduces Emery Clarke's *Fortress of Solitude* cover from the October 1938 pulp, while our variant edition showcases James Bama's 1968 cover art for the Bantam paperback. The dynamic and cohesive look of Bama's covers was a major factor in the success of Bantam's Doc Savage revival, giving the series a unique look all its own.

James Bama's art was a fixture in popular culture throughout the 1960s and early 1970s. The most revolutionary and influential paperback artist of his day, Bama also provided the package art for Aurora's Universal monster model kits and the original NBC *Star Trek* promotional art which was later used as the cover of the first Trek paperback.

Bama had grown up with *The Shadow* and

Walter Baumhofer's cover for *Doc Savage Magazine* #1, March 1933

James Bama's 1964 cover for the first Doc Savage paperback

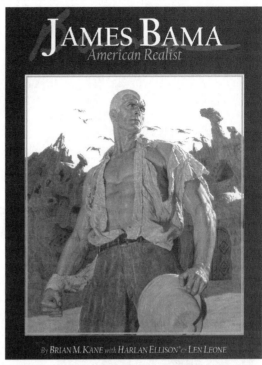

The artistry of James Bama (left) is showcased in Brian M. Kane's book.

Doc Savage pulps. "My uncle used to get pulp magazines," he recalled. "I was 12-13 years old, and I remember the *Doc Savages*. It seemed like he was always in the jungle with jodhpurs on, his shirt torn. That's all remembered 25 years later. That's why I conceived him that way. And when I look at the first *Doc Savage Magazine* cover today, I wasn't that far off!" Though the pulp covers of Walter Baumhofer, Robert Harris and Emery Clarke may have more accurately approximated Lester Dent's descriptions of Doc Savage, Bama created the iconic image that baby boomers would forever recognize as the Man of Bronze, just as Walter Baumhofer had for an earlier generation. For that reason, we're proud to include James Bama's superb imagery in our relaunching of Doc Savage.

We'd like to thank Brian Kane for his assistance in obtaining James Bama's approval to reproduce his classic cover for Bantam's *Fortress of Solitude* on our variant edition. Kane is the author and designer of *James Bama: American Realist,* which was recently published by Flesk Publications (www.fleskpublications.com). The book reproduces 260 classic Bama illustrations including all 62 of his Doc Savage covers, and also features an introduction by Harlan Ellison, the acclaimed fantasy author who began his writing career during the final years of the pulp era.

James Bama: American Realist is available in both the standard $34.95 hardbound edition, and a $74.95 deluxe slipcased edition, limited to 1000 signed and numbered copies (which also include a one-hour DVD documentary on Bama).

In selecting stories for our new Doc Savage reprints, contributing editor Will Murray and I are deliberately avoiding novels like the best-selling *Brand of the Werewolf* (which sold some 185,000 copies in its numerous Bantam printings) and are instead focusing on outstanding Doc Savage stories that had lesser distribution in rarer editions. Our next book will showcase two of Lester Dent's greatest thrillers. In *Resurrection Day,* the Man of Bronze perfects a method for resurrecting a dead human being, but only a single person can be revived. Who will Doc choose? In *Repel,* a strange new element expelled in a South Pacific volcanic eruption falls into the hands of Cadwiller Olden, Doc Savage's most unusual foe. *Doc Savage #2* also includes a foreword by Peter David *(The Incredible Hulk, Star Trek),* the original pulp covers by Robert Harris, interior illustrations by Paul Orban and background articles by Will Murray. We hope you'll rejoin us next month for the continuing adventures of Doc Savage, the Man of Bronze.

Series editor Anthony Tollin co-authored The Shadow Scrapbook *with Walter B. Gibson, and was colorist of DC Comics'* Doc Savage *and* The Shadow Strikes *series and Historical Consultant for the SCI FI Channel documentary* "Martian Mania: the True Story of *The War of the Worlds."*

Lester Dent (1904-1959) could be called the father of the superhero. Writing under the house name "Kenneth Robeson," Dent was the principal writer of *Doc Savage,* producing more than 150 of the Man of Bronze's thrilling pulp adventures.

A lonely childhood as a rancher's son paved the way for his future success as a professional storyteller. "I had no playmates," Dent recalled. "I lived a completely distorted youth. My only playmate was my imagination, and that period of intense imaginative creation which kids generally get over at the age of five or six, I carried till I was twelve or thirteen. My imaginary voyages and accomplishments were extremely real."

Dent began his professional writing career while working as an Associated Press telegrapher in Tulsa, Oklahoma. Learning that one of his coworkers had sold a story to the pulps, Dent decided to try his hand at similarly lucrative moonlighting. He pounded out thirteen unsold stories during the slow night shift before making his first sale to Street & Smith's *Top-Notch* in 1929. The following year, he received a telegram from the Dell Publishing Company offering him moving expenses and a $500-a-month drawing account if he'd relocate to New York and write exclusively for the publishing house.

Dent soon left Dell to pursue a freelance career, and in 1932 won the contract to write the lead novels in Street & Smith's new *Doc Savage Magazine.* From 1933-1949, Dent produced Doc Savage novels while continuing his busy freelance writing career and eventually adding Airviews, an aerial photography business.

A real-life adventurer, pilot, world traveler and member of the Explorers Club, Dent wrote in a wide variety of genres for magazines ranging from pulps like *Argosy, Adventure* and *Ten Detective Aces* to prestigious slick magazines including *The Saturday Evening Post* and *Collier's.* During the pioneering days of radio drama, Dent scripted *Scotland Yard* and the syndicated *Doc Savage* series. He also contributed to the legendary *Black Mask* during its golden age, creating Miami waterfront detective Oscar Sail. His mystery novels include *Dead at the Take-off* and *Lady Afraid.*